JEFF
ABBOTT

AN AMBUSH OF WIDOWS

CANELO

First published in the United States in 2021 by Grand Central Publishing

This edition published in the United Kingdom in 2023 by

Canelo
Unit 9, 5th Floor
Cargo Works, 1-2 Hatfields
London SE1 9PG
United Kingdom

A CIP catalogue record for this book is available from the British Library.

Print ISBN 978 1 80436 239 6
Ebook ISBN 978 1 80436 238 9

Look for more great books at www.canelo.co

Printed and bound in Great Britain by Clays Ltd, Elcograf S.p.A.

1

Jeff Abbott [illegible] bestselling author of 21 suspense novels including UK bestsellers *Panic* and *Fear.* He is published in over twenty languages. He is a three-time Edgar Award nominee and a past winner of the Agatha and Thriller Awards. He lives in Austin with his family. You can read more about Jeff and his work at at www.jeffabbott.com

J. T. Abbott [illegible] bestselling author of [illegible] novels including [illegible] bestsellers [illegible]. He [illegible] over twenty languages. [illegible] and a past winner of the [illegible] Thriller Award. He lives in [illegible] with his family. You can [illegible] about him and his work at [illegible].

For Wes Miller

1

Thursday evening

Kirsten North was doing what she normally did when Henry was gone on a business trip: finishing her own work on her laptop on the couch, ordering in Chinese food from that place Henry didn't much like, and watching a British baking show that was like a televised tranquilizer.

She was on the second episode in her mini-binge when the phone rang. She glanced at the screen; it was Henry's number.

"Finally, sweetie," she said. "How's New York?"

There was a silence for five seconds.

"Henry?" she said.

"Kirsten North?" The voice was muffled, indistinct, a whisper.

"Yes?"

"You're Henry's wife?"

A coldness fell on her skin like sudden rain. "Yes. Who is this?"

"Your husband has been killed. In Austin. Texas." She couldn't tell if the voice was male or female, and it didn't matter, because it spoke madness.

"This isn't funny, Henry," she said, at the same time she thought that this wasn't the kind of joke he would ever make. Henry's phone must have been stolen and this was the sick thief's idea of a prank.

"He was shot." And then the caller hung up.

Kirsten North stared at the phone. Cruel and sick, that's what it was. Her husband was in New York, not Austin. She texted Henry: did u lose yr phone? Some sicko just called me from yr number.

And then she realized the sicko was reading the text now because they'd called from Henry's cell.

There was no replying text.

Think, she told herself. She pushed down the anger and the rising fear. What hotel had he told her he was staying at? She tried to remember while in the background one of the baking show judges gently chided a contestant for an undercooked crust, and the woman's lip trembled like her whole world was falling in on her.

The Van Vleck, a small, quirky hotel not far from Times Square. Yes. He'd stayed there before on business.

She googled the hotel, called its main number.

The polite young man who answered checked and told her there was no Henry North registered there. She thanked him automatically and ended the call. *But he arrived in New York Sunday night, and he's due home tomorrow*, she thought. *He must have stayed at another hotel.* She hurried through her emails and texts, in case she'd missed a message from him, telling herself when Henry called and explained he'd lost his phone she'd laugh at her silly worry.

He was shot.

Something in the voice...that awful voice. Like it was glad.

There was no mention of the New York hotel in his emails from last week.

Who was the client? What was the company name?

Henry had been trying hard to land clients beyond his few in New Orleans. Had he told her the name of his hotel and she hadn't been listening? Sometimes she wasn't a good listener.

She searched her emails and the texts from him once more. Nothing mentioning this New York client's name.

Austin. She and Henry didn't know anyone in Austin. They'd talked about moving there once, because it was growing so fast and there were lots of tech jobs, but Henry said there were so many freelancers it would be more competitive than New Orleans, which was just sort of emerging as a tech area and there were more chances here to make an impact....

In Austin. He was shot.

Instead of looking for hotels in New York that sounded familiar, she entered in the search engine an awful phrase: "austin shooting."

The results popped up, the most recent at the top. POLICE INVESTIGATE DOUBLE HOMICIDE. The related headlines: TWO MEN FOUND SHOT TO DEATH AT WAREHOUSE. LEADING BUSINESSMAN KILLED. The stories were tied to local news stations. The victims had been found two days ago, in the early hours of Tuesday morning.

He'd left early Sunday afternoon. "Got an early Monday morning meeting. I'll text you," he'd said. And he had, that all was fine, the meetings were going well. But if these headlines were about him, he was dead, and someone else had texted her from Henry's phone. Nausea churned her gut; her chest felt tight. This couldn't be.

She clicked on the first result and watched the news video. The reporter was young and eager and said two bodies had been discovered in the warehouse by a homeless person who had found an unlocked door and entered.

More details had emerged since Tuesday.

One of the men was named Adam Zhang. An entrepreneur of some note who had launched multiple start-up tech companies in the crowded Austin landscape. The other man had not been identified. Those active in the tech scene were expressing shock and dismay. "More to come," the reporter said. The police were asking anyone who might have seen anything or knew anything to come forward.

If Henry was the other victim...why would an anonymous person call her? Why tell her this?

Had the call come from the murderer? Did the killer have Henry's phone?

She started to shiver, her mind reeling in shock. She forced herself to take several deep breaths. *No. Don't just sit here. Do something. Be like Henry. Act when it seems impossible to act.*

A back corner of her mind took over. She logged on to an airline website and found a late-night flight to Houston, connecting onward to Austin.

She could just make it if she hurried.

2

Nothing on this job had gone quite right; none of the normal protocols were followed, and now having his next target walking directly toward him in the airport was a sure sign to call off the hit.

Mender caught his breath. Here she was, hurrying toward a gate in the New Orleans airport, just as he'd come off his flight from Austin.

He stopped and looked at his phone and she rushed past him, her carry-on bag nearly hitting his hip.

Kirsten North was leaving town, just as he was arriving to take care of her.

His mind literally went blank; he nearly laughed. He normally felt emotionless about his work, but this job was testing his nerves. He followed her to the gate where she waited. The flight that he'd taken from Austin would soon be reboarding, getting ready to head back via Houston. He'd just come off the plane; if he tried to buy a ticket to get back on, wouldn't that flag the system? Be suspicious? He could not be noticed.

Why was she flying to Austin?

Because she knew. How could she know?

He watched her, but he was careful to flicker his gaze because a woman could sense a stare. She was shivering. Anxious. Like she'd gotten bad news. But that wasn't possible. Not yet.

He saw there wasn't a change of crew. So if he got back on the plane, the flight attendants might notice him, might even jokingly comment.

He had no idea how to trace her once she made it to Austin. But this was a bonus-driven job and he had to risk it. He went back to the gate counter. Waited behind people trying to buy a lower boarding pass number. He put a beaten, sad look on his face.

"I just flew in on this arriving flight, but there's a text...." Mender held up his phone like it had all the answers. "My dad's had a heart attack in Austin; I need to fly back....Can I get a ticket back on this flight?" His voice quavered.

The gate agent said, "I'm so sorry, let me check," and Mender put on an expression of muted grief, one that wouldn't draw attention. He glanced over toward the target. She was sitting, staring at her lap, not looking at anyone. Lost in real grief, where his was pretend.

"Yes, there's a seat," the agent said. Mender wordlessly shoved a credit card toward her. It didn't have his real name on it.

"Thank you so much."

"I hope your dad's okay. You'll be in the final boarding group, though. Sorry."

"It's fine."

He didn't have a checked bag—he was to get a weapon, courtesy of his handler, here in New Orleans. He dumped the weapon he'd used in Austin, per standard protocol. He got his boarding pass—a number so high it guaranteed a middle seat—and sat down, where he could see the target but she wouldn't notice him.

It suddenly occurred to him that she would be in his boarding group; she must have been late in booking her flight as well. He hoped not. He did not want her to notice him. He had on a baseball cap and sunglasses; it was the best he could do to minimize being noticed or recognized.

The plane was readied; the groups lined up per the airline's policy, with boarding group A first, numbers one through thirty.

The target and the killer both kept their seats.

"Group B," the agent brightly announced, and more people rose. The plane, he guessed, might be full. It would be close. He should try to sit so he could deplane before her, so he could follow her when she left.

Then group C. The stragglers got up, worrying about whether there would be any remaining overhead storage; couples resigning themselves to not sitting together. The rest bracing themselves for the little hell of the middle seat.

They ordered themselves by number. The target was immediately ahead of him. Of course. She didn't look back at him. They were the last two in line. He hoped she wouldn't look at him.

They boarded the plane. The flight attendant gave them each a bright hello and neither the target nor he responded. The flight was nearly full. He scanned the seats, hoping she would pass up a middle seat toward the front of the plane and leave it for him so he could exit in Austin ahead of her and more easily follow her. But all the seats were taken.

He could see the last two seats, in the back row. Next to each other. A middle and an aisle, an older man already in the window seat with his neck pillow, reading a book.

The target glanced back at him and he froze. "You're tall," she said. "You can have the aisle."

He found his voice and said, "You sure?"

She nodded. "It's a short flight."

"Thanks." He glanced away as if embarrassed, but he didn't want her looking at his face. Something had gone so bent on this job and he'd have to turn this to his advantage.

She had already turned away, shoving her carry-on into the overhead bin. He put his bag next to hers. She settled into the middle seat and he sat down in the aisle seat.

He had to decide how to do this. He could try to engage her in conversation, maybe in the Houston airport—they would have to change planes for Austin—then draw her somehow away from people and end her.

But if she was heading to Austin on a last-minute flight, she knew about her husband, and she wouldn't be in any mood for some guy chatting her up, not with all the terrible thoughts that must be swirling in her head. He sat very still, looking ahead, sunglasses in place. She did the same.

He wondered: *What is she thinking?* He needed to just be the guy sitting next to her on the flight, faceless, voiceless. Unremarkable. He would not interact with her again; he would not give her reason to remember him.

The plan had been to make her look like a suicide. He couldn't do that in an airport. Far too dangerous. Best to not be noticeable, to not engage.

How did she know?

He kept his gaze straight ahead. He heard the man in the window seat offer her a drink coupon when the flight attendant came around to take orders. She accepted.

The profile said she used to drink a lot but had stopped two years ago. She must be in shock right now. If she got drunk, maybe the hit would be easier when she got to Austin. Follow her to wherever she was going, pour more alcohol down the grieving widow, and then end her.

He smiled at the flight attendant and ordered a ginger ale.

3

Morgan cried and howled, as though he could feel Flora's pain. She walked and patted the child, murmuring to him, wondering: *Can a one-year-old know that his father is dead? Does he feel the shift in the world?*

Flora Zhang had hardly slept since Adam and the unknown man were found shot to death. She had given Morgan an early dinner and then lay down on her and Adam's bed with their son. She'd just drifted off, exhaustion taking its toll, when Morgan suddenly awoke, squalling, restless, and she stumbled to her feet, scooped him up, made her checks. Diaper dry, nose clear. She began her weary procession of walking back and forth.

The door to the nursery cracked open. Her next-door neighbor, Jeanne, stood in the doorway. "Flora? I can take him...."

"Thank you, Jeanne, I have him."

"Are you sure?" Jeanne was in her sixties, silver hair fashionably cut short, bright blue eyes behind stylish red eyeglasses, always calm in a crisis. She had been a steadfast friend since Adam's body had been found and Flora's world unraveled. Jeanne had brought over the first meal in the initial shock, held Flora's hand while she tried to process the impossible, been a constant, reassuring presence for Morgan.

"I have him," Flora said and Jeanne nodded and shut the door. Jeanne meant well. But Flora couldn't hand over her child right now. Adam was dead and Morgan was all she had left. She needed to hold her baby.

But Morgan wouldn't stop crying. Flora shuffled back and forth, trying every song he loved, the old lullabies, the ones Flora had heard Jeanne sing for him, fumbling over the lyrics because she wasn't sure of them, and while his crying would subside it would not cease.

Adam. Sometimes he would stand in the doorway, watching her walk Morgan when he was fussy, as though the crying were an inconvenience and he was judging her job performance. Once when Morgan was asleep on her shoulder but she hadn't wanted to set him down yet, Adam had said, "I know I'm not good at this dad stuff. I wish I could be."

He had said that as though he'd forgotten himself, almost shyly, and then he'd taken Morgan from her and set him down in the crib and taken her back to bed. He had wanted a wife and a child and then once he had them, she sensed a growing indifference. As though he'd realized: Is this all there is to it? And she was in love with him, and she found herself wondering if he still loved her. She should have talked to him. Asked him.

And now the doorway was empty. It would always be empty.

Morgan kept crying, wriggling in her arms.

The door opened and for one moment she expected it was Adam, and the past two days had been an unmanageable dream. But it was Jeanne, again.

"Please, let me help you. I know you're exhausted...."

"I need Morgan to want me right now. To not cry..." She managed to keep her voice under control. "Why doesn't he want me? Is he sensing how I feel?"

"Oh, Flora. He's just a bit fussy and out of sorts. Sweetie, you can't help him if you're exhausted. I'm here, let me help."

And exhaustion won so she gave Morgan over to Jeanne. Who cooed and rubbed his back in a way different than Flora had, and his cries started to soften.

He responds to her more than me, Flora thought, and it was just another way for her to feel crushed. *He can feel all my fear and my grief.* It would be so much easier not to feel.

She eased the door shut and walked down the stairs to the kitchen. She looked at the counter. More food. The neighbors, including Jeanne and her husband, Milo, just kept bringing food. Teddy Chao was on his laptop at the table, but as she came into the room, he put it aside and stood. That was one way you knew your life had forever changed; now people didn't look at their phones or their tablets or their laptops if you were around. They looked at you.

"Morgan all right?" Teddy asked. He was young, early twenties, a little too handsome for his own good. Adam's assistant strategist, protégé, and distant cousin. He had been living with them since he graduated from college two years ago.

"Yes. Jeanne seems to be able to calm him." She tried to keep the bitterness out of her voice.

"Can I get you anything? Tea?"

She thought she had been offered more tea in the past two days than in her whole life. "No. What are you doing?"

"Dozens of people who work for the companies Adam helped launch have been emailing me about Adam. Offering condolences, support. I've been responding to them. I'll keep all the emails for you to read if you like, when you feel up to it."

"Thanks." Maybe it would be comforting to read words of sympathy from people who knew him, who actually got to spend time with him. More time than they'd had together lately. She pushed that thought away. His business. She had hardly thought about it. "His company...I haven't asked what everyone is doing." Adam was gone, but the things he'd built, the lives he'd touched, remained.

"You don't need to worry about it. Shawn and I have everything under control." Shawn was Adam's business partner in their venture capital firm, Zhang Townsend.

"All right. At some point, we have to talk about what happens next."

"I think Shawn will want to buy out Adam's partnership. He hasn't said so, but..."

Flora sat down and she realized that Morgan's crying had stopped. He'd fallen asleep. For Jeanne, not for her.

"I'd like to stay on and work with Shawn," Teddy said.

There was plenty of money, and she didn't have to worry about that, but she had worked when Adam was in grad school, and she had worked as he built up Zhang Townsend from two guys with their desks pulled together to one of the largest venture funds in the South. She wasn't so sure she wanted to sell her ownership shares. "We'll see," she said. Teddy nodded.

"The funeral…," Teddy began, as if hating the word. "We don't know when the police will release the body….Do you want to have a memorial service first?"

Flora rubbed at her temples. "I can't decide right now."

"All right," Teddy said, in a tone that made it sound like it wasn't all right. She didn't care. Teddy was a lot like Adam, in that things needed to be done a certain way. Precise and proper and businesslike. But until she knew why he died, what had happened, it seemed bizarre to think about gathering with people and talking about him. It felt like rushing him into his grave.

Teddy said, "I didn't mean to pressure you. I'm sorry."

And of course he was just trying to *help*. Everyone was. But there was no help. Literally none. There were times in the marriage when she'd felt so alone, but this was a new kind of alone. She didn't know what to do. The first two days had been numbness, her on autopilot, but now the reality was setting in that Adam was *gone*. And the rest of her life stretched out like a long, fogged road that she couldn't see.

She glanced at the stairs as Jeanne came down them. "Morgan's fine….He cried it out."

Flora started to say *I'm glad he would sleep for you*, but the words didn't come.

"We were talking about the memorial service, Jeanne," Teddy said. "That we're going to wait."

"Flora, can Milo and I do anything to help you with that?" Jeanne asked.

"No. I'm not ready to have an actual memorial like a church service yet. Maybe the fund-raiser on Saturday…maybe it could be like a way to honor him. A lot of people he knew will be there."

"Yes, of course," Jeanne said noncommittally. She glanced at Teddy. "I can stay over if you need me, Flora."

"No, we'll be fine," she said. "Give my best to Milo and thank you again for everything." She gave Jeanne a quick, grateful hug and Jeanne left, telling them she'd be glad to come over in the morning if they needed her and wishing them a good night.

"Do you still want to go to the fund-raiser? I know it mattered a lot to Adam, but..." Teddy's voice trailed off.

"All I want to know is why this happened." Now she looked up at him. "Why...did this happen? Why is Adam gone; why does Morgan not have a dad? Why?" she repeated, and then she felt like a child for asking the question.

"I don't know."

"You knew...you knew the people he dealt with. Was there someone who could have wanted to hurt him?"

"No. Of course not. Everyone loved Adam."

"Someone didn't, Teddy. He was killed in an empty building he owned. He went there. To meet someone...a deal that went bad, someone resenting him..."

"No, I think this had to be some random...act, Flora. I know you want it to make some kind of sense, but it's not going to. Someone might have spotted him near the warehouse, guy in a nice Mercedes, decided to rob him." Teddy opened one of the casseroles and started to put food on plates.

Flora got up and went to the window. From their hilltop Lakehaven mansion that overlooked Lady Bird Lake, the lights of downtown Austin gleamed on the other side of the water, to the east.

She picked out the tower where he'd surprised her with the keys to a penthouse he'd bought three weeks ago. They had planned to move in two months. Or rather he had. She loved their Lakehaven home, having thoughtful neighbors like Jeanne and Milo, and the quiet. Lots of people lived downtown now, but there was traffic and honking horns and she had wondered how a baby would do, even in a penthouse. They wouldn't have a yard. Adam thought she'd be delighted and she remembered her automatic smile feeling a bit frozen on her face. He couldn't have even talked about it with her? What had he really thought of her, to assume she'd just accept a new home, sight unseen? Had he thought he knew her so well, when he didn't at all?

The penthouse purchase meant that maybe she didn't know him so well either. She didn't like to ponder that thought.

"It won't ever make sense to me," she said.

"I'm not saying that.... I know the police will catch whoever did it. We have to have hope," Teddy said.

Hope is a cruel thing, she thought.

Teddy brought her a plate with some chicken casserole on it, as well as salad and broccoli. "People have brought so much food, Flora, and you've got to eat."

"I'm not hungry."

"You didn't eat lunch."

"I'm not..."

"For Morgan. Do it for him. Please."

Teddy was right. Flora sat down and ate dutifully. She barely tasted the food. She drank a glass of water Teddy brought her. Through the huge window she looked at the tower, where they were supposed to live....

The penthouse light was on.

She was sure of it. Why...why would it be on?

No one was supposed to be there.

But someone was.

Why did this happen? Why? Maybe the answer was there, in the lit-up place he'd bought for her without even telling her.

She grabbed her purse off the table.

"Where are you going?" Teddy asked.

"I have to get out of here," she said. "Just for a bit. Keep an eye on Morgan for me." She decided not to tell Teddy she'd seen the light. He would call the condo management, ask questions. She wanted out of this house.

"Okay, I'll drive you." He stood. "I'll get Jeanne to come back."

"No. I want to be alone." She'd felt stuck and mired for the past two days. She needed to do something. To not feel numb. To be in fresh air.

"Flora…"

She shut the door on his words.

4

Short flight to Houston. Kirsten had the next-to-last boarding pass number and she stuck herself between two men on the row right before the bathroom. If she had been sitting between two women, she might have confided in one: *I think my husband might have been killed*. It would be crazy to tell it to a stranger. She closed her eyes.

When the flight attendant came by and asked if they wanted a drink she didn't answer at first. A beer would be nice. The older man next to her, in the window seat, ordered one.

"I got drink coupons," the older man said. "My treat." He even showed her the coupons, like cards in his hand. He had a low, gravelly voice.

"I'll have a beer," she heard herself say, lowering her tray. "Please." Her voice sounded like someone else's. The man in the aisle seat asked for a ginger ale.

The flight attendant took the coupon and marked her tablet and vanished.

"Thank you," she said to the older man.

"Sure. You okay, miss?" He looked at her, one eyebrow raised.

"My husband's taken ill while on a business trip. I've got to get to him." The lie was easy on her tongue, but in a way, wasn't it true? It was like the truth. And it let him know that she was married and she had her mind on important matters, in case he thought a drink coupon was an invitation to full flight-time chatter.

The man in the aisle seat cleared his throat and started working the crossword in the back of the airline magazine.

"I'm sorry to hear that," the older man said.

"I'm sure he'll be okay," she said, because if he wasn't, she shouldn't be drinking.

The flight attendant returned with the tray of drinks and set the beer down on her tray, with a plastic cup atop the can.

"Thank you," she said to the man with the coupons.

"Really, are you all right?" he asked. She realized she was staring at the beer.

"Yes," she heard herself say. "I'm fine."

He was shot. Maybe with a rich man she'd never heard of, in a city where he wasn't supposed to be.

She took the cup off the top and opened the beer. She drank from the can, the first cold taste of it like a door slamming open from a strong wind. For a moment, her mouth full of lager, she didn't swallow. She thought she could spit it back into the cup. But she gulped and felt the first sweet surge of the beer move in her blood. She drank again, a generous gulp.

We'll laugh about this. A prank. Because he's not dead. This can't be real.

"You're thirsty!" the coupon man said.

Her fingertips trembled against the cold of the can.

-

Kirsten lucked out. Her connecting gate at Houston Hobby Airport was right next door to her arrival gate. Wasn't that a good sign?

And there was a bar right there, by the gates.

She sat on the stool. The bar wasn't crowded.

She summoned up every possible ounce of courage and called Zach.

He answered on the third ring. "Hey," he said. "What's up?"

For a moment, shamed and scared, she couldn't breathe.

The bartender set the martini she'd ordered down in front of her. Two olives, a whisper of vermouth, the glass perfectly chilled.

"Kirsten?" Something in Zach's voice, as if he'd heard the shift in her breathing.

"I'm going to ask you a question and I want a direct answer."

Zach was quiet on the other end of the line.

"Has Henry gotten involved in something bad?" she asked.

Silence for five beats. "Bad?"

"Something he shouldn't have."

"Why would you ask me that?"

"Just answer the question."

"Do you mean has Henry gotten involved with something involving me?"

"Well?"

"No. You know Henry and I don't talk much. Why would you ask me this?"

"I'm in Houston. Waiting for a plane. Someone called me on Henry's phone and said Henry was dead in Austin. Henry told me he was in New York. On a business trip. But I've not heard from him except via text for a couple of days."

Zach let out a long, slow sigh. "And you believed this person?"

"I can't find that he's in New York. Nothing in his emails, or on his credit card, that he bought a ticket or reserved a hotel room."

"It's some sick joke."

"It was his phone. The caller said he was shot in Austin and I looked online and there were two men shot there Monday night. Their bodies were discovered early Tuesday morning. It's all over the Austin news."

"Whoa, slow down. Say again."

"You heard me." She stared at the martini. It looked so good.

"Have you had anything to drink?"

"I ordered a mineral water."

"Don't drink."

"I'm not an alcoholic and the bar's just a place to sit."

"So's the gate area. Go there. I'm listening to you walk there right now. Please."

"Zach. What if it's true?" Aside from Henry, Zach was the closest thing to family she had.

"It's not true. Just don't panic. It can't be Henry."

She still sat on the barstool. The martini gleamed. She took a sip: it was icy steel on her tongue. She was careful not to slurp so Zach couldn't hear.

"What are you doing?" Zach said. Like he could see her through the phone.

His voice made her put down the drink. She pushed it away, threw cash on the bar to pay for it, and walked toward her gate. "I'm walking to my gate. Happy?"

"I'll come to Austin," he said.

"Not until I know it's true."

"I don't want you doing this alone. You don't ever have to do the hard stuff alone."

"I know. I'll be fine. You've done enough for me." And she stopped, because they weren't ever supposed to talk about *that*.

"You're right. If someone had called me on your phone and said what they said, I'd be racing to wherever I thought you were."

She stopped walking. "I know you would."

"Call me as soon as you know something." He coughed. "No matter how late, you call me."

"All right."

Kirsten glanced back toward the bar. The bartender had cleared away the martini. She said good-bye to her foster brother, ended the call, and sat down to wait for her flight.

-

Mender followed her, hanging back, staring at his phone screen like most of the people walking through Houston Hobby. She walked into a bar across from the gate for the Austin flight. It didn't look as busy as the flight from New Orleans had been.

He kept walking. Found a vantage spot where he could watch her. She ordered a martini and then got on the phone. She appeared badly shaken still.

His phone buzzed. Annie.

"Hi, babe," he said.

"I miss you," she said. "How was your day?"

"Complicated but all right. How you feeling?"

"She's kicking up a storm," she said. "Back's killing me. And I'm out of ice cream."

"I'm sorry." Mender wished he was home, curled up next to her on the bed. She liked to lay on her side; month nine and it was the only way she could get comfortable. He'd spoon into her, his palm on her swelling belly, feeling the baby stir. He thought he would have been home by now, but the job had taken this extra work. And it was more money.

He could quit. Not receive the full payment. But babies were expensive, and he'd promised Annie he wouldn't work the first six months after the baby was born. They needed the money, so he needed to see this job through.

"It's okay. How did the client meetings go?" Annie asked.

"All right. They might keep me a couple more days."

"Oh, babe. What if this baby comes early?" Her voice rose slightly. Annie was not the type to get rattled and this surprised him.

"She won't. I'll be home soon."

"All right," she said, but she didn't sound convinced.

"You call me if you can't sleep," he said.

"You need your rest to stay sharp," she said. "You do the job right and then you can worry about me."

She was right. "Love you."

"Love you too. Sleep tight." She hung up. She always hung up first because she believed there would always be a tomorrow. He knew better.

He'd kept his gaze on Kirsten North during the call. He watched her not drink her martini—*she must be rethinking getting drunk, unfortunately*, he thought—and make a phone call. She was upset.

She knew. How did she know? He realized maybe he should have sat closer to her during her phone call, tried to eavesdrop, but that was a huge risk. He could not be seen showing any interest in her or have her notice him again.

Kirsten North sat down at the gate. He sat a row over from her, with her back to him, but where he could watch her.

Airports were busy, with lots of security. Lots of witnesses. It was more of a challenge than ever to follow someone from one: she could have been calling someone to pick her up, taking a rideshare, grabbing a cab, renting a car. Telling a rideshare or cabdriver to follow her would be memorable and normally you had to tell them your destination—he didn't know where she was going.

Mender had to think. How could he follow her?

5

The press had been at the bottom of Flora's gated driveway the day after the murder. She hadn't looked at the news channels, but she'd heard from friends in Lakehaven that they'd seen a news report, that the reporter broadcast from her front gate, that at some point Teddy had asked the TV crews to not set up right in front of their driveway. It was strange, she thought, people letting her know that her husband's murder investigation was on TV, and what was happening at the end of her driveway. Did that make it more real for them? Did they think she needed to know her husband's death was on the local news?

She had looked at the headlines on her phone. They felt like bits from someone else's life, an odd reality that had invaded her own.

TECH INVESTOR MURDERED IN LOCAL WAREHOUSE.

ZHANG SLAIN WITH UNIDENTIFIED MAN.

FLORA ZHANG WIDOWED, DOESN'T KNOW WHAT THE HELL SHE WILL DO NEXT. OR EVER.

That last headline was one she wrote herself. She was alone now, even with Teddy and Morgan, alone in a way she hadn't felt before.

The press weren't there, but there was a car parked by the gate. Teenagers taking pictures with their phones. They moved aside as she drove her Mercedes by, and one of them actually raised his phone and took a picture of her. She nearly stopped the car to yell at him, but she knew they all would just take more pictures. And post them, and then strangers would feel entitled to comment on her—her grief, her bad luck, her wealth.

Murder meant an end to privacy.

She drove down the hill, past other gated mansions, down to a road that crossed over a narrow bend of Lake Austin, close to where it became Lady Bird Lake—the name for the Colorado River as it ran past downtown. She drove down Cesar Chavez Street on the north side of the lake into downtown proper, then turned and parked in the tower's garage.

The residential high-rises had blossomed over the past decade as Austin grew and grew, and the downtown area now held more than the state capitol and a few large office buildings and entertainment districts that catered to the tourists and the UT kids. Adam had always wanted to live downtown, although they were just across the narrow water and already close…and Lakehaven had a great school district. Adam told her they would send Morgan to private school anyway. Decision made.

And she had just stood there in her shock, and nodded, and gone along. Why? She would not have done that before her marriage. But she had, and now she didn't have to go along anymore.

She got out of the car and checked her keys. Maybe it was the police there. Suddenly she felt a tremble of fear. Maybe she should have brought Teddy. Or told Teddy. It was probably the police.

She entered the code and the elevator took her straight from the garage to the penthouse.

The doors opened.

The lights were off. She had been so certain they were on. She stepped off the elevator into the foyer of what should have soon been their new home. She flicked the screen on her phone, found the flashlight app, and tried to remember where the light controls were. There. She pressed the button and the lights came on.

"Hello?" she called. Her voice wavered a little. "Is anyone here?"

She could hear a distant noise…music. Not surprising in downtown Austin, where there were many venues offering live music. She walked through the penthouse, turning on more lights. It was grand and glorious and now she'd never live here. The penthouse took up the entire top floor. It was, even more than the Lakehaven mansion, a sign of how well Adam had done. That, Flora thought, was why he wanted it and why he was sure she'd want it too. The windows of the main living room faced west, toward the dark rise of the Texas Hill Country.

The music came from the floor below. She peeked over the balcony off the main living room. Lights, brightly glowing beneath her. She decided she must have misjudged—it had been the floor below, not hers that was lit. The lack of sleep, the constant worry, it was undoing her.

She walked through the rooms, trying not to imagine the life here that she and Adam wouldn't have. The rooms were mostly empty, but he'd stocked basics in the kitchen. There was wine and champagne, presumably for when they moved in, and takeout from his favorite lunch places in the fridge. Had he eaten here?

She went down the hall from the kitchen toward the guest rooms. One he'd already made into an office, with a desk and bookshelves and photos from home.

Had Adam stayed here to work? He hadn't mentioned that to her.

What else didn't he tell me?

The office here was much like the one at their Lakehaven house. A high-end Danish desk; a photo on the corner of him and Flora and Morgan, taken on Morgan's birthday. She thought with a jolt that it might well be the last photo of Adam that was taken, at least that she knew of.

She walked out of the office and back down the hallway. She walked onto the penthouse's balcony—this one among those located on the east side of the building. It was thirty stories up. She didn't like heights, but the wind felt good in her face and the music on the floor below had stopped.

This was where Adam had wanted to be. She thought she would have learned to be happy here. But then she was glad Morgan wouldn't be playing out on this balcony. She'd sell the penthouse soon. No way she was leaving her house now.

She looked up at the scattering of stars and closed her eyes. The night was silent and she took several calming breaths. It was the first time she'd been physically alone in days, no one else in the house, no one hovering near her.

You're free, she thought. It was a terrible thing to think. She pushed the thought away. She felt suddenly cold, then hot. She couldn't think like this, she couldn't.

You get to make your own choices. For better or worse. He's not here to interfere.

Then she heard it.

A noise.

A footfall, or the sound of something dropping.

There were no rugs on the hardwood and marble floors and thus nothing to mask the sound.

Someone was in the penthouse.

She felt a chilly terror slide up her spine. She stepped from the balcony back into the living room.

"Hello?" she called. "Hello? I'm calling the police."

Silence again. She dialed building security; the guard at the front desk said he'd be right up.

Now she moved through the rooms, toward the elevator where the guard would arrive.

His office? Is that where the sound came from? She dialed the phone for Teddy.

"I'm at the penthouse," she said as soon as he answered. "I think someone's here. I called the guard."

"Leave," Teddy said immediately. "Just go downstairs. I'm on my way."

"No, stay on the line with me," she said. She headed down the hallway. The light in his office was on. She had turned it on, but had she turned off the hallway light? She couldn't remember.

"Just leave."

"The guards are coming," she said loudly, in case the intruder hadn't heard. She made it plural too.

Flora stepped into the office. No one here. There was a shut closet door. She opened it and it was empty—save for a few boxes and binders and office supplies still in the shopping bags.

She went back out to the hallway. The guard had arrived. He was fortyish, bespectacled. She hadn't heard the elevator arrive. Was it always so quiet? "Mrs. Zhang? You all right?"

"Yes. I was sure I heard a noise…." Now she felt foolish. "Teddy, the guard's here. It's all right," she said, and she hung up before he could answer.

"Let's check then," he said kindly, and he proceeded to check every room, every closet, even the cabinets in the kitchen where a person could hide. She followed him.

They found nothing.

"I feel so dumb," she said.

"Please don't," he said. "Now, there's two ways out of the penthouse. The elevator and the stairwell, in case of fire."

She nodded.

"That door is locked from the other side?"

"Yes, ma'am. You have to have an electronic passkey to get in from the stairs. Or the elevator."

"Is there a security camera in the elevator?"

He cleared his throat. "That's a private elevator for y'all; and no, the camera's not activated as you haven't moved in yet."

But could someone have snuck out while she was exploring? She thought not. "My imagination then. I'm sorry to have troubled you."

The guard cleared his throat. "If I may, ma'am, I'm very sorry about Mr. Zhang. I met him a couple of times and I helped him carry a box up here last week. He was so nice. My condolences."

"Thank you."

"Would you like me to stay up here with you until you're ready to leave?"

"I'm ready to leave now." They walked to the elevator. "Have the police been here? I know they must be talking to everyone who knew Adam."

"Not while I was here, ma'am, but I can check the logs."

She turned off the lights and they stepped into the elevator.

"He'd moved his home office here already," she said. "Did you see my husband here much?"

"No, ma'am," he said, looking straight ahead.

Something in the tone. "Did you see anyone coming up here in the past couple of days?" She thought of that guest room, made up and furnished for no reason other than Adam might be using it.

"No, ma'am. I can check the visitor's log if you like."

"Yes, please."

They entered the downstairs lobby. He went to the computer terminal. "Visitors…guy delivering furniture a week ago."

The furnished office he hadn't mentioned to her. Why? Did he need a place to escape from work and from her? Tears danced at the back of her eyes. "All right. Thank you so much for your help."

"Yes, ma'am. Again, my condolences."

She went back down to the garage and got into her car. She had to get some rest. She was imagining things, she was creating unneeded drama in her head.

She drove home, feeling more embarrassed, more certain that she had to get a grip on herself. She'd sell the high-rise; she didn't want to be there.

She'd go home, watch Morgan sleep in his crib for a minute, and then get some rest. She had to figure out her life.

Flora didn't notice the car following her at a distance from the high-rise. It turned right at the last light before her house.

6

Mender and Kirsten were again holding the last two boarding passes. But the flight going to Austin wasn't crowded, and he was able to secure a seat a couple of rows ahead of her by choosing a window seat. Kirsten went farther back and got an aisle.

The flight from Houston to Austin was like an elevator, up and down quickly, barely time for beverage service. Once they landed, he was off the plane before she was. He glanced back, seeing her about thirty feet behind him. She was walking in a hurry. He exited the secure area of the airport and nearly took the escalator down to baggage claim, but at the last second he saw the sign for taxis and rideshare pickups. He backstepped off the escalator and hurried toward the sign. He slowed a bit, checking his phone, glancing back. She was studying her phone, now about ten feet behind him.

She had to be doing a rideshare app. He slowed and she passed him up, gaze still locked on the phone.

They both followed the signs, him careful to keep a few people between the two of them. The signs guided them to the rental car facility and then to a pickup area for rideshares and taxis. She went toward the rideshare side. He watched her, studying her phone, heading toward a white subcompact.

He ran to the taxi stand, which was less busy. The first driver waiting raised a hand in a friendly wave.

He got in.

"Where to, sir?"

"I need you to follow a car coming out of the rideshare lot."

"Why?"

He produced a private investigator's license, one he always carried with him while on a job. "Because I'm following a woman who's flown here to cheat on her husband and he's paying my bill and your fare. I'm not a creep; I'm just doing my job, same as you."

The cabdriver turned to study him. As if not entirely swayed by the PI license.

"If you won't help me, I'll get in another cab, sir," Mender said.

"All right, all right." But he took a photo with his camera of the PI license before handing it back.

Damn it, he thought. *Okay.* With his own camera he made a point of taking a picture of the taxi's ID and license.

The cab roared out of the lot and headed toward the highway. He saw the white car the target had gotten into turning onto Highway 71, headed into Austin proper. The cab followed.

Then the white car took the exit toward downtown. The taxi followed.

He leaned forward, watching.

Several minutes later the white car turned into the entrance of a building off Interstate 35 and pulled up to the front. The target got out.

"That," the cabdriver said, "is the Austin Police headquarters."

Oh, hell. But he kept his voice calm. "Makes sense. She's been seeing a detective there. Drop me off here."

He glanced at the man's eyes in the rearview. It didn't matter if he was or wasn't convinced; he seemed to have decided it wasn't any of his business.

Mender paid the cabbie, adding a hugely generous tip. He got out. He found a spot where he could watch the headquarters front door and not draw attention to himself. And wait.

-

Kirsten took a rideshare into downtown. She had heard Austin was cool and trendy, but all she saw along the first stretch of the highway were lots selling mobile homes and many billboards, three of which featured Milo's Gin. A smiling bald man hoisted a bottle and a different well-known actor or athlete on each billboard had a friendly arm around the man (who must be Milo). The billboards worked: she wished she had a bottle of gin, but she pushed away the thought. As they approached downtown, the lights of the city gleamed, and downtown was much bigger and taller than she'd imagined it would be, all that tech money having built luxury office buildings and gleaming condo towers.

The driver dropped her off at the Austin Police Department headquarters, located in downtown Austin on Eighth Street close to I-35. She approached the front counter and told the officer on duty that she might have information about the double shooting.

The officer took her name and asked her to wait. After ten minutes a detective came out and walked her to an interview room to take her statement. He said his name was Jones and he was one of the detectives on the investigation. Kirsten told Jones about the phone call, about looking up a shooting in Austin online and then coming from New Orleans. Jones—young, male, and drawing the late-night shift—seemed to study her, as though measuring whether or not she seemed credible.

"Have you filed a missing person report on your husband?" Jones asked.

"No. Since I thought he was on a business trip."

"But you felt that you should come all the way to Austin first? Did you call here?"

"I couldn't sit at home. What good would a call have done? I needed to be here."

He looked at her as though she might be slightly stupid. "Do you have a picture of your husband?"

He's seen the bodies, Kirsten realized. This was about to cease being a weird theory and perhaps turn into an awful reality.

She pulled her phone from her purse, opened the photos icon, and thumbed through the pictures. She found a good one of Henry; it was from last summer, just him, leaning against the front door in a Louisiana Ragin' Cajuns T-shirt and khaki shorts. They'd gone out for dinner with Zach, a rarity, because Henry and Zach didn't always get along so great. Henry looked handsome in the picture. Nice smile, very slight gut he was working on getting rid of, tall, brown hair, brown eyes, Clark Kent eyeglasses.

She handed the phone to Jones; he didn't react or say nope, not the guy who was killed. He looked and then he handed the phone back and asked her to take a seat, please.

"If the dead man's not my husband, you can just tell me," she said. "Can't you just tell me?"

"I'm sorry, you need to speak with the chief detective on the case. I'll be right back." He left the room and shut the door.

A staffer stuck his head in and offered her coffee—did Jones tell him she'd be here awhile?—and she accepted, feeling a numbness begin to creep over her. Jones could have just said, *It's not him*, but he didn't. He couldn't.

Then she realized with a shock that maybe the victims had been shot in the face and he couldn't tell. She fought down a tremble.

She waited and sipped her coffee. Soon a woman entered, wearing jeans and a blazer, dark hair pulled back in a ponytail. Eyes bright, alert, sharp.

"Mrs. North? I'm Detective Bard. Would you mind if I asked you a few questions?" She had a soft Southern accent, her voice a bit scratchy.

"I already gave a statement. I just want to know if my husband is dead. And if he is...I want more than that. I want whoever hurt him caught."

"I understand." Detective Bard made Kirsten go through her story again. She listened as carefully as a psychiatrist. "You're sure the caller used your husband's phone?"

"Yes. His name appeared on my screen."

She went to the door, spoke to someone out in the hall, and then returned to sit across from Kirsten. "And so you decided to fly here. Tonight."

"Yes." Kirsten paused. "I showed Detective Jones a picture of Henry, but he didn't say anything."

"Will you show me?"

She did. Bard studied the photo. She handed the phone back to Kirsten. "Mrs. North, would you be willing to view the victim and see if you can identify him as your husband?"

Kirsten felt the words punch holes in her soul. She didn't speak but nodded.

"It's about a twenty-minute drive to the medical examiner's office."

Kirsten slowly rose from her chair.

-

Bard drove. They were silent on the way. Kirsten wanted to get her phone out and text Zach, but it felt strange to be on her phone in front of a detective. So she closed her eyes and tried to steady her breathing. She thought of Henry, always calm in a crisis. Even during the worst crises.

Be like Henry.

I can't do this if it's you. I need you. Please don't be there. Please call me in a minute and tell me this is all a bad dream.

She said nothing as Bard escorted her inside the Travis County Medical Examiner's Office. It was very modern and clean and nice, like a health-care clinic. An attendant walked them down a hallway to the morgue itself. She had only seen morgues in movies and on TV; this wasn't like that, with worn tile and dim lights. But the room did feel cold. The attendant walked them to a sheeted body; there were three others there and Kirsten didn't look toward them. Wouldn't he have been in cold storage? But then they knew she was coming because Bard surely called, so the staff would have gotten the body ready for her to view.

"All right," Kirsten said, steadying herself. She crossed her arms as though she expected a physical blow. "Go ahead."

The attendant gently pulled back the sheet to reveal the unmarked face.

Silence for long seconds. Kirsten found her voice. "That's my husband."

"That's Henry North?" Bard said.

"Henry Kenneth North," Kirsten said. "He was named for his two grandfathers." This wasn't happening. Henry lay dead before her. Some nights she had watched him sleep, marveling at the miracle that a decent, loving guy loved her. Fought for her. Did the unimaginable for her.

She stared at him, and when she swayed Bard steadied her. The attendant covered Henry's face and Bard escorted her out. Kirsten did not cry. Bard escorted her to a private room with a sofa and a chair and Kirsten sat down heavily on the sofa.

I should be crying, Kirsten thought. *They'll want me to cry. No, not in front of them.*

"I'm sorry, Mrs. North, I'm sorry for your loss. Can I get you some water?"

She shook her head. She took in four deep breaths and when she spoke her voice sounded shaky. "Henry told me he was in New York. He never said anything about coming to Austin."

Bard sat down across from her. "Do you know why he wouldn't have told you the truth about his travel?"

"No. I can't think of any reason."

"Pardon my bluntness. Was your marriage a happy one?"

"Yes," she said. "I thought so."

"Could he have been here to see someone you didn't know about?"

"You mean like a girlfriend?"

"Yes."

"That's not Henry. I mean, he's not the type."

Bard looked at her blankly, and Kirsten knew the detective must think her naive. But she knew Henry, and Bard didn't.

"I had no reason to believe he would cheat on me," Kirsten said, fighting the urge to grab the detective by the blazer lapels and shake her to make her understand.

"Lots of people visit New Orleans. Could he have met someone there from Austin?"

"We both work at home. We're together…a lot." No, it wouldn't have been easy. "He wasn't shot in the head. How did he die?"

"He was shot once in the shoulder, three times in the chest. One bullet nicked his heart. I don't think he suffered."

You can't know that, Kirsten thought. It sounded like a meaningless reassurance that a detective would offer to a new widow. But she said nothing.

"Was the other man shot repeatedly?" She wasn't sure why the question fell out of her mouth. She could not imagine anyone wanting to shoot Henry.

Bard gave her a look that was hard to read. "Twice in the head. It's possible that your husband rushed the shooter, or they grappled. We're still investigating."

Kirsten didn't want to picture Henry's last moments, but the possible images rose in her brain and she pushed them away.

Bard asked, "And what do you and your husband do for work?"

"He is a software consultant. He specializes in computer security. Stopping hackers, finding vulnerabilities in his clients' networks so they can be fixed. His company is called North Star Consulting."

"And does he have employees?"

"No, it's just him. He's a freelancer."

Bard made a note in her notebook. "And you?"

"I'm a freelance information researcher."

Bard stopped writing. "I don't know what that is."

"I do research. Into people, into companies. Some clients hire me to vet people for executive or sensitive positions. I dig into their pasts and make sure there are no concerning issues. Sometimes I get hired to research firms that might be attractive acquisitions for other companies."

"You find the dirt."

"Facts. Dirt, if it's there to be found. Why…why is this happening? Why is my husband dead?"

Detective Bard put down her pen. "We don't know that yet. Do you have a place to stay in Austin?"

"Not yet." Her voice shook. "I haven't made a reservation."

"Do you have any friends or family in town?"

Kirsten shook her head. "I will find a hotel. When...when can I take him home to New Orleans?"

"I don't know yet. This is an active investigation...."

"He had no enemies. Everyone loved Henry, he..." And then the sheer weight of the horror hit her and she doubled over as she sat on the couch, fighting for control. She did not cry in front of other people. That was a lesson she'd learned young. She. Did. Not. Cry. In. Public.

"Okay. Okay, Mrs. North, I can find you a place to stay. Give me an idea of your budget." She looked pained at having to say this to a woman who'd just confirmed she was a widow.

"I don't want help. Thank you. You focus on finding who killed him."

"To do that, we need to know about his life. What brought him here."

"I don't know!"

"Was he having money problems? Did he know Adam Zhang?"

"No and no. I can't do this right now. I can't."

"I understand." Bard actually sounded like she did. "We can give you some time. Can you come back tomorrow and talk to me? I'll call you to set up a time."

Kirsten nodded. They drove back to the APD headquarters. Bard brought her back to her office and she signed a statement. A police officer appeared to escort her. Bard told Kirsten that there was a good, clean budget hotel a couple of blocks away and given that it was midweek, they might have rooms.

The officer walked her there. He tried to make light chatter with her, but Kirsten never heard what he said. He waited to make sure there was a vacancy for her. The hotel did have a room available. When she was checking in, the desk clerk asked how long she was staying and she started to say *I don't know; my husband is dead* and *I don't know how long this will take*, but she couldn't say those words: *My husband is dead.* So she said, "Three days, and maybe longer. I don't know yet."

"I'll make a note on the reservation. Ma'am, are you okay?"

Kirsten managed to nod. It was as if her body was waiting to be alone and let her grief explode, and as she got closer to privacy the howl waiting inside her was straining for release. She got her room keys—she asked for two; she and Henry always got two—and took her small suitcase to the ground-floor room.

She closed the door behind her; the room was small but spotlessly clean. Walking into a hotel room was vaguely reminiscent of her years in foster care, stepping into a new bedroom, evaluating it and letting it tell her something about her foster parents: whether they would treat her with decency or if she was simply a check from the parish to them.

Hotel rooms didn't tell her anything.

She sat on the end of the bed and she said Henry's name, once, and the grief came not like the eruption she expected, but a slowly rising heat, and that was somehow worse, because it felt like it was permanently attaching itself to her, a lump on her shoulder, a disfigurement on her face.

She fell back on the bed and she cried, for minutes, hours, days it felt like and then the emptiness took the place of the grief and she stared at the blank ceiling and thought: *I'm going to kill whoever killed him.*

No you're not. Of course you're not.

I am. Watch me.

You cannot risk it. The police will handle this.

They'll look at you. Your life with him. They'll suspect you. They have to. They'll dig into your life with Henry....

Let them, she thought.

Who had called her and sent her on her way to Austin?

Someone knew he was dead and reached out to her? Why bother?

Why did someone care that she knew?

The other man. The one he died with. Adam Zhang. He was some investment bigwig. He must have hired Henry. Brought him here. But why would Henry have concealed that from her?

Did the caller feel bad about Henry's death? Told her out of pity? Could someone who shot two men dead feel remorse?

It was this Adam Zhang's fault—it had to be. She would have to learn everything about him. *I'll need money. Information. Leverage.* Henry had died with a rich man and the whole world was organized to protect rich men.

She'd need a gun. To end whoever did this.

She was supposed to call Zach. She couldn't. He would try to talk her into coming home. She could not. Would not. Until she knew the truth. She saw on her phone he'd left texts. Messages. She turned off the phone. Tomorrow she'd talk to him. Now she was too raw.

She went to the small business center at the hotel and connected her laptop to the available Wi-Fi. She started searching the internet and the information databases she relied on for her work. Printed out photos, articles, anything to help her understand the man who had died with Henry. Material on his life, on his wife, on his business. All the accounts of the murders that she could find. She stole the center's tape dispenser and took it back to her room, where she began to put the pictures and articles up on the wall where she could easily browse the information and perhaps spot connections.

She stood in front of the pictures of Adam Zhang. The biography was impressive. He'd grown up in Houston, the son of immigrants. Valedictorian, full scholarship to Rice. He'd gotten his MBA, worked for a couple of start-ups that had done well (one went public, the other didn't, but both were bought by much larger companies for premium prices). He'd taken his money and started Zhang Townsend, known for funding the companies that hit at the right time and helping to nurture them through their rocky beginnings when many start-ups stumbled and never recovered. He'd done very, very well for himself and Flora.

Next she read a series of profiles a guy named Marco Hernandez had written on Adam Zhang.

"What I do," Adam was quoted in one of the profiles as saying, "is assess potential. My partner and I look at a company, or even just an idea, and try to assess what market it could meet, how the idea could grow into something huge. Could it grow enough to be sold to a larger company? That's frankly the more likely outcome rather than a successful public stock offering. It's often the most desirable. But then at the same time, when every promising company gets bought up by larger ones, you lose that chance to truly grow something great. I look at the history: How did the company start, how did they first make their money, what ideas worked for them at the beginning, and can that magic be manifested and multiplied?"

She studied the companies he'd funded—there had been a list of them on the Zhang Townsend website, and she'd gone to the companies' individual websites. Mostly tech companies, but he'd invested in two consumer goods companies—one a cider company here in Austin, another an organic dog food company in Houston. There were pictures of Adam every time he had a success, but his wins had aged him. Silver had arrived early in his dark hair. It was a high-stakes game he played. She looked at the tech companies, wondering if any were clients he shared with her husband. But she saw nothing to connect him to Henry, and she didn't recognize the names as being among Henry's few clients. One a network management firm, another centered on creating and managing digital content for huge-scale e-commerce sites. A third was focused on a new way to analyze financial trends for banks and stock traders. All had been bought by bigger, better-known tech firms who wanted to fold their technology into their product offerings. Bought for tens of millions of dollars. Adam was good at his job.

She also taped on the wall the pages she'd printed about Flora Zhang. She found a certain amount of biographical information on a leadership page for a foundation that funded research into cures for rare diseases that didn't always get attention from pharmaceutical companies. Flora was the chief mission officer of Zhang Global Rare Diseases Foundation. She was born in New York to an American father and a Chinese mother who were both professors at Columbia. She had graduated from Columbia, got a master's in journalism at the University of Texas, and met Adam Zhang there. Kirsten wondered why she'd left New York for Austin. An adventure? Tired of New York? Hopeful of a job in the booming Austin tech economy that had transformed the city? She and Adam were apparently supportive of local charities.

Nothing much about the person she was. Kirsten looked for her on social media; she had a Faceplace account as Flora Graham Zhang, mostly consisting of pictures of herself with friends at gala events, or having coffee, or at a girls' night out. She didn't smile a lot in the pictures. There weren't a lot of personal insights shared. In several pictures she stood with an attractive blond woman who was tagged as Taylor Townsend.

The investment firm's name was Zhang Townsend and Adam's business partner was Shawn Townsend. Taylor must be his wife.

Kirsten went farther down the page until she found a few pictures with Flora and her husband, Adam. They looked…moderately happy. She thought of pictures of herself and Henry, goofily smiling, enjoying life, not holding back. They had nothing compared to the Zhangs and yet the Zhangs looked like fully posable mannequins to her. Almost awkward with each other.

Her Henry was one in a million. Billion.

Research should have been a way to fend off tears, but it didn't work. The tears came back and she couldn't see the printouts and the pictures anymore, so she curled up on the bed, alone. She hated to sleep alone. She was used to Henry being by her side.

Kirsten North lay awake for hours, unable to sleep, until she closed her eyes again and had one last thought before exhaustion claimed her: *When you wake up you're not this weepy sad widow. You're a bullet. You're going to end whoever did this. You might not be you anymore.*

Then she was in the blessed blackness.

7

Mender watched Kirsten North come out of the police headquarters and even in the thin light of the entrance he could see her world had crumbled. A police officer walked with her and they turned onto Eighth, away from the highway, and continued down a few blocks. He followed.

They went into a modest hotel. He waited. A few minutes later the officer headed back toward APD headquarters.

If she'd identified her husband, then she'd be depressed. Maybe suicidal. A hotel, with its security cameras and guests coming and going, was not an ideal site to do his work. There would be cameras in the lobby. And he'd need to find her room. There was a way to do this and a way not to. It had already been a risk to sit next to her on the flight. Being at the same hotel—no way.

He walked on to another hotel, a nicer one two blocks away, and got a room. He went upstairs and assessed the job. He was on unexpected ground, and the situation with the target had changed. He needed a weapon, he needed to assess her locale, and he needed to find out what her plans were. Because if he messed up now and got caught, Annie would never forgive him.

He could see the top of the target's hotel. *Both of us in our rooms*, he thought, *missing someone we love.* He got undressed for bed and was nearly asleep when he wondered again, *Who told Kirsten North to come to Austin? Who else knew?*

That, he decided, was another problem. One he'd have to solve after he'd figured out the best way to deal with the target, and depending on how the days ahead unfolded. It was like he thought he was playing one chess game and then suddenly everything on the board changed.

He ought to raise his price.

He turned over and thought again about the target. He tried not to think about the targets too much. It was strange, to have sat next to her and felt the anxiety and grief coming off her in waves. That was the most time he'd ever spent with a target alive.

That would end soon enough.

He opened his secured laptop and contacted his handler via email. Every hit man working at his level had a handler: a sort of assistant/researcher/provider who took care of the details that allowed him to move like a death in the shadows, unseen, unknown, untied to the criminal elements that could betray him to the police. His handler gave him what he needed to know about the client, about the target's locale, about schedules, about habits, about the weaknesses of the target. This arrangement allowed him to do his work with caution and care and let him focus on the kill rather than hunting down needed information or depending on chance.

In the near-immediate reply, his handler—using a code name of Garrison, as he was code-named Mender—gave him the link to a document hosted on an online service; Garrison told him what the password would be to access it. They could each type in it at the same time. When their conversation was finished, the document would be deleted.

Mender opened the document and wrote:

> —The target left NOLA to come to Austin. I saw her in the airport, turned around, flew back here. She was distraught and had bought a ticket last minute. She went straight from the airport to the police HQ. Who else knew it was her husband? You, me, the client.

His handler wrote:

> —The client has no reason to talk.
>
> —The job just got a lot more complicated. If I take care of her here it will be a news story. Unless I make her vanish.

—You can decline to continue.

—Not really. I need the money.

He waited. No response for several moments. Then Garrison wrote:

—Is it too dangerous?

—I need to know if client is cracking. No one else knew. Or we need to know how target knew to come to Austin.

—There could be any number of reasons.

—Not really.

—What do you need?

—My thought is not to kill her like her husband and leave a body behind. That feels like a big news story. She's distraught, grieving. Maybe she takes off. Vanishes. That's less of an impact. It could even make her look like she had something to do with the deaths, maybe.

—Suicide. Overwhelmed by grief. Some will be suspicious but that's always true.

—She's at the La Condra hotel on 8th. I need to know her room number. I need to know if she's planning on returning to New Orleans. If she has a flight reservation. I need a car and I need it delivered close to there. And I need rope, zip-ties, and a firearm. A way to sedate her for the suicide and a weapon in case I can't.

—I'll do what I can and will let you know. For sure the car first. Weapon and pharma may take a few more hours.

—I need to figure this out. Some other factor has entered this job. She's a freelance researcher. Maybe she dug into her husband's life and found out something we don't know. Maybe she found a source who talked to her. Now she's a risk.

—Don't get paranoid.

—I'm not.

—Client requesting photo confirmation once job completed.

—Understood.

—You're nearly done.

—Sure. But this job was supposed to be done last night, and I have other obligations.

—Ah yes. How is she?

—Craving ice cream. Text me a name and a password when you know something.

He leaned back. He could see as Garrison—there was an icon for each of them in the document's menu bar—selected all the text in the document and deleted it. And then Mender closed the document, after which his handler would delete the document itself.

He got back into bed. He hated when a job went wrong or required him to deviate from his plan. He never slept well for a week after a kill, and he'd hoped to stock up on sleep before the baby arrived. He cordially hated Henry and Kirsten North for the change in plans. He wished he had her room number and a gun because maybe he'd do the riskiest thing possible, knock on her door, get her to open it, fire two shots to end her, and collect the payment.

But he'd gotten rid of the gun he used for the work here in Austin as protocol dictated. He didn't have another one, and he'd just have to wait.

Sleep your last night, Kirsten, he thought, but then he decided she probably wasn't sleeping at all.

8

Friday

The next morning, Flora got up later than she'd intended. She had slept heavily for the first time since the murders. Usually Morgan's crying awoke her and now she rose to his silence in a sudden bolt of fear. She hurried to Morgan's room, but he wasn't there, and as she descended the stairs she could hear her neighbor Jeanne softly singing to him. Teddy and Jeanne had let her sleep. It had been a kindness. She sighed in relief, went back to her room, and showered.

Flora put on a nice suit, as if she were going into her office. She stared at herself in the bathroom mirror. She applied her makeup, as carefully as daubing paint on canvas. She looked immaculate. She felt broken.

She raised a pair of earrings to her ears and considered them in the mirror. Adam had given her these, of course. It would be best in the days ahead to wear things he had given her, not the things she had picked out for herself. A brief way to honor what had once been between them. Before he started to change.

I'm free. The ugly thought crowded into her head again and she pushed it away. *I can be who I want. I don't have to think about what he thinks.* It was strange, that she could both miss him and yet feel like a weight had slipped from her. It was confusing. She didn't want to be confused.

She put on the earrings and patted her dark hair. Calmed her face once more in the mirror and turned away.

Flora went downstairs and walked into the kitchen. Morgan sat in his high chair, Jeanne cleaning food off his cheeks; Teddy was reading the news on his tablet and drinking coffee. For a moment it felt to Flora like they were the family who belonged here, and she was the intruder....She froze and watched the scene for a moment. Morgan giggled.

"Good morning," Flora said.

"Morning," Jeanne said. "I brought some kolaches for y'all for breakfast. Teddy and I talked and we decided to let you sleep. I hope that's okay. You didn't have an appointment on your calendar. Teddy checked."

"Thank you both," she said. "I was exhausted."

"You look nice," Jeanne said, making way for Flora to sit next to a cleaned-up Morgan. Flora took Morgan's hand and smiled brightly, and Morgan smiled back.

"How's Mommy's little man?" Flora wrinkled her nose teasingly at Morgan.

"Hungry," Jeanne said. "If you're fine for a few minutes, I'll run next door and check on Milo, then come back before Teddy's gone to work if you need me to keep Morgan today."

"That's awesome if you can watch him. I do have an errand to run. Thank you, Jeanne." Jeanne nodded and hurried off.

Teddy poured her a cup of coffee. "What errands do you have?" He couldn't keep the surprise out of his voice. Like she should just be lying on a bed, broken. She'd done that since Adam died. Today she felt like doing *something*.

She sipped at her coffee. "I decided to go make the funeral arrangements today. I felt that I had to look pulled together." She wasn't sure when she would even get Adam's body back, but planning the funeral was an activity, and she needed that today. It had to be done, with dignity, and she would do it.

"Oh," Teddy said, as if she'd announced she was performing some herculean task. "I'll go with you."

"I can do it myself," Flora stated.

"You don't have to do that alone."

"I'll call Taylor. She'll go with me."

"I'm happy to help you....It would be an honor."

"Teddy," she said, and she realized her voice sounded sharper than she intended. "I know you mean well, but your hands are full at the office, I'm sure, and this is my job to do."

"Sure," he said with a nod. "Of course." His gaze broke from hers and he sipped his coffee. She could tell he had something else to say.

"What?"

"It's nothing." He set down his mug. "Jeanne and I watched the news this morning. No arrests yet. But they did release the name of the man found with him. Henry North, from New Orleans."

Henry North. "How did Adam know him?"

"I don't know. I checked: he's not in any of Adam's emails or his contacts listing. Do you recognize his name?"

Flora shook her head. "No. But Adam must have known him. He would not have gone to that warehouse with a stranger."

"I did a search on his name." Teddy's finger glided to another browser window on his tablet. "There is more than one Henry North in New Orleans, but this guy's profile on LinkedIn says he's a software consultant. And the news said the…other victim was in his thirties."

"What kind of consultant?"

"Security and hacking prevention. Which means he knows how to hack, to defend against it." One of Teddy's eyebrows arched. "Maybe Adam thought someone was trying to steal a business idea or sabotage one of our start-ups."

"Had Adam been hacked?"

"He never mentioned any concern like that to me," Teddy said. "I could hire a private investigator, see what they can find about this North guy."

"Won't the police do that?"

"Yes, I'm sure they will. I thought you might want to have your own source of knowledge. Because the police have told us nothing whatsoever."

She took a deep breath. "Let the police do their job. I don't want us to get in their way." Flora turned and drank her coffee.

She texted her friend Taylor Townsend: May I come see you? I need out of the house.

Of course, the answer came.

"I'm going to Taylor's," she said. She kissed the top of Morgan's head. "I might get her to go with me to the funeral home." Where she didn't have an appointment. Did you need one? Did funeral homes take walk-ins? The things you wondered at times like this.

Teddy said, "I'm sure Taylor will be a help. Before you go, you should know...there's a reporter down at the gate. Just one. I saw him on the security camera. He's sitting down there drinking coffee. There's not a TV crew. I think it's that guy who interviewed Adam for some magazine pieces. I can tell him you have no comment and open the gate for you."

Questions, Flora thought. *Are you really ready for questions? Are you ready for what you might say? Put on your grieving widow face, say all the right things, and then drive on. It's just one person, no cameras.*

9

Adam had jokingly called the cul-de-sac where they lived the golden circle, because the people who lived there were, to be blunt, successful. Flora thought it tone-deaf and arrogant. But the golden part aside, it was decidedly a circle, a close one, and they looked out for one another.

Two of her neighbors were at the bottom of their driveways as well, one with arms crossed, the other with his phone raised, aimed at the solitary member of the press who sat on a curb just outside her gate with two coffees and a bag of bagels.

Flora drove the Mercedes down, opening the gate remotely, and the reporter got up and out of the way. He was on his phone, listening with an intent look on his face.

He nodded at her and lowered his phone as she slowly drove through the opening. Flora recognized this reporter, a young freelancer named Marco Hernandez; he wrote for some of the largest business publications in the country. He had interviewed Adam for a series of articles for a business magazine, and another time onstage at a tech event here in Austin. Marco was prepared and thoughtful; Flora liked him, and so had Adam, who normally thought of the press as a useful megaphone for his companies.

So she stopped and lowered the window.

"Mrs. Zhang?" Hernandez stepped forward tentatively. "I'm so sorry. I'm just so very sorry."

She felt like she'd heard *He's in a better place* and *I know how you must be feeling* so many times that this simple, sincere declaration of sorrow moved her.

"I appreciate that. Adam enjoyed the interviews he did with you. But I didn't think you covered criminal investigations."

"I'm not writing a story right now."

"We're always writing stories."

"We?"

"What?" she asked.

"You said we. You're still a journalist."

"Well. Not anymore." Her face felt hot. "Those days are long gone."

"Hey," a voice called. "Don't you have anything better to do than bother a fresh widow?"

Flora peered past Marco to see her neighbor, Jeanne's husband, Milo, arms crossed, glaring at Marco.

"I'm not bothering her, sir," Marco said.

"Milo, it's fine; it's okay," Flora said.

"Milo?" Marco said. "Wait. Milo from Milo's Gin?"

Flora nodded.

"It's an outrage," Milo said, "that they won't leave you alone." He sounded more regretful than angry.

"This reporter knew Adam, Milo; it's all right," Flora assured him. She appreciated Milo's defense, but it wasn't needed. Milo was sixtyish, the self-styled "Gin King of Texas" ("Milo's Gin, Texas's Favorite," the ads read), and he and Jeanne liked to parent the whole cul-de-sac.

"I brought coffee and bagels." Marco held up a bag. "Would you like one, sir? I'm a fan of your gin." He gave Milo a polite smile.

Milo seemed mollified by Marco's words. "No, thank you. I just wanted to be sure you're okay, Flora. We're all so worried about you. We saw on the news they know who that other man was. Do you need anything? I don't want to pry. We just want to be here for you, hon. Jeanne told me she's going to watch Morgan today for you."

"And I appreciate it so much, Milo, thanks. I'll call you later."

Milo nodded and went back to his house, walking up the driveway. Flora gave the neighbor with the phone camera a wave and he nodded and returned to his house.

"My neighbors are being protective," Flora said.

"It's nice that they care about you." Marco's phone buzzed and he glanced at the incoming text message. "Do you know this Henry North they've identified? Was he a friend or colleague of Adam's?"

"You said you weren't writing a story...and no, I don't know Henry North, and that's the only question I'll answer."

"Oh. Because a source of mine on the police force says Henry North's widow is at the, um, crime scene right now and she's making a fuss."

It was such an odd thing to say, a tidbit offered, and Flora stared at Marco. "Why would you tell me that?"

"I thought you might want to know. Maybe Mrs. North knows why this happened."

And if you point me toward her, maybe I'll give you an interview. Or you're about to bolt over there yourself and you're luring me along to see what happens when widow one encounters widow two. Suddenly Marco didn't seem so nice anymore, with his coffee and bagels.

"Did Adam know this wife of Henry North's?" he asked.

"No...wait. What are you saying?" *That my husband died over a married woman?*

"I'm not saying or suggesting anything. I'm trying to figure out why these two men who apparently didn't know each other ended up together. I thought maybe you knew the Norths." He hesitated. "Maybe they were working on some project together."

"I don't...I don't know the Norths. Excuse me."

She drove away. Such an odd term Milo had used: "fresh widow." She couldn't think of herself that way.

Her thoughts turned to what Marco had just told her: *Henry North's wife was making a fuss at the murder scene?*

Flora hadn't gone to see where Adam died. She forgot about going to Taylor's and instead headed in the direction of the crime scene, which was only fifteen minutes away.

She ran two stop signs without noticing.

10

Kirsten woke from sleep feeling like her body had been pounded with rocks. It turned out grief could physically hurt. She staggered to the bathroom and showered, then put on a change of fresh clothes—jeans, blouse, jacket. And thought about her next step. She stared at the wall she'd covered with notes and printouts on the Zhangs and their business. She told herself to look at it as a problem to be broken down, a section of an intel report for a client. Analyze the information, synthesize it, and then put a bullet in whoever was responsible. Simple. Except for the last part.

She looked at her phone. Two more voice mails and a text from Zach, asking her what was happening. Saying that it was on the news that the Austin police had released Henry's name as the second victim. She texted him back: I am broken. But I have things to do and I'll talk to you later. Then she silenced the phone.

The caller had gotten their wish, she thought. Someone wanted her to be here. Someone wanted Henry identified sooner rather than later. Why?

The answer was here in Austin, and the questions Detective Bard had asked last night made Kirsten feel as though she had to stand up for Henry, defend him.

Bard had implied Henry was the reason for their deaths.

Like a powerful wealthy man such as Adam Zhang couldn't have enemies.

They always wanted to blame the easier target. She knew that from her days in foster care. Whoever could fight back the least was the easiest to blame. And that blame made her livid.

Often when she had to write a profile of a person for her clients, she didn't go to an internet search engine first. She went to where they lived or worked. She looked at their surroundings. You could learn a lot about a person from the world they built at home, where they were employed, and what they did when they arrived at their job and after they left.

This could apply to where they died as well. The thought was terrifying. But she had to do it.

He did it for you, she thought.

She logged in to a private website that hosted a discussion group of people who did work like hers: information analysts who would share strategies and resources useful for creating profiles of people and companies. Sometimes they shared…cheats. Ways around the system, or useful tech hacks, or scripts to do phone interviews if you needed someone to admit something they might not if you asked directly. It was all done anonymously, and they were careful not to reveal too much.

If she wrote that she was looking into her husband's murder in Austin, it would not be hard for someone to deduce her real name. And that would be the end of her participation in the group.

She considered and then typed: May need support in the next few days for information related to computer hacking. Not in support of illegal activity but in creating a profile have come across troubling behavior. Will notify police anonymously if I find evidence.

She called up a rideshare driver on her phone app. Then she summoned all the bravery she could muster and headed out to the hotel parking lot.

11

Mender awoke, checked his text from Annie: had an ok night, baby kicking so that's good, and I just miss you so much. Come home soon. I don't want to guilt you but I don't want to be alone right now.

Soon, baby, he thought. *Quick as I can.*

An email from his handler indicated that the car was ready, but not yet the gun. He felt a surge of frustration. How hard was it to get a gun in Texas? He could only guess that on short notice his handler's trusted source of untraceable weapons hadn't been available. The email included the car's make and license plate.

He went down to the parking lot and walked down the street. At a public parking space on the street was the car with the license plate mentioned in his handler's email. He felt under the bumper, found the magnetic box with the key, and checked the hood. In the trunk was a medical sedative with syringe and kit, rope, zip-ties, and a Taser.

Tools of his trade. He immediately felt better, more focused. Get this done, get home to his girl.

He filled the syringe with the relaxant, then capped the needle and pocketed the syringe. He drove down to the La Condra and parked. If she came out, he could follow. His handler was excellent, but there was no replacement for eyes on the ground. He did not want to rush into a mistake.

Soon enough he saw Kirsten North come out of the hotel. She looked worn and drained, like she hadn't slept at all. Probably she hadn't. For a brief second he thought what it would be like to lose Annie—would he look as devastated as this woman?—and he shoved that thought away.

She got into a waiting rideshare car at the hotel's entrance.

He followed, at a cautious distance, hoping she'd be heading back to the airport. That would make his life easier. Follow her back to New Orleans, revert to the original plan to make it look like the suicide of a grieving widow. *Please*, he thought.

She wasn't heading to the airport. He realized it when the car turned onto Congress Avenue and headed south past the exit for Highway 71, which would have taken her to the airport.

Kirsten North was going to the warehouse.

That was a cardinal rule—you never returned to the site of a kill. Ever. He cussed under his breath.

He had to decide. Gritting his teeth, Mender followed her.

-

The rideshare car headed down the major thoroughfare of South Congress Avenue and turned left. A quarter-mile down stood a set of older warehouses. They seemed likely candidates to be replaced by the encroaching gentrification of the growing city. A building next door that was obviously once rental storage units had been converted into food stops, a hipster bar/café, and small office pods for "the creatively inspired," according to the sign. Another lot had been cleared and turned into a ten-story condo development, with retail on the first floor. Along with the warehouses a car repair shop hung on, as well as a tattoo parlor.

Had Henry come to one of these upscale joints and somehow ended up at the warehouse? By accident or by design? Maybe Henry was just in the wrong place at the wrong time. That thought—that he could have been taken from her due to cruel and random fate—made her heart hurt.

She asked the driver to let her off at the bar because police tape hung across the front of the warehouse driveway.

Henry died there. Just walk over there and duck under the tape.

She couldn't face it. Was his blood still there on the floor of the warehouse? Would the police clean that up? Or leave it for someone else?

She took a couple of hesitant steps toward the warehouse, then turned and walked over to the hipster bar.

12

Kirsten had been in bars since she'd stopped drinking; and she usually did just fine. She liked ginger ale with a lime slice; it looked like a cocktail and she liked the taste—and mostly she liked having her wits about her. There had been a long tunnel in time of not having her wits about her, and Henry had helped her out of that. Helped her find her strength.

In the café, a few people were eating breakfast tacos and pancakes. It was nearly eleven. She didn't sit at a table or booth but at the bar. She wasn't hungry. There wasn't a bartender but one of the waiters came over: a young man, goatee, dark hair, elaborate Japanese-art-inspired tattoo snaking up his forearm. She ordered her safe choice of ginger ale with lime. He gave her an appraising look but then noticed her wedding ring and shrugged himself back into neutrality.

She drank half the ginger ale. *Just go over there. Walk where he last walked. Breathe where he last breathed.*

She gestured to the bartender, thinking of the single beer last night on the plane, and that she'd had only a sip of the tempting martini at the Houston airport, so *that* was okay, it wasn't a real slip, she could handle it, clearly, and the rotten little voice inside her said, "Could I have a Bloody Mary?" It was mostly tomato juice, wasn't it? Hardly any vodka, and it had vitamins. Practically a salad of sorts. She would just have the one, like the solitary beer, to steady herself. But it hadn't been the rotten little voice that ordered it, it had been her voice, and the bartender was already making the drink.

Just the one, for courage. She opened the laptop; if she started searching, learning, even before the drink was set before her, all would be fine. She drank it down quickly.

Then she ordered another one. The bartender nodded and made it.

Her phone beeped. Zach. A text: Are you ok?

She didn't answer as the second Bloody Mary was set down in front of her.

I'm here in Austin. Just landed. Coming to help you. Where are you? Please answer me.

She texted him back: I can't talk right now.

Her phone started ringing. After two rings and one cussword she answered it.

"Zach."

"I'm so sorry. I am so, so sorry," he said. "Where are you?"

"At a bar near where his body was found. The police tape was up, and I couldn't go in there....I'm just sitting here." Oh, why had she called it a bar? It was a café. Damn it. Slip of the tongue.

"What's the name of this bar?"

"It's a café, so calm down."

Zach was silent. "I need to see you, Kirsten. And you don't need to be at a bar."

"I can't deal with you judging me right now."

"I'm sorry," he said instantly. "I'm sorry and you're right. I'm just trying to help."

"I know. Zach. I know you...know people."

He said nothing.

"You could find out where he stayed. There's no credit card record of him being here, but he was here for a couple of nights; he had to stay somewhere."

"I'm seeing you first," he said. "Where are you? Please."

She told him. He said he had a rental car and he was on his way. She drank down the second Bloody Mary, fast, as if he might screech into the lot at any second. Both had been made strong and she felt a lovely wooziness inch through her. She hadn't eaten since dinner last night. This was a bad idea. Then she paid the tab and told the bartender that she'd like a Virgin Mary, and to start a new tab, in case Zach looked at it.

She didn't want him to know how weak she felt. She didn't want a lecture from him.

"Oh, there he is. The celebrity. He's still not coming in here," she heard the bartender say to another customer, who was drinking a respectable iced coffee and working on a laptop. She glanced through the front window and saw a man pushing a shopping cart. He was tall but bent, gray-haired and bearded, wearing a battered, faded cap.

Just some homeless guy.

She turned back to her laptop. Best to look busy, with her nonalcoholic drink, when Zach got here. Adam Zhang. She opened up a new tab, searching again, now in AllConnect, a popular social media site for professionals, trying to find overlap between Adam and Henry. They had no contacts in common on this platform. Another dead end.

She looked over at the warehouse. There. The last place he saw. The last place he knew. The answers were there.

13

Mender parked in what he hoped was the best inconspicuous spot to watch the café. This was a hard area to surveil and not be noticed, but he held his phone up to his face like he was talking. The front of the bar was glass and Kirsten North was the only customer sitting at the bar. He didn't understand why she'd come here if it was just to drink, but the profile said she'd had a problem with alcohol and now that seemed to be holding true. He watched her down two drinks, fast. He wished she'd get drunk; it'd make his life easier.

He had few options without a gun. It was better to just make her vanish. The sad widow, who took herself off somewhere and ended it all. Right now she must want to see where her husband died. Maybe he could grab her when she left here. Use the sedative in the kit—inject her, dump her in the car trunk, and drive out to the Hill Country, where she'd never be found.

But a kidnapping was dangerous to try here. The police might still be investigating the scene at the warehouse. She might be meeting a detective here. Better to do it at the hotel. He'd just have to follow her back.

He waited. She kept sitting at the bar, but he saw she had a laptop open. The profile said she was a freelance researcher, but he wasn't sure what that meant. What did she research? Was it like being a detective but investigating a certain topic?

In his rearview mirror he saw motion—an old guy pushing a shopping cart, head bent down. Mender frowned.

The old guy moved on and Mender put him out of his mind.

Mender at one time thought he'd do this work for a while longer and make his small nest egg bigger, but when Annie got pregnant he started to think he should stop. It felt weird enough to kill people and come home to Annie and cuddle up on the couch with dinner and Netflix on the TV. His work and home lives were separate, but he didn't like it when thoughts from either encroached on the other.

He saw a car pull up and park in front of the bar. A guy got out. Big, muscled, short hair, in a blazer. He glanced around and then he looked right at Mender.

Who kept his phone in place, like a guy just sitting in his car, having a chat.

The big man walked into the bar.

Through the glass wall he could see the big man go up to Kirsten North and embrace her in a hug.

She leaned against his shoulder.

Oh, no. She wasn't alone anymore.

Mender had missed a chance. If his handler had come through with the gun…if this job hadn't had this last-minute change…if he'd acted last night, taken the greater risk…

He'd have to be less cautious or this job wouldn't get done.

14

Kirsten had told herself she wouldn't cry when Zach arrived and it was a struggle, but she didn't. He closed his arms around her and for a second she nearly gave in to the emotions swirling through her, but instead she closed her eyes and leaned against him. She would not cry.

"I am so sorry," he said. "What can I do?"

She appreciated his words, because Henry and Zach didn't always get along, mostly because of Zach's work. Like they were on opposite sides of a divide. She hadn't thought of what to say to Zach today, but now her mind was a blur of past and present: Zach telling her it would be okay; Zach telling her no one would ever know; Zach telling her they'd protect her…

He had come here today for her. Of course he had. They were bound together always, Kirsten and Henry and Zach….

She turned away from him and sat down.

"Are you drinking?" he asked.

"Are you really asking me that right now?" She regretted the words immediately, but she didn't want to admit her bad choices. Nothing was normal now.

"I really am."

"Why? Scared what I'll say if I drink too much?" Her words were like a knife. She pressed her fist to her mouth. What was wrong with her? He was here to help.

He sat down next to her. "That's not it and you know it."

"I know. He can't be gone," she said. "But he is. I saw him. They showed him to me." Her voice wavered and Zach gestured to the bartender, who, given the awkward show of emotion of their reunion, had retreated to the far end of the bar. "Two waters, please."

"It was a Virgin Mary," she said. She showed him the tab for the single drink before he started asking questions. "See? I had to keep my wits about me."

Zach gave her a doubting frown. "Let's go back to your hotel. Being here isn't doing you any good."

She closed her laptop as the bartender set down the waters. "No. I want to go over there. I have a right to see it."

"They're not going to let you in."

"Maybe they will. Will you go with me, Zach?"

"I'm here to do whatever you need me to do."

She looked past his shoulder, through the window and across the street to the warehouse. "Let's go."

15

Flora could hear the voices as she entered the warehouse.

A woman yelling, crying, another woman trying to calm her. A man's deep voice, asking someone to please calm down.

An officer tried to stop her and she pushed past him, saying, "I'm Flora Zhang. Detective Bard called me." She was amazed at how easily the lie fell out of her.

The officer reached out again to restrain her and she said, "I'm the widow of the victim. If you'll take me to Detective Bard, she'll say I should be here." Flora wouldn't normally ever bluff like this, but some strange heat in her chest formed the words and she just kept walking, so the officer walked alongside her like it was his idea.

This is where Adam died, Flora thought. This was the last walk he made. For a moment she thought if she breathed in she might catch a hint of his shampoo, the smell of his skin, his sandalwood deodorant. But her breathing was ragged and there was only the smell of an old dusty warehouse.

She could see Bard—the detective who hadn't been particularly forthcoming on any details—and a woman, a few years younger than Flora, arguing in the back corner of the warehouse. The woman was frowning belligerent, yelling. She was taller than Flora, dressed in jeans and a blouse two years out of fashion, her hair in need of a brush and a quality cut, unsteady on her feet. Near her, but not too close, stood a tall, well-built man, dressed in jeans and a blazer. Maybe another cop? Dark hair, handsome face. He glanced over at Flora as she approached, and he reached out a hand to the woman and touched her shoulder as if to warn her.

Bard had her back to Flora; the other woman saw Flora and she stopped yelling.

She stared at Flora. Her voice was low: "You're the other widow. Flora. I looked you up. And your husband."

"Hello," Flora said, uncertain of what to say. She should say she was sorry for the woman's loss. Of course. But the other woman gave her no time.

"So why is my husband dead?" the woman said.

Bard had turned to Flora. "Mrs. Zhang, you should leave."

"No. I want to talk to her," Flora said.

"This isn't the…right time."

"I'm standing right here. And the time," the woman said, "is perfectly fine." She took a deep breath. "Why is my husband dead?" She looked now at Bard. "I mean, you're supposed to detect stuff, yeah? So detect that."

"Mrs. North?" Flora said.

Kirsten glanced at her.

"What's your first name?"

She dragged a hand across her lips. "Kirsten."

Flora looked to the man.

"I'm Zach Couvillon. I'm her foster brother," he said.

"I have no idea why they died, Kirsten," Flora said. "And I'm so sorry. But my husband is dead, too, and I would like to know why. You tell me."

"Me tell you? My husband…wasn't a rich guy. He was a regular guy. With no enemies. Your husband, well. I researched him and you last night and this morning. You don't make forty million without pissing off some folks and burning a few bridges. So, my husband didn't even know anyone in Austin, and so…he couldn't have made anyone mad here. Your guy, though; well, forty million can make some serious enemies."

"Are you saying this is Adam's fault?" Flora tried to force herself to calm down. This woman was grieving; a fight would accomplish nothing. But Flora felt she had to stand up for her husband's memory.

"Well, it's not *my* husband's fault," Kirsten North said.

"This isn't productive, Kirsten," the man—Zach—said.

"Ladies, please," Detective Bard said. "Mrs. Zhang, would you kindly wait outside?"

"What, I can't ask her a few questions?" Kirsten North demanded. "We're citizens; we get to have a conversation if we want."

"My husband died here...." Now Flora's voice wavered. "I wanted to see..." She didn't want to admit she'd come because Marco had told her Kirsten North was here, not with the woman being so combative.

"Your husband's been dead for two days and you are just showing up here?" Kirsten North's voice was like a knife skimming along Flora's skin.

"Kirsten, don't," Zach said.

She paid him no heed. "Wow. Impressive. Real devotion there. Nothing I wouldn't do for Henry. It just hurts so much."

"I have a small child....I have to take care of him...." Flora's voice drifted off and she felt her face burn with shame. Why was this woman making her feel awful?

"She's angry," Zach said unnecessarily.

"I know. I am too," Flora said. "You don't know me or Adam. What's wrong with you?"

Silence fell heavily. Kirsten put her face in her hands. Flora started to say something, but the tears blurred her eyes and she turned away.

Bard spoke: "Mrs. North. Let's go talk outside, all right?"

"I think Flora here knows what happened," Kirsten said, her finger shaking as she pointed at the other widow. "Someone came after her guy and my guy was in the wrong place at the wrong time."

"You said your husband told you he was in New York," Bard said, and Flora thought, *Her own husband lied to her about where he was.* Her suspicion that this was somehow Henry North's fault deepened.

"His plans obviously changed and he couldn't reach me." Kirsten announced this with attempted dignity. Her voice broke at the end and her face contorted in grief. Flora took a step toward her and Kirsten North fixed her with a look of such resentment that Flora stopped. "We're not from here! She is! Her husband is! Talk to her!"

Kirsten North was a wreck, a mess, and Flora wished *she* could just... yell at people. It was impossible to believe she could ever feel better. She had been controlled, reserved, the way Adam would have wanted her to be, the way she wanted to present herself to the world. This woman had a freedom Flora lacked.

But this little grieving idiot couldn't say this was Adam's fault. That was Flora's line that could not be crossed. She knew Adam, and she knew this could not be his fault.

"But her," Kirsten said, "her...Hey, did you have to go to the morgue too? See your dead husband?"

Flora wanted to ignore her, pretend this loudmouth wasn't here, but she nodded. Teddy had wanted to do it for her, spare her, but she'd said no. Adam had been shot twice in the face, precise-looking wounds two inches apart. She had looked at him for five seconds and then turned away, pushing the image out of her mind, trying to remember him smiling and handsome.

"Then you know how I feel," Kirsten North said. "This happened on your property. Your husband owns this building. You must know why they were here."

Flora said to Bard, "I'll wait outside." She looked at the concrete floor and behind a ribbon she thought she saw blood. Or maybe just something dried there from long ago, dark in the dim light. She turned away and hurried toward the door.

"What are you hiding?" Kirsten North called to her back. "Answer me!" Flora kept going. She let the air hit her face as she stumbled out into the daylight.

The officer who had walked her in followed her out. "Ma'am, are you okay?"

"Yes. Do you think she was threatening me?"

"No. She's distraught. She and her brother, I guess he is, came over here from that café, they said. They slipped past another officer and got inside and refused to leave until Detective Bard got here. We could have arrested them, but…" He shrugged.

"I think it's best I wait in my car. It's the gray Mercedes. Will you please tell Detective Bard I'm waiting there for her?" Suddenly Flora thought, *Why do I always sound so formal? Like I'm talking down to people?*

"Yes, ma'am."

She saw Marco talking to someone in front of the bar/café, probably gathering the sad story of semidrunken Kirsten North. She hurried to the car. He'd followed her here, of course. All he wanted was a story.

She heard the door of the warehouse open behind her. The big man, Zach.

"Kirsten's completely distraught right now," he said as he walked toward her. "She doesn't mean anything by it."

"Sure she does," Flora said. "People always want to excuse emotion. You're her…foster brother?"

"Yes."

"I'm sorry for your loss. But she cannot go around accusing Adam. They're both dead; they're both victims."

"And they didn't know each other, so why were they here?" Zach asked.

Now that he was closer to her, in the light, she could see a hardness to his face. A thin scar marred his jawline. He looked…intimidating. She felt a quickening beat of fear in her chest.

"I don't know why."

"If you should think of a reason…maybe we could share information." He handed her a slip of paper. His phone number was written on it. Reluctantly, Flora entered the number into her phone and texted her number to him.

"Thank you. Kirsten and I, all we care about is finding who did this. She's just having a hard time. I'm sorry for how she talked in there. She's better than that."

"I'm having a hard time too," Flora said. But she had to force herself to say it.

"I'm sure," he said. "I'm truly sorry for your loss too."

"You tell your foster sister that my husband was innocent in this. And I will not take any suggestion that he wasn't very kindly."

"I'll tell her that. But maybe you could just answer her question. What do you know?" he said softly.

"I don't know anything. I don't know why this happened."

"Any theories?"

"No!"

"Odd. I have at least one theory." He gave her an enigmatic glance and turned to go back into the warehouse.

"What do you do in New Orleans?" she asked.

He stopped and turned back to her. "What?"

"What job do you have?"

"How could that be of possible interest to you?"

"I'm trying to figure out how our families connect. How Adam and Henry knew each other. No one knows."

"Kirsten is self-employed. I work as a VP of business development for a private firm."

"What company?"

"You wouldn't know it. It's small and local." The soft smile on his face faded. "Forty million your husband had and is leaving you, presumably. Wow. *Cui bono?*"

"What?"

"There's my theory."

She walked away from the warehouse, feeling shaken. *Cui bono?* She remembered suddenly what the Latin meant: "Who benefits?"

The answer was *her*.

She benefited from her husband's death more than anyone else. By far.

Flora got into her car.

Is that what people would think? The thought should have occurred to her right after the murder, but she'd been in a haze of shock. She'd been worried about Morgan.

Were people—or the police—going to think she had forty million reasons to wish Adam dead?

16

Flora started the car and turned up the air-conditioning; the day was humid. After a moment she tapped the audio button—she had driven twice since Adam's death and done so both times with no mood for music—and it was set to CD so it played Frank Sinatra, Adam's favorite, because a week ago it had been his birthday and she'd driven him to dinner. It had to be a fast dinner, he apologized, because he had to make phone calls. Business deals. Business had always come first, come before their marriage, and now all his worry about business meant nothing. The economic world would spin on without him. No more money to make, no more ideas to promote, no more companies to launch.

She listened to Sinatra singing "More." It had been a thing to tease him about, his love of the old crooners. Adam's musical taste had been out of a grandparent's stereo cabinet. *It's straightforward. I listened to it when I was young because that's all there was in the house*, he'd say. She listened to the smooth velvet of Frank's voice wash over her.

Adam. Adam. Adam.

She waited for the tears, but there was nothing there. How could she feel grief and shock and yet a weird...relief? He hadn't cheated on her or abused her or their child. He had never hit her. He had just...*reshaped* her.

The word fell into her brain like a suddenly remembered song.

She opened her eyes. Kirsten North and Zach and Detective Bard stood outside the warehouse now. She watched, wishing she could hear what was being said. Kirsten and Zach spoke to Bard, and Bard shook her head, and then Zach offered his hand to Bard and she shook it. They weren't going to get in trouble for trespassing? Flora felt a hot burst of anger in her chest. She watched Zach and Kirsten walk across to the bar's parking lot, get in a car, and drive away.

Flora saw Marco observe their departure and hurry to his own car. No doubt to follow.

Bard watched the police car leave and then walked over to the Mercedes. She got in on the passenger side of Flora's car.

"Are you not arresting Kirsten North and her brother?" Flora asked.

"Why would I do that?"

"Well…weren't they interfering with a crime scene?"

Bard sounded tired. "She's a grieving widow. The scene has already been processed. They got in and were immediately stopped and held there until I arrived. I think, perhaps when she's calmer, she might be able to answer some important questions for us."

Flora steadied her voice. "Do you think she knows what happened?"

"I couldn't say."

"How did you identify her husband?"

"She did."

"She…wait, you said she thought her husband was in New York. How did she know he was in Austin?"

"I cannot go into details about the case. I'm sorry, Mrs. Zhang."

Kirsten had known to come to Austin. So Kirsten knew *something.*

But Bard would tell her nothing, so she tried another tactic. "Her brother seems to have lots to say. He practically accused me of killing Adam."

Bard said nothing.

"Which is ridiculous. And I don't have to take that."

Bard's silence continued.

Flora couldn't hide the frustration she felt. "It's all a one-way street with you. We tell you everything and you tell us nothing."

"Have you told me everything, Mrs. Zhang?"

Flora felt her muscles tense. "Yes."

"Tell me again. Tell me about that night."

"Why don't you go question Kirsten about why she trespassed on a crime scene? Also, her brother looks like a thug."

"We have talked to them and we will continue to. That night. Let's go through it again."

Now Flora was sure Kirsten North or her awful brother had said something that made Bard look again at Flora's memory of the terrible evening.

Fine. She could do that. She'd been a journalist once; she could keep her details straight. She was scared of contradicting herself given the pressures and the emotional upheaval of loss. Of what that would look like for her. *Cui bono?*

She cleared her throat. "Okay. Fine. I spent the day in meetings for my foundation. We raise money for research into rare diseases that don't always get enough funding. I was either in face-to-face meetings downtown or on the phone. I expected Adam home for dinner around seven; he texted me that he would be home but had a last-minute meeting come up and would be about an hour late. I assumed the meeting was at the office."

"Was it normal for him to text you rather than call?"

"Yes. Texting is more efficient." *If he had called, I would have heard his voice one last time*, she thought. *But we are all so busy. Too busy to hear each other.*

"So what did you do?"

She paused. What had she said before to the detective? "I put in the dinner to stay warm, poured a glass of wine, and sat on the floor to play with Morgan. He was fussy, but he likes *The Jungle Book*, so I put that on for him and he was entranced by it. I watched the movie with him and drank the wine. I got a couple of text messages from friends, one from Adam's assistant."

"That's Teddy?"

"Yes. Teddy Chao."

"And he…lives with you all as well?" She said this as if it seemed unusual.

"Teddy's a distant cousin. He's like a younger brother to Adam." Is. Was. She could not yet make the change. "I know it's unusual, but we like having Teddy around."

Bard said nothing.

Flora forged ahead: "Teddy was working late on a presentation at the office and I think he meant to text Adam, not me. He asked if I was home yet, and when I got home could I call him. I texted him back and he said oops, I meant Adam. So I thought Adam was on his way home. It's a ten-minute drive." She cleared her throat. "But Adam didn't show up. I called Teddy. He said Adam had left thirty minutes ago."

"And Teddy thought Adam was headed home."

"Yes, as indicated by the mistaken text."

Bard didn't ask another question. She just waited.

"So, I texted Adam...asking, where are you? No answer. I figured he was driving. But then it got even later, so..."

Bard waited and said, "So?"

"I thought...maybe he'd stopped for a drink or gotten a phone call that was about business and he'd pulled over to talk....The start-up companies he funds and advises, they're very important to him. He loves, I mean loved, his work." Past tense. She had to deal with this. No point in staying in present tense. Soon it would seem very weird to do so, like she was in an unhealthy denial that he was gone. "So, I waited. I put Morgan to bed. I drank another glass of wine. Then another. I should have eaten the dinner, but I wasn't hungry." She felt embarrassed admitting to the three glasses of wine after seeing how Kirsten North had behaved under the influence. "Then I fell asleep on the couch. The wine probably helped."

"Did you think Adam was maybe doing something he shouldn't have been?"

This was a new direction. "I don't know what you mean."

"He wasn't with you; he wasn't at his office. Where else would he go?"

"Meeting this Henry North, I guess." Flora sounded snappier than she meant. She didn't like what Bard was suggesting. "I tried to call him again. Text him again. I've shown you my texts to him. He didn't respond. I don't even know if he was dead by then. Teddy went out and had dinner...."

"Does Teddy usually eat at home with you and Adam?"

"Usually Adam or I cook for us all. But sometimes Teddy dines with his friends, and other times he wants to give us privacy so he goes out."

"Teddy have a significant other?"

"No. Teddy's consumed with his career. He's ambitious, works long hours. He's like Adam in that way." Flora coughed. "But...Teddy said he went and had dinner by himself at a place on South Congress. He watched a basketball game at the bar and had a burger and a beer, and then he came home and saw I was asleep on the couch. He realized Adam wasn't home yet and he woke me up." She had been looking at the steering wheel, but now she looked at Bard. "Is this matching everything I told you before? Have I left out anything?"

"My questions aren't a trap, Mrs. Zhang."

"The police won't do anything if someone's not missing for twenty-four hours. We started calling and texting. I had Teddy text him....I thought maybe if he was mad at me, he'd answer him...."

Flora realized, too late, she hadn't admitted that in her first statement.

"Did he have a reason to be mad at you? Had you argued?"

Bard couldn't know. No one knew. "No, of course not. I just...I didn't want to pester him with another text. But I thought maybe I'd irritated him." He had seemed a little irritated with her lately.

"Was he hard to live with sometimes?" Bard asked. "Most people are."

Flora studied the steering wheel. "Adam was intense, driven, focused. When he was focused on you...you were the whole world. When he was focused on a project, you didn't exist." She shrugged. "I was used to it."

"And where was his focus that night?"

"He was occupied with work, but he didn't tell me specifics and I didn't ask."

"Did he often just go off without telling you?"

She felt a spark of anger. "This isn't about us...it's about why he was here with Henry North at the warehouse."

"Henry North. Do you know him?"

"No, I've never heard of him or his wife."

"They're from New Orleans."

"Adam and I don't have business or family or other ties to New Orleans." She looked at her lap.

"We'll look through Adam's computer and phone to see if there's any communication with Henry North."

Suggesting there was a connection Flora didn't know about. She didn't say Teddy had already done a search on Adam's backup data and found nothing about Henry North. "Do you suspect her? Kirsten?" Flora asked.

"I can't say."

"Where's she staying?"

Bard studied her. "Why do you ask?"

"I don't know, I just thought...we're both fresh widows...I don't know."

Because I want to talk to her. I want to see what she knows.

"Fresh widows?"

"Just a term a neighbor used with me," Flora said. "It's awful, isn't it?"

Bard didn't tell her the name of Kirsten's hotel. She gave Flora a measuring glance. "So, your husband was overdue that night and you started calling and texting people."

"Yes. Friends of Adam's. He doesn't have...a lot of close friends. His life is his work. So we called people he worked with. A school classmate he sometimes meets for drinks. No one had heard from him."

"Why does your husband own a warehouse? It doesn't quite fit into his growing business portfolio."

"I don't know....He bought it a few weeks ago." And then that struck her as odd. "He'd bought that penthouse; he'd bought this old warehouse. Maybe he'd decided to get into real estate."

"Your husband not telling you things; Henry North lying to his wife about being in Austin...lots of secrets, Mrs. Zhang. What secret brought them together?"

"I don't know."

Bard frowned at her. "If you know something, tell me."

Flora thought: *Adam went to this warehouse after leaving the office. So something happened to veer him onto the path to his own murder. Something happened.* "Maybe Henry North called him. What about Adam's cell phone log, or surveillance video at the warehouse?"

"So far no record of phone communication between them. There is no security video system in the warehouse."

No record of his being there.

No record of what was happening there.

Meeting a man he apparently didn't know.

Flora said, "One of my first thoughts, when we couldn't find him, was kidnapping. That I would get a ransom call." She took a deep breath. "Maybe this was a kidnapping scheme that went wrong."

"And a kidnapper brought Adam to an empty building he owns?"

"Maybe they somehow lured Adam here. And Henry North's plan was to kidnap him. I'm just thinking aloud. And at the warehouse Adam fights back—maybe there's a struggle for a gun. Adam gets killed. Then there must have been another kidnapper, and he kills Henry North, because he killed Adam, or he messed up the plan...."

"Henry North has no criminal record."

Flora said: "It's just a theory. We always worried about kidnapping. You do, after..." It sounded gauche to say "after you've made a certain amount of money," but it was the truth. "After a certain level of financial success. But he was always more worried it would be me or Morgan who was kidnapped."

"We're looking at all possibilities," Bard said. "But Henry North had to have a reason to come to Austin, and it must have been a business reason."

"What about the guy who found the bodies?" A man experiencing homelessness had tried the door on the warehouse, gone inside to use the bathroom when he discoved it was unlocked, and tripped over one of the bodies. He rushed over to a nearby coffee shop, yelling for someone to call the police. Flora was grateful he hadn't just walked away.

"He's not currently a suspect."

Currently? Flora wondered. Maybe that was a standard disclaimer. "All right."

"When you couldn't find Adam...what did you and Teddy do?"

There was an implication under the words. Bard had asked a lot about Teddy. Like she suspected him, or she thought there was more to the story. The young man living with the married couple. "Teddy drove back to the office. Adam wasn't there. Teddy texted me and I told him to come home because we'd tried everyone we could think of. So I just waited up, and I fell asleep finally around four a.m."

And that was where her first statement had ended. Bard watched her.

"Did you think perhaps he was off with another woman?" Bard made no apology for her bluntness in asking the question she'd only hinted at before, and Flora wondered if this had turned into an interrogation, if she should have her lawyer present. But she didn't want to look uncooperative.

"He was faithful. And no, since he'd told Teddy he was headed home, I wouldn't have thought he was off for some rendezvous. He would have made another excuse."

"If there is anything else you know that you haven't told me..."

"I want you to stop asking me the same questions and find the people who killed him," she said. She realized she'd said it more harshly than she intended. But she didn't feel like apologizing. "I've told you everything."

Bard said nothing and Flora thought: *Cui bono? I benefit and that's all they can see right now. She thinks I could have done this. Maybe Teddy helped me. She's considering that and it's insane. If it had just been Adam who was killed, would I have been arrested by now?* The thought was terrifying.

Bard said in a calm voice, "All right, Mrs. Zhang. Thank you for your time."

"What are you going to do about Kirsten North?"

"What do you mean?"

"You're going to question her, yes? What if *she* knows what this is about?"

"As I said, we're pursuing all options. All of them."

That felt like a warning. "I look forward to hearing of an arrest soon. And justice for my husband."

Bard got out of the car. Flora watched her walk back into the warehouse.

She hated to admit it, but if Henry North had no ties to Austin, then Adam was somehow the catalyst for the murders. It was unthinkable, but…she had to accept the possibility.

Her phone beeped. A text from Taylor Townsend, her friend she'd contacted this morning: Are you still coming by? Are you ok?

Shawn Townsend's wife. *What about Shawn? Could he benefit from Adam's death?*

Look at it fresh, Flora told herself. The office Adam shared with Shawn was the last place Adam had been before the warehouse. Who else, aside from her and Teddy, spent the most time with Adam? Shawn, his business partner.

She answered Taylor's text: can you meet me later at the penthouse? Have the guard let you in if I'm not there yet. I'll call him and tell him to expect you.

She never put off Taylor. Her best friend. She ought to be leaning on her now. But she was tired of leaning.

What are you going to do with your life now? she asked herself.

What were her options? Adam had wanted her to stop writing—but he'd never said that, had he? But she had, somehow, heard it. And known it. And she had silently agreed, and put down her pen, and why? She couldn't say why. She had just…agreed. To make them both happy, she thought, moving on to a new phase. Sometimes writing was hard and boring and…she could do anything, like help start a medical research foundation, which was hard, all-consuming yet vital work. And then once the foundation was expanding and she felt like she was making a difference, he'd wanted her to be a full-time mom, nagging her but with a smile.

And suddenly Adam was gone, and it was like a hand was no longer pressing on her shoulder. Pressing on her heart.

She had money, and she had freedom, and she felt her stomach twist that he was gone, because she had loved him even when she resented him, and not worrying about his approval any longer was like a cage's door unlocking.

She could do…anything. Now.

Unless the world thought she'd killed him in cold blood. Then she would never be free. Ever.

Cui bono? But in a deeper way no one knows or suspects.

Flora drove toward downtown.

17

"I still want you to find out where Henry was staying. I want to find it before the police do," Kirsten said.

Zach turned his rental car into the hotel lot and parked. "Why?"

"I want to find the person who killed him."

"Why?"

Silence.

"Why, Kirsten?" Zach's voice rose.

"They don't get to walk. They don't get years more than he got."

"Kirsten." He stared down at the steering wheel. "You cannot contemplate this. You can't."

"He took care of me. He..."

"So did I," Zach said. "So did I, and if someone kills me, I do not want you killing them in revenge and going to jail for the rest of your life."

She didn't speak. She closed her eyes. Zach and Henry, reassuring her, while her eyes could barely register what she'd seen.

"Kirsten," Zach said. "You cannot...kill his killer, and I will not help you."

"I drank a beer on the plane. I ordered a martini in the airport. But I only took a sip. I drank two Bloody Marys before you showed up." She cleared her throat. "If I can make whoever did this pay, then I'll be at peace. Otherwise, I won't. And you know what I'll turn into. And if you don't help me, that's on you."

"Spare me this self-indulgent emotional blackmail," he said. "Hell no."

"You do violence all the time for your boss."

He gave her a disbelieving look. "No, actually, I don't. I make sure it doesn't get to violence. *That's* my job. Violence is bad for business."

"Henry did it for me. The whole reason I even have a life is because he did it for me."

"I was there too. You act like no one ever helped you but Henry."

"I'm not asking you to do anything wrong. Just to find where he was staying. The police will be calling every hotel."

He seemed to flinch slightly. "How am I supposed to do that?"

"You have contacts."

"Contacts." He raised an eyebrow.

"Yes. With the police, in New Orleans. Can't they check credit cards or hotel registries?"

He shook his head. "What…what contact do you think I have?"

"I'll bet your boss owns a few cops. Are you telling me they can't run a credit check—see if there's another credit card of Henry's I don't know about? Please. Please ask."

Zach took a deep breath. "Why exactly do you think he was here in Austin and lying about it to you?"

"I don't know."

"Well, since I'm a guy, I can tell you. It was either a woman or money. If it was a woman, he stayed with her. If it was money, he'd just use his regular credit card."

"So you're saying it was a woman. You're saying maybe he cheated on me. I am a new widow and you are suggesting that to me. Brothers are supposed to be assholes sometimes and you are being my foster asshole."

"I'm being honest with you when no one else will. Maybe he was involved with this Flora Zhang. Maybe that's why he and Adam Zhang met."

The utter calm with which Zach said this unnerved her. "And she…she killed them both?"

"Maybe her husband was going to leave her with nothing if she cheated on him and Henry betrayed her to him. Or Henry was an inconvenient witness."

"You think Henry was capable of cheating on me."

"Okay, maybe he wasn't cheating. Different angle. Maybe *she* hired Henry to find out what was on her husband's computer."

The thought chilled her. "But why lie about it? Why say New York?"

"I don't know. I'm just throwing out possibilities. Maybe there was something illegal about the job." Zach took a deep breath. "We both know what he's capable of."

She didn't have an answer. She wiped her cheeks with the back of her hand. "You never wanted me to marry him."

"Of course I did. But stop looking at him like he's some golden boy. Henry was capable of stuff most people aren't."

"We're all capable of the unimaginable to protect someone we love."

"He's out of money," Zach said. "Did you know that?"

"No, he's not."

"I know because he asked me for a loan. A month ago. He asked me for twenty thousand."

She wanted to slap Zach for those words. But she didn't. She grew still. Henry hadn't been sleeping well. She'd hear him get up in the night, pacing the floor, surfing the web. He told her he was just sweating the consultant deals. He kept the money he made in a separate account for tax purposes and moved it into their joint account when needed. The joint account had been getting low, but she'd been busy and she always put her money in there right away when she was paid for a project.

"You have picked the greatest possible moment to share this news with me," she said.

"It's not my place to tattle on Henry to you," Zach said. "But I'm so sorry now that I didn't before."

"Got to love that male solidarity." If Zach had told her...would things be different now? Would Henry have told her he was coming to Austin? "The job here must have promised him something big. But that was still no reason to lie."

"Unless he was breaking the law. Hacking into computers in places he had no permission or business to be. If you didn't even know he was in Austin, then I'd say he was protecting you in case he got caught. You couldn't be an accessory."

"I take it you didn't loan him the money then."

"No."

"Why not?" Her voice rose.

"Me saying no is not why this happened," he said.

"He asked you for help and you said no."

"I'm not allowed to loan money," he said quietly. "My employer doesn't allow it."

She stared at him. "What, out of morals?"

"No."

"Oh, because he has people whose job is to loan desperate folks money. And to take his cut. Zach, I just can't with you."

"You're sitting here contemplating murder yet critiquing the man I work for because you don't like him." Zach took a deep breath. "I'll see if I can find out where Henry was staying and see if there's an explanation for why he was here. But I'm not going to help you ruin your life. You cannot play executioner."

"My life's already ruined," she said. "You know what I'm like. You think I can ever be happy without him?" She pressed her fists to her eyes. A whirl of memories: The first time Henry kissed her. The first time they made awkward love; the first time they made love when it was good; the marriage in the pretty church, Zach beaming, happy for them both; the ring right now on her finger that Henry could barely afford.

He took her hand. "Your life isn't over and Henry wouldn't want you to say or think that."

She looked out the window. "He wouldn't have cheated on me with that Flora woman."

"You asked me what I thought. Usually these things are simple. He lied to you. Money or a woman. I hope it's money."

"He died with a rich man. That tells me it was more likely about money."

Zach said, "Maybe Henry found sensitive information that he could sell to Adam Zhang. It could be something Henry found while working for another company. Who were Henry's recent clients?"

"Right now, a few law firms, some insurance companies, and an energy company in Houston." Usually his job was to attempt to hack his way in and then show them how to avoid being compromised.

"Let's take this one step at a time. Henry needed money. He's doing security work for someone else. He learns something about Adam Zhang. Or maybe about Flora Zhang. Something valuable, maybe dangerous. He comes here to share it. Or sell it. Maybe someone knew Henry had this and followed him here and killed them both. We have to fit them together somehow." Zach bit his lip in thought.

"His backups are passworded. I can't get into them."

"But he would have brought his laptop here. Does it have that 'ping' ability, or locator, or whatever it is?" Zach asked.

"No. He disabled it. Said it was a security risk."

"So I'll do as you ask and I'll try to find out where he stayed. And if he had another credit card. I know a detective in New Orleans who might help me. He…owes me a favor."

Your boss owns him, Kirsten thought, but she said nothing. It was awkward when your foster brother worked for a criminal family organization.

"Thank you."

"Kirsten…"

"I mean, this is my hour of need, and you say you came here to help me, but you can go home if you won't."

"I just said I would."

"And, you'll stay to make sure I don't drink."

His mouth twisted and she saw he was fighting down his emotions. Zach didn't show a lot of emotion generally and so she squeezed his hand.

Zach said: "I protected you. Before Larry, after Larry. I supported you. I know this is the worst time of your life, ever. So you can be mad at me, if you've got to be mad at someone. You can yell at me when I offer to help you. You can act like you're not hurting and I'll look away to protect your pride. You're a grown woman. Make your choices. I'm not your savior or your boss."

She didn't speak for a moment. "Thank you for coming. For helping me."

"You're my sister," he said.

"Not really."

"Always really."

They sat in silence for several seconds and then she said: "All the police are looking at Henry, not at Zhang. You and I know Henry, but they don't. They'll start digging into his past. They'll find out about Larry…."

"There's nothing to find."

She said nothing for a long minute, just taking deep breaths. The smell of the dusty attic. The open cooler. The shock of knowing her own life was over.

"Kirsten?" Zach stared at her.

"Money or a woman. I refuse to accept those are the only two alternatives," she said.

"Lust, love, loathing, or lucre. Those are the reasons for…violence." He didn't want to say murder.

"Is that what they taught you in Crime Family 101?"

He ignored her. "Flora gave me her phone number. Here it is." He pulled an Austin map from his rental car's glove compartment, tore part of it off, wrote the number down for her. "Maybe you should talk to her."

Kirsten accepted the number in silence.

Zach took a deep breath. "I can put both of us in a better hotel than this place."

"Courtesy of your boss."

"Well, yes. They own a couple of properties here."

"I'm fine. You stay where you please. I'm going to go research the Zhangs. Maybe lie down. I didn't sleep hardly at all last night."

"I don't think you should be alone. Let me get us a suite at a better hotel. We can work together. Turn it into our HQ."

And he could keep an eye on her that way, talk her out of taking her revenge. No, thanks. "I don't need your charity."

"You can push me away in anger all you want, I'll still be here when you need me."

There are real brothers who aren't this loyal to their real sisters, Kirsten thought. She squeezed his hand again, then let it go. "I appreciate you being here and helping me." She handed him the extra key to her room. "Here, in case you need the room and I'm not there." She got out of the car. "Where are you going now?"

"You gave me a job, I'm going to go do it. Get some rest," he said. And he backed the car out as she headed to her hotel room.

She didn't want to fight with Zach. He wouldn't lie to her about Henry asking for a loan. Henry was in some kind of monetary bind. She trembled at the thought. Another secret he'd kept from her. She went to the laptop, signed into her bank. Henry paid the bills; he was better with money than she was. She'd forget to balance the account. The figures popped up. Their checking was low, and their savings was nearly empty—there had been twenty thousand in there a few months ago. That was what he'd asked Zach for.

She stared at the computer.

The clients. She remembered their names. She googled them, started making calls.

And heard the slow unraveling of her husband's life: *I'm sorry, we stopped using North Star Consulting last year.... Sorry, we haven't used Henry for a project in months.... Sorry for your loss. No, we hadn't worked with him in a while....*

Then she decided to take a different tack when she called the last one, an energy company in New Orleans. After being connected to Brenda Lugg, head of IT security, Kirsten said she worked with Zhang Townsend in Austin, and was thinking of hiring Henry North.

"Wait, is Henry North using me as a reference?"

"No. I just saw a client list and he included your company. It was in confidence, of course."

"We did use him. Smart guy. But we didn't renew with him."

"May I ask why?"

"We got some anonymous complaints about him."

"Anonymous?"

"Well, that we should check his work. That he was sloppy, unprofessional. There was a link to a forum where he was getting slammed."

"It could have been someone with a grudge."

"Maybe. But security consultants are a dime a dozen. I don't need the hassle of working with a problematic one. Reputation is everything. Sorry, I've got another call." She hung up.

Her husband's business, ruined, by steady innuendo. By someone posting anonymous reviews about his work, undermining him. No big deal to get rid of a single security consultant charging inexpensive rates. Look up the reviews on North Star Consulting, see they're bad, move on. Don't take the risk. Get rid of him, hire another one. Gig economy at its finest.

"Someone did this to you, baby," she whispered aloud.

Was it Adam Zhang, or someone else in Austin, and was that the reason for Henry's trip?

Her phone buzzed. An Austin number, one she didn't recognize. She answered.

"Mrs. North? It's Detective Bard. I would like to schedule a time for you to come in later today and answer some questions for us that I think will assist us in our investigation."

"Okay," she said. "Yes. Of course." She cleared her throat, steadied her voice.

"How about three o'clock, here at the department?"

"Do I need to bring a lawyer?"

"You can if you want, certainly. But that's your decision."

"Okay. Three."

"Thank you, Mrs. North." And Bard hung up.

Kirsten had started to realize that Bard could have arrested her or detained her for trespassing in the warehouse, but hadn't. Either out of decency…or maybe to see what dumb move she'd make next. Should she have asked if *she* was a suspect? She could prove she was in New Orleans the past few days.…But wait. Could she?

Henry had left for New York, or so she thought. He'd taken himself to the airport at his own insistence (had he driven to Austin or flown—she realized she had no idea). Sunday she'd been at home when he presumably flew or drove to Austin. Monday: She worked from home, as she always did. She hadn't gone anywhere, not even to the grocery. No one would have seen her. Tuesday: She worked from home, napped in the afternoon because she never slept well when Henry wasn't in the bed beside her. No one would have seen her that day either. She could be a bit of a hermit; she missed Henry when he was gone but she liked her alone time. Wednesday and Thursday: the same.

Then Thursday night the call had come.

She felt her heart catch in her chest. What if…what if they asked her to prove she had not been in Austin?

She poured herself a glass of cold water and drank it down. Then another one. Then a third. She needed food and coffee and to get ahold of herself.

How could you have been so stupid to act the way you did this morning? What if they had arrested you? Or Zach? Justice was never a guaranteed thing.

She found some ibuprofen in her purse on the bed, gulped it down. Whoever killed her husband was out there, free, breathing air, thinking he or she was smart as hell and getting away with it, while Kirsten had indulged in cowardice, drinking because she was scared to face the truth.

No more. No. More.

She threw the glass at the hotel door and dropped to her knees as it shattered. Stupid. She was accomplishing nothing.

There was a knock on the door. Oh great. Probably the maid, hearing the glass smash. Could they throw you out for breaking a glass?

She put her eye to the security hole. She didn't know the man on the other side.

18

The past

Zach had already been living with the Melancons for six months when Kirsten arrived. She was in her bedroom, unpacking, when Zach came and stood in her door. He didn't enter the room, he just stood there watching her.

She hadn't had to change schools with the foster reassignment, which she was glad of, because St. Gentian was the best school she'd ever gone to. Some anonymous grant had made it possible for her and Zach Couvillon, foster care kids, to attend. It gave them a greater hope for the future. She had read that the majority of foster kids did not go to college. She wanted to beat the odds.

She knew who Zach was from school; he played football. The St. Gentian players were paraded at the school spirit rally ("We've got spirit; yes we do! We've got spirit; how 'bout you?"—naturally the response was predetermined); attendance was mandatory, and she couldn't get away with reading a book during all the school spirit programs, people would think that she was odder than they already did. She was certain Zach didn't know who she was before they'd been introduced as part of her assignment to the Melancons. She was not popular; but he was one of the good-looking boys who played freshman football with high school kings like Paul Fortunato and Jake Girard, so he thus occupied a higher social station than a loner bookworm like her.

She expected him to say something like *Don't talk to me at school* or *Let's pretend we don't know each other.* He looked at her and she crossed her arms and waited.

"They're nice people," he said quietly. "Larry and JJ." His voice was low; he seemed older than a freshman to her. But she knew he wasn't. Being in foster care was what made you seem older.

"They don't make you call them Mom and Dad?"

"No. They told me I could if I wanted. But I remember my parents, so I call them Uncle Larry and Aunt JJ." He shrugged.

"My last fosters made me call them Momsy and Pop."

His face showed a slight frown of distaste.

"There was lots of praying. So much praying," she said.

"Is that why you ran away?"

"No. He started touching my shoulder. Like, a lot, like every time he asked me to think about my actions or to look into my heart or to apply myself to my studies. I asked him to stop and he wouldn't. I know where that goes."

"Larry won't do that."

She wanted to say, *And neither will you*. She nearly told him that as a warning. But he'd probably laugh at the thought of her (looking like she did) thinking that of him (looking like he did and being a football player). She knew how to scream, she knew when to scream, and she knew how to break a finger.

She knew already that at school there would be those simpering girls who would say to her on Monday, *Oh, wow, you get to live with Zach Couvillon? What's he like?* She dreaded it. She just wanted to get through her classes and read books in the library and not get picked last during gym or have some smart-ass decide her name was Cursed and not Kirsten. At least with Pop and Momsy she'd been the only kid. That had its own perils but also its own rewards.

She hoped the Melancons would leave her alone; feed her and give her shelter, but not...bother her. She just had to stay here until she was legally an adult.

"I walk to school," Zach said. She didn't answer, but she supposed the foster parents would expect her to walk with him. Maybe he wouldn't talk to her. Maybe he'd pretend he didn't know her. She wasn't sure what would be worse.

"Good for you," she said with her default thorniness.

He shrugged and walked away without another word. She got the odd feeling that he hadn't expected any more from her.

JJ came up and checked on how she was doing. She seemed nice enough, a bit cool, and that was preferable to Kirsten over Momsy's fake and constant sugary kindness. Where Zack had leaned in the doorway, JJ hovered. Kirsten reluctantly put down the book she was reading (an Ursula K. Le Guin novel). Reading science fiction and fantasy novels had not been allowed with Pop and Momsy, and she'd checked this out from the library immediately on her reassignment to the new family.

"We hope you'll be happy with us, Kirsten."

"I hope so too." She should be more diplomatic with JJ than she'd been with Zach. She attempted her version of a smile. "I know Zach calls you Aunt JJ. Is it all right if I call you that too?" He had been here longer, and it would be easier to follow his lead in this important and sensitive matter.

"Sure, sweetie."

"Okay, I'll do that." She felt a sudden lightness and realized Zach had done her a favor.

"It's not good to read too much," JJ said. "I mean, you want to get outside and get some exercise too. Zach likes to go to the park or toss a football. I'm in a book club, so it's not that I'm against reading; I just think there are other activities."

Probably she was described as a bookish loner in the file. She sighed at the thought of being JJ's makeover project.

"You're right," she agreed with a smile. "I'm reading this for advanced English, though." She didn't think JJ looked the type to check a syllabus, but she should be cautious. There was a "free reading" book choice Kirsten would perpetually use as a shield.

"Got it! Studies first," JJ said brightly.

"Yes, ma'am," Kirsten said.

And after a moment, JJ went back downstairs. Kirsten decided JJ would not be a problem and could be handled with faux optimism.

Kirsten finished reading a chapter. Then she stared up at the ceiling for a while. The doorbell rang and she could hear Zach and the voice of another boy. Then the back door opened and closed. She was learning the sounds of the house in case she needed to know if her own door creaked or if a tread on the stairs (the master bedroom was downstairs) meant danger.

Zach was probably having a friend over. She should make an effort. It was good to have a positive start. She missed her mother and wondered what her father was doing in Denmark right now—probably sleeping, due to the time difference. She was sure he wasn't thinking of her.

She wandered downstairs a few minutes later. Larry was in his recliner, reading a thick book that she guessed, from the cover photo and title, was a history of Chicago mobsters. Zach, she could see through the den's window, was sitting on the shady back patio with another boy, talking. The boy looked familiar, but she didn't know his name. Glasses, brown hair, nothing special about him.

Larry glanced up from his book. "Hey, Kirsten. You getting settled okay?"

She nodded.

"I know you like to read. You can borrow any book on the shelves."

She glanced at the shelves on the wall—more books than she'd ever seen in a person's house, at least one hundred. She knew Larry was an accountant; it must pay well. She liked math; maybe accounting was a job she should think about. She thought a lot about life after foster care. "Thanks," she said. She pointed at his book. "You interested in the mob?"

"Oh, just saw *The Godfather* a couple of times too many." He laughed.

She wasn't good at laughing when other people laughed because she didn't really find what they said that funny. Or she didn't get it. He kept his smile in place. "Do you like to fish? Sometimes Zach and I go, just take a couple of coolers, have a quiet day. JJ hates fishing."

"I'm not really into fishing."

"That's fine. If you change your mind, you're welcome to come." He reopened his book to continue reading. "You could go out to the patio and talk with Zach and Henry. Henry's the boy next door."

She shrugged. "I'm reading a good book, too, so I think I'll just go back to my room."

"Sure. I want you to know, though, that Zach's a good kid."

She had to figure out how to make living here with these people work, so it was best to take their advice at the beginning. Once they saw she really preferred to be alone, they'd let her be—it was easier on all of them. So, after a moment she did as Larry suggested and walked out onto the patio.

The boys were laughing about something—probably her, because they suddenly stopped and Zach gave her a smile and a nod.

"Hey, Kirsten," Zach said. "You know Henry, right?"

"Hey," she said, like she did.

"Hi," Henry said, and he stood, like it was a formal thing. He offered his hand to shake. "I'm Henry North."

She thought he probably stood because his parents made him go to cotillion, the class a lot of St. Gentian kids took for social graces, manners, and dancing. She shook his hand. "Kirsten Plumm." The only chair was between the boys and she sat.

"I live next door," Henry said as he sat back down. He smiled, like that was an accomplishment.

What a geek, she thought. "I live here now."

Henry squirmed slightly in his chair, as if unsure of what to say.

"Henry's real smart," Zach said. "He's my tutor for math. And science. And whatever else I need. Which is practically everything."

"That's cool," she said. Henry North was looking right at her in a way that didn't seem shy or geeky. She looked away. "Are you having a tutoring session now?" She didn't see books out.

"No, just talking. About school and stuff."

"Cool," she said again and Henry was still looking at her, so she just looked straight back at him. The boys went back to talking about freshman football (Henry also played, but on the B team and not as a starter); and Kirsten sat and thought: *This place might not be so bad.*

-

Zach needed a lot of help with his homework, and so Henry was a regular presence. Kirsten could see it wasn't a matter of Zach's intelligence—he was bright but not particularly bookish—but that he was behind. On everything. He'd been promoted through when he wasn't ready. He didn't talk much about his life before the Melancons, but once, when he was coming out of the bathroom without his shirt on, she'd seen a constellation of what looked like cigarette burns along one shoulder, and a bad scar across his back—the kind she thought a belt buckle might leave.

It made her feel sick. He seemed so quiet and gentle. She would have been full of rage. *You* are *full of rage*, she told herself.

Henry was a real help to Zach. Sometimes they studied together at the dining room table, and when Zach got stuck Henry was patient, showing him how to break down a problem—whether math or history or biology—into smaller steps, to make it easier. At first Kirsten felt funny seeing this—she thought it might embarrass Zach. He didn't seem to care that Kirsten knew where he struggled. Henry would just say, "Step-by-step, break it down," and Zach would seem to get it.

"If you need extra tutoring in math or English, those are my best subjects," she said to Zach at dinner one night. She saw Aunt JJ and Uncle Larry glance across at each other, with a look she found hard to read.

"Thank you," he said. "I'll let you know."

"Sure," she said. She had noticed that Uncle Larry and Aunt JJ asked her about her grades—which tended to be excellent, because she would not stumble—only when Zach wasn't around. Like it might make him feel bad. She glanced up at Aunt JJ's kind smile and smiled back, just for a moment. It was a bad idea to care about anyone, but it was hard not to care. She stared down at her plate, not wanting to look at any of them.

"That's kind of you to offer, Kirsten," Uncle Larry said, and she realized she'd done something right. And then Aunt JJ started talking about this goofy new coworker of hers at the microbrewery down near the Quarter, and they moved on.

Kirsten and Zach and the Melancons fell into a pattern, and patterns in her life—predictable, settled things—were unusual for her. Football season was over, so Zach didn't have early morning or afternoon practice. She and Zach did walk to school together, and he was always friendly to her without being pushy about it. She did not think the other kids at St. Gentian realized how odd it was to move into a house with strangers and have to navigate through those relationships. They walked to St. Gentian and they walked home together, but they didn't have any classes together and only nodded to each other when they passed in the hallways.

Three weeks after she moved in with the Melancons, the one friend Kirsten ate lunch with every day was absent for a doctor's appointment, and she remembered this as she came out of the cafeteria line. She would have to sit alone. She didn't feel like she could join another group of girls; she hardly ever spoke to anyone if she could avoid it. Sitting alone at lunch was social suicide at school and she didn't *want* it to matter to her; she liked to think she was above such concerns, but it *did* matter. She stood in indecision, thinking that maybe she'd just skip lunch and dump her tray, although she was hungry, and then she saw Zach standing, waving her over to where he'd been sitting with a coterie of football players and cheerleaders.

No, thanks, she thought. *No.*

But she couldn't ignore Zach, so she walked to him.

He'd pulled a chair over next to his and he said to the group, "Y'all know my foster sister, Kirsten." And the other kids nodded, even if they only knew her by sight, and said hey and she sat down, unable even to look over at Zach with gratitude. *Foster sister.* He hadn't said those words before and she hadn't thought of him as her foster brother, but there it was. She thought she could wolf down her food and make an excuse to go do homework because the other kids would all be awful, and while one cheerleader seemed kind of snooty the other two were friendly, and they talked about the science projects that Mrs. Danley assigned that were too hard and for which they weren't allowed enough time, and an upcoming Black Eyed Peas concert everyone (with money, so not her or Zach) was trying to get tickets for. Some of the St. Gentian kids were rich, at least by her standards, and she doubted any of them had wondered where the next meal or bed was coming from, or had been asked to move in with complete strangers for a long stretch of time.

But, that day, she didn't have to sit alone.

The group broke up as the lunch period ended and she took her tray to the conveyor belt, Zach behind her.

"You can sit with us whenever you want." He said it so no one could hear.

"I sit with Molly. She just wasn't here today. I couldn't leave her."

"Well, Molly can sit with us too. If you want. It's no big deal."

"I know it's not," she said. "You didn't have to call me your sister."

"But you are now."

"Not really."

"Always really."

She felt the heat of unexpected tears behind her eyes. "Whatever."

"Later," he said.

She watched him walk away, saying hey to another table of kids, then walking out of the cafeteria with Paul Fortunato, easily the most popular freshman at the school.

The next day Molly was back at lunch, and Kirsten sat with her, but a month later Molly got a boyfriend Kirsten couldn't stand and so she left them alone, feeding each other potato chips and overripe glances, and began eating each day with Zach.

The difference was that Henry was eating with them too. And he kept looking at her.

She decided she didn't mind that.

19

Mender followed Kirsten back to her hotel—he knew he had to get ahead of her and see what room she went into, then he could deal with her in privacy. The big guy parked and they stayed inside the car, talking. Mender pulled his cap low—*she might remember you being her seatmate on the plane if she sees your face*—and went into the lobby to wait. He'd follow her back to her room. He still didn't know her room number and his handler had not acquired it for him. Parking lots were less than ideal, even with a sedative. Everyone had a camera in their phone.

"May I help you, sir?" the desk clerk asked and Mender smiled and said, "Oh, no, just waiting for a friend." The clerk nodded and went back to his computer as another guest checked out.

Mender sat and studied his phone like a good citizen would but kept his gaze on the car.

The clerk went into the back. It might just be the two of them in the empty lobby. Finally, his break.

Kirsten got out of the car; the big guy drove off. For a moment she stood there watching him go.

Come here, Mender thought. *Come here to me. And let me be done with you.*

She crossed the parking lot just as a bus pulled up to the entrance and a group of high school girls dressed in athletic attire got off and entered the lobby, Kirsten trailing behind them. Too many people.

He thought the girls would all be checking in, but no, they all walked past the elevators. He followed them down a main hall—with several going into rooms. He kept his eye on Kirsten among them and saw which room she entered.

"May I help you?" a woman's voice said. He turned and one of the coaches was looking at him, with a polite smile but suspicion clouding her eyes. Like: *Why are you following my players?*

"Sorry, took a wrong turn," he said and immediately reversed direction. Great. Another pair of eyes on him. Improvising sucked. He always used a battle plan, and he was having to make this up as he went along. If he went to her room now and there was a struggle, the athletes might overhear. Too risky. But teams came to play and so they wouldn't be in the hotel for long. Then Kirsten would be alone in this long stretch of rooms.

He went back to the lobby, where the desk clerk gave him a friendly nod, and sat again, staring at his phone's screen. He needed to think. But he needed to know if she left again. Or if she headed home.

The big guy wasn't in the target's file as a possible concern. He had taken a picture of the friend when they walked toward the warehouse and sent it to his handler via text, saying, I need to know who this is.

So she'd gone to the murder site, loitered at a nearby café—Who did that? If Annie had died, he could never have hung out for drinks close to the murder scene. It was offensive—and then she'd gone to the warehouse where the men died. He thought there was something fundamentally wrong with this woman and that made it easier in his mind to eliminate her.

This big guy had come and found her and driven her home. What was he to her? If Mender was to make Kirsten North vanish, then he'd need to avoid dealing with this guy. If the big guy was based here in Austin, a local relative or friend, then perhaps he'd have to wait for the target to go back to New Orleans, and that meant how many more days away from Annie? The thought made him tense. He should be home painting the nursery, buying whatever Annie asked for, looking at that baby name website where she'd tagged possibilities because they still hadn't decided.

A man—black T-shirt and blazer, stylish eyeglasses, dark hair—walked through the lobby, glancing at him, heading toward the rooms.

Mender waited. Maybe she'd leave the room for lunch, and if she cut across the parking lot, already heading in the direction of his car trunk, well, that would be a gift and his work could be done quickly.

He got a text just then from his handler: My regular gun contact in hospital with appendicitis. Working on a backup. Be patient.

It wasn't his day. But he had the syringe, and the urgency to end this felt like a fire in his gut.

20

"Yes?" Kirsten called through the door.

"Ms. North?"

"What do you want?"

"My name is Marco Hernandez. I'm very sorry for your loss."

"Who are you?"

"I'm a freelance writer."

"I don't have any comment, Mr. Vulture," she said. "Leave me alone." How did he know she was here? He must have followed her from the warehouse. One of the reporters hanging out near the crime scene, looking for a crumb on the murder case, watching her leave, watching her talk to Bard, maybe figuring out who she was. Or a cop told him.

"I'm not a vulture," he said. "I've covered Adam Zhang and his business ventures. I knew him somewhat well."

Now she recognized the name. She'd printed out some of his articles about Adam Zhang for her wall last night. She went to one of the printed articles and checked the byline to make sure she'd gotten the name right. "Then go talk to his wife," Kirsten said, coming back to the door. "I have nothing for you."

"I thought I could help you...," he said. "Don't you want to know more about Adam Zhang?"

Well, she did. The *more* was bait. Maybe she could find out things from him. Like did Flora have a motive beyond millions of dollars to kill her husband. Or if some connection between the men had gone undetected. Or what this guy planned to write about Henry. "Just...just a second." She carefully picked up the chunks of glass and put them in the trash can, then opened the door.

Marco Hernandez was about her height, dark hair neatly cut, eyeglass frames that looked like what a model would wear, dark T-shirt and jacket.

"I am truly sorry for your loss," he said.

"Thanks. So, what about Adam Zhang?"

"I don't mean to be forward, but have you eaten?"

Maybe someone at the bar, or a cop, told him she'd been drinking earlier. She didn't want to eat with this man, but she was suddenly hungry and she didn't want to wait for Zach to come back, whenever that might be.

And she realized she would get no answers just staring into her scrambled eggs alone. "I have not eaten today and that was a mistake."

"There's a really good café about a block away. My treat."

"You don't have to treat me."

"Has anyone been nice to you since you got to Austin?"

Zach, but I sent him away, she thought, though she wouldn't say that to a reporter. "Okay," she said. "Let's eat and talk."

They walked out. She noticed a man in a ball cap sitting in the lobby, watching his phone. He turned his back to her as they passed, but she didn't give him another glance, her mind full of how she could pry some useful information loose from Marco Hernandez.

As they exited, she didn't see the man in the ball cap rise and head back toward her room.

21

Flora drove to her husband's downtown office. Thinking.

She didn't like Kirsten. She felt sorry for her, which wasn't the same as liking her. She needed to text Taylor back, and she needed to return her friends' calls, but she just couldn't bring herself to bother or care right now. She was unused to grief; it was a stranger who had taken her hand and was leading her off the ordered path of her life. For a moment she wondered what Adam would have done if she had been the one who died. He was so relentlessly competent at business and so clueless about everyday life. He would have figured it out, though, and so would she.

She thought: *I need to know more about the Norths. And that brother of hers—he's trouble.* She could hire a detective, maybe, but would that seem...odd? What would the police think? She did not want to make an enemy of Bard.

She took the elevator up to Zhang Townsend. The venture capital operation had half the floor; the other half served as incubator office space for the various early-stage start-ups the partners were funding, a mix of software and consumer product firms. In the elevator area there were framed logos of the companies Adam had launched. For a moment she thought of the hundreds of people employed now by those firms, the millions he and their founders had made, the value he'd created, the products they'd brought to market. It was overwhelming for a moment. It was as if *this* was Adam more than the life he'd made with her and Morgan.

She walked toward the side where the venture capital staff worked. The office was quiet, subdued. She had thought that

Shawn might close their offices for the week, in honor of Adam, but he hadn't. The office was mostly cubicles, which contained lots of young people eager to make their mark in the world. It wasn't fancy or glamorous, but it had made Adam a millionaire many times over. As soon as they saw her, a small parade of employees came forward, offering condolences, telling her how special Adam was and how much he would be missed, asking her what she needed. As if any of them could fix it. She wasn't sure what she needed. She kept on her brave face and thanked them all.

She asked to go see Teddy first; she realized she didn't know where he sat. One of the employees steered her to a cubicle in the back, far from Adam's office. Teddy was creating a presentation on his computer and got up immediately when she stood in his entryway.

"Hey. How did it go at the funeral home?" he asked. His eyes looked red. She saw tissues in the wastebasket. He'd been crying.

"Change of plans. May we talk for a minute?" she asked.

"Sure." He steered her into an unused conference room and closed the door. "Why are you here?"

"Oh, Teddy. Have you been crying?"

"No," he said, glancing at the floor. "Allergies."

"I know you miss him too." She felt heartsick that she hadn't thought more about Teddy's grief for his cousin and mentor. "I know you're hurting."

"I'm fine. I'll be fine," he said, forcing a nod, starting to smile, and then thinking better of it.

She told him about the morning's events: talking to Marco Hernandez at the gate; going to the warehouse; encountering Kirsten and Zach, who implied she had more motive than anyone else. She waited for Teddy to look at her with suspicion, but none showed on his face.

"So, Henry North lied to his own wife about where he was and she's a mess and her foster brother came across as a thug," Flora said. "If Adam is dead because of them, I want to know it. I want to know their history, their work, how they came into Adam's life."

She was about to add, *I'm going to hire an investigator, like you suggested*, but Teddy said, "Let me see what I can find out about them."

She frowned. "You. Play detective."

"I researched businesses and technologies all the time for Adam. It's not that different to do it for a person. And given what you said, I think the first person I should check into is Kirsten North."

"You think she hasn't been honest?"

Teddy raised an eyebrow. "Her brother's suggesting you have the best motive. Well, she could have a motive as well. We don't know that she was in New Orleans when…it happened."

Flora crossed her arms. "And she killed them and now is pretending to have just arrived in town?"

Teddy said, "It's a possibility. One the police should consider if they're going to be looking at you as well, Flora."

"The police *are* looking at me," Flora said, as if she were still two statements back. "Did they ask you…"

Teddy gave her a measured look. "They asked me if yours was a happy marriage. I told them it was. And they asked me where you had been that night. I confirmed your story."

"Yes," she said quietly. They were each other's alibis. But Teddy had been at a restaurant, and no one had seen her but Morgan. For a moment, panic crossed her face.

"Flora," he said.

"Yes."

"We trust each other, don't we?" Teddy took a step closer to her.

"Yes," she said.

"We have to stick together," he said. "I'm worried Adam's going to be dragged through the mud before this is over."

"What mud?"

"Anything bad the press can find, they will."

That made Flora feel like he knew bad press was coming. "What are you not telling me?"

"Nothing." He met Flora's gaze.

"Speaking of the press, Marco Hernandez has got someone giving him tips on the police force. That's how he knew Kirsten was at the warehouse."

"Do not trust him right now." He hesitated. "Is there anything you want to tell me?"

"Tell you?"

"Anything between you and Adam I need to know about?" His voice now was neutral.

"No." She cleared her throat. "Find out what you can about Kirsten and Zach. Of course you have your work here, but if you have time…"

"I'm just making a presentation for Shawn."

Shawn. Presenting and pitching just days after his partner was murdered. Life and business went on. And what was Shawn doing to keep Zhang Townsend on a steady course with Adam gone? She should ask, shouldn't she? She would hold Adam's ownership stake now. Was it wrong to ask before Adam was even buried?

"I can dig into Kirsten and Zach," Teddy said. "Hopefully before they leave town."

She didn't want Kirsten leaving town, not yet. Not before she could learn what she needed from the woman. So how to keep her here, and close? She'd have to think of something. "Thank you."

Teddy nodded. "I'll get right on it."

She hugged him. She thought he trembled for a moment under her touch. Teddy wasn't a hugger, wasn't emotional. Her voice went hoarse. "I've got to talk with Shawn. We're going to get through this."

Teddy stepped away from her and sat down at his computer. He ignored the PowerPoint file on his screen and opened a browser. Flora watched him for a moment and then turned away.

22

Flora walked to Shawn's corner office but he wasn't there.

She could hear his booming extrovert's voice, though, and she realized he was in Adam's office, at the next corner.

She found him sitting at Adam's desk, talking on a speaker phone, paging through a bound notebook.

She recognized Adam's handwriting in the notebook.

"Let me call you back," Shawn said into the phone as soon as he saw her in the doorway, and tapped the button to end the call without waiting for a response. He stood. "Flora."

"Why are you in his office?" she said, and immediately thought, *This can't matter; don't let it upset you.*

"The police took his laptop from here....I was just calling a company he'd planned to invest with...and his notes were in here." He pointed to the notebook. She knew Adam took handwritten notes in his meetings a lot of the time; he said he remembered more if he wrote rather than typed.

"I'm sorry," she said instantly. She stepped inside and closed the door. "It was harder to come here than I thought it would be."

"Can I get you a water? A coffee?" She shook her head in answer. "Here, sit." And he gestured her toward Adam's chair where he'd been sitting, and he went and sat on the visitor side of the desk. Shawn was a bit taller than her, broad-shouldered, hair longish. He looked a bit more like a college professor than a venture capitalist.

Flora realized that although his wife, Taylor, had come to the house shortly after the murders to comfort her, Shawn hadn't.

Odd that she hadn't registered his absence before. He must have been busy dealing with the impact of Adam's death on the firm.

"Everyone here is devastated," Shawn said. "I don't have the words."

"Thank you," she said. She took a deep breath. "I feel like we need to talk. If I can find the words." She didn't mean to sound petty; he must be grieving as well. She realized, rather suddenly, that she resented him. Sitting in Adam's office, talking with Adam's possible investees. Adam was dead and Shawn was still here. Her resentment made no sense. But she felt what she felt. She didn't need to be angry at him.

"Of course." Shawn leaned forward, the picture of devoted listening.

"Have you talked to the police?"

"I gave some woman…uh, a Detective Bard…a statement." Shawn moved his chair to the edge of the desk and closer to her. As if discussing the police needed to be whispered between them. She leaned back; she didn't feel the need to be closer to him.

Stop this, she thought. *What's wrong with you?*

"And what did that statement include?" she asked. *What did you say about my newly dead husband?*

He studied her for a long moment, as if trying to read the odd tone in her voice. But she could tell that he was wondering whether or not he should tell her how the statement went. "Well. They asked the last time I'd seen Adam, they asked where I was that night.…I was at home, by the way…and, full disclosure, they asked about the state of your marriage."

His words felt like ice sliding along her skin. And, *full disclosure*, like it was an investment deal.

"I told them I'd seen Adam late that afternoon, but I'd gone home early since Amelia had dance practice and I took her"—Amelia was his and Taylor's six-year-old daughter—"and I told them after dinner I was home with Amelia and Taylor, and I told them your marriage was happy and secure," Shawn said.

"Thank you." Of course they asked about the spouse. She thought of Bard, asking her again about their marriage this morning, and Teddy revealing to her that he had been asked the same question. "I suppose they have to ask that," she said. But in her head she heard Zach's words: *Cui bono?* The police knew she stood to benefit…but what about Shawn?

"I suppose they do," he agreed.

"I'd like to know what investment deals Adam was working on."

She never asked about the deals when they were socializing. "May I ask why?" Shawn said.

Like her husband hadn't been murdered.

And then…she saw him glance at his phone on the desk. Checking the time, like he had somewhere to be.

Like this didn't matter. Sparing her a few moments.

She steadied her gaze on him. "I don't want to keep you from your appointments, or your busy day, or whatever presentation Teddy is prepping for you. But I would like to know about all Adam's deals, in light of…my now being a stakeholder in this firm."

Shawn leaned toward her, very slightly, his mouth set in a puzzled frown. "Stakeholder? Flora, this firm isn't for you to worry about right now. You're…we're all in mourning."

Are you? she thought. Something here, with this man she'd known for years, felt so off it was nearly like a sound underlying their voices, a hum whose source you couldn't identify.

Shawn Townsend was afraid. She could see it in his trying-too-hard gaze of sad empathy, in his voice.

Flora found her voice. "Adam built this company, and I want to be sure it holds true to his vision."

It was a punch and she knew it and so did he. "Did Teddy put you up to this? Flora, you're going to be a very wealthy woman, and I want to be sure people don't take advantage of that."

Oh. Do you not like Teddy for some reason? That's news to me.

"Shawn, that's ridiculous." She leaned back in the chair. "I want to know what deals he was working on. I want to know if there's anyone he might have angered by not investing in their company. I want to know who could have hurt him."

Shawn stared at her, then shook his head. "Oh. Flora, this isn't one of those TV dramas full of corporate intrigue. We…don't have enemies that way."

They asked you about my marriage? Why didn't they ask me about how your partnership was going? You spent more time with him than I did.

She kept her voice low because she realized the office door was open and she didn't want the staff to hear her. "There are people who resent investors like you and Adam who say no to funding their dreams. A strong hate can grow from a small seed."

"And they go on and get money from someone else who believes in them. Flora…his death has no connection to my business."

My business. My. It wasn't just his. He looked abashed, though, as if realizing he'd chosen his words poorly.

"This man who died with him. Henry North. Did you know him?" she asked.

"No. Never heard of him."

"Austin is full of software consultants; why did Adam hire this guy from New Orleans?"

Shawn stiffened. "If Adam hired this man, it wasn't to work for us. I've checked our email servers since the news about Henry North broke this morning. We don't have any record here that they were in contact through our office."

Flora stared at the floor.

"I can't imagine what you're going through," Shawn said. "And I know you need closure. But we may never know the answer."

Closure. She hated that word. Like she could ever have that. People were always in such a rush for closure. Adam wasn't buried yet. It was just a bit too soon.

"You'll have a lot to think about as we get through these difficult days," Shawn continued. "I'm sure when you've had a chance to collect your thoughts, you'll want to sell me Adam's stake in the firm. I know right now's not the time for major decisions. I just want to reassure you we'll deal with all that fairly whenever you're ready."

"I just want to be sure we're understanding each other," she said, slowly and deliberately. "You are saying nothing happening in this business is connected to my husband's murder."

He nodded. "I swear that to you."

She nodded mutely.

"I know Taylor wanted to talk to you about postponing the fund-raiser…," he began.

"No," she said, because she felt like being contrary to him. "We'll still have the event. Do it to honor Adam. It's to help kids. They need help; it should go on."

"What? Flora, I know how dedicated you are to your causes, but that's not a good idea."

He seemed determined to contradict or patronize her at every point and she tried not to let it irritate her. Or at least not to let it show. "Well, you and Taylor will do what you want, but the fund-raiser meant so much to Adam…he would want it to go on. I'll be there to honor Adam."

"Are you sure?"

"Yes. It'll be a way for me to say hello and accept condolences."

"Flora…I understand this is important to your foundation, but…"

"I have no idea when they will give me back his body, Shawn. I can't have a funeral. Maybe people will donate more if I'm there. In his honor. If you're no longer comfortable hosting it at your home, then I'll see if I can make other arrangements."

"Okay. We won't cancel." He raised his hands in surrender—like he was indulging her. She felt a hot flush of anger with him. This whole talk had gone wrong.

She was mourning. Taylor and Teddy and Jeanne and Milo were mourning. But Shawn, she realized, was speeding on to his post-Adam life. Adam was gone, so he was in charge, and now was not apparently a time for reflection or slowness. Busy, busy. Money to be made. And he was going to try to shut her out from her rightful role. He had made that decision with no consideration for her.

She glanced down at the open notebook. At Adam's handwriting. Careful notes on the prospect start-up's chances, their marketing opportunities, their competitive edge that no one else had grabbed yet. He was careful in his thoughts, in his choices. Seeing the words in his hand suddenly strengthened her.

Flora got up and stopped at the door. "Thanks for your time and your sympathy. If you could prepare a briefing for me…maybe next week, I'll have Teddy set up a time so I can get up to speed on the investments and the opportunities under consideration and also the personnel. I'd like to get to know everyone here. Oh, and our financial standing."

Shawn's astonished expression quickly retreated behind a look of concern. "I thought you'd want me to buy you out."

"You didn't listen. I told you I'll remain at Zhang Townsend as a stakeholder. It's what Adam would have wanted." She wasn't sure at all she wanted to do this, but she wanted Shawn to *think* she did.

And she thought: *Did you want him out of the way, Shawn? Did you want all this for yourself?*

"Being a partner…" Shawn's face paled. "Well. Of course you should consider that option."

She leaned against the office door. "I don't know what's going on with you, if it's grief or shock or concern about your precious business. But you know something, Shawn."

Now he simply looked startled at her words.

"Do you know why he died?" she pressed.

"I told you it couldn't have anything to do with our work."

"I didn't ask you that. I asked if you knew *why*. Because if you do, and you haven't told me, I'll find out."

He looked at her in shock. "No," he said. "I do not, Flora, and if I did, I would have told you immediately."

"The past that you and I had," she said carefully and quietly, "is small and meaningless. We were over as soon as I met Adam and you met Taylor. We both knew that."

He nodded. Silent, his face reddening.

"I just want to be sure there's no resentment. Nothing lingering. Nothing simmering. Because we were a casual, just friends thing, and we both found someone better for us and we're happy for each other, right?"

He nodded again.

"So. That has nothing to do with whether or not I sell my interest to you or whether I don't and assume my duties as a partner."

"My concern is that you have no experience in this area and millions of dollars are at stake. The position requires insight and judgment that take a substantial amount of time to develop."

"I once had a profession. I'm sure I'll manage."

"Journalism isn't the same."

"I can see the parallels. An analytical mind, the need to ascertain facts, the need to employ judgment, the need to read people when they might not be honest with you."

His mouth worked for a moment as he stared at her. "There's a lot more to it than that, but I'm sure you'll be a fast study."

"Adam had set up a home office in our new condo downtown. Without telling me."

"So?"

"So, was he coming to this office as often? You just alluded that you two weren't together as much as I thought. Maybe he was working on a project you didn't know about."

"He could work on any project he pleased right here."

"Okay," she said, trying to be polite. But then whatever had been revived in her when Adam died, after the worst of the shock passed, wriggled a little freer. "Everything just changed for both of us, didn't it? I want to believe you, but…I don't really know you."

He looked shocked. "We've known each other for years. I'm just going to put this all down to your grief."

Like she owed him an explanation. Something must have shown in her face because he said instantly, "I didn't mean that the way it sounded. I'm sorry."

"We're all raw right now," she said. "I'll see you and Taylor later."

"Flora. I have a buyout clause," he said suddenly. "If I pay ten percent above market price, I can buy you out. That might be for the best. For both of us. All Taylor and I want is for you and Morgan to…to know that we care for you."

She didn't answer him. She walked out of the office, and immediately encountered more people offering condolences. These people saw her husband more in a day than she did. She suddenly resented them all, but she nodded and accepted their kindness. She glanced over her shoulder once and saw Shawn watching her.

The most likely connection between Adam and Henry North was their mutual work in software. Which meant the connection had something to do with Zhang Townsend, but it was clear that Shawn was sealing up the walls, protecting the firm.

Protecting himself.

You thought someone was in the penthouse last night. Maybe it was Shawn. Maybe he does know. But how would he get in?

Something was going on here, something beyond denial of an unpleasant possibility. He had wanted to rattle her, telling her the police asked about the marriage. *We may never know the answer.*

Sounded like he didn't want the questions asked.

She summoned the elevator. On the opposite side of the lobby, the side where the start-up businesses worked to emerge from the Zhang Townsend cocoon, a door opened. An attractive young woman, dressed smartly and holding a laptop, walked out but stopped full when she saw Flora.

"Mrs. Zhang? I'm Melinda Alari."

"Hello," Flora said, trying to remember if she'd met the striking young woman at an office function.

"We haven't met before. Adam funded my company."

"Oh, I see."

"Adam was the most remarkable man I've ever met," Melinda said.

"Thank you," Flora said. Melinda's suit was high-end, she was well-styled, and Flora thought of a time when she used to face the world like that each day.

Melinda Alari looked as if she wanted to say something more, almost staring through Flora, but then the elevator doors opened. Flora stepped on and turned back to face the woman.

She waited for condolences or sympathy, but Melinda Alari was silent. Just…studying her.

"I wondered what I'd say to you…," Melinda started, but the elevator doors slid shut.

What did that mean?

People were odd; they didn't know what to say in moments of grief.

She texted Taylor: I kind of had an argument with your husband.

Then she added: sorry I keep ignoring you, I met the other widow

Taylor texted back: You know I love you and what do you need from me?

And Flora had texted back: I just need to talk.

A few seconds later, her phone rang. Taylor. "Hey," Flora said.

"Hey, how are you? Don't answer. You're doing awful."

"It's been a long morning."

"Are you still at the office? I was heading in to have lunch with Shawn. He's been so down. Well, obviously. What thoughtless thing did he say to you? You know he didn't mean it. Can you join us for lunch? Whatever happened, we'll mend it."

"No, I left. I'm about to head over to the penthouse. Hey, will you meet me there before you go see Shawn? Tell him you'll be a bit late? He's busy right now anyway." That was a little vicious jab, but she couldn't help herself.

"Of course," Taylor said, sounding a bit uncertain. "You know he's not the most diplomatic soul, Flora. Whatever he said, I'm sorry…" Taylor's voice trailed off.

"It'll be all right. I'll see you there." Flora ended the call. She took a deep breath.

Her husband was dead, and she felt she couldn't trust his closest friend and business partner. This was what murder did—exposed all the seething emotion beneath the polite connections. Then the thought occurred to her: If Shawn was lying and the reason for the murders was connected to Zhang Townsend, was she putting herself in danger by assuming Adam's place in the company?

23

The Right Now Diner had a hippie atmosphere and Kirsten wondered if this was a chunk of genuine Austin or a re-creation of the city's former vibe—that was the kind of question Henry would ask and the thought of him not being here to ask it made her chest hurt. Marco Hernandez did her a kindness: She ordered a cup of hot black coffee and drank it down and he said nothing to her. Just...waited for her to collect herself. She thought he would pepper her immediately with questions, but he didn't. Instead he watched the pedestrians passing on the sidewalk. She set down the coffee cup and said, "I really needed that." The waiter refilled it immediately, then took their order and hurried off.

"Thanks," she said. She drank more of the coffee. "I forgot to eat. And then I drank on top of the not eating. Don't write that down, please." She thought she'd test his answer.

"I won't. And it's shock. It's grief. I can't imagine what you're going through."

"People always say that, yet they think they can imagine it."

"Tell me about your husband."

He didn't get out a tape recorder or a phone to record their conversation. Or a notebook to write in.

"I thought you were going to tell me about Adam Zhang. That was the invite."

"Okay. I'll answer your questions then. What would you like to know?"

The coffee was helping clear her head and center her thoughts. She finished the cup and waved at the waiter, who refilled it, and she told him how good it was and thanked him. When the waiter left she said, "You told me you'd written about Adam Zhang."

"Yes, for national magazines. I freelance. Usually I'm a business reporter."

"And you want to cover homicides now." It was such a strange word to use in connection with her husband. Who was dead. She missed Henry with an ache that felt like a shove from inside her heart.

"I'd only consider writing about it because of my connection with Adam," Marco said. "I'm just wondering why they were together."

Their food arrived: migas for him, scrambled eggs with cheese, peppers, and tostada bits; and for her two fried eggs, pan sausage, toast, grits, and grapes and pineapple in a side bowl. She fell on the food. They each made a dent in their lunches before she spoke again. "So tell me three things about Adam Zhang."

"Smart. Ambitious." He stopped.

"That's two and it sounds like a press release."

Marco took a deep breath and a sip of coffee. "He's both those things. One way to write about these hyper-successful types is to identify their fatal flaw, you know, like they're a character in a Greek tragedy."

"What was Adam's flaw, then?"

"If you were in business with him, Adam would make sure that he ended up with all the advantages. Adam couldn't help himself—he had to feel he was ahead of you. Even when the stakes were small, he had to have more leverage, more power. This…need had soured big deals and ruined important partnerships for him, ones that could have made him even richer. Some of his investees told me he wasn't entirely fair to the companies he helped fund—that the founders could have held on to more of their ownership. That maybe, as well, he had taken ideas started by others and folded them into his other companies. It hurt his rep to a degree, but nothing could be proven—people come up with similar ideas all the time."

"Could someone he'd burned that way have killed him?"

"There are lots of other ways to get funding. He's not the only game in town. So did Henry work in software?"

Marco asked it like he knew the answer. Henry was on those business networking sites, so Marco could have found his profile and figured out it was a software connection between the two men. She wasn't about to tell this man that she didn't know her husband was in Austin. "Yes, he's a software consultant, primarily in security."

"Was your husband trying to start a company? Maybe he had pitched to Adam."

She nearly said no, of course not. But then she thought, *Maybe he had. Maybe he'd reached out to Adam Zhang and somehow it had horribly gone wrong.* If she could just find out where Henry had spent the time between his arrival in Austin and his death, she might have an answer.

"Henry never talked about a start-up to me," Kirsten said. "If Zhang was meeting him, I'm guessing he'd want to hire him as a consultant to defend against breaches and hacks. Was Adam Zhang a man who would worry about being hacked?"

"Every prominent businessperson worries about it. They can be targets. Corporate espionage or having their embarrassing secrets aired. Sex pics on their phone, stuff like that," Marco said.

"And so he hires Henry, and Henry comes here and they both get killed," she said. "Or maybe Henry found out something that was valuable to Adam Zhang." She put her elbow on the table, her fist resting against her forehead. She had some possible theories in mind, but she needed proof. Chasing answers this way was like chasing shadows.

"You mean information Henry found out about Zhang, like, damaging?"

"Maybe. I'm just throwing out thoughts."

"And Henry came here to…sell it to him?" Like blackmail.

She realized she'd made a serious misstep. "No, not at all. Henry wasn't an extortionist. Maybe he came here to warn him. Maybe it wasn't about Zhang." Now she looked at Marco. "This wife of his. Tell me about her."

A woman. Or money.

"I don't really know Flora well."

"Did you interview her when you wrote about her husband?"

"Not formally. I've talked with her a couple of times, but more like conversations, not interviews. We conducted the second interview for my article at his house. She was there. She seemed pleasant. Kind of a…" He stopped.

"What?"

"Kind of a person who fades into the background."

Henry had been the same way, but she had loved that about him. "Adam was the star and Flora was the scenery."

He shrugged. "She's a nice woman. She's smart. She used to write for major business magazines before she met Adam."

"What, she quit once she got married?"

"Yeah. She had a career I wouldn't have minded having. Now she runs a medical research foundation that does a lot of fund-raising."

"So she does goody-goody work to make herself feel better about buying Louboutin shoes."

"Have you met her?" he asked.

"You should know. You followed me back to the hotel. She was at the warehouse."

He gave her a smile that admitted he'd underestimated her. "I didn't know that you talked to her." He shrugged.

"Could she have killed them?"

"Why would you think that?"

"Because Adam Zhang was worth millions and they always look at the wife. Who benefits? She does."

"True. But if it's her, she killed your husband just for being there. Pretty cold."

"Him being there makes it look like it's business-related. Maybe it's personal."

"Maybe, but I think all the drama in Adam's life was in his businesses. You don't know why they were meeting?"

"Henry didn't tell me details of his work."

"Did you know he was specifically meeting with Adam Zhang?"

"No."

Marco moved the fork around his empty plate. She had the sudden sense that he wanted to tell her something, rather than just buzzing her with questions, but it would be like showing his hand in poker.

"Were you working on a new article about Zhang? When all this happened?" she guessed suddenly. It was a fair deduction. Like, he'd started a story and now it had taken this murderous turn, and he wasn't sure how to finish his article or even if he should. He wasn't a crime reporter. He was trying to play the hand he'd been dealt.

Marco nodded, and she felt a little tickle in her brain. She'd read Marco right. She bet he hadn't gone to the police yet. He'd wanted to break his story. So maybe this wasn't something Bard knew. Or even Flora Zhang.

Money or a woman.

"What about?" Kirsten asked.

He looked at her, studying her, and she guessed he was trying to figure out how much their mutual interests aligned. "My interviews with him were never just one meeting. It usually took three or four talks. He wasn't that eager to be interviewed, but I think someone had told him he had to do it. Although he was reticent, I was able to get him to open up. He knew I'd be fair with him."

"Not adversarial," she said.

"No. Look, if he wasn't giving me a straight answer to a reasonable question, I'd push. . . ." He stopped suddenly. "I wonder if you might do me a favor."

"What?"

"Can you access your husband's emails or texts? You have his password?"

"The police already said there was no sign that they had contacted each other."

"They would have searched Zhang's emails, but they didn't ID your husband until you came to town. Are they searching his emails? Zhang may have deleted his, but your husband might not have been so careful."

"I don't know. They must have a warrant because it's a murder case." Henry's laptop was missing and she couldn't access his backups, so as far as she knew no one had looked through his emails.

"I'm just wondering.... This will sound odd."

"Ask me."

"Did he ever mention a *green key*?"

"Green key? As in a key that is green?"

He looked at her with such urgency that she closed her eyes and thought for a moment. "No. I don't recall Henry mentioning a green key. What does it mean?"

Of course he didn't answer. He sipped his water.

"Really?" she said. "This can't all be one-way, Marco. I can look and see if there's a mention of a green key, but I'd need some context. Is it referring to an actual key? Is it a company name, like one word?"

"He just said it to me, I guess like it was one word. He'd reached out to me, called me last week, asked me if I would work a story that wasn't intended solely for the business press." He lowered his voice. "I asked him what it was about, and he laughed and said, 'green key,' then he told me we'd talk more later."

"Not *a* key or *the* key. Just 'green key.'"

"I researched it. There was a Greenkey company here in town that did software for environmental systems. Their website went dormant about six months ago, but I haven't yet found a connection to Adam. If Adam hired Henry, maybe this was what Henry was going to work on."

"I'll look. Have you told this to the police?" She lowered her voice, as though someone was listening. But she wanted him to think that this information was shared. Their secret. They were in it together.

"No," he said after a moment. He looked uncomfortable. "If you found a mention of this Greenkey company in your husband's stuff, then it would have context. We could go to them then."

"I'll see what I can find. And what if I find out my husband knew about a 'green key' in some way?" she said. "We go straight to the police."

He nodded. It would help his story, and he'd be the hero for having uncovered the connection. And if it got her to the killer before the police…well, she was fine with that.

She stood. She felt recovered now from the morning drinks. "Who else have you interviewed for this?"

"Flora won't talk. I haven't tried yet with his business partner. I'd like to talk to the homeless guy, but he won't talk to me."

"Homeless guy?"

"He found the…he found Adam and Henry. His name's Norman."

And then she remembered Bard mentioning that, and at the café, hearing the bartender say "the celebrity" as the old man pushing the shopping cart went by.

"Oh. Yes," she said. "Thanks for lunch. We'll talk soon."

She'd originally planned to go straight back to the hotel, work on unearthing more data about the Zhangs, and wait for Zach to return. She'd learned some of what she needed to know.

Massive change of plan, she thought to herself as she left the café.

24

Kirsten walked from the diner to a car rental office downtown and got herself a subcompact. She didn't want to rely on rideshares or Zach anymore. She drove off the lot and headed down South Congress. She drove past the turnoff to the warehouse, and three blocks farther down, she saw him. An older man with a grocery cart, trundling down the road. He seemed to go a little faster when he walked past the new, renovated buildings that housed the gentrified businesses. He slowed as he got to an older body shop that was holding its ground against the encroachment on South Congress Boulevard. He stopped and searched in one of his bags.

Kirsten pulled up behind him. He glanced at her as she got out of the car and she could see in his face he was already trying to decide how much trouble she was going to be.

"Sir?"

He gave her a look that said, "I know you want something because I don't get called sir often."

"Are you the gentleman who found the bodies in the warehouse?"

"I don't have nothing to say," he said, turning from her and continuing to walk.

"One of them was my husband. Henry. I just want to talk to you. I'll pay you for your time."

"I'm sorry for your loss." He kept walking. He had a strong voice, resonant.

"If you won't take money for your time, can I buy you lunch?"

He stopped. Glanced back at her, seemed to consider. "Sorry for your loss. What do you want to know?"

"First…what's your name?"

"Norman."

"Hi, Norman, I'm Kirsten."

She offered her hand and he shook it, looking a bit surprised.

She could see now that he was older than she'd thought. Maybe close to sixty. "Are you hungry?" she asked.

"Around here they don't like it when I come into places."

"You'll be with me. We can even drive to someplace that's not around here."

"I can't leave my cart."

"Okay. Where would you feel comfortable?"

He named a fried chicken chain, told her there was one half a mile on down the road.

"That sounds good. I'll give you a ride."

"I'll meet you there," he said, patting his cart.

"All right."

She drove to the fast-food place, parked, and wondered if he would show. She got out of the car and stood by the front doors, waiting for him.

Norman came eventually, pushing the cart, keeping his eyes down, and she wondered what his life was like. She had run away twice from her first foster home, each time spending one night out on the streets, and both times she'd been terrified, but the cops had found her and taken her back to the foster family. She thought most people couldn't understand the sheer level of vulnerability you felt. Her clearest fear those two times had been of sleep, even after finding an alley that was deserted and quiet. For the first time she thought what the loss of Henry's income and depletion of their savings might mean to her. She couldn't afford their apartment on her earnings alone. He didn't have life insurance…he was so young; they hadn't imagined needing it for a while. That had been a mistake. She had no one to help her, no cushion to shield her from the blow. Well, Zach, but Zach worked for an organized crime family called the Fortunatos, and her fear was that one day Zach would go to prison for a very long time. Once, they had offered her a job, but she'd begged off. She couldn't go to work for the Fortunatos, no way, no how. She didn't have a set of real friends—she didn't worry about making or keeping friends. She had Henry and a job she could do from home and books to read and TV to watch and that had been enough for her.

She lacked…connection.

Would she end up like Norman? Maybe she should ask him about which shopping carts were best. Suddenly she felt fear, sharp and silvery, sliding down into her gut as if settling in for a stay.

He parked his cart at the edge of the parking lot and straightened his jacket and cap. "If we sit on this side, I can keep an eye on it."

She nodded and they went into the restaurant.

"I can get us our food if you'll find us a booth," Kirsten said. "Do you know what you want?"

"Just a chicken sandwich, please." He bit at his lip.

"How about two? Or three?" He might want to save one for later.

"Won't argue."

"Fries? Coleslaw? Red beans and rice? All of them? What to drink?"

"Fries and a sweet tea, please."

She stood in line behind a uniformed police officer who glanced back at her once, maybe recognizing her from this morning's incident. She placed the order, getting a sandwich and water for herself. She saw Norman vanish into the men's room and return a few minutes later, hands and face washed, beard damp. He sat and watched his cart through the window. He didn't look at the other people in the restaurant.

She collected their tray and sat down across from him.

Kirsten watched as he dug into the food. She tended to plow through meals, eager to get to the next activity, but he savored the spicy fried chicken sandwich as though it were haute cuisine. She didn't know what small talk she should try to make—asking him about his life felt like intruding or judging how he had ended up here. So they ate in silence until he finished the second sandwich.

"You're from New Orleans," he said. "I could hear your accent, although it's slight."

The New Orleans accent was rather distinct from the rest of the South, more like a New York accent. She'd never thought there was just one accent in New Orleans, but she knew hers was there. "Yes," she said. "So was Henry. Can you tell me what happened?"

"I can, but you seem like such a nice young lady I don't want to upset you."

"I really need to know."

He sipped at his iced tea. "Behind the warehouses, there's a thick growth of oaks they haven't cut down—left over from when the train tracks there were active. They'd muffle the noise for the neighborhood when the trains passed. Sometimes I go back there to sleep. That night I did. Now, I didn't hear nothing in the night, no shots or arguing or anything. I watched the stars and I slept fine in my bag."

She waited, letting him take his time.

"So I didn't see anyone arriving or leaving."

"I see," she said. Trying to keep it conversational.

He got up suddenly and went to the condiments stand and pulled out a stack of napkins from the dispenser. He came back and pushed them toward her and she realized, *He thinks I'll cry*.

"I woke up in the early morning, and I needed the facilities. Sometimes that warehouse is open, sometimes not."

"It's not consistently locked up?"

"No."

"That seems odd."

"I don't look a gift horse in the mouth. It had a bathroom I could use. Restaurants don't like me using their facilities. So that restroom gave me a little dignity to start my day if I was lucky and it was unlocked." He cleared his throat. "So I turned on my little flashlight and I walked down to the warehouse. I went in. The bathroom is on the other side, so I have to cross the warehouse to get to it. This was maybe four a.m., did I say?"

He stopped.

"It's all right, Norman. I need to know."

"I was walking in the dark with my flashlight, but I tripped. I saw a foot, in a shoe.…It was the Asian gentleman. He was on his back. Then I saw the other body, your husband. He was facedown."

He stopped. She nodded. "It's okay. I can take it."

"They'd both been shot. Mr. Zhang, two shots to the face. Your husband had been shot in the chest, not the head. I checked for their pulses. Then I went back outside, but it was early and all the businesses were closed still except the all-night café a ways down the street. So I walked down there and told the manager there were two people dead in the warehouse. At first she didn't believe me, but I kept telling her and she called the police. She let me use their bathroom too." He paused, as if sorry he'd noted that.

She said nothing. A pair of young men sat in the booth next to them and she saw one frown at Norman, as if he had no business being there.

"Thank you for telling me."

"The police came, they asked me questions, I told them what I told you. That's all I really know." He looked down at the third sandwich and slid it into his pocket.

"Did you see their phones?"

"Their phones? Like, lying by them? No."

"Or a backpack? Like one to carry a laptop."

"No. Just them. I didn't really inspect the scene."

"Were they lying next to each other?" She wondered if they had been shot at the same time.

He took a pen from his jacket and drew on one of the napkins. Two stick figures, not lying parallel, but their feet closer together than their heads. "The Asian gentleman was closer to the door. Your husband was here."

Maybe Adam running for the door, maybe Henry standing his ground? She didn't want to picture his last moments. She felt certain he would have thought of her.

"Norman, my husband told me he was going to New York. Not Austin. He was not one to lie to me. So he didn't want me to know why he was here and then he ended up dead with a man he didn't know and had no connection to. I got an anonymous phone call and the caller told me he'd been killed here. Someone called me on his phone."

Norman stared.

"So, this is...extra weird. And I'm wondering if there's anything you noticed, anything you didn't tell the police because it didn't seem important or maybe in all the awfulness of the moment you forgot."

Norman closed his eyes. She waited.

He kept his eyes shut. "Will you buy me some cigarettes? Just a pack, not a box?"

"Sure."

He reached into his pocket and pulled out a cigarette, partly smoked. It looked bent, a little worn. "Once I went into the warehouse and saw...them, my mind's kind of a blank. But I found this in the woods when I walked down there with my flashlight. It's some fancy brand. See?" He pointed at the name and the logo on the cigarette, close down to its filter. A little fleur-de-lis and a name below it, in blue.

"What brand is that?" She and Henry had never been smokers.

"It's French. Gaudet," he said, pointing to the tiny print below the fleur-de-lis.

It sounded vaguely familiar to her, but she couldn't remember where she'd heard of it.

"Now, that's not likely a cigarette that I or someone else like me is going to smoke, unless someone hands it to us. And maybe that's what happened. Has to be a lot of a cigarette left for me to pick it up; I don't like to see waste. Live out on the streets and you'll see how much folks waste. How much they take for granted. Even here, look at how much food is still on the trays, being tossed into the trash. So I picked this up. But that means someone was in the woods smoking it and maybe watching the warehouse. Maybe…waiting for them? And they showed up and so he didn't finish the cigarette and that's why so much of it was left. I don't know. Maybe it means nothing. Might have nothing to do with the killer."

"Why didn't you tell the police?" she said after she'd found and steadied her voice.

He didn't answer. He looked embarrassed.

"I won't tattle on you."

"Because I'd have to say how I found it, where I'd been sleeping, and they'd turn me out from there. It's a safe spot. The city has changed so much…there's so many more homeless here than there used to be. Fewer places for me to rest my head."

"Can I keep this?"

"Yes, but maybe tell the police you found it in the lot. Not the trees, not where I sleep. So they'll let me be."

"Sure," she said, and she suddenly felt like crying. She pushed down the feeling.

"It's just a cigarette," he said.

She wrapped the cigarette in the napkin. She walked with Norman, and his cart, to a convenience store and bought him two cartons of cigarettes, which he said was too much, but she insisted. She bought a box of plastic sandwich bags and put the Gaudet cigarette in it. She should give it to the police. Could DNA be lifted from it? Maybe. Then they'd know who the murderer was, and she would have no chance to get to him or her.

To make them pay.

She walked back out onto the street with Norman. She'd bought him some baby wipes and deodorant and toothpaste as well.

"I have a daughter, you know," he said quietly. "About your age. We don't talk. I'm not even sure where she is."

"Wouldn't she like to hear from you?"

"She said she wouldn't, the last time we talked. I used to be a teacher. Math, middle school. I got tired of it."

So much unsaid in that last sentence, Kirsten thought.

Kirsten said, "I'm sorry, Norman."

"It is what it is. Thanks for the lunch and the stuff."

"Thanks for talking to me." She tried to give him a quick hug, but he backed away, startled, then turned back to his cart and pushed it away.

She could call Bard. She wondered if the cigarette would be considered compromised evidence anyway. And there was nothing to connect it to the case. Yet.

She did a search on her phone for "Gaudet." Edgy-cool French brand, with a distinctive gold-and-blue package; and then she remembered stores in the French Quarter selling them when she was younger because the package used a fleur-de-lis and that was also the New Orleans Saints logo. But she couldn't remember seeing them in a while. According to her search results they weren't sold in the US stores anymore, but still in France and the rest of Europe.

Had someone bought them on a trip? Or ordered them online?

She wondered if any of Adam Zhang's friends smoked these kinds of cigarettes or had made recent trips to Europe.

She would *really* like to know that. But this could also be meaningless, a false trail.

How could she get access to the Zhang house? Or this penthouse they'd recently bought, which she'd found mentioned on a high-end real estate blog during her internet search last night?

Pretend to need to talk to Flora Zhang. Share information with her. Be a widow, together. Apologize for how she acted.

End the hostilities.

The penthouse was closer; she could try there first.

She got in her car and headed to the Zhang penthouse.

25

Mender was getting tired of waiting for his target to return. The hotel room closet was small and he'd started to worry that his muscles would cramp when Kirsten North walked back in and he'd stumble out of his hiding place, more comical than terrifying and she could scream before he was back on his feet. He would be between her and the only door, and so if he could just gain control of her in those few critical seconds, all would be well.

He'd managed access via pure luck. On the hallway floor, he'd seen one of the paper envelopes containing a key card, with the room number written within. One of the high school athletes must have dropped it. Quickly he used a pen to change the 3 to an 8 on the room number, matching it to Kirsten North's, dumped the lost key in front of the room where it belonged so it would be found with no worry, and walked down another hallway, seeing a housecleaner and putting on an apologetic smile while flashing the key envelope at her.

"Hi, I'm Mr. North and I grabbed my key envelope when I went out and it didn't have my key in it…there's a long line right now at the front desk, I guess there are teams staying here?"

She nodded and let him into the room, and he thanked her with a ten-dollar tip. But he might not have long. The housekeeper might say something to her supervisor or to the front desk. Kirsten should come back here after her lunch and then he could deal with her.

He hated making kills in hotel rooms. He thought of Vancouver, the time he'd come out of hiding to stretch his legs and in walked the victim, still talking on his cell phone. Such a mess. He could never go back to Canada.

And Annie kept buzzing him. He normally didn't keep a cell phone with him during a kill that she could contact him on—he didn't want anything traced back to her if it went wrong or he got caught. But he felt that he had to stay in touch.

He looked at her last text: I had pains last night. Mom came over. I'm ok. But I'm nervous. Thought labor was starting. It's too early.

His heart jumped at that, but he read on: I miss you. When will u be back? Thought u were about done.

He wrote: Miss u 2. Trying to finish job today. Maybe home tonight. Can't promise. Give my best 2 yr mom. He actually liked his mother-in-law. She didn't ask too many questions about his work and his travel, and as long as it looked like Annie was taken good care of, she seemed fine.

He had just slid the phone back into his jacket pocket when he heard the hotel door open. He tensed. He could inject her with the sedative here, take her out the back to his car trunk. It was risky, he might be spotted. He could tell anyone who saw him that she'd collapsed and he was rushing her to the hospital a few blocks away. Then out to the Hill Country, where she'd disappear forever.

The closet door was barely cracked, and he waited for Kirsten to cross his line of vision. Spring out, hand over her mouth before she could scream, the needle finding the sweetness of her flesh...

Not Kirsten North.

Mender froze.

It was the big man he'd seen meet Kirsten at the café across from the murder site.

The man moved out of range. Mender could hear his footsteps. Could hear the rustle of paper—he must have been looking at all the printouts Kirsten had taped to the hotel room wall.

How had he gotten in? She must have given him a room key. Who was this guy? Boyfriend? She hadn't been a widow for very long. Relative? Friend?

This guy, when Mender had seen him at the café, had the air of a protector. Mender was careful to be still. He was worried the slightest movement would produce a sound and give him away.

He didn't slide the closet door closed the few inches he'd opened it. He slid, very slowly, back and felt the bulk of her carry-on suitcase, sitting upright. It started to fall over. He grabbed it, froze. Listened.

He heard nothing. Then the man's voice. "Hey, I'm just checking in." Low, deep, New Orleans accent that always sounded vaguely New Yorkish to Mender.

Mender steadied Kirsten's suitcase. She had clothes in the closet on hangers. He had to be careful not to brush against them or the big man would hear.

"Yeah. Yeah. Well, email him back," the big guy said. "Tell him no, he knows what the deal is. If he needs a reminder to pay on time, I'll pay him a visit."

Mender wondered if the syringe would be enough. The big guy outweighed Kirsten by a hundred pounds. Or knock the guy out and kill Kirsten the moment she walked in. The client was being very picky about how this job was done, and it had gotten complicated.

He was going to have to improvise, and he hated improvising.

Silence, and then what sounded like a new conversation. "Hello, Detective. Zach here. How's the wife and kids?" Pause. Mender decided not to attack him while he was on the phone with the police. "I need your help. We need to find out where Henry North was staying in Austin, Texas. Can you run a check on any credit cards in that name used here in the past week?"

Mender thought again: *Who is this guy?*

"Yeah, that's your problem. Say you got an anonymous tip about a New Orleans citizen killed in Austin. Make the ask understandable. Do this for me and we'll cut some off your debt."

Your debt? Mender felt a cold finger tickle his skin.

"Henry North. No, he didn't go by other names; he was a respectable citizen." Pause. Mender waited. The pause got longer. "Okay. He had to be staying somewhere, and I've got to find out where before someone else does." Pause. "Yeah, pretty sure he drove here. What? Really? Yeah, I think their car had that. Well, try that too."

Mender clearly had to get Big Guy out of the way to fulfill the contract and make Kirsten vanish.

"Can you do it or not? And in a hurry? Thanks, Lieutenant." The last part was sarcastic.

Mender held his position. Maybe the man would leave now. But he was sure that this guy was waiting here for Kirsten to return.

He had to decide.

Then he heard movement. The man went into the bathroom but didn't shut the door. He washed his hands noisily. Then silence for thirty seconds, then he heard him speak again.

"Yes, can you connect me with Detective Bard?"

Mender knew Bard was the detective in charge of the case. His handler had relayed that information to him.

"Hello. Oh, okay, thanks, Officer. I'm Zach Couvillon. I met Detective Bard this morning at the Zhang/North crime scene. I'm Kirsten North's foster brother...."

Foster brother. So he viewed Kirsten as a sister. That complicated everything. He wasn't going to vanish. There was another pause, probably him being put through to Detective Bard.

"Yes. I have information on the case. Henry North was in serious debt. He had asked me for a loan that I was unable to give him. I don't know how he knew Adam Zhang, or why he might have approached him as well, but it's a possibility. Kirsten was unaware of the debt; I think Henry kept this from her. Which would explain why he lied about his destination. I think that's the reason he didn't tell her."

Pause again.

"Yes, ma'am. This is all going to be devastating for my foster sister. But you have to know this and I wasn't comfortable keeping it from you." Pause. "Yes, ma'am. Please don't tell her I told you. I mean, you have his name now, you can investigate his assets, right? She'll be mad at me, but I'm just trying to help her. If that makes sense."

Pause again. Mender found himself wondering if Henry North had owed the client money. This might be a thread that could lead back to the client, and then to him. What to do?

"Okay. You're talking to her at three? Yes. All right. I don't know if she'll let me come with her. Okay. Does she need a lawyer to give a statement? Sorry, I'm not familiar with police procedure."

Hmm, the conversation he'd just had with some "lieutenant" would not support that contention.

"She won't want a lawyer. She'll just want to tell you what she knows, but having spoken with her I feel safe in saying Henry deceived her, kept information from her. Kirsten...has had a hard life, ma'am. She loved Henry something fierce. He was her world." Pause. "Yes, ma'am. Let me give you my number." He did. "Yes, I also live in New Orleans. Yes. Yes." Pause. "Thank you. Good-bye."

Mender calculated the angle of approach. Thought about whether to take the risk. Then he heard the big man again. "When's Martinez back? Okay. Okay. Here's what I need: Her name is Elise Bard. She's a police detective in Austin. I need the full workup on her." Pause. "I need to know her weaknesses, her secrets, who she owes money to, what trouble her husband or her kids are in, I need to know can she be bought, I need to know what leverage I might have on her."

Mender stayed very still. This wasn't a concerned brother. This was someone working an angle, influencing this mess, and he was an unknown factor. Mender knew unknown factors could get him killed.

"No, just the information now. Same for a woman named Flora Zhang." He spelled the last name. "All right."

Pause again. "Hey, it's me. Where are you? I came to your hotel room and you're not here. I'm going to go get lunch. Call me."

And ten seconds later the big man was out the door. It closed with a click.

Mender slowly unfolded himself and crawled out of the closet. He thought this would be simple, despite the change in plans to take her in Austin instead of New Orleans.

Maybe he should cancel the kill. But then he wouldn't get the full amount of money, and he and Annie needed that with the baby coming.

He needed to think. He needed a new plan. He'd thought of leaving her a note, but the fact that someone had been in her hotel room would scare her.

He needed to pull her out of this crowded hotel, away from the brother.

He needed to make that happen.

Mender looked at the notes she'd put on the wall, the printouts. He'd heard the papers rustling, the brother going through them. Examining them? She had grouped some…like the ones on Flora Zhang, the ones on Adam. On the room's small desk were pens and pencils and a stack of sticky notes.

This could be like throwing a firecracker into a theater, he thought to himself. But he wanted the big guy out of the picture. It was a risk.

Then he wrote on one of the sticky notes: "YOUR BROTHER IS LYING TO YOU." He attached it partially under one of the pages about Flora Zhang, where the words weren't visible but the edge of the note was. It might not scare her to read it, but it would raise questions. Maybe create trouble, split them up. He could take advantage of trouble.

He walked past the table, not noticing he'd knocked a jacket draped loosely over the back of a chair off and onto the floor.

He stepped out of the room. The housekeeper he'd bribed was in the hallway. She smiled and nodded and he smiled and nodded and went on his way.

She was talking to the police at three. She'd probably come back after that, but the brother might be with her or waiting for her here again. He needed to be sure he understood what the brother was…who he was. He'd give that problem to his handler.

Because Zach sounded like someone who had resources and Mender didn't want someone capable of hurting him coming after him now.

He needed to handle this in a way that left the brother either dead or powerless. He wanted to get home to Annie—and not be looking over his shoulder.

26

The past

Three years as foster siblings. Mostly happiness. Mutual respect. Kirsten didn't spend so much time in the library. She had made friends beyond Molly, including the cheerleaders she'd previously dismissed as vacant airheads. They were nice to her, initially because of Zach, but then because she'd help them with homework and her wry sense of humor made them laugh. They helped her, introducing her to more people, getting her involved in the student council and volunteer projects, and helping her find her own style with clothes and makeup.

Kirsten didn't change who she was—quiet, bookish, studious, and a bit aloof—but she found ways to widen her social circle. She and Zach had grown close. He could still irritate her: be thoughtless; tease her about her friendship with Henry (they weren't dating, but if another boy had asked her out, she would have said no); and she never liked how close Zach was with Paul Fortunato. Paul gave her the creeps; there was an emptiness behind his eyes and his smile, and she wondered how Zach could not see it.

She was nearly through. Nearly clear. Nearly ready to start the life she'd dreamed of. She would soon turn eighteen, and she and Zach would stay with the Melancons until their departures for college.

She wouldn't have said the words aloud, but she loved Zach. As the brother she'd never had and now did. She didn't love Aunt JJ and Uncle Larry—she was fond of them, and grateful, but she sometimes wondered how often she would see them after she left. They would probably take in new foster kids and they'd be fine. Neither had suggested she and Zach come back for Thanksgiving or Christmas, and that was fine with Kirsten—they might be welcome, but they hadn't been asked yet. She sensed that their affection for her and Zach had a limit, and it had been reached. The care had been a transaction, a business arrangement at heart. Her family now was Zach, and she had an unspoken fear that he'd forget about her or ignore her or not be there for her anymore after they went their separate ways.

And she didn't want to think about Henry, probably bound for college out of state. He'd gotten into Tulane, ULL, and LSU, but she suspected he wanted to go up north, experience a locale other than Louisiana.

One day during their senior year Zach started afterschool spring practice for baseball. Kirsten walked home from St. Gentian by herself that day—she was one of the few seniors who didn't have a car—but the second day Henry offered her a ride. This made her happy, though she couldn't really say why.

But he had an agenda.

"How are the Melancons? As foster parents?" he asked suddenly. Henry had never asked her this before.

"Fine," she said, and they were. Polite and thoughtful. They didn't water down the milk or make her do unreasonable chores. And Larry had never said or done anything that made her feel uncomfortable or scared to be alone with him. "Aunt JJ takes good care of us. Uncle Larry works a lot of late nights."

"Has he ever mentioned any clients of his, who they are?"

"No. He never talks about his work. He doesn't want to bore us, I guess."

"It might not be boring. I heard Paul tell Zach that Larry's only client in his accounting business is Paul's dad."

She knew Paul Fortunato's dad was wealthy and sometimes there were whispers about how he'd made his money. She'd heard kids say the Fortunatos were tied to the mob up in the Northeast, but she noticed these claims were never, ever made in front of Paul himself.

Paul always acted nice to her at lunch. He had this joke he always made that Zach would come to work for his family one day, and if she was lucky she could get a job with his family too. She didn't care for Paul's tone, like Zach would never be as good as him—that he wasn't a friend but just a future employee. Like Paul was stooping, the rich kid befriending the pair in foster care. She just thought it was a weird comment for Paul to make, although Zach appeared unbothered by it. But Zach didn't generally show a lot of emotion. He'd give his tight smile and nod.

"I don't know anything about Larry's work," she said, and she didn't, and she didn't want to know. An accountant for a reputed mobster. No, she didn't want to know anything about that. "Why are you even telling me this?"

"I heard Paul and Zach talking about it. In a back corner of the library where I tutor Zach during our free period. I was going there to meet Zach and before they saw me...Paul told Zach to look for the money Paul's dad thinks Larry took. That Larry's been *stealing*."

"That's ridiculous."

"You know the Fortunatos are a"—he lowered his voice—"crime family. I mean, their front businesses are real estate. But Paul's grandfather and uncle both went to jail for fraud and tax evasion and racketeering."

Suddenly she remembered one of her first days at the Melancons and seeing Larry reading the book about gangsters. She felt cold. "Where was Zach supposed to look?"

"I guess in your house."

"So, what, Paul thinks there's some large amount of cash just hidden in the house somewhere? That's silly. Paul's dad should be talking to Larry, not Paul telling Zach."

"Paul made it sound like his dad hadn't talked to Larry about it yet. Paul was telling Zach to look for it. To spy on Larry. Because they're friends."

She tried to imagine Zach at dinner that night, saying to Uncle Larry, *Hey, are you stealing money from my friend's dad, the mobster?* The whole thing was so bizarre and odd it scared her. It wasn't the kind of thing Paul or Henry would make up to tease her. They weren't pranking her.

They turned the corner and reached Henry's house, with the Melancons next door. She never thought of it as "her" house.

"Why are you telling me this?" she asked again.

"I just want you to be careful," he said. "If you ever feel scared, come to my house, all right?"

Kirsten nodded.

When she went into the house no one else was home. JJ was at work—she was a secretary at a local microbrewery and she'd be home late tonight because the brewery was launching a new beer at a press event and tasting, and Kirsten had promised to cook dinner—and Larry was at his office. Zach was at practice.

And Henry was telling her that her foster father was involved in something out of a mobster movie. Maybe Henry misheard. Or misunderstood. She decided to take what she called "the Henry approach"—break the problem down. First step: confirm the story.

She put down her books. She went to the master bedroom, looked in the closet. She spent the next hour going through all the rooms, careful not to disturb anything or leave it out of place.

She found nothing.

She went up to the attic.

It was a jumble of old boxes and trunks, dusty. Rolled-up rugs, framed pictures, a baseball bat leaning against one stack of boxes. But she could see a path of sorts had been made; boxes and junk moved aside so someone could get to a back corner.

She noticed footprints in the dust.

She walked down the path. Nothing back here but a stack of coolers. Like the ones you'd fill with ice and take to the park or the pool. Four or five of them. She'd seen Larry taking coolers out to the car, sometimes with Zach for what he called "man time," sometimes alone. Her first day here, she remembered, Larry talked about taking a couple of coolers and going fishing and he'd invited her, but she'd told him she didn't care for fishing.

She opened the top cooler.

Bricks of cash. Tidy. Organized by hundreds, fifties. There must have been thousands in the one cooler. And there were five others stacked here, and how many had she seen Uncle Larry taking out to his SUV for his fishing trips. So much money...where would he be taking it?

Mobster money, if Henry was right.

She texted Henry: YOU WERE RIGHT. And immediately regretted it. She should say nothing. Keep her mouth shut. Pretend she never saw it. But what if Larry had stolen this money from the Fortunatos and they came looking for it?

What if they hurt her or Zach or JJ trying to find out where the money had gone?

Her world had collapsed in seconds. She finally had a good life. Nice place to stay, a school she could love, a cool foster brother who thought a geek like her was all right. And Henry, who looked at her like he saw *her*, not just the girl with her nose in a book.

She heard voices. She'd left the door unlocked. But two male voices, and not Henry.

She shut the cooler. She turned off the attic light.

"Hey, you don't have to cook," she heard Uncle Larry's voice saying, and a frozen bolt of terror went through her. "Kirsten? Did you hear me..."

And of course he could see the attic stairs, unfolded down into the hallway, right outside her bedroom.

She could hear him scrabbling up the stairs. She knelt by a box, yanked out an old sweater, knocking over a dusty, wooden baseball bat that was leaning against it. Larry's head came through the attic opening and they stared at each other in complete silence.

A knowing silence. She had never come up to the attic before.

"Kirsten. Hey. I got Chinese takeout. You don't have to cook." His voice was low and flat.

"Okay. I love Chinese." She heard the quiver in her own voice. She, who could be so distant, so unemotional, so guarded, now when she needed to sound normal her voice trembled.

"What are you doing up here?" Larry's voice was cold now. He climbed into the attic. Standing over her. He looked taller and bigger. His hands were huge. One closing into a fist, then opening again.

"Nothing. We're..." *You have a sweater in your hand, dummy. Use it.* "We're having mismatched clothes day at school, and I thought I'd see if there was anything of JJ's I could borrow." She tried to meet his gaze and then she looked away. St. Gentian required uniforms and had never had a mismatched clothes day in its history.

"Oh. Sure." Then his gaze betrayed him. He looked straight down the little open path that led to the coolers. And his gaze widened.

She turned. She could see the cooler she'd opened.

It still had its lid up.

"Kirsten," Larry said.

She made a noise in her throat, but it wasn't a word.

"Let's go downstairs." His voice was flat. It had gone flat the way her former foster parent Pop's would go when he told her that he didn't believe she was praying hard enough and perhaps they should pray alone together.

"They know," she said. "The Fortunatos, they know about the money. Please..."

He could not have looked more surprised at her words if she'd thrown ice water in his face.

Then—she saw Zach's head coming through the attic opening, staring at her, at Uncle Larry.

"Get up," Larry Melancon said to her.

"I won't say anything, but they know," she said.

"How?" He glanced at Zach.

She couldn't pull Henry into this. "They suspect you're taking money. Paul told me."

"Paul Fortunato," Larry said, "wouldn't tell *you*."

He turned and grabbed Zach by the throat, yanking him upward with an unexpected, brutal strength. Kirsten could see Larry's thumbs digging into the soft flesh of Zach's throat.

"You ungrateful little bastard," Larry said. "What did you tell them? What? You'll get us all killed. Did you tell them about the others? Did you tell them about her?"

Zach, strangling, his face purpling, tried to pull free. He tried to force Larry's hands away. He had no leverage, Larry's rage-filled strength holding him above the opening, Zach's feet dancing.

"No!" Kirsten screamed, grabbing at Larry's arm. He powered his elbow into her throat, shoving her away, harder than anyone had ever pushed her. She sprawled over the box.

Zach started making noises no one should ever make.

No. Not Zach. She saw the dusty baseball bat she'd noticed earlier propped against a stack of boxes and she, the girl who got picked last in gym, grabbed the bat, took a solid grip, kept her eyes on Larry's ribs, and swung hard. The bat connected and Larry howled. She swung again, scored again.

He let Zach go. Zach fell down the attic ladder, tumbling to the hallway below.

Larry's normally taciturn expression was gone, replaced by something she hadn't seen before. A rage, a fury—and even with broken ribs he was lurching toward her. She just wanted him to stay away.

She drove the bat into his stomach like a jousting pole, sending him reeling, and watched in horror as he fell, headfirst, out of the attic. Then there was a cracking noise she could not have imagined, even in a movie, a sound that made her cringe involuntarily, every muscle in her body seeming to contract.

She dropped the bat and peered down through the opening.

Larry's head didn't look right. It was twisted around and she shouldn't have been able to see his face, but she could, his eyes full of blank surprise. He lay next to Zach, who was not so purple now, holding his throat, breathing hard and staring at Larry.

Henry was kneeling next to Zach and looking up at her with complete and total shock. She hadn't heard him arrive, in response to her text, with all the fighting in the attic.

None of them seemed to be able to move.

Henry reached over and touched Larry's wrong-way neck and then his wrist.

"He's dead," he said and Kirsten made a mewling, gasping noise of horror and shock.

"Kirsten…Kirsten…," Zach managed to say, as if struggling to find the strength.

This would end everything. Why had she come up here? Why had Paul Fortunato come to Zach with what was a problem between their parents? How would they tell JJ?

Now Henry was staring up at her. "It was an accident. You didn't mean to."

She shook her head. She could just stay and hide away in the attic. Pretend it all never happened. That in saving Zach she hadn't destroyed her carefully imagined future.

"The police may not see it that way," Zach gasped, grabbing Henry's arm. "Do we risk that? Kirsten in juvie? Kirsten carrying this on her for the rest of her life?" He slowly got to his feet. "Or the Fortunatos coming after us for their money?"

"What do I do?" Kirsten said in a ragged whisper. This ended everything. *Everything.*

How could she go back to school? She couldn't. How could she look Aunt JJ in the face? *Sorry for killing your husband after you took me in.* And she knew the Fortunatos' secret now; they could kill her…they could get rid of her.…

Henry looked at Zach and then looked at her. Steady as a rock. "We fix it."

27

"You should take Shawn's side," Flora said. "I mean, I get it. He's your husband."

"I don't agree with how he handled you," Taylor Townsend said. "He's not really the comforting sort. Or the sort to let himself be comforted. It may not seem so, but Shawn is…just numb right now."

There was no furniture in the main rooms of the penthouse, so they sat near one of the floor-to-ceiling windows that looked out over both downtown Austin and the hills to the west, a gorgeous view that probably convinced Adam to buy this, thinking Flora would love it when she just wanted to stay in their Lakehaven home.

He didn't know you that well to think you wanted this. How can you be married and not know someone that well? She should have asked him that while he was alive.

Flora had told Taylor all about how the morning had unfolded. Taylor had thoughtfully bought them each an iced coffee on her way. She listened without interruption and Flora thought again what a rare kind of focus that was. Her other friends (Flora included) would have interrupted with comments and questions. Taylor just listened, and Flora felt a surge of gratitude for it.

"Do you think Kirsten North is dangerous?" Taylor finally asked.

"Did I make her sound that way? I gave her brother my phone number. I just felt I needed to be able to reach her. Her brother looks like trouble. Like he's waiting for a fight."

"She accused you of knowing more about the…um…"

"Murders. You can say the word."

"I'm just trying to do better than my beloved husband and not say the wrong thing." Taylor took Flora's hand. Taylor was dressed in stylish dark jeans and a thin textured purple sweater, her blond hair pulled back into a ponytail.

"Saying the wrong thing doesn't much register with me right now," Flora lied. She had blinked and nodded at people who said, *Oh, he's in a better place*, or *He's at peace*, or *I know justice will be done*, when to Flora, none of those things were assured. Or were designed to make her feel better.

"If anyone is a suspect, it ought to be Kirsten North," Taylor said.

"She wasn't even in Austin."

"So she says. Do we *know* she was in New Orleans?"

"You sound like Teddy. I don't know if the police have checked that," Flora said slowly. "I don't know for sure when she arrived in town, but I think it was last night."

Taylor frowned. "And she says her husband lied about coming to Austin? Doesn't that seem a little…forced? Like she's establishing that she can't be a suspect if she didn't even know where he was. Then how did she even know to come here?"

"I don't know. The police didn't tell me."

"And she goes to see where her husband died, and she ends up drinking at a bar. In the morning. I know she must be a mess, but that is not a person who makes good choices."

"She's grieving."

"Or she's putting on a good show."

"What, you think she came from New Orleans, killed them, and then went home and made up this story?"

"I'm just saying that the police both here and there ought to be checking to see if she has an alibi. This whole 'I didn't even know what city my husband was in'…I don't buy it." Taylor shook her head.

"There's just nothing to connect Adam and this Henry North."

"They both work in the software industry, you said. That has to be it."

"So why meet at the warehouse? Why not at the office?"

Taylor straightened her ponytail. "Because Adam didn't want someone at the office to know about the meeting. Maybe he didn't want Shawn or Teddy to know."

"I didn't really ask Shawn how he was holding up. I guess I was surprised to see him at work."

"Work is his security blanket, pacifier, and mistress. I'm lucky that way."

"I know, but...he and Adam were so close."

Taylor said nothing.

"What?" Flora asked after the silence grew.

"Nothing."

"Tell me. Shawn got very defensive when I talked about staying on as a partner with my shares."

"Things aren't going terribly well," Taylor said and for a moment Flora was sure she misheard.

"Wait, what? I don't understand."

"Well, they've not been getting along. Shawn and Adam. The partnership was strained. I guess they weren't agreeing on which companies to back. I don't really know details."

"Why didn't Adam tell me?"

"I don't know, sweetie. Because he didn't want to worry you, because he thought he could turn it around. You know men and their endless confidence."

"And...Shawn told you this?"

"Yes." She cleared her throat. "This is awkward. And this is not the time or the way I would have told you. You're dealing with so much. I mean, you know what venture capital is like. Reputation is everything. If they don't agree on which companies to fund, there's not much point to the partnership."

How was your day, honey? she'd ask, and he always gave the rote answer of *Fine*. What if it hadn't been fine? Adam would never tell her. He would not have let her help him navigate a hard time. She felt sick.

"Whatever is between them, or was, it doesn't affect us," Taylor said.

Flora felt shaken. She realized she had gotten very, very comfortable in her life. "Okay. So what would any of these troubles have to do with Henry North?"

"Maybe Adam wanted to invest in Henry North. Maybe he didn't want Shawn to know about it."

"Why would he keep a deal from Shawn, though?"

"Shawn had broached the subject of dissolving the firm with him. So maybe he was already starting to look for outside deals if he ended up on his own."

"Dissolving Zhang Townsend."

"Yeah. I'm sorry."

"Why would you not have told me this before?" She pulled her hand away from Taylor's.

"Because it's between them and it has nothing to do with our friendship. We're not dissolving. They weren't blaming each other, or angry with each other. Business is business. If they felt Zhang Townsend had run its course, if the problems had gotten worse than the rewards..."

"He never told me any of this, never even hinted at it," Flora said and stood.

"I'm sorry. And I'm sorry to tell you all this now, but...there's probably not going to be a partnership for you to join."

"I don't care about that. I care that Adam didn't tell me."

Then she realized that if Shawn could get Flora to sell her shares to him, as he'd mentioned, he wouldn't have to start from scratch. Shawn would be in a far better position financially.

She glanced back at Taylor, whose face was slightly red with embarrassment. Taylor blew out a long breath. She knew more about the mechanics of Flora's life than Flora did. Shawn shared with Taylor in a way that Adam never did with Flora. It was strange, Flora thought, how you could slip into thinking every marriage was just like your own.

"When were you going to tell me all this?" Flora asked.

"When you were stronger. After the funeral, I guess. Shawn wanted to tell you and I said it was too soon. I'm sorry. I'm the worst friend ever."

"No. I get it. I'm glad to know now. Is there anything else I should know?"

After a moment, Taylor bit her lip. Like she was weighing something.

"Taylor."

"I wouldn't hurt you for the world," Taylor said.

"What?" She couldn't breathe.

"It's only because it's a murder that I'd say anything. I know Shawn talked to the police about it. But I don't know for sure. Don't be mad at me. Nothing was confirmed."

"Just say it," Flora said.

"There was a rumor that Adam was seeing someone. I think this might have fueled part of the feud."

Ten seconds ticked by. "You're saying he was cheating on me?"

"Nothing confirmed. It was just talk. In the office."

"Who is she?"

"She's heading one of the start-ups. Her name's Melinda."

"Melinda Alari," Flora said quietly.

"You know her?"

"She spoke to me at the office when I was there this morning. She gave me her condolences. She said...she wondered what she would say to me." Her voice shook. "I thought she meant the condolences."

"Shawn asked her if something had happened between her and Adam. He'd spoken to Adam about it. Adam denied it. So did she."

"How long had this been going on?"

"Well, there was nothing going on. They said."

She felt her stomach twist. "I went to a divorce lawyer a couple of months ago, Taylor."

"What?" Taylor's gaze widened.

"I did. I thought...he didn't love me anymore. He didn't seem interested in me or even in Morgan. He was like a man going through the motions of being a father and a husband. So…I just went to one I know through the foundation board. Once. Talked. Then I decided that I was imagining it and that it was silly." *But part of me knew*, she thought. *Some part of me knew.*

"It was just a rumor. If Shawn had said something like, 'Yeah, I caught them kissing in the break room,' yes, I would have told you. But I wasn't going to hurt you needlessly."

Flora sat back down. "Do the police know about her?"

"I think Shawn mentioned it. He couldn't have concealed it."

"So she's a suspect?" *And does this make me more of a suspect now than I was before? This increases my motive.* Could she prove that she didn't know, that Adam hadn't told her or asked her in private for a divorce? She felt sick.

"I don't know."

And then she remembered what Shawn and Teddy had both said: *They asked me about your marriage.* "The angry wife. I'm even more of a suspect now."

Taylor shook her head. "You have an alibi."

"Yes." She had been home with Morgan. But no one else was in the house. She could have left a sleeping child, gone to the warehouse if she knew Adam was there…The police might consider that a possibility.

Taylor said, "Shawn told me…when I called him after y'all talked…that you wanted to keep the fund-raiser on as a memorial to Adam. If this changes your mind…"

"If you don't want to host it now…"

"Of course we will. But you don't have to put yourself through being there."

"No. It'll honor…everyone's image of Adam." She forced down her anger. It was just a rumor. And even if it was true…she loved him still and he was dead and it was all too much. He wasn't here to see or hear her rage. And then Flora wondered: *What if this…mistress* (she could hardly wrap her thoughts around the word) *killed him? Maybe he wouldn't leave me and she killed him in anger? But then why kill Henry North? Innocent bystander?* How could she pull these threads together?

"Oh, Flora," Taylor said. "What do you need from me? Because I wanted to give you support and I feel I've only given you bad news."

"You're the one being honest with me. Does Teddy know any of this?" If there were rumors swirling in the office, surely Teddy would know.

And he hadn't told her.

Living in the same house as her and he hadn't told her. Not even of the business's difficulties.

Failing business, mistress, secret hiring of a security consultant...She had been surrounded by secrets and...

No one had told her.

"Do you want lunch?" Taylor asked. "You need to eat. I doubt there's anything here, but I can order in or go get something."

"No." She thought of Kirsten North. What could she possibly say to Kirsten if Melinda was the killer? *Sorry my husband's screwing around got your husband killed.* "There's a ton of food back at the house. I just want to be with Morgan."

Taylor nodded. She stood and gave Flora a hug. "I love you. We'll get through this together."

"Do you think this is where they were meeting?" Flora said into her shoulder.

"Um. No. There's no place to..."

"There's an office. There's a futon in there." She would be throwing that out, then.

The intercom buzzed. Flora went to it and pressed the button. She hoped it wasn't more bad news.

"Mrs. Zhang? It's Carl, the front desk guard. There's a Kirsten North here. She wants to know if you'll talk to her."

28

Kirsten rode the elevator up to the penthouse.

The doors slid open and she saw Flora Zhang standing there, along with a very attractive blond woman who looked like she was heading to an audition for one of those reality shows set in a wealthy suburb.

Kirsten stepped off the elevator, suddenly conscious of her old blouse and worn jeans. "Hi. Thanks for agreeing to talk to me."

Flora nodded, a bit stiffly. "Sure. Maybe it will be easier to talk without the police hovering around us."

"I've been compiling data on your husband." That sounded wrong, and Flora started to frown. Kirsten said: "Let me try again.…I've been trying to find out how our husbands were connected. What brought them together." The two women were staring at her and she realized she'd skipped a step. Social cues were such a pain.

Kirsten cleared her throat. "I want to apologize for my behavior earlier. It was…I wasn't myself. This has been a terrible shock. I mean…for both of us."

Flora's expression softened, just slightly. "I'm sorry, too, Kirsten. I am very sorry for your loss."

"And I'm sorry for yours," Kirsten said. *Unless Adam got Henry killed.* She glanced at the other woman, who was staring at her, and almost looked like she wanted to bolt past Kirsten and take the elevator.

"Hi," Kirsten said. She forced herself to be extroverted. "I'm Kirsten North."

"Kirsten, this is my dear friend Taylor Townsend."

Kirsten recognized her now from the photos with Flora on social media, and nearly said so, but realized that would sound a bit weird. So she just said, "Hello. I'm sorry to intrude on your time together."

"Oh, we were just talking." Taylor blinked, as though coming out of a stupor. "I'm Taylor. Hello." She stepped forward, offered her hand. "I am so sorry for your loss."

"Thank you," Kirsten said as she looked around the empty penthouse. She glanced at Flora. "You haven't moved in yet?"

"Adam had set up his home office here, but we were going to move here soon. We were still living at our home in Lakehaven. It's on the other side of Lady Bird Lake."

"Is that the lake that looks more like a river?"

"Yes."

"So…are you over here a lot, getting ready for the move?" Kirsten asked.

It was such an odd question, Flora wasn't sure how to answer and Kirsten said, "I don't know where Henry was staying. There's no record of a hotel charge. It occurred to me if they were working together that Adam might have put Henry up somewhere. I saw on a real estate blog that y'all had bought this place and then I did a tax record search last night for the address and thought maybe Henry had stayed here."

"You've been busy," Taylor said.

Kirsten nodded. "I couldn't sleep."

"There's one room where a person might have stayed." Flora walked across the living room and down a hallway. Kirsten followed, taking in the spectacular view from the windows. Taylor hurried behind them.

Kirsten followed Flora into a bedroom that seemed to be doubling as an office. It was spare: a nice desk and chair, a futon couch. A bookshelf, with a few books on business, photos of Flora and a cute little infant, the happy family all together, Flora beaming, Adam with a restrained smile. He was one of those men who didn't look right smiling.

"Henry packed a bag," Kirsten said. "Did you find that here? Or any sign that someone was staying here?"

A strange look crossed Flora's face.

"What?" Kirsten asked.

"I was here last night and I thought someone else was in the penthouse. Like…I heard a noise, like someone else was inside, with me. The guard came up and checked, but there was no one here."

Kirsten didn't ask permission. She opened the closet door, scanned the space inside. No bag of Henry's.

"Has the futon been slept on?" Taylor asked. "Usually there's a hair on a pillow, you know. Not to be awkward."

They checked. No sign someone had slept there. Kirsten started looking in the drawers of the desk. "Henry could have left something here. Let me know if you see something that's not your husband's."

Together the two women searched. Pens, legal pads that looked unmarked, highlighters, spare phone chargers. Nothing unusual. Kirsten went into the full adjoining bathroom. There was a tub with a shower but no soap, no shampoo, no towel hanging to dry. She came back and moved the desk chair out of her way and set her bag down in it. "Nothing of Henry's here."

Kirsten glanced at Taylor. "Did *your* husband know mine?"

"No. We only learned your husband's name this morning," Taylor said. "I asked and Shawn told me he didn't know him."

"I should…I'm sorry. Did you want some water?" Flora said. "Have you eaten?"

"I just had lunch with Marco Hernandez," Kirsten said. She might as well play that card.

"Oh. Marco. Yes," Flora said. "He told me you were at the warehouse."

"He seems very well informed for someone who isn't really writing about our husbands," Kirsten said. "Do either of you recognize the term 'green key'?"

Flora shook her head; Taylor crossed her arms. "What is it?" Taylor asked.

"I don't know. It might be a project of Adam's that he mentioned to Marco. Something big. It might be what brought Henry here."

"Green key. Sounds environmental," Flora said. "I don't know it."

"Environmental. Like a green key. Got it," Taylor said. "No, I've never heard of it."

"Adam wanted to talk to Marco about it," Kirsten said. "If your husband doesn't know, maybe it doesn't relate to their business."

Flora said, "Adam might have been pursuing a project and not telling Shawn. Their partnership was in trouble."

"Flora," Taylor said in a voice that clearly meant that information was private.

Interesting, Kirsten thought. *Zhang Townsend was troubled. Maybe Henry got hired to look into this Shawn Townsend.*

Flora said, "I wonder why Marco didn't mention it to me."

Kirsten knew she was taking a chance by telling them. If they knew what the green key meant and it was the reason for Henry's and Adam's deaths, they could have destroyed all the evidence already.

"Marco thought I would know," Kirsten said. "Because I suppose he assumed Henry had told me why he came to Austin."

"But he didn't."

"Henry didn't want me to know about this trip. I can think of a few reasons."

Flora said nothing and behind her Taylor shifted from one foot to another.

It was humiliating, but Kirsten couldn't care less now. "One, Henry was having financial difficulties. I'm not sure how that would relate to Adam. Second, I have to find out if there's any overlap between the companies Adam funded and the clients Henry had. So far, from the companies mentioned on the Zhang Townsend website, I haven't found any in common."

"Okay," Flora said. "Earlier, Kirsten, I shouldn't have said your husband was to blame. Whoever shot them was to blame."

It was a peace offering. *But was it you?* Kirsten wondered. "We want the same thing. I'm sorry too," she said. Henry often coached her on social niceties and now what would she do without him? Her chest felt tight.

"So, what do you think you know?" Taylor said. "That the police don't know."

"They both went to that meeting in the warehouse without telling anyone where they were going. Henry knows hacking, knows security, so it must have been related to that. Maybe someone had hacked Adam or one of the start-ups and he hired Henry to find out who. And whoever that was…killed them." That possibility ignored Flora's motivations, but Kirsten didn't want to accuse her. Not when she could get closer to Flora and learn more. "That seems the simplest explanation."

"How did you know to come to Austin if Henry hadn't been identified yet?" Taylor asked. Flora glanced at her.

"I got an anonymous phone call. Telling me Henry had been shot to death in Austin."

"Like…from the killer?" Taylor asked. Her eyes widened.

"I don't know. It was from my husband's phone, but it can't be traced now, so I guess they destroyed it. Or they're calling from a cloned phone because they suspected I wouldn't answer a call from a number I didn't recognize."

"What would they gain by calling you?" Flora asked.

"I don't know," Kirsten said.

Flora said, "Where are you staying, Kirsten?"

"I'm just at a hotel downtown."

Flora folded her hands. "Do you want…do you want to stay here?" This was the idea she'd had earlier—a way to keep an eye on this woman, keep her close, learn her secrets. It was a risk but one worth taking. Kirsten might share more if Flora showed her generosity.

"Flora," Taylor said, "Kirsten might want some privacy."

"No one is here; we can get you food and supplies."

Kirsten said, "I appreciate it, but…you don't even know me."

"Our husbands died together," Flora said. "We're linked for life now, so we might as well get to know each other."

The silence grew and became awkward. Kirsten didn't know what to say. She wasn't good with hospitality.

But if Flora Zhang had killed Henry and Adam, this was a way for her to keep Kirsten under watch, under her thumb.

That went both ways, though. Kirsten could watch Flora. Bide her time. Find the evidence, whether it pointed to Flora or someone else.

"That's really kind of you," Kirsten finally said.

"Flora," Taylor said. "I can get some furnishings here. I've got friends who stage homes for sale, who decorate. I can make some calls if you'll give me a passkey, and we'll get it set up for Kirsten."

"Thanks," Kirsten said. "The futon is fine for me."

"Plates, silverware, all of that. Let me make a couple of calls."

"Could I get a glass of water, please?" Kirsten asked.

"I don't even know if there are glasses here...," Flora said. The women went into the kitchen and she opened a cabinet. "There are. Two of the place settings from our house. Maybe he planned to move here in small boxes." Her voice sounded bitter.

"Oh, my bag," Kirsten said, as if forgetful. She went back into the office and picked her purse off the chair where she'd purposefully put it and stuck her hand down between the back-support pillow and the cushion in the chair. She'd thought she'd seen something when she moved the chair and she wasn't wrong.

A flash drive. Maybe the police hadn't searched the empty penthouse that he hadn't moved into yet. Or they'd missed it. Or...someone else had left it, thinking it was hidden.

Kirsten stuck it in her pocket.

And then she heard the voice, distant but booming. Coming from the street. She went to the window and peered down. She could see cars, news vans along the road. And she heard one word: "justice."

She went back to the kitchen, where Flora was standing holding a cold bottle of water. "There's some leftover food in the fridge," Flora said. "I saw it last night. Maybe Adam did have your husband stay here."

"Something's going on down on the street in front of the building," Kirsten said. "There are news crews." She pulled her phone out of her pocket, went to her browser, and opened the window where she'd followed the news coverage about Henry's murder. She studied the screen.

"What is it?" Flora said.

"Someone named Melinda Alari is having a news conference about your husband's death," Kirsten said. "Downstairs."

29

Out on the balcony, Flora looked over the railing. Kirsten did the same.

Far below, in front of the building, they could see the figure of a woman with a bullhorn, the tops of several news vans, and three men with cameras aimed at her.

And the voice from the bullhorn drifted up to them: "I believe Flora Zhang killed her husband because of me."

"So I guess the rumor was true," Taylor said behind them. "That's unfortunate."

-

Flora hurried back to the penthouse office and turned on the TV. Found the twenty-four-hour local news channel.

The young woman Flora had seen at the elevators was giving a statement. She held a sign that read "JUSTICE FOR ADAM." She was still in her impeccably styled suit.

"My name is Melinda Alari. My software start-up was funded a year ago by Zhang Townsend; and for the past four months I was in a romantic relationship with Adam Zhang," she said. "I am coming forward because in the final week of his life, Adam confided in me that his wife was aware of our relationship and that he feared for his life."

"This is total insanity," Flora said, sounding dazed. What had Bard asked her: *Did you think Adam was maybe doing something he shouldn't have been?* Nausea churned her stomach.

"Flora, stay here." Kirsten hurried out of the penthouse and to the elevator. The lobby was empty, except for the guard, who apparently was on the phone to Flora, saying, "Mrs. Zhang, the sidewalk is public. I can't chase her off."

Kirsten walked out the main doors. There were three camera crews, a few bystanders, and a thickly built man standing off to the left, his gaze locked on the woman. She had put down the bullhorn she'd first used to attract attention from those walking by and was talking into the microphones.

"Adam and I had been involved for four months. Flora Zhang was aware of our involvement, and Adam said she had threatened him should he attempt to divorce her." Melinda Alari glanced at Kirsten, having noticed her come out of the lobby, then turned her gaze back to the cameras.

"Do you have any proof of this…relationship?" a reporter called.

"I have texts from him. He had a separate phone to use in contacting me. That phone wasn't on his body, and I can think of exactly one person who might have taken it. His wife."

"Will you produce these texts?"

"I will be providing evidence to the police at the appropriate time. Adam Zhang was supposed to meet me the night he died. Instead, he was killed."

-

Upstairs, Flora leaned against the chair as she watched the TV screen.

"Why…why is this woman accusing me? What have I ever done to her?" She glared at Taylor. "You said…it was just a rumor."

"I'm sorry, Flora," Taylor said helplessly.

"Morgan can't see this," Flora gasped, as if a one-year-old would understand. "Melinda is basically accusing me of murder. I have to go down there."

"Flora, no. Kirsten is right. Stay here; don't add to the circus. And don't give her accusations the power she wants you to give them. Don't dignify them."

"She can't say these lies about me."

"She's going to look foolish. You can destroy her in court."

"When I went to the divorce attorney, I just wanted to know…where I might stand. I didn't pursue it. But I didn't go because he was having an affair! I didn't know!" Her voice shook. "How will that look now? Like I wanted to be free and clear of him and I didn't like my legal standing so I took another way?" Flora's voice cracked. She reached for her phone.

"Who are you calling?"

"The police chief. I know him. This can't happen."

"Flora, don't!"

But Flora turned away from her, thinking of Morgan seeing this one day, hearing this vileness directed at her. *No!* a voice inside her screamed.

-

Kirsten watched the media circus. Adam Zhang's murder was a lead story, and the press couldn't afford to *not* cover this woman's announcements. If Kirsten interrupted or intervened or said, *Oh, hey, I'm Kirsten North, the other widow*, then she'd be part of the story, and that wasn't what she wanted right now.

Melinda Alari might know something about Adam that Flora didn't know. Maybe Flora really knew nothing about why Henry had died. The answers might lie with Adam's girlfriend.

So let her talk, and then play nice.

A reporter asked then, with a slightly mocking tone, "Were you involved with Adam Zhang when your start-up got funding?"

Melinda shook her head emphatically. "Absolutely not. My company was funded on its own merits. I only got involved with Adam well after that process was complete and we'd started working closely together."

Another reporter: "Why are you so sure that Flora Zhang is responsible?"

"Let me be clear: I'm not saying she's responsible. I'm saying Adam didn't have enemies. And Henry North was a security expert, and as Adam was afraid and concerned about Flora, he might have hired Henry North to look into Flora's activities. No one's motive comes close to matching Flora's."

"Flora Zhang could have simply divorced him," another reporter said. "She didn't have to kill him to get her share."

"I'm sure she felt anger and rage."

"What about the other victim? Henry North?" the first reporter asked. "Did you know him as well?"

Melinda Alari's pause felt like three seconds too long and Kirsten felt a tightening in her gut. "No. I didn't meet him, but I'm sorry he died with Adam. I think the reason Adam hired an out-of-town security expert was to protect himself from his wife's jealousy, to find out what she knew and what she planned to do if he left her for me."

Melinda Alari took two more questions, then she and her apparent bodyguard walked away, the bodyguard putting himself between Alari and the press with a raised palm to signal no more questions, and the reporters began to disperse.

No one followed them.

Except Kirsten.

Kirsten walked along Fifth Street, past another high-rise that was a combo of residential and business on another glossy block of the new and worldly Austin, and as she crossed the next street she saw the pair enter one of the restaurants on the ground floor of another high-rise. She stopped. Hesitated. Then followed.

30

The restaurant was named Leav, and Kirsten wasn't sure if it was a hipster play on the word "leaf" or "leave" or "leaven" or maybe someone's name. Austin was full of this odd bull, she'd noticed, a town trying to be as hip as the towns it was trying to join or replace—or as hip as it once was. A full glassy front, a huge oaken bar, a supermodel-ish host working the welcome stand. Kirsten just smiled and pointed toward a barstool and he nodded. "I'm waiting for a friend," she said as she walked past.

Melinda Alari and the big-shouldered guy were sitting at the bar, whispering, talking. Melinda looked stressed. There were only a few other people at the bar: a trio of young men, an older couple. Kirsten sat closer to the older couple, and from that vantage point she could see Melinda clearly.

Kirsten looked at the wine list. She wanted a glass very, very badly. But she asked for ginger ale with a lime slice and put the wine list where she couldn't see it.

The bartender brought her the soda and she was careful to not look toward Melinda and Big Shoulders. She sipped at the drink and pretended to check her phone.

She looked up. Big Shoulders was leaning toward Melinda Alari and whispering. He got up and headed to the back of the restaurant.

Kirsten took her ginger ale and walked toward Melinda, who was looking at her phone and smiling slightly. She noticed Kirsten when she was two steps away.

"Oh," Melinda said. "You were at the press conference. I'm not doing interviews yet."

"Okay." Kirsten had decided how to play this. "I'm Henry North's widow." Funny way to say it. When he lived she never would have said she was Henry North's wife. She wouldn't have described herself in terms of Henry. But she wanted to hold Henry close to her. Make him matter because someone had thought he could be erased.

"Ah," Melinda said. And for all her confidence at the press conference now she seemed, for exactly five seconds, unsure. Then the self-assured woman was back, straightening her spine on the barstool, closing her grip around a wineglass. "I'm very sorry."

"Why are you so sure Flora Zhang killed them?"

"Why were you at Flora Zhang's building?" she countered. "She doesn't live there."

"She and I met this morning. At the crime scene."

"Awkward."

Kirsten decided to twist the truth a bit to make it sound like she and Melinda could be allies. "I was trying to talk to her again. I wanted to talk to her about how Adam knew my husband."

"Did she talk to you?"

"Not really. She claims to know nothing."

"Of course not. She's a cordial little monster." Melinda took a sip of her wine, glanced toward the back where her friend had gone.

"I get that she's grieving, but so am I," Kirsten said. "You're certain enough to make a public accusation...."

This seemed to warm Melinda to her sudden appearance. "Sit. Again, I'm so sorry."

Kirsten knew she had to be very careful in what she said. One wrong word and someone like Melinda, who picked words like a bomb-maker picked components, would bolt.

Kirsten sat. "I'm sorry for your loss too. I just don't understand what could have happened to Henry and Adam."

"Flora happened to them."

"I get it. But why hurt Henry? He had nothing to do with their miserable marriage." She needed this woman to think of her as an ally, a friend. She tried to imagine doing a press conference with Melinda, standing next to her, accusing Flora.

Melinda lowered her voice. "I believe Adam hired your husband to investigate Flora."

"Do you have any hard proof?"

"No. But he had exactly one person he wanted investigated, and your husband is a security expert from out of town. Someone she wouldn't know. Someone his business partner or their friends wouldn't know."

"But Henry's not a private investigator," Kirsten said. "Why wouldn't he hire someone who was an investigator to investigate?"

Big Shoulders returned from the back, his glare locked on Kirsten.

"Hello," he said to Kirsten. "Is there a problem?" His voice was a low rumble.

"No, none," Melinda said. "This is Henry North's widow."

Big Shoulders said nothing and Melinda added, "The other victim."

"Oh. I see."

"This is my friend David."

Kirsten thought David had an oddly blank look. He looked like he might be comfortable fighting; she noticed a scar on his hand and another on his nose.

"Flora's powerful in this town. She's connected. The tech people love philanthropy, and she's got a homegrown charity. Buddies with the mayor, the police chief. Just watch if there isn't an arrest soon, and it's not her."

Kirsten said, "I'm going to ask you specifically. Did Adam ever tell you he was bringing my husband here to help him investigate his wife?" Her tone had hardened and she saw David draw himself up, like he was ready to escort her away from Melinda.

"He didn't tell me your husband's name. But I knew he was finally going to shed himself of her. And he wanted to control that process, not let her do it."

"Why kill Henry?" Her voice held controlled anger and pain.

"Because he was in her way. Maybe he was in the wrong place at the wrong time." Her mouth narrowed. "Or maybe he found the truth out about her. Maybe he had the proof that Adam needed to shut her down. So he had to die."

If Melinda didn't realize her words were a knife, Kirsten felt them as such. This didn't have to be complicated.

"How would she have known they were meeting? You say she has motive, but how does she have opportunity?"

"She could have followed Adam that night. Maybe she thought he was meeting me. Her whole story about being at home could be a lie."

"Does she carry a gun?"

"I'm not sure about her, but Adam had one," she answered. "I don't know if the police have found it. Shawn and I both told them in our statement. And it's not like a motivated woman with money has trouble getting a gun."

Then Melinda said, "I think he had a concern about Teddy and Flora."

"Who is Teddy?"

"Teddy Chao. His cousin. A distant one. Adam pulled him up from nothing, sent him to college and gave him a job. He lives in the house with them. Which I always found odd. But Adam told me once that Flora insisted Teddy stay with them. I wonder why."

"That's a terrible way to pay back Adam."

"Teddy's sweet but kind of naive. Flora could have seduced him."

She had to think. Decide how to play this. She felt David's gaze on her. She glanced up at him. His stare was steady.

"You look like a bodyguard," Kirsten said.

"Melinda needs protecting," he said. "Until the police arrest Flora."

"You could have had any guy you wanted," Kirsten said to Melinda. "Why Adam, a married one?"

"You disapprove."

"I'm just asking what made him special."

She shrugged. "I'm driven, I'm ambitious, he admired that in me. Flora lost all her ambition when they married, he said. He told me once that I reminded him of how she used to be—ready to take on the world. She got comfortable and boring. Adam and I understood each other's ambitions. We fueled each other. I never thought I'd get involved with a married man, but he said it was a marriage in name only."

"But you think the firm will try to shut you up?" Shawn Townsend couldn't be happy about this publicity.

"Shawn has told me that the firm would stand behind me."

"I guess they don't want to have wasted their investment," Kirsten said. It sounded harsher than she intended, and Melinda frowned.

"Did you ever hear Adam mention a project called Greenkey?"

Melinda said, "David, go outside for a minute. See what the weather is."

David got up and went outside. Through the window Kirsten could see him squint up at the sky.

"David's precious," Kirsten said.

"He cares about me. I threw him over for Adam. Worst mistake ever. He stands by me now and I realize he was and is a real friend. He knows he has my loyalty now."

And you can use that, can't you? Kirsten thought.

"What is Greenkey?" Melinda asked.

"A reporter told me that Adam wanted to discuss it with him, for a story."

She shook her head. "Adam wouldn't have talked to a reporter about a project that wasn't announced. He certainly wouldn't share an internal code name with him. You must have misunderstood."

This was a brick wall. "He told the reporter it would be a big story."

"Who?"

"Marco Hernandez."

"Yeah, I know who Marco is. Read his pieces on Adam. Maybe he was just trying to get you to share what you knew by dangling that this had something to do with Zhang Townsend and not Adam's train-wreck marriage."

"It seems an odd thing to make up. I heard Zhang Townsend was on the verge of breaking up."

"That's not true. I don't know what Greenkey is and I think this reporter is stringing you along." Melinda sounded irritated. Kirsten figured she was mad because Adam told a reporter something of interest but not her.

"Let's exchange phone numbers," Kirsten said, and they did. "I think you and I should make a trade."

"For what?"

"You find out what Greenkey is. Get me that, and I'll find out Flora's secrets."

"I know the current projects list, and Greenkey's not the name of one."

Or maybe you're full of it, and you're covering for the firm that funded your company, Kirsten thought.

Melinda looked past Kirsten to David, still outside the window. And saw Flora and Taylor walking up to David, Taylor saying something to him.

"Taylor recognizes David," Melinda said. "I brought him to last year's holiday party."

Kirsten saw Flora move past David and presumably toward the front door.

"Forgive me," Kirsten said. "But if you're telling the truth, you'll thank me later." And she hauled off and struck Melinda hard, a resounding slap that sounded across the whole bar. Melinda screamed and clutched at her cheek. Stared at Kirsten in dismay.

Kirsten winked at her.

Kirsten turned and walked away from her. She turned and saw Flora standing in the bar's doorway, looking at her in shock. She'd timed the slap perfectly.

"What the hell is going on?" Flora said as Kirsten approached her.

"Let's go. You don't want a public confrontation with her." Kirsten put her arm around Flora's shoulders.

She steered Flora out into the sunshine; David moved past Taylor and the two women, not looking at them.

"I found out what I needed to know from that liar," Kirsten said. "Yes, I'll move into the penthouse. Thank you." She looked at Taylor. "Can you get Flora out of here before Melinda comes out? I'm due to answer questions with Bard; then I'll go get my things and move in, if the offer still stands."

Of course the offer still stands, Kirsten thought. *I just slapped your husband's mistress.* But Flora, still amazed, said: "You slapped her! What did she say to you?"

"We'll talk when I get back." She wanted to be gone before Melinda and David came out of the bar.

Flora pressed a key card into her hand. "This will get you into the penthouse."

Are you a murderer, Flora? Did I just put my trust in you? Kirsten wondered, but she nodded and turned and walked in the direction of police headquarters.

31

Elise Bard waited in an interrogation room for Kirsten. She arrived alone, without Zach or a lawyer.

Detective Jones, whom Kirsten had met the night she arrived in Austin, was also in the room and turned on a recording device when Kirsten sat down. He announced the time, and the names of those present in the room.

"Thank you for talking to us, Ms. North," Bard said. "How are you holding up?"

This was one of the moments where you were expected to give a polite answer, not the truth. But she couldn't. She took a deep breath. "The reality that Henry is dead is starting to settle in. That this isn't just an awful dream."

"I'm a widow too," Bard said unexpectedly. "Three years ago. My husband died from cancer."

"I'm sorry," Kirsten said.

"You and me and Flora Zhang. It's an ambush of widows."

"Pardon?"

"That's the collective noun for a group of widows. An ambush. You know, like a parliament of owls or a troupe of acrobats."

"What an odd word," Kirsten said. "Do you think it's because we feel ambushed by what's happened to us?"

"I think it's because widows can be dangerous," Bard said. "Why make us wear black for so long, back in old times? Marking us. Because we might be capable of anything."

It was an odd comment, and Kirsten felt some of the rage and anger she'd been pushing down bubble up inside her. But under the table she clenched her hands and didn't answer.

"I'd like to know more about your husband and his work. We're trying to determine why he came to Austin."

Kirsten waited.

"Are you going to help us, Mrs. North?"

"I really don't know anything."

"We'd like access to your husband's phone and laptop."

"I don't have either of those things. I told you, the person who called me about Henry called from his phone. Or a cloned phone. It was his number."

"And you don't know where in Austin he stayed."

"Not for sure. He might have been hired by Adam Zhang, so Adam may have put him up somewhere. I don't know." The little flash drive she'd found in the chair and hadn't had an opportunity to look at yet dug into her pocket as she shifted in her seat. She should give it to Bard. But if it had the proof…then the police would arrest the person and she'd never have her chance for revenge.

Is that who you are? Is that who you're going to be? Henry's voice piped up in her head.

"Did he make regular backups?" Bard asked.

Kirsten leveled her stare at Bard. "He was a security expert. Of course, you can have access to his backups online or back in New Orleans, but they'll be passworded and encoded and will be a challenge to crack. I'm sorry I can't help you."

"Do you *want* to help us?"

"Yes. But I already told you everything I know."

"I thought you might have come across further information since I last saw you."

"I haven't. I don't know why he lied to me or why he was here."

"You've lived in New Orleans your whole life."

"Yes." She could sense the questions that were coming.

"Your foster brother who was here with you, Zach…"

"Zach Couvillon. He was close to Henry too. He flew here this morning when I called him and told him about Henry."

"Your foster brother. So you grew up in a foster home? Or where, exactly?"

"What does that have to do with anything?"

"I'm just interested in yours and Henry's backgrounds."

"Yes. Zach and I had foster parents. Henry lived next door, so we went to the same high school. That's how we met. Henry and I were friends for a long time before we dated. We married right out of college." She waited. What if they googled her? Her name wouldn't come up, but Zach's might. He had been quoted in a news article about Larry several years ago. A series on New Orleans cold cases. The thought of it made Kirsten sweat.

"And you're both self-employed?"

"Yes."

"That can be a challenge at times. Did you or your husband have financial problems?" Bard had asked that last night. It was distinctly unsettling to have a cop ask you about an aspect of your private life that you had just learned about. *She's asking again because she knows*, Kirsten thought.

"Yes," Kirsten said. "I've just learned that some of his clients had decided not to use him again. We'd gone through our savings, apparently. He kept that from me."

"Did Henry know Flora Zhang?"

"Not that I am aware." She tensed. She couldn't help it. "You know Adam Zhang's girlfriend believes that Adam hired my husband to ferret out the goods on his wife in preparation for an expensive divorce and Flora found out and killed both of them."

"We are aware of Ms. Alari's accusations. We'll be having a discussion with her."

"Do you think it's true?"

"We're pursuing all lines of inquiry." Bard wrote something in her notebook and Jones remained silent. An officer opened the door; Jones went to speak to him, and Kirsten heard whispers. Jones returned to his seat and Kirsten felt something shift in the air.

"Why do you think your husband concealed this financial problem from you?"

Why were they back to this? "Male pride."

"Why did he conceal this trip to Austin from you?"

"Probably saw it as the way to fix the financial problem." It was all so petty and small. If Flora had done it…it would be hard to kill her, what with living in her penthouse. She would be a suspect. She pushed the thoughts away, wondering if the detectives could see the idea of murder on her face.

"Can anyone confirm that you were in New Orleans the night of the murders?" Jones asked.

Now Kirsten glanced up. "No. I work at home. I didn't go anywhere or see anyone."

"See…it's just strange, the killer presumably calling you and alerting you to the fact that your husband was dead," Jones said. "Why help the investigation along? Why call you?" Kirsten didn't answer and then he said, "Tell us again what was said."

She didn't want to revisit the words, but she did, eyes closed, remembering. "They asked if I was Kirsten North. Then they asked if I was Henry's wife."

"Odd. I mean, they're calling on his phone, you said. Maybe they saw you in the list of contacts and deduced you were his wife."

"It sounds like someone who wasn't sure of who we were," Kirsten said. "But if they weren't sure of who I was, why go to the bother to call? How would they benefit?"

Bard didn't answer, so Kirsten added, "Then they said: 'Your husband has been killed. In Austin. Texas. He was shot.' That was it. I mean, I thought it was a prank at first, that someone had stolen his phone. And I'm in his phone's favorites list, so it wouldn't be hard to figure out I'm his wife. But…I can't explain this. Why they called."

"And you cannot think of any reason Adam Zhang and your husband knew each other. No mutual connections?"

"No."

Jones pushed a list at her of the things they wanted: computer hard drives, online backups, client lists… Good luck cracking Henry's security. But the police could track payments made to Henry, and that would give them a client list.

She was running out of time for revenge.

"I'll do my best. Flora Zhang, could she have done this? Don't the police always say the simplest answer is the most likely?"

"Is it the simplest answer?" Jones said. "Tell us about your talk with Norman Murphy."

"How did you know I talked with him?"

"One of our officers saw you having lunch while picking up his own. He was on duty at the warehouse this morning and had finished his assignment there."

The uniformed officer in line ahead of her. "I just wanted to know what Norman had seen, what he knew."

"What did he tell you?"

Kirsten told the story as he'd told her, except not mentioning his sleeping place or the French cigarette. She was so torn. She thought of showing it to them. Being a good citizen. But she had to find the killer first. For Henry.

They didn't tell her if her account matched Norman's. "Did you know Norman Murphy had a criminal record?" Bard asked.

"No. He seems very mild-mannered. He said he was once a teacher."

"Until his drug addiction, he was. Burglary of a habitation, several years ago. He got off lightly. But he has owned a gun in the past. We stopped him and did a search on him twenty minutes ago." The detective paused. "Your husband's phone was in his cart."

It felt like the floor dropped out from underneath her. "He could have taken it when he found the bodies," Kirsten suggested.

"Maybe. Or he might have gone in to burgle the warehouse, surprised Adam and Henry, and it went wrong."

She was trying not to think: *I bought chicken sandwiches for Henry's murderer. No. It couldn't be.*

"Did you find a gun?" she managed to ask.

Jones wasn't going to answer the question. "He's been arrested; he's being charged."

What had Melinda said about Flora's connections? *Buddies with the mayor, the police chief. Just watch if there isn't an arrest soon, and it's not her.* "Do you think Norman called me on that phone?" she said after a moment. "Why would he?"

"I think he might have felt bad that no one knew who this man was. He had the phone, and you're the only woman listed in Henry's favorites. He called you so you could know the truth."

"The phone has a passcode."

That seemed irrelevant to Jones. "The point is he's in possession of it. He has a record, and he admits he was there."

"Hours after they were dead."

"You're very protective of Norman."

"I just think you have to be sure you have it right," Kirsten said. Norman was an even easier solution than Flora. She felt sick.

But he had the phone.

He'd lied to her. "How did he explain having the phone?" Kirsten asked.

"He claimed not to know it was in his pack," Bard said.

"They always do," Jones said.

"We would like access to everything on that list." Bard tapped the paper. "We can arrange for the New Orleans Police Department to take custody of this evidence and ship it to us. We would still like to know of any legitimate business reason Adam and Henry might have had for being together."

Kirsten nodded. If it was Norman and he was arrested, then he was out of her reach. Would she have leveled a gun at him? Fired it at him? She put her face in her hands. "I bought him lunch and you're saying he killed Henry."

"Let this be a relief, Mrs. North," Jones said. "He did it and we have him."

"But why?"

"There is no why," Jones said. "Because one of them told him he was trespassing. Or he wanted their wallets. Or he was high.

Those are the whys. They're never enough. They are what they are."

"You know what a group of tigers is called?" Bard said suddenly.

Kirsten stared at her. "No."

"Also called an ambush, same as a group of widows. An ambush of tigers. Widows and tigers. Maybe they're more alike than we think. I think we're done here, Mrs. North."

32

Flora had gone back to the penthouse and searched through it again, but she found nothing that suggested it had been a hideaway for Henry North or a love nest for Adam and Melinda Alari. She felt tired and empty and she dreaded seeing people after Melinda's publicity stunt. When she got home, after driving past two news crews parked in the circle, her neighbors—Jeanne and Milo—were already in the kitchen. Milo had cooked more food—a lasagna—and Jeanne had been reading a story to Morgan while he had a snack of sliced fruit.

Jeanne went straight to her and hugged her.

"I don't want to talk about it," Flora said. "That woman. I just can't."

"You just have to hold your head up," Jeanne said. "You did nothing wrong."

"I can go chase off those reporters," Milo announced. "Like I did that one this morning."

"They'll leave when they get bored. Or maybe I should take them this lasagna. We can't eat all this, Milo," Flora said, "and I don't want it to go to waste."

"Then freeze it; it'll keep. I don't want y'all worrying about dinner." She could hear the ache in his voice, the concern, and she wondered what she would do without the two of them.

"Shouldn't y'all be at the distillery, though?" She worried she was taking advantage of them. Milo had founded and still ran a gin distillery that had become the "it" gin after he garnered celebrity endorsements from multiple stars attending one of Austin's many film festivals. Milo's Gin became part of Austin cool (his billboards with celebrity endorsements marked much of the roadway coming in from Austin's airport) and had become what the beautiful people ordered from coast to coast, and their small, niche, unnoticed business had exploded. Jeanne still worked at the distillery with him, keeping the accounts and answering the phones. They were good surrogate grandparents to Morgan.

"We've got smart employees; they've got it under control," Milo said. "Jeanne wants us here for you."

"How are you holding up, Flora?" Jeanne asked, handing Morgan to her after she'd washed her hands.

"I'm all right." Morgan felt wonderful in her arms. "Tired. Thanks for everything you've done today. Have you two eaten? I know it's a little early, but have dinner with me and Morgan and Teddy." She suddenly thought she should call Kirsten, probably eating alone in the penthouse, but wouldn't it be strange? No, she would likely be with her brother.

They both nodded.

"Teddy's not back yet," Jeanne said. Flora felt a spark of hope; maybe he'd found something on Kirsten and Zach that would be helpful.

As Flora got down plates and silverware, she suddenly realized she was famished. She told the Hobsons to help themselves. They loaded their plates and Milo opened a bottle of Sangiovese and poured them each a modest glass.

"Flora, we just want you to know that we're here for you," Milo said. "If there's anything you need, I mean anything, you let me or Jeanne know."

She nodded.

"Honey…are you going to move downtown still?" Jeanne asked.

"I haven't decided."

"Well…we'd love for you to stay here, of course."

"I don't think I want to live downtown right now. Too much change for Morgan." She gulped down salad.

"What more have the police said? I saw on the news they said the man found with him was from New Orleans," Milo said.

Flora told them about her day: from her encounter at the crime scene with Kirsten North and that she had no idea why Henry North was with Adam, to Kirsten slapping Melinda Alari after the press conference.

The Hobsons looked at each other. Stared. Flora suddenly felt nervous.

"Now I wonder," Jeanne said.

"I'm not sure how to say this," Milo said.

"It's not our business," Jeanne said. They looked at each other again.

"I just don't want it to be a shock," Milo said. "You've suffered so much already. And maybe it doesn't mean anything. It was just odd."

Flora waited. She thought she could use some of Milo's gin right now.

"Adam came over to the house last week," Jeanne said. "You and Morgan had gone somewhere, I don't know where Teddy was or if he didn't want Teddy or you to know about this. I was reading and Milo was watching a talk show on the sports channel." Jeanne bit her lip. "He asked us to witness a document. Just sign our names and date it."

"What…was the document?"

"I believe it was a transfer of property," Milo said. "But I didn't see that it *said* that."

Flora blinked. "You mean Adam was giving property to someone?" Melinda Alari. She felt a sharp rise of rage in her chest.

"I don't know, honey," Jeanne said. "I didn't know what to think. And then he gets killed. He'd turned to the page where I was supposed to sign and his hand slipped. So I saw more than I was meant to, but I pretended not to." Jeanne sipped nervously at her wine.

"What exactly did you see?"

"It was about his ownership shares in Zhang Townsend."

"What about them?"

"I don't know, I just saw what I saw," Jeanne said. "You're married, so isn't it all yours?"

"He founded Zhang Townsend before we were married. His original set of shares is not joint property," Flora said. Her stomach began to shift. "What did you think you saw?"

"I don't know. I saw Teddy's name, but all spelled out. Edward Chao."

"Why would Teddy's name..." She stopped. "Have you told this to the police?" She knew the police had spoken to all the neighbors on the circle, even if just for background information.

"Yes. Because it was the last time we saw Adam," Milo said. "But we didn't say anything other than it was a legal document, no matter what Miss Eagle Eye here says."

"Okay," Flora said. Could he have shared his stake in the company with Teddy? And then he died. And what would the police think? Did this make her look worse? She flashed back to every expression of suspicion Bard had made today, watching her.

"I appreciate you telling me," Flora said in an even voice.

Milo took Jeanne's hand. "Maybe it was for something minor."

Did Teddy know this?

She felt a chill. How would she find this document? Adam had to have kept a copy close by. She needed to call the lawyers anyway about Adam's will. It would have to be probated. He had left her everything and she was the executor. But the shares in Zhang Townsend...those were worth millions. Where was this document? Maybe here in the house, or at his office, or...She suddenly felt pressed down by all Adam's secrets. How had they even lived in the same house?

-

While Milo insisted on cleaning up from dinner and loading the dishwasher, Jeanne distracted Morgan with a song. Flora went to her laptop and sent a note to their family lawyer, asking him to call her.

She did a quick internet search. Texas was a community property state and she was entitled to half their community property. Which would include the house, the penthouse, anything acquired after the marriage…but he was free to do what he wanted with *his* half of the property. Why would he move his shares to Teddy? He'd asked her to sign a prenup, and she had, and she'd had a lawyer look at it and they told her it was all standard…*standard*. An odd word for her reality.

He had a mistress.

He was giving critical property not to her or their son but to his protégé—and not telling her.

Nothing in her life was standard.

She went and washed her hands again. *What do you think the police will say*, she thought, staring into the mirror, *if they think he was moving millions and you knew about it right before he died?* Norman Murphy didn't look so interesting then, did he?

She went back to the kitchen. Jeanne and Milo both looked miserable. They told her to call if she needed them, she thanked them again, and they left.

Flora found a cartoon Morgan liked on a streaming service, poured another glass of the Sangiovese Milo had opened, sat Morgan on her lap, and waited for Teddy.

It couldn't be. He would have discussed with her.

Like he did the penthouse?

Jeanne said she wasn't even sure; she must be mistaken. Didn't such a document need a notary present, witnessing the witnesses?

Like that would have stopped Adam. He would have bribed someone to help him keep his secrets. She knew it now.

Morgan crawled off her lap and stretched out on the floor, his favorite television-watching position. She went into Adam's home office and searched through the drawers, feeling her heart grow heavier. She found nothing.

She heard Teddy arrive and went back down to the kitchen.

33

"They made an arrest," Teddy said as Flora came into the kitchen. "I thought the police would have called you."

"I turned the phone off. I needed to think. Was it Melinda Alari?"

"No. The homeless guy who found them."

"Why...why would he..."

"A robbery that went out of control, I guess."

Flora sat down heavily in a chair. All this talk with that odd Kirsten, all this drama over the business and this mistress and it came down to...a mugging. How utterly pointless. She would weep if she didn't feel so exhausted. "They're sure? They're sure?"

"They arrested him," Teddy said as he knelt by her chair. "So yes."

"I called the police chief and the mayor. I asked what they were doing to move the case forward. And this happened."

"That call didn't result in the arrest."

"Maybe it did. They don't want the rich people in Austin thinking they're not safe," she said, and her voice sounded brittle. "Oh. Taylor told me not to do this. What if this is for show? I mean..."

"Flora, they must have had evidence."

She turned on her phone. Immediately saw a text from Kirsten: They arrested Norman, homeless guy. He had Henry's phone in his cart. Phone that I was called on. I don't know what to say. I fed him lunch today.

"Hey," Teddy said. She looked up at him.

"I don't know where to start in what we need to talk about," she said. "Arrest or no arrest."

Teddy sat across from her.

"Melinda Alari," she said.

The seconds passed. His face betrayed nothing. "She flirted a bit with him. I don't know that it ever went further than that. He didn't confide in me. I know he loved you."

"Did he? I think there's a lot I didn't know. What about the partnership possibly breaking up?"

His mouth narrowed. "Shawn told you."

"Taylor did."

"Of course."

"What's that mean?"

"Taylor sure seems to know a lot of stuff for not being an employee." Teddy frowned.

"Is the partnership breaking up?"

"There have been difficulties. The recent investments haven't gone well."

"Was the affair with Melinda affecting the partnership? Shawn knew about it and disapproved. Bad PR if it got out."

"I think…it might have contributed."

The surge of anger she felt rocked her in the chair. "Was anyone ever going to tell me this?" she yelled.

"I'm sorry…."

"You could have told me any of this, at any time." She had this mad urge to hit him, to shove him.

"Adam asked me not to repeat gossip to you. Surely you can understand that."

She jabbed a finger into his chest. "I welcomed you into my home, Teddy. I treated you like family."

He looked down for a few moments and then raised his head and met her gaze. "I know. I'm so grateful to you both. But I didn't know for sure, for sure, and it wasn't my place to interfere in your marriage."

"You've always put him on a pedestal." She cleared her throat. "I can't be shielded anymore, so I need the truth from you, Teddy. Are there any other unpleasant surprises?"

He shook his head. She wondered if she could trust him, and that was not a question she would have ever asked herself in the time Teddy had lived with them.

"Do you know why he was meeting Henry North?"

"No. I swear I don't."

"Could Melinda have shot him? Jilted lover, angry mistress?"

"I don't believe she's capable of it." Teddy's handsome face was impassive.

"What about Shawn? How angry was he about this?"

"I…I don't know. I'm not in his confidence."

"Were there any other women?"

"I don't know."

Her anger was a sudden heat in her chest. "Did you know Adam planned to give you shares in the firm?"

He could not have looked more surprised. "Wait, what?"

She repeated the question.

"No. Why would he?" He glanced away from her.

She told him about the Hobsons' visit and their witnessing of a document for Adam.

Teddy shook his head. "I cannot imagine for a moment he would do that without discussing it with you and me both."

"Like how he discussed his affair with us? Why is my husband giving you shares, Teddy?"

"I don't know."

"I don't believe you." Flora couldn't keep the sharp edge of accusation out of her voice.

"The last thing in the world I have ever wanted to do is hurt you," Teddy said. "I'm sorry. I'm so sorry. I swear I've told you everything I know. I don't know anything about him giving me shares."

In the den, Morgan began to cry. She didn't know what to say to Teddy. What if it had been extortion? Teddy, all innocent.

Maybe he'd threatened to expose the affair.

Maybe the shares were buying his silence. Would Adam do that? Or give Teddy the shares to keep her from acquiring them in a divorce?

Maybe Henry North had gotten pulled into this scheme, working for Teddy, not Adam. And once Teddy had what he wanted, he'd silenced them both....

Teddy blinking at her.

He was living in her house. He had kept Adam's secrets. Maybe done worse. But this was *Teddy*. Who helped her with Morgan, who made Adam and her laugh, who was family in his own way.

Flora hurried to her son; the TV show had ended and Morgan fussed. She held him and soothed him and he was this lovely warm weight against her shoulder.

Morgan was all that was still right with the world.

You didn't know Adam. Why do you think you know Teddy?

34

Kirsten walked back from the police station to where she'd parked her rental car near the penthouse.

She weighed her options. She had to decide: go back to New Orleans; or move to the Zhang penthouse, stay here, and see what Zach found.

They had arrested Norman. So, case closed.

"Thank you for the lunch," Norman had said. So politely. Killers could be polite.

She opened her hotel room door and stepped inside, thinking that now she could look at what was on this flash drive. If it was all Zhang Townsend stuff, she'd just return the drive to the penthouse office, put it in a drawer, and never mention it to Flora.

She took six steps into her room and stopped.

Someone had been in her room.

She saw it as soon as she stepped inside. Not the maid—the room hadn't been made up yet because she'd forgotten and left the Do Not Disturb hanger on the door. But she'd pulled on a jacket, decided not to wear it, and left it on the back of the chair.

Now it was on the floor.

Maybe it fell off.

Maybe someone knocked it off.

You're imagining this. The jacket slipped off the chair.

She sat down and slid the flash drive she'd taken from the penthouse into her own laptop.

There was only one file on the flash drive. It said REPORT. Nothing else in the title.

She double-clicked it. The document opened.

REPORT ON FLORA ZHANG SURVEILLANCE

Dear Mr. Zhang:

We have completed our surveillance on your wife. We were unable to get incontrovertible video or electronic evidence that she is having an extramarital affair with anyone, including your house guest and employee, Edward "Teddy" Chao.

Kirsten's mouth went dry.

We observed at your home and followed Mrs. Zhang on dates from 12/15 through 1/15, including during the holidays when you were called away on an emergency business meeting. Only once did Mrs. Zhang and Chao leave the house together, to a local hamburger restaurant where they ate dinner and immediately returned to the house. Your minor child Morgan accompanied them. Our operative did not observe any hints of a romantic relationship between them. (photos attached).

The access you provided us in your home did not reveal that there were any intimacies between your wife and Chao. You can see the attached hidden camera footage from Chao's bedroom, but there is nothing to see. He is either working on his laptop, watching television, reading, or sleeping. Chao appears to have a very limited social life that does not coincide with Mrs. Zhang's absences from the house. We removed the camera per your instructions.

Adam allowed these people to put a hidden camera in his assistant's—his cousin's—bedroom. Because he suspected his cousin and his wife of having an affair? Why not just throw out this Teddy guy?

We did observe your next-door neighbor, Mrs. Jeanne Hobson, visit the house repeatedly and twice play outside with Morgan while Ms. Zhang and Chao were both inside and you were not present. Our understanding is that Mrs. Hobson often helps your wife with Morgan; we are unsure if her help allows for private moments between your wife and Chao in unmonitored areas of the home.

Although your request to us centered on her relationship with Chao, we did not see any evidence or behavior suggesting that she is having an extramarital affair with anyone.

Kirsten scrolled on:

Regarding your concerns as to any digital impropriety, we suggest hiring a consultant who can discreetly access and investigate their emails and in the case of your wife, her finances as they pertain to her charitable foundation. We can suggest several.

There it was. How Adam came to Henry, possibly. She read on, expecting to see him mentioned…but he wasn't. The list of possible hires was small, all local to Austin. She read past it:

We did find that Mrs. Zhang had an appointment with an attorney in Austin who represents spouses in divorce proceedings. She had one meeting lasting at least an hour. The firm has experience handling high-stakes, high-dollar divorces.

Our operative overheard her on the phone in the lobby of one building. Apparently, she called a friend or confidante and while she did not share that she had met with an attorney, she stated she loved you and just wished you would be more attentive to her and to your child. Our operative could not hear more of the conversation without becoming obvious.

We cannot find evidence that she engaged the firm or paid a retainer, but it's possible she did so using funds from accounts you do not have access to check.

We also cannot find evidence that she retained her own investigators to follow or surveil you.

A detailed summary of her activities that we observed follows:

Kirsten read through the detailed summary. The private investigators had followed Flora to meetings of her foundation's board, to her lunches with Taylor Townsend and other friends, to her volunteer work at a homeless shelter as well as a literacy event, and to a fund-raising lunch for literacy. To yoga. To the movies. To a bookstore, several times. To the airport, where she took a flight to New Orleans....

They'd followed her to New Orleans. Two months ago.

Kirsten read on:

> ...and spoke at a conference on foundation governance. She had dinner with two of the other featured speakers and the conference organizers at a restaurant off Canal, returned directly to her hotel, did not leave her room again that night, and spoke on a panel the next morning. Afterwards she left the hotel and took a flight back to Austin and went straight home.

Adam had Flora watched, and Flora came to New Orleans. But this report wasn't exactly damning.

Had these investigators already gone to the police and told them that Adam Zhang suspected his wife of adultery with the young man who lived with them? It gave Flora a motive: kill him before he could divorce her. All this money...all this money...and maybe a love affair...She closed her eyes. And maybe someone, her own Henry, had been pulled into this scheme and ended up dead.

Maybe Flora did kill Henry. Henry dug and found the dirt, and he was delivering it, and she caught them both and killed them.

She started to tremble. This wasn't a smoking gun...but she had to find out the truth about Flora Zhang.

She hid the flash drive in her luggage, deep in a zippered pocket she never used. She tried to think of a better place, but then decided Flora had no reason to search her bag.

She had been in New Orleans.

There were so many conferences and conventions there. It might be coincidence.

It might not be.

What about Henry's days when Flora had been in town? Had Henry somehow met Flora?

No. She was followed. A meeting with Henry would have been in the report.

Unless they hadn't met in person. Maybe she googled security experts and found him, or found him through a client.

And then a devil's voice, whispering in her ear: *Maybe Flora hired Henry.* Maybe that was the secret. He was helping her, somehow, to set up her husband for death. And then he was a loose end, dealt with.

And you're moving into her penthouse.

She let the thought simmer in her head. Okay. It was a possibility. It seemed a remote one. If Flora was having an affair and wanted free of her husband, she could simply divorce him. She might not get as much money, but it was far less risky. Flora didn't strike her as a violent person.

And Henry didn't strike you as a liar, yet here we are.

A knock at the door. She answered.

Zach. "I found where Henry was staying." He entered the room and she shut the door.

"Where?"

"I had no luck with the credit card. But another guy who works for the Fortunatos has a contact at a satellite radio company."

The dark web of the Fortunatos' reach never ceased to amaze her. "Henry canceled his car's satellite radio service last year."

"Yeah, well, I had my contact temporarily reactivate it and use their stolen vehicle recovery mode—it pinged the car's location. He gave it to me. You owe me."

"Where was he?"

"Parked in a long-term lot near the airport. But I got the navigation history of where the car had been the previous days from the stolen vehicle mode."

He showed her the list—he'd already cross-referenced it with location names. Their home in New Orleans. Various points along I-10 through Houston and then Highway 71 to Austin. A hotel in south Austin, where he must have stayed. A home address in Lakehaven, an Austin suburb. Then a restaurant, the hotel again, and then the warehouse. Then the airport parking lot.

Her first urge had been to race to his hotel room. But this was much more information, and she needed to think.

"Someone moved his car from the scene," she said. The police hadn't been able to discover how Henry got to the warehouse.

"Yes."

"Where's the car now?"

"Still where it was parked. I don't have the keys to move it and I can't exactly tell the lot how I found it."

"Norman took his phone, supposedly." She updated him.

"But not his laptop? I think we can assume the killer took everything of Henry's to keep the trail cold. So no phone, no laptop, no wallet, no parked car with Louisiana plates nearby. Maybe that's why you got the phone call. How much longer would it have taken the police to ID him?" Zach said. He sat on the edge of the bed.

Kirsten wondered about the phone call. The reason for it still seemed completely uncertain. The killer wanted her to know her loss. Why? It might have been more time for the evidence to grow cold or an arrest to be made if she wasn't on the scene, identifying Henry. There had to be a reason for the phone call.

"I'm moving into the Zhang penthouse," she said to Zach.

One eyebrow went up. "Why would you do that?"

She wanted to say: *I'm going to find out who smokes that brand of cigarette. If it's Flora.* But instead she said: "If I get close to her, I might find answers."

"You think Flora killed them."

"I don't think she would have actually done it. I think she would've hired someone."

"Well, can I have this palatial room then? I haven't booked a place to stay."

"Yeah. I have it reserved for two more nights."

He gestured at the wall. "You can leave up all your notes. I know that matters to you."

"I'll take them with me."

"Won't Flora object to being analyzed in her own penthouse?"

"We'll see. Maybe she can add context."

"What do you want me to do?"

"That home address in Lakehaven that the navigation tracker said Henry drove to."

"Yeah. On Summerhill Trail."

She opened her laptop, found the Travis County tax assessor rolls, did a search when Zach gave her the house number.

"Oh," she said.

"What?"

"The property is owned by Drew and Jill Grimes. I don't recognize their names." It was a high-dollar address, appraised at several million.

She found them quickly on social media. She was a partner at a major law firm in Austin; he was CEO of a large regional bank. "I don't see a connection to us."

"The map data just tells you where he parked," Zach said. "Try the other house addresses."

She typed in a variety of addresses and then she said. "Shawn and Taylor Townsend's house is three lots down from that address."

They stared at each other. "Maybe it wasn't Adam that hired him. Maybe it was Shawn."

"I've met his wife. She's, like, you know, suburban-nice." She almost called her a trophy wife but then thought that was unfair. "She's setting up the penthouse so I'll be comfortable there."

"Have you met Shawn Townsend?"

"I haven't. Taylor said he hadn't heard of Henry. Melinda said there was no contact trace for Henry in their network, but maybe Shawn erased it all. I need to see this Shawn guy."

"You're not going over to their house," he said, "at least not alone."

Of course I am, she thought. "I need to get my things moved over to Flora's penthouse."

"I don't much like that idea either."

"I didn't ask," Kirsten said. "Either support me or go home."

"I'm going to get my stuff from the car."

"Okay." She started pulling the taped pieces of paper off the wall as Zach left the room. She quickly gathered all the information—printed articles, pictures, sticky notes—and stuck them into a folder.

There was a lot going on at Zhang Townsend—failed investments, sexual indiscretions—and she'd thought only of Adam's potentially bad behavior and not of his partner's. She had to think how to play this. If it was Shawn who was responsible, then she had her chance because it felt like the news and the theorizing were swinging toward Flora or Melinda. No one was looking hard at Shawn and how he might gain from shedding himself of Adam as a business partner.

She stuck the folder of papers into her carry-on bag and zipped it up.

Zach came back with a surprisingly large suitcase. *Men*, she thought, *they never can pack*. He also had a pizza and bottled water from a restaurant down the street.

They ate like people who didn't have time to enjoy their food, just needing fuel.

"Thanks for this. And everything," she said. "If you're going to stay here, I thought you should know I thought maybe someone had been in the room today."

He lowered the slice of pepperoni pizza he'd been about to bite into. "You mean other than the housekeeper."

"Yeah. A jacket I left was on the floor; I had hung it on the chair."

"I was in the room. I made some calls from here." He shrugged. "I probably knocked it over."

"Oh, okay," she said. "But right now I want to go to Henry's hotel room."

"If it's under his name, the police will know about it."

"But his laptop might be there. If they don't…"

"How exactly are we supposed to get into a room if we don't know what name it's under?"

She looked for the hotel name on her phone's browser with the address Zach supplied. Hotel Byte. Odd name. She dialed the hotel and asked to be connected to Henry North's room. The clerk said there was no guest there by that name.

And then hung up on her.

"That's odd."

"Hotel Byte," Zach said. "I've heard of that. There's one in New Orleans."

"Well, do you want to go with me to check it out?"

He nodded.

35

Hotel Byte sat off South Congress, a small old-fashioned building that sported a lit No Vacancy sign. The parking lot was mostly empty. The place itself looked deserted.

The front door wasn't glass, like you'd expect, but steel. Zach tried it and it was locked. A sign announced "Members Only." It didn't give hours that the lobby (presumably on the other side of the door) was open.

"What kind of hotel is this?" Kirsten asked. She pressed the intercom button.

A tinny voice on the other side said, "Reservation code?"

"I don't have one."

"Then password, please."

"I don't know your password."

"Sorry, members only." The voice was male, youngish, a bit hoarse.

"We have reason to believe that my husband stayed here. Henry North. Can you at least tell me if there's a room here in his name?"

"I cannot and you are trespassing."

"Henry North was murdered and the police are investigating. We can go and get the police and bring them back here."

No answer. After a minute, she walked away from the lobby door and toward the other doors along the courtside of the building, which had a 1950s roadside motel architecture to it. All the doors were steel. They had no numbers. The windows were reflective—she couldn't even see if there were curtains on the other side. She returned to the lobby door.

"What is this place?" she said to Zach, who had walked down the other side of the hotel and returned.

He shrugged and took out his phone instead of answering and stepped away from her, talking softly.

She got annoyed and pressed the intercom button again.

"I really cannot help you," the young man said again. "Please leave."

"I get the feeling this place doesn't want a parking lot full of TV news crews and police cars," Kirsten said.

"Who are you?"

"Kirsten North. Henry's wife. Henry's widow. We know his car was here. We've tracked it." She watched Zach end his call, punch another number into his phone, and begin talking again.

"This is a private establishment," the voice said. She saw Zach walk up to her and put the phone close to the intercom. And then she heard a voice come out of the phone.

"This is Paul Fortunato. Account 230, password tko93bv. Admit my guests, please."

Silence, and then they heard the sharp click of the lobby door unlocking. They entered into a small fifties-style motel lobby, with at least one notable exception: a wide-screen monitor that sat behind the check-in desk and displayed financial futures and cryptocurrency prices.

No one was in the lobby; the door was electronically controlled.

"I'm officially weirded out," Kirsten whispered.

"We just fell down a rabbit hole," Zach whispered. "It's a hotel for hackers."

"A what?" she said, but then a back door opened and a young man came out, dressed in a Pokémon T-shirt and jeans. Glaring at them.

Zach whispered, "The Fortunatos have an account at the one in New Orleans."

"This is really truly not permitted," he said. He wore a name tag that said Xeno.

"I don't care," Kirsten said. "I need to know if Henry stayed here and if his room is still available."

"Our guests aren't registered by their names. So I don't know a Henry."

She pulled up a photo of him on her phone. "Do you recognize him?"

She could tell from the man's reaction the answer was yes. "So, he did stay here," she said.

"He still has two days on his room reservation."

"Can you let us in his room?"

"This is most unusual. I need to check with Central on this. . . ."

Kirsten thought. A hotel that didn't use names, tracked cryptocurrency in the lobby, and was for members only. For hackers. So it was a very niche audience, and one that put a lot of trust in their anonymity. That trust could be quickly eliminated.

"I know a journalist who's writing about the murder case and would love this mysterious, edgy angle," she said. "And if you don't..."

Zach touched her arm gently. And then she saw the gun at the concierge's side. Holstered, but there.

"We don't want to threaten anyone. But you'd rather deal with us than the police asking more about what goes on here," Zach said. "I mean, my boss is a member and he'd agree with me. If you ask higher-ups, it escalates. We look, we leave, you don't get any unwanted attention. Maybe the police never need to come here."

Xeno considered. He said, "Follow me."

"I'd prefer that you show us to his room unarmed," Zach said.

The hacker concierge stared at Zach. "Who do you work for again?"

"The Fortunatos of New Orleans."

Count of three, then Xeno removed his weapon and secured it in a small safe under the counter. "All right. I haven't given this much special treatment in a long time." He sounded peevish.

They followed him, not back outside, but down a hallway that also featured steel doors. Kirsten realized that the original motor court layout of the building had been modified—there was a privacy hallway to access the rooms that ran parallel to the parking lot. It wasn't large, and they had to walk in single file, but it meant a room could be entered without being visible from the street.

Xeno held the door for them.

"Can we have some privacy?" Zach asked.

"No," the concierge said. "You may not. I'll wait right here."

Kirsten walked to the closet. Henry's clothes, hanging up. Underwear, folded and stacked on the shelf. She leaned into his shirt before she thought and she could smell him, the scent of his soap. And for one moment tears threatened to overwhelm her.

She felt Zach's hand on her shoulder. She stepped away from the shirt. The bed was messily unmade.

"I assume there's not traditional daily housekeeping," she said. "Given the obsession with privacy."

Xeno said, "I handle that. We don't have a housekeeping staff. It has to be requested. He has made no requests." So—Henry didn't make the bed.

Henry had made their bed every day of their marriage.

She looked on the desk. No computer, but a charger sat there, waiting to be used.

"His laptop is gone," she said.

"He must have taken it with him," Zach said.

To the warehouse.

"Do you have a record of his browsing history here?" she asked Xeno.

"No, obviously not," Xeno said, managing to sound horrified. "That would be considered a grave security risk. Our internet servers do not record history or activity. We guarantee anonymity."

Henry stayed here because he needed to be invisible.

Because he had work to do.

That could not be discovered.

And something he found while he was here led him to the warehouse. And Adam Zhang.

She and Zach searched. No sign of a handy, convenient second flash drive. Surely he backed up whatever work he did here. But there was nothing.

"This isn't like him," she told Zach.

"Then he made a different choice for a reason," Zach said.

Xeno looked bored. "Are you done yet?"

Zach took a step toward the concierge and Kirsten stopped him.

She packed Henry's clothes, carefully, trying not to cry in front of this jerk concierge. Henry had packed himself for this trip. He had come here and checked into the most secure hotel in the city. He had done something, apparently, for a millionaire. He had driven to a warehouse. He had died. None of it made sense to her.

"You have to have some digital record of his activity," Kirsten said to Xeno.

"Ma'am, not having any digital record is the entire point. This is an invisible zone." He crossed his arms. "I'm really sorry for what happened to him, but I can't show you a blank slate and expect to be helpful to you."

"Has this ever happened before? A guest killed?" Kirsten asked.

"Not while I've been here. We're not criminals. We're digital explorers."

"Kirsten," Zach said. She turned toward him. He was kneeling by the bed, on the opposite side from where she and Xeno stood. He held a thick sheaf of papers that he had pulled from under the mattress. "They were pushed under here."

"Well, that's retro security," Xeno said. "Did he hide money under the mattress too?"

Zach looked at the pages and she saw his mouth tremble before he handed them to her. He walked over to the concierge and shoved him out and slammed the door. "Just give us a damn minute," he yelled through the steel. "I'll punch your face in if you open that door. It's private. She's his widow. She's in mourning."

Kirsten's gaze went down the first page as she sat on the edge of the bed.

The cover page indicated it was a report compiled by North Star Consulting, Henry's company name. She noticed the pages were numbered and stapled together.

She read on the inside of the report:

> Mr. Zhang:
>
> Per our discussion, I accessed your wife's computer through your home network. I also accessed her work computer at her workplace. Here are my preliminary findings for your review. The most concerning section is at the end.

Kirsten scanned the first pages. The next pages detailed Flora Zhang's finances—her bank balances, her credit card payments.

"Why hire Henry for *this*? He's not a private detective! Adam already had her followed."

"So you said," Zach said. "And when he didn't get any satisfaction, he decided to look at her digital life."

The next page was an analysis of her home email patterns. Nothing interesting.

"If he got hired, is this the whole work product? He was only here a day, so maybe he was working on it before he got here. And then...he got..." She could not finish.

Zach's voice was gentle. "We know Henry was short on money. Maybe he took on this kind of work."

"Unlicensed?"

Zach shrugged.

She got to the final pages. She read. She sat down suddenly on the edge of the bed.

> Searching through the folder structure on your wife's personal laptop I found an encrypted folder marked as "system_software_7B," a meaningless term that does not apply to your wife's operating system. I performed a password hack against the folder and gained entry. There I discovered a large cache of PDF files, all articles and news accounts on women who had been caught, tried, and sentenced after

murdering their husbands. There were fourteen articles in all, including six that referenced women who hired killers to eliminate their husbands. There were an additional eight files on cases involving women suspected of murdering their husbands but who had successfully avoided prosecution. The files are attached for your reference.

She went through the cases. They had an unsettling pattern. The husband was often rich, often abusive, and the wife had reached a point of no return. She had either enlisted a boyfriend, a former boyfriend, a man who wanted to be her boyfriend, or a paid killer. Several of the articles described how the wife had solicited the services of a hit man. Friend of a friend. Anonymous ad on the internet. Asking a criminal acquaintance for a reference. It was a sad litany of suffering and murder.

She handed the sheaf of papers to Zach.

He read through them. "I told you. *Cui bono?* She has the most to gain."

"Does she strike you as the type?"

"She would hire it out if she was going to do it."

"And who benefits if Flora's blamed for this?" Kirsten asked.

Zach frowned. "What, you don't believe Henry found this?"

"I don't believe Henry would get involved in this."

"God only knows what Zhang offered him."

"I could take this to the police. Say I found it on his computer backup, printed it out."

"You could. That sounds like an excellent idea."

Kirsten paced the floor. "And then they'll arrest her, maybe, and she'll hire a bunch of fat-cat lawyers and she'll walk. Some of these women walked. Adam was an asshole."

"But Henry wasn't."

"Bard said something. That Adam was killed with two shots to the head. Like it was precise. But Henry was shot four times. In the chest." Kirsten stopped pacing and looked at him. "Why would a hired killer do that?"

"Why do you want to believe this woman is innocent?"

"I want to be sure. I want to know it. She's letting me stay at her place. I can get the truth out of her."

Zach shook his head. "If you kill her, you'll be the prime suspect."

"Will I?"

"Likely."

Kirsten narrowed her gaze. "Can you find out if a hit man's been hired?"

"How…"

"Your boss. He knows people."

"It's not casually discussed. No. Not without a name, a face."

"If she hired him, she has a way to contact him. I want them both. It's no good if I just catch her."

"The best ones don't interact with their clients. They have handlers. Go-betweens."

"Do you know who the go-between might be? Would the Fortunatos know?"

"Kirsten. Let me take you home." An ache in Zach's voice, one she'd never heard before, nearly made her want to cry. "There is nothing for you here but misery and regret."

"There's nothing for me at home. I can't imagine going back to that house knowing he's never coming home. I can't…"

The door opened. Xeno was back, holstered gun on his hip. "I'm sorry for your loss, but I want you to leave."

Zach took a step toward the concierge and she stopped him with a hand on his chest.

"Answer this question for me," she said, "and if you're lying, I'll take my hand away and my brother will beat you within an inch of your life."

Xeno stood firm, but his bottom lip trembled before he stilled it with a frown.

"Has anyone else come here looking for Henry?" Kirsten asked. She showed him a picture of Flora Zhang on her phone's web browser. "You ever see her?"

He stared at her, then at the picture for ten long seconds. "No. Please take his things and go. We had a deal. I let you in and you don't talk," He glanced at Zach. "If you break our deal, your boss's membership will be forfeit."

"I understand," Zach said.

Kirsten made one last glance at the room. She thought, too late, she should have taken a picture, but she couldn't with the concierge standing there. Henry slept his last night here.

A surge of grief rose in her chest.

She followed Zach down the hallway. She looked up at the ceiling. No security cameras. No trace of who else came to the room.

Kirsten got in the car and burst into tears. Zach said, "Oh, Kirsten," and patted her and she sobbed, for Henry and everything she'd lost, for what she was bracing herself to do. Zach nudged his shoulder under her head and held her and made brotherly reassuring noises, trying to calm her.

36

It had taken Mender's handler more time than usual to acquire a gun for him, but now he would be able to attend to business, armed with the knowledge he'd gathered. That would make having had to wait into an advantage and he could get home to Annie.

His handler had provided him with more vital information. He opened a file on Zachary Xavier Couvillon: six four, 210 pounds. Majored in business at LSU. Grew up in foster care when orphaned at age eleven, no other relatives who would take him. Characterized as "violent," was put into boxing and martial arts programs to channel his energy; played football, basketball, and baseball at St. Gentian Catholic School in New Orleans. His foster father, Larry Melancon, had vanished. Larry's disappearance remained unsolved. Couvillon was the foster brother of Kirsten Plumm North. He was employed as a VP of business development for Magali Investments, a front company owned by the Fortunato family in New Orleans, one of the best-connected criminal families in the South. The Fortunatos were suspected to be deep into money laundering, online fraud, and other financial crimes. They were very polite criminals, until they broke your arms or made you disappear. The vanished Larry Melancon had been an accountant working for them.

VP of business development. Mender could guess what that meant for an organization like the Fortunatos. Zach Couvillon was likely an enforcer, who could either negotiate a new deal or put a bullet in you.

And if Mender killed Zach's foster sister, Zach might well come looking for whoever was responsible.

He might be backed by the resources of the Fortunato family.

He alone was dangerous. With a crime family behind him...Mender was afraid now.

I should have been informed of this connection to the target before I took the job, he told his handler via encrypted text. It should have been part of the assessment. I need to know if the relative of a target is connected to organized crime.

Sorry, his handler responded. You know the job scope expanded. If you want to say no, then say no. Let me know when you have her. The client wants to be informed.

But Mender needed the money. He just had to make her vanish. And it would help if he could serve up a suspect to Zach Couvillon and any associates who wished to stand by him.

A false trail for them to chase that would never lead back to Mender.

Maybe Flora Zhang, who already had to be seen as a suspect in her husband's death.

Mender could have this done tonight and then drive back to Dallas to be with Annie. Annie was strong—he loved that about her—but her texts in the past day had become more impatient and pleading. She needed him. He could not let that cloud his judgment. But this job hadn't gone right since the beginning, and he needed to have it done and be shed of it.

Mender parked in a lot across the street from the hotel. He had seen more squads of high school girls entering, returning from dinner or some nearby tournament, he guessed being played at the University of Texas. He didn't like it—students would be going between rooms, visiting, talking, laughing. Chaperones or coaches keeping an eye out. It would be easy to be noticed if he wasn't careful.

In his car he was prepared: Gun in holster under his blazer. Syringe, full of sedative, in his blazer pocket. New passkey that his handler had assured him would work in any room in the hotel, keyed for the same access as housekeeping. The ID in his wallet identified him as Frederick Mender, a person who had died five years ago and whose identity he had appropriated. Neatly secured in the cuff of his black pants was a small, thin Japanese blade, honed to a fine edge, useful as a last resort if he was disarmed. It had saved him once before when a target, a Brazilian military attaché, had gotten a momentary advantage on him.

He went to Kirsten's room and finally got a lucky break. The hallway was for the moment empty, but he could hear laughter from one of the rooms. A coach walked past him, gave him a friendly nod as she headed toward the nook where the ice machine was. He waited for her to turn the corner. He used the passkey; the light turned green. He pushed open the door, ready with a quick apology that the front desk must have made a mistake, so sorry, but the needle would be in Kirsten North within seconds, and seconds after that she'd be doped to the gills. He'd help her stagger out to the car, like another person who'd overindulged on Sixth Street.

He heard the shower running. Oh, even better.

He eased the door shut behind him so it closed silently. The bathroom was to his right, the door open, the shower at full blast. He took two steps in to survey the bedroom area to be sure the foster brother wasn't here; the room was empty. He saw the big suitcase open at the floor of the bed; he saw her notes were gone from the wall.

Wait. The big suitcase. He didn't remember that from his previous visit. It hadn't been in the closet. It hadn't been in the room.

The shower kept running. He stepped into the bathroom. One more step to the shower. He pulled the syringe from his pocket, took the cap off the needle. He glanced at the countertop. Shaving cream, men's razor.

She wasn't here. This was either a new guest and she'd checked out or...Mender fumbled for the gun, never mind the syringe.

The shower curtain suddenly parted and a huge fist caught him hard as he turned.

Mender slammed back against the sink. The foster brother, naked, conditioner in his hair, pulling his fist back for another punch. He tried to slip the syringe into the big guy's neck, but instead Zach Couvillon knocked it from his hand. Mender's off-balance punch landed but didn't slow Zach down.

Mender kicked hard, catching Zach in the upper hip, and Zach's eyes widened in fury as he slammed another fist into Mender. Hard, a blow right to his heart that staggered him, and then a blow to the throat. Mender went down, panicking, thinking, *Not like this, not like this.* Stunned, he tried to get back on his feet.

Then Mender felt the needle pierce his neck and he cried out.

"So what is it, sunshine? Poison? Sedative?" Zach had him by the throat.

"Sedative," Mender managed to say. He was not sure he'd ever been hit this hard in his life.

"Let's have a talk," Zach Couvillon said, "about why you're trying to kill my sister."

Gun gone, syringe gone. He tried to pull his ankle up toward his hand, to get at the hidden Japanese razor, but Zach depressed the plunger and darkness washed over him.

37

When Kirsten arrived at the Zhang penthouse, the key card to the elevator worked, and there was now a small dining table, chairs, a sofa, and a coffee table facing the spectacular view. All modern and expensive-looking. Taylor had delivered on her promises; and Kirsten, exhausted from her crying jag, felt a surge of gratitude. Groceries to last a few days were in the refrigerator and the pantry; fresh sheets were folded to put on the office futon. A note from Taylor read:

> I hope this is a help to you. Flora is a good person for letting you stay here, I hope you see that. Working on getting you a bed from my house stylist.

This was nicer than her hotel room. But it could also be an elegant little trap.

So what did she do about Flora?

Kirsten could confront Flora with the report. She could take it to the police. She could question her without revealing what she knew, hoping to find out more.

She read the report again and then she noticed it.

The format, the layout of the report wasn't...right.

Hey, babe, can you proof this? He'd sometimes asked Kirsten to look at longer reports, to catch any typos or awkward language, and she would. He'd always used a template to lay out and organize the data for the client.

This report wasn't in the template. It was the kind of thing no one but her would notice.

Maybe he forgot. Maybe he didn't have time to format it right. Maybe he switched formats, but she suspected he would have asked her opinion. It was his simple logo on the front of the report. Who else would have written this?

But why hide it under the mattress? Zach said the pages were peeking out from the edge.

He hid the report, then didn't make his bed as was always his habit? Maybe he simply didn't know there wouldn't be housekeeping without a request at that hacker hotel.

Maybe. She thought it likely that all the hacker amenities and the lack of normal ones were explained to him.

He'd apparently written the report, hidden it in his room, and gone to his death.

Cui bono? But who benefited if Flora was blamed?

Cui bono? could be answered with the name of more than one person.

It was either a frame of Flora or it wasn't. If it was, the killer was sitting happily. Flora was suspect, but the cops had arrested Norman. No one looking the killer's way. If it wasn't, then Flora would be happy Norman had been arrested and imagining herself getting away with this.

Right now, the killer might be feeling relief that at the end of this long day, a poor old guy was in jail.

Of course, if Norman had killed them, then this was all sound and fury, nothing more.

So what are you going to do? She could drive to Flora's house and confront her. She could physically overcome Flora, force her to tell the truth. And then what? If she didn't kill her, Flora could press charges. Without proof—and a bunch of articles lifted from her computer wasn't what Kirsten pictured as hard evidence that a good lawyer couldn't dismantle (*she's a journalist who was researching her first article in years, Your Honor*)—Flora might not admit to anything.

Kirsten heard the elevator ping and here came Flora, holding a toddler, the toddler Kirsten had seen in the photos.

"Hi. Are we intruding?" Flora asked. She offered a thin, quick smile.

"It's your house so you can't intrude...." Kirsten's voice trailed off. She turned away from Flora and put Henry's report facedown on the coffee table. Then she turned to face her.

Kirsten looked at Flora's son. She wasn't good with little kids; they made her nervous. And she didn't want a kid here as she confronted this woman.

"This place doesn't feel like it's mine. I...I wanted out of the house for a bit. I thought Morgan might like the view."

Or you wanted to see what I was up to and you're using your kid as a shield, Kirsten thought.

Kirsten didn't connect much with kids, but Morgan Zhang was a cutie. He gave her a speculative look and then, noticing the lights of the city and the view, his gaze sparkled with delight.

"See the lights? All the lights?" Flora walked him to the window and he said "lights, lights" repeatedly. Kirsten joined them.

"This is Mrs. North. Say hello to her."

"He can call me Kirsten. If he can say it," Kirsten said, surprising herself.

Kirsten thought Flora seemed somehow...less severe while holding her baby. And that was ridiculous. Mothers could be murderers.

Morgan looked at Kirsten as though she were extremely interesting, then looked again at the lights.

I thought if you killed my husband, I'd kill you.... She couldn't look at Flora holding the child. She turned away. What was it that she owed Henry? Vengeance? Or justice? They weren't always the same thing.

"Did you get some dinner?" Flora asked. "I know I sound like a mother."

"I honestly don't know what a mother sounds like," Kirsten said.

That made Flora pause, but then Flora said: "Taylor said she was having groceries delivered. I should have brought you food…we have so much at the house. Our neighbor won't stop cooking."

You have so much, period, Kirsten thought. "Yes, Taylor kindly left milk and bread and stuff. But I had a pizza with Zach." She decided: *Just talk to the woman. Test her a bit.* "Listen, I know I apologized before, but I'm truly sorry you saw me like that. Earlier. At the warehouse. I don't have a good history with booze. Or with cops."

"Oh." Flora frowned. "Like you have a police record?"

"No, like I ran away from my first couple of foster homes and the cops gave me a dumb lecture every time."

"Oh." Flora touched Morgan's hair, and Kirsten wondered if she was imagining her own son in the foster system, what it would be like for him. She could guess at the next question—*what happened to your parents?*—but Flora didn't ask it. Most people did.

Kirsten waited until Flora's gaze met hers. "So. We're widows. It's weird, isn't it?"

Morgan had stopped watching the lights and was playing with an old flip-style cell phone Flora had pulled from the backpack. Probably pretending to make little venture capitalist deals. "Yes," Flora finally said.

"I'd like to know any possible reason that my husband had for being with your husband," Kirsten said.

"As would I."

"My husband was good at breaking into computers. You have anything in yours you want to hide?"

"No," she said after a moment.

"Maybe your husband was trying to see if there was any dirt on you before he got into a messy divorce battle."

"Not in front of my kid, please."

"He's too little to understand."

"He's very gifted. He understands more than we realize."

"Let's not live in a bubble. Tell me about Shawn Townsend." Kirsten had decided to try to keep her off balance, switch topics without warning. Henry had gone to Townsend's house. If he was just investigating Flora, then why? There was no reason.

"I actually met Adam through Shawn. Shawn and I had dated, briefly, nothing serious, and he introduced me to Adam—they had just formed Zhang Townsend."

"Wasn't that awkward?"

"Not really," Flora insisted. "Shawn soon met Taylor, and he and I were never an item anyway."

"What if Shawn still had feelings for you?"

"Then he would have pursued those when he had the chance. Shawn and I wouldn't have made a lasting couple. He's much better matched with Taylor."

Is there any other secret from your past I should know about before I make accusations? "Did you date Norman too?" But she said this lightly, so Flora wouldn't get mad.

"Perhaps it would be easier if we both shared our backgrounds. And our husbands' backgrounds. Perhaps we'll find a common thread."

Kirsten looked down at the blank back of the report. Flora hadn't even glanced at it. "All right. Henry grew up in New Orleans. He lived next door to my last foster family, went to high school with me and Zach. He got a computer science degree at the University of Louisiana at Lafayette. Came back to New Orleans and got a couple of jobs with small software companies. Neither company flourished. So he went freelance. He would do test hacks sometimes and write customized security code. Energy companies, hosting companies, law firms, e-commerce sites, stuff like that. Not exciting. Not dangerous. Not criminal."

"And you?"

She sipped at her lemonade. "We both studied computer science. Henry was great at breaking problems into steps and solutions"—her voice wavered here for a moment—"and I liked the order of it. That if you entered in all the factors and variables, it would give you the answer. But I guess I don't work well with others, because I got fired from two jobs, so I went freelance as a researcher. Henry and I were each other's lives outside of our work. His parents died a couple of years back in a car accident and I don't have any family outside of Zach."

"Not your foster parents?"

"We…weren't close. And my foster father took off when I was a senior in high school. It wasn't a good situation."

"What about your biological parents?"

Kirsten's voice was steady. "My dad was a Danish med student at Tulane. My mom worked there as a secretary. He got her pregnant and he didn't tell his parents until after I was born. They married secretly, but when his parents found out they made him come back to Denmark—they had control of all his money. He left us. I'm named for his mother, which is weird since she wanted nothing to do with me. I guess it was my parents' attempt to get his parents to accept me. I've never met the Danish side of my family. They weren't interested in me. I didn't look enough like them." She set her jaw, met Flora's gaze, hated the pity she saw there.

Kirsten took a deep breath. "My mom got hurt in a fall down some stairs. It messed up her back and her doctor got her onto opioids for the pain. They killed her, eventually." She cleared her throat. "I wrote to tell my dad, but he didn't write me back or come for me."

For a moment the only sound was Morgan opening and shutting his old plaything phone. Flora looked absolutely stricken. She said: "Oh, I am so sorry, Kirsten. So sorry. That's just unforgivable."

Murder is worse, Kirsten thought. She shrugged, like she often did when she spoke about her family. "Henry was literally the boy next door. The incredible man that helped me find who I was. He was my everything." She waited for Flora to say the same about Adam, but of course she didn't. Because, as had become clear, he wasn't. "So tell me about Adam. Like what I won't read in an article." *Tell me how much you wanted him dead. Make me believe you're capable of this.*

Flora cleared her throat. "So, Adam started a software company here that made it much easier to manage network security. They got a number of huge corporate accounts. A bigger company bought them out. He went into venture capital work then with his own money, and with some of Shawn's money, they started investing in select companies. Most of the ones he backed did well. That's what he was still doing when he died." Flora realized she was twisting one of Morgan's plush toys in her hand and Kirsten's gaze had drifted to that. She set the toy on the floor; Morgan grabbed it.

"I said what I wouldn't read in an article, Flora. Was he just his résumé?"

Flora's gaze met hers. "When we met, he didn't want to talk to me. I was working as a journalist. Mostly for larger business magazines, in-depth feature. As I mentioned, Shawn introduced us; I asked Adam for an interview and he said no, we were going to go out to dinner instead, and...he...he could dazzle you. It was like he could take over a room—and he took over my brain, my heart. It sounds so stupid now. He had a forceful personality. He knew what he wanted and he knew how to get it." Flora stopped, closed her eyes for a moment. "I think I mistook all that interest and all that energy directed at me for love. I'm not sure he knew how to love. I think he...prized me and Morgan. I was the kind of wife that was acceptable and more than a trophy. And Morgan...I'll have to guess on how he would have been with Morgan as he got older." Her voice steadied. "He cheated on me and he deceived me and it's all a shock because I didn't see it coming, so how dumb am I?"

Are you playing a role? Kirsten thought. *The shocked wife. Oh, she knew nothing.* She decided to show sympathy. "You're not dumb, Flora. You loved him. I can tell you loved him. Love makes us do things we wouldn't otherwise."

"I don't know what he thought he was going to get from Melinda he couldn't get from me."

Kirsten decided there was no point in sharing Melinda's insights as to why the affair had happened. "Men often don't know," Kirsten said. "They do it...because they can."

"I still loved him, despite all that. I feel so stupid. But...if we don't love, if we don't risk, we have nothing."

Kirsten watched her with her son, the gentle way Flora brushed her fingers through the boy's hair. Kirsten stood and looked out the window for a moment and gathered her courage. She turned back to Flora. "Is there a reason why Adam would investigate you?"

"Me?"

"Yes. Like having you followed. Or having your computer hacked."

"No. I've never given him reason to doubt me."

"Nothing with Teddy Chao?"

"Teddy?" For a moment she looked startled, then she nearly laughed. "No. And our neighbors told me they witnessed some legal document for transferring some shares of Zhang Townsend to Teddy. Adam wouldn't have done that if he thought Teddy and I were having an affair."

Now she was the surprised one. "Adam was moving shares?"

"So they said. But no one has found this document yet."

"Has Teddy been acting oddly?"

"These are odd days."

"How about in the days before?"

"Teddy keeps to himself sometimes. I guess he's been a bit more withdrawn." Flora said this as though just realizing it. "I don't understand any of this. His giving part of the company to Teddy, having an affair, why he was with Henry..."

"Flora. You understand, to the police, this all amps up your motive to kill him."

"But I never would have hurt him. It's not in me. I would have just taken Morgan and left him and...lived my life. If I hurt him, I would risk losing Morgan, and I never, ever would risk that."

Kirsten stared at her. Studied her.

And a back corner of her heart believed Flora.

"What?" Flora said.

Kirsten pulled some papers from her bag. "Well, let's go all the way. I found this. Here, in Adam's office, on a flash drive. It's a report on you from a local investigator."

Flora read it. "He had me followed." The words were like stones falling from her mouth.

"Did you confide in anyone that you were meeting with this lawyer?"

"No. No one at the time." She tried to think. She had called the lawyer a couple of times, but not when Adam was home.

"Somehow he knew. And he was trying to get ahead of you."

Flora read the report twice. Her voice rose. "He thought Teddy and I…He let them put a camera in Teddy's room? *In our house?*" The report fell from her hands; disbelief contorted her face.

"I'd get Teddy his own place, real soon," Kirsten said. "And I'd take that to the police before someone else does."

"But this confirms that if I wanted to get away from him, I had an avenue. I didn't have to kill him."

"Did you have a prenup?"

"Yes, but so what? As long as I had Morgan…" She stopped. "Was he looking for a reason to take Morgan away from me? This ridiculous accusation about Teddy…"

"But you have nothing to worry about. They've made an arrest. Although it feels like an arrest for public opinion's sake. Whoever killed them and took Henry's phone could have planted it in Norman's cart."

"I didn't tell Bard to arrest Norman Murphy."

"Why would a homeless guy kill them?" Kirsten asked. "They would just give him the money. Henry wouldn't fight a guy with a gun. And why did Adam have a warehouse?"

"He hadn't had it that long."

"Why did he buy it?" Kirsten hadn't wondered previously. Rich people owned real estate. But for a guy who did most of his business in the tech sector, it seemed an odd choice.

"He said it was for a new investment, but he didn't tell me more. He was closemouthed about his work."

Kirsten seemed to digest this answer. "Do you smoke?" she asked suddenly.

"Me? No."

"Does anyone you know?"

"No. I don't really know anyone who smokes. Why? You found this report. And did you find a cigarette at the crime scene the cops somehow missed? What are you doing?"

Kirsten didn't want to tell her about the cigarette butt Norman had given her. "Just wondered."

"You don't ask without a reason."

Kirsten picked up the report Zach had found in Henry's room. "Here's chapter two." She handed the papers to Flora.

Flora looked at her and then read the pages. She slowly sank into a chair. "I…I don't understand. Henry thought this was on my computer? It's not. I've never researched killing a husband. And if I had, I wouldn't be stupid enough to leave it where it could be found!" She stormed to her bag and for one moment Kirsten thought, *She could have a gun.* But instead she pulled out a small, sleek laptop, opened it with fumbling hands. Typed.

"What's your password?"

"MorganAdam."

"Really?" Such a simple password did not make for a secure laptop.

Flora was trembling. "That file isn't here…it isn't…oh, oh, oh."

Kirsten sat down next to her.

Flora's voice grew ragged. "It's here. Labeled like the report said. It's asking me for a password. I don't know it."

Kirsten watched, impassive.

"If I wanted him dead…and I wanted to hire someone…I wouldn't have left this on my computer. Hidden file or not. I wouldn't risk losing Morgan. I wouldn't."

"Mommy…," Morgan said in a worried voice, and she dropped the computer and scooped up her child. She cried into her son's shoulder. "You can call the police. Okay? You can give them that report. And they can get some computer forensics person to say it was faked, because that's the truth. I didn't kill them. I didn't."

Kirsten got a glass and filled it with water. As she handed it to Flora, she said very quietly, "The format is wrong."

"What?"

"The format of Henry's report. It's his company logo. But that's not the format he used for his analysis reports. Ever. And he'd used the same one for five years. And it was hidden, under a mattress, in a bed he slept in that wasn't made. He made his bed every day that I knew him. That's why you and I are even having this conversation."

Flora shook her head. "I swear to you…I didn't kill them. I know you don't know me and I don't know you, but I swear…"

"Did you hire someone to kill them?"

"No. No."

Kirsten watched her. One widow looking into another's eyes. Trying to see what was in her face, in her heart.

"Then someone planted that on your computer. Who has access?"

Flora took a deep breath. "Adam. Teddy. My neighbors, they help me with Morgan."

"Did you ever take your laptop to the Townsends?"

She started to say no and then remembered: "A week ago. I was over there to see Taylor. Shawn was there too. My laptop was in my bag."

"What about Melinda? Could she have gotten access to the house through Adam?"

"I don't know. I wouldn't think he would bring her around the house."

"Do you use your laptop every day?"

"No…well, usually. But I have a different one for work. Sometimes I might skip a day."

"So if Adam was thinking of leaving you for his mistress and wanted to plant something bad on your computer, he could have taken it during the day. Melinda's a computer whiz, right?"

Flora got up, staggered to the bathroom, and Kirsten heard gagging sounds. She followed after a moment, held Flora's hair back for her, got her fresh water.

"Mommy sick," Morgan announced.

"I brought the laptop so he could watch cartoons on it while we talked," Flora said. "I don't think I can touch it right now."

"He can watch on mine," Kirsten said. She found a cartoon on a streaming service that Morgan giggled at. Flora sat on the couch, a lank of hair hanging in her face.

Kirsten sat next to her.

"Do you know what it's like to have your life vanish in an instant?" Flora said.

"I do. Flora, I want your help."

"My help. Why? I'm the idiot who didn't know her own husband or what he was capable of."

"Obviously, I don't think Norman killed them. I think we need to keep looking."

"You are telling me the people I'm closest to in my life might be capable of framing me for murder. Teddy or Shawn? No."

"All this seems designed to make you look like you have the biggest motive and were taking steps to get rid of Adam. Norman's arrest aside."

"If neither Norman nor I did it, then someone is trying to frame us both, which makes no sense," Flora said. "Wouldn't you pick one person to frame?"

"Henry's report hadn't been found yet. Maybe the killer panicked because you hadn't been arrested. Maybe they thought the frame against you was falling apart. Maybe Norman did take Henry's phone. But that phone call to me doesn't make sense either. I can't see him calling me on it and disguising his voice to tell me my husband was dead. And Norman wouldn't have kept the phone for long, or…been willing to help me. I keep thinking I'm looking at it from the wrong angle." Kirsten leaned forward. "I want to find out who killed Henry. And why they thought they could do that. And then I'm going to make them pay." She didn't mean to say the last part, but she did. Because it was just the two of them, Morgan crouching by the laptop screen, the lights of the city beyond them. For a moment it felt to Kirsten as if she and Flora were the only two people in the world. "Make them pay...forever."

Flora's mouth thinned. "That's what the courts are for."

Kirsten didn't answer. "I read once that when the French Resistance needed to get information from captured Nazis, they left them alone in a room with the widows they'd made. That the Nazis would beg and cry not to be left alone with the widows."

Flora stared at her.

"If I'd been a French war widow, a Nazi would not want to be left alone with me." Kirsten watched Morgan crawl toward her—the short cartoon had ended—and he clambered into her lap. Kirsten looked surprised for a moment, then let him settle onto her. The two of them looked back at Flora, Morgan smiling.

"Why are you telling me this?" Flora whispered.

"Whoever killed Henry killed Adam. They shot Adam neatly and they shot Henry messily. And maybe Adam was being a jerk in his last few weeks, but he was still your jerk. He was this baby's father. And whoever killed them was quite happy to send you to prison for life, away from your child. Do you want justice...or do you want *justice*?"

"I want them to be found and to go to prison forever."

"See, I don't want them to suffer, because they're still existing then. They don't get to live while Henry is dead."

Flora hesitated. For a moment Kirsten thought she was going to snatch her child away from Kirsten's lap. "I could tell the police what you're planning," Flora said in a low voice.

"What am I planning?" Kirsten said innocently. Morgan showed her his flip phone that had won back his attention, and she nodded at him.

"You're basically telling me you're going to kill the killer. And that you have evidence, of a sort?"

"Well, my evidence all points to you. I could tell the police what I've found. I'd tell them I think it smells like a fake, but I could tell them."

Flora's gaze locked on hers. Now Kirsten could see it: that Flora had been a journalist once long ago, and that Kirsten's words had wiped away something that had been on Flora—a film, a shade—and she didn't seem quite so cowed by her grief, or dulled by her shock. "Who do you think it is?"

"Oh, you might go tell the police my theories."

"This is so high school."

"High school just repeats itself again and again—college, job environment, family life, old folks home. High school is training for the world we live in."

"High school didn't train me for this," Flora said. She watched Morgan playing with his toy phone in Kirsten's lap. "I think maybe you're a little unhinged."

"Maybe I am. You think you've lost everything, and you're wrong." Kirsten stared at her as Morgan turned and put his head on Kirsten's shoulder. "You lost a guy you loved who didn't deserve you. But I don't have millions in the bank and a fancy house and a spare penthouse. Or dozens of friends wishing me well or bringing me food. I had Henry. Okay?" Her voice quaked and she brought it under control. "He was everything. And someone with no right took him away from me. Maybe Adam was just…one of the many things you had and so you won't miss him so bad. But I'm going to get whoever really did this. And I'm not risking the police not catching him or expensive lawyers letting him or her walk."

Silence in the penthouse. Then Kirsten said: "Because…I have nothing else to do. Nothing to distract me. This is what I live for now. Do you get it?"

"Yes," Flora said after a moment.

Kirsten stood and handed Morgan back to her.

"I don't have it in me to kill someone," Flora said, folding her arms around Morgan.

"You never know," Kirsten said.

38

The past

The crisis became, under Henry, a series of steps and problems to solve without review or discussion, because there was no time.

"We can't get away with this," Kirsten said, her voice shaking. "We can't. It won't work. The two of you will get in trouble."

"You saved Zach," Henry said, "and I'm not letting anything bad happen to you. Okay? I got this. We just break it down into smaller problems. Solve a step at a time."

A step at a time. Like it was a tutoring session for Zach or starting a service project at school.

Henry said, "He's in trouble, clearly, with his boss. So now he's running. That's our solution. Let's get moving." Kirsten and Zach stared at Henry in disbelief, but they followed his crisp instructions.

They wrapped the body in an old blue-and-gray rug that had been shoved into the back of the attic, one JJ wouldn't miss. Drove Larry's car into the garage, shut the door, put Larry in the trunk of his own car.

Henry drove Larry's car; Zach drove Henry's car and followed him.

Leaving Kirsten alone in the house, waiting for the unknowingly widowed JJ to return.

They left Larry's phone on the dining room table where he'd set it down next to the congealing kung pao chicken and broccoli beef.

"Trust me," Henry had said. "Leaving his phone here will work for the story."

"Story? What story?" Kirsten had said. Like the three of them could build such a convincing lie.

"When JJ gets back, if she gets back before we do, here's what you say and do, step-by-step," Henry had said, and his recommended series of lies became a glowing checklist in her mind.

1. Larry came home, dropped off the food, and left. He didn't eat, but he told you he had to go to his office for a bit. Larry was acting oddly. You say *nothing* about the missing suitcase or clothes that JJ will soon notice are gone from his closet.
2. Zach and Henry had a school project to work on; you say we're at the library or some other kid's house. (Henry was considered an extremely positive influence on Zach and Kirsten, so if Zach was with Henry, JJ would not be concerned.
3. Do not touch the money in the attic. Do not mention the money in the attic to JJ. She might know about it and she might go up and look for it. If she does, stay out of her way; you know nothing. If the police search the house, and find the money in the attic, you know nothing about it. If she doesn't look for it, she doesn't know, and we don't want more trouble from the Fortunatos.

More trouble, she thought. Would...would Steve Fortunato hurt JJ to find out where Larry had gone? Or her or Zach? She tried not to think of it.

There was no blood except one spot on the pull-down attic ladder, and she bleached it as much as she dared, then folded the stairs back up.

She went downstairs and heard Larry's cell phone ringing. She let it ring.

She couldn't bear to eat the food Larry had brought, but they needed some of it to be gone to support the story she'd been eating when he left so she ate and chewed and tasted nothing. She put the rest of the food in the fridge.

His phone began to ring again. She did not answer.

She tried to imagine looking JJ in the face and not losing her composure entirely. She thought about what Larry said to Zach: *What did you tell them? What? You'll get us all killed. Did you tell them about the others? Did you tell them about her?*

What did any of that mean?

The doorbell rang. Hopefully Henry, back.

She answered the door.

He was a dark-haired man, in khakis and an Izod golf shirt, with two large men standing behind him. She knew who he was from the St. Gentian football parent tailgates before the games, although she had only spoken with him a few times.

Steve Fortunato, Paul's father.

The mobster Larry worked for.

"Hey there, Kirsten."

She put on a smile and kept it there. "Hi, Mr. Fortunato."

"Hey, is your uncle Larry home?"

He knew what she and Zach called Larry. "He isn't, sir. He told me he was going to his office to do some work." That was what Henry told her to say, and they'd all thought she'd be saying it to JJ first, not this guy.

Fortunato turned to the two men, muttered something Kirsten couldn't quite hear, and the two men retreated to a black SUV. "How about JJ, she here?"

"No, sir, they're launching a new ale at Magnolia Beer tonight and she's helping them with the event. She's not back yet." Her voice was steadier than she had imagined it could be.

Fortunato frowned. "That is very interesting. I stopped by Larry's office and he wasn't there. He's working on some tax documents for me and it's urgent. He's not answering his cell phone."

"Oh, he left his cell phone here. I think he set it down when he brought me and Zach our dinner and then he left and he must have forgotten it." *This sounds like a lie*, she thought, *it all sounds like a lie.*

"Huh," Steve Fortunato said. He gave her a hard look, but she was a kid, a friend of his son's, so it became a smile. "Okay, Kirsten; well, I really need to get in touch with him."

"Yes, sir, I'll tell him as soon as he's home." And then she improvised. "If he wasn't at his office maybe he's on the way home now? Or maybe he went by JJ's launch party in case she needed help?"

"Well, if he's on his way home, then maybe you wouldn't mind if I came in and waited for him."

She felt a sick tickle along her spine and knew she should have kept her mouth shut. "Sure," she said.

He followed her into the house, through the foyer and into the den just off the kitchen.

"Smells like Chinese food," he said. "From Red Lotus?" It was a popular restaurant close to St. Gentian.

"Yes, sir. Are you hungry? We have plenty." *No no no don't stay and eat; don't stay...*

"You're a sweet girl, thank you, no. But I will take a glass of water."

She nodded and got it for him. The cell phone started ringing again. Steve came into the kitchen, holding his own phone. He picked up Larry's and saw it was his own name on the screen. He stopped the call.

And then he slipped Larry's phone into his pocket, like he had every right to it.

Kirsten made sure her hand wasn't shaking when she handed the glass to him. He went back into the den and she followed him. He studied the bookshelves. "Larry read all these?"

"Yes, sir. Most of them." She knew the ones on the bottom shelf were the ones he hadn't read yet and now never would.

"I don't trust someone who reads so much. I like people who live in the real world, you know what I mean."

The real world. None of this felt real.

He sipped his water. Looked her over. She wasn't sure what to do so she sat down on the chair and he sat down on Larry's recliner, but he didn't recline.

"Paul says you're real book smart."

"Oh, well, I want to go to college and so I need good grades for a scholarship."

"Your biological father was from Denmark, right?"

How did he know that? It wasn't something she ever discussed with Paul. Henry and Zach knew, but she'd told them only after knowing them for two years. But she pushed down her fear of this man and just said, "Yes, sir, he is in Denmark."

"And your mama passed?"

"Yes, sir." She kept her expression neutral.

"So what do you want to study?"

"Computer science, maybe."

"Good jobs in that field. You and Zach are close, right?"

"Yes, sir."

"He's going to come work for me when he's done at LSU."

"Oh. I didn't know he'd already decided that."

Fortunato laughed. "Well, I'm paying his college tuition and so he's an investment for me."

No, no, Zach, she thought. *Don't.* But she just nodded and said, "That's very generous of you, sir."

"Where you going to school?"

"ULL. In Lafayette," she added unnecessarily, because she was anxious.

"That is where it is," he said smoothly. "You seem a little nervous, sweetheart. I don't bite."

"I'm not nervous."

"You know, the reason you and Zach are at St. Gentian is me. I paid the tuitions for the foster kids there." He laughed at her surprised reaction. "You didn't know. I keep it anonymous. I only tell people when I want them to have a good opinion of me."

"Yes, sir. Thank you. I love St. Gentian. It's meant a lot for me to go to school there." That at least was a truth.

"You're very welcome. Paul doesn't even know that, so it's our secret."

She nodded. She felt all twisted inside. She owed him now.

"Computer science, huh? I could use a smart cookie like you too. You gonna come back here after college? Some don't." He shrugged. "They want to go to Houston or Memphis or Austin. They don't appreciate New Orleans."

"I don't know if I'll come back yet," she said. "I don't really have any family except Zach." She hadn't meant to say that.

His glance seemed to burn into her. "Larry and JJ aren't family to you, opening their home for all these years?"

For some reason she decided to be brutally honest with him. "They're really nice, and I'm grateful, but they're not my parents. It's money to them."

"Well, Larry does like his money." Fortunato gave her a crooked smile. "You'd think Larry would be home by now."

"He normally is." She could not believe she was able to keep from falling apart right now. But she was afraid, and she was afraid of this man. She wondered what he would say if she said, *Some of your cash is upstairs; would you like to take that? And oh, Larry won't be stealing from you anymore.*

"Are you all right, sweetheart?" he asked, but she could hear a chill in his tone.

She decided to parry bluntly. "I'm socially awkward," she said. "Paul may have mentioned."

At this confession he laughed. "Ha, Paul wouldn't say that about you, he said you were cute."

Paul thought she was cute? She was sure that was a lie.

The garage door opened. *Oh don't come in announcing you got rid of the body don't don't*, but Zach and Henry had seen the black SUV outside and they came in all smiles.

"Mr. Fortunato, sir!" Zach said, stepping forward to shake the man's hand. Smiling brightly.

"Hello, Zach. You're a bit bruised up there." He gestured at Zach's throat.

"Collision in practice today," Zach said. "Sir, this is our neighbor, Henry North. He's also a senior."

"You're his tutor," Fortunato said. Kirsten wondered if he paid for that as well.

"Yes, sir," Henry said, shaking Fortunato's hand. He glanced at Kirsten.

"Mr. Fortunato's looking for Uncle Larry. He told me he was heading to his office, but he forgot his cell phone. Have y'all heard from him?"

"Uh, we went to a study session, sorry," Henry said.

"Well, Larry must be working hard for me." Steve Fortunato glanced at his watch. "I'll let you all get back to your evening. Kirsten, great to talk with you, young lady. Zach, please tell Larry he needs to call me right away." He nodded at Henry. Just like he was a family friend stopping by, just for a casual hello.

"Bye!" Kirsten said in the brightest voice she'd ever used. She shut the door behind him. Counted to ten so he would step far enough away not to hear and then locked it.

Hurried back to the den; both boys were collapsed on the floor.

"What happened?" she asked.

Henry said, "We got rid of him."

"Where? How?" she asked.

"You don't need to know; it'd make you an accessory. I saw that on TV."

"I killed him," she said and the words, and the shock of it, overwhelmed her and she burst into tears.

"You're steel," Henry said, shaking her and looking into her eyes. "You didn't crack with that guy here and he's a tough test. You'll be fine."

Kirsten felt dizzy with delayed shock. "Him? How am I supposed to act around JJ? How do I even look her in the face?"

"Day by day. Step away from her when you need to."

"Henry, you don't have to live with her. But what I did...How do I deal with what I've done?"

"Larry was a bad person," Henry said. "He was stealing from crooks. He was a criminal. He would have killed Zach and then killed you. You did what you had to do. You'll act just fine because if any of us crack, we all go to prison. And if Steve Fortunato finds out we know what Larry was doing, he won't like us knowing his business. We're trapped. So the only way out is to stay quiet and act normal."

The hard truth of it hung in the air.

Henry embraced her and then Zach embraced them both. Zach whispered to her: "It will be okay, no one will ever know, we'll protect you."

"I'm going to wait here until JJ gets home," Henry said. "To help you both. This is the plan. Kirsten, go upstairs and go to bed."

"I haven't done any of my homework. I'm not sure I could," she said dully.

"Go to bed. Tell JJ you're sick if she asks. Upset stomach," he added helpfully. "He's not coming home and eventually she's going to panic; she's going to call the police. We stick together on our story."

The three of them repeated their story: Larry came home (true); he brought Chinese food (true); said he was going to his office to work on something (lie). Just the one little lie.

"Zach, you and I are going to play video games until JJ's back. Okay? I'm sticking with you."

You got rid of a body. You stayed calm and got rid of a body. You're saving me and Zach. You're saving us. She grabbed Henry's hand. He squeezed it back.

This will never work, she thought. *But we have to try.*

–

But Henry's step-by-step plan did work. Sort of.

JJ got home late. She came up and checked on Kirsten, who lay fake-asleep in the bed. JJ touched the back of her hand against her forehead to see if she had a fever, which of course she didn't. "The boys said you were sick."

"It's just my stomach. I think dinner disagreed with me," Kirsten murmured. *Also, I killed your husband. I'm sorry. I didn't mean to.*

"Okay, honey, do you want something for nausea?"

"I took some medicine. I just want to sleep." What a liar she was. Henry had been a genius telling her to go to bed; if she got shaky, JJ would think it was the illness.

"I wish Larry hadn't forgotten his phone. He's not answering at the office," JJ said.

Kirsten didn't answer, just burrowed into the bed.

"Good night, honey."

Honey. She heard the sound of Larry's cracking neck. "Good night, Aunt JJ."

JJ shut the door and went back downstairs to wait for a man who was never coming home. Kirsten lay very still. She tried to read her book, but she was afraid if she associated reading with tonight it would be forever ruined for her. She turned off the light and just stared into the darkness. She heard Zack and Henry coming up to Zach's room and her door opened and shut very quickly.

"It's me," Henry said softly. "JJ is watching TV. She's curled up with a blanket over her. She's just waiting for him to come in. Hopefully she'll fall asleep on the couch and won't raise the alarm until morning."

Kirsten sat up in the dark. She heard him kneel by her bed. "How? How? I have to know."

"Bayou Sauvage. Weighted down. The gators..." Step-by-step, and she didn't want to hear about that final step.

She was glad he couldn't see her face. Then he said: "We left his car parked on a street near the airport. They'll think he dumped it there. No trace of him on a flight, but the Fortunatos are going to think he knew he got caught and ran."

"How are you capable of this?" she whispered. And she thought: *He's wondering what you're capable of. He'll always think you're a murderer.*

"Because it's my fault. I shouldn't have said anything to you. You wouldn't have gone up into the attic if not for me, would you?"

"This will never work," she said.

"It will. I think quick. I break things down into problems and solutions. I've thought of everything."

Except that I'm weak and Zach and I have to live with the woman I widowed in this house for the next several months. "But you were just a witness. Now you're deep into this. You broke the law."

"I'm helping my two best friends."

"Henry."

In the dark his thumb found her cheek and wiped the tears away. He put his forehead against hers. "I will never let anything bad happen to you. Never. Okay?"

She nodded.

He got up and went out.

This was why she *had* to hold it together. For Henry.

-

It unfolded.

JJ fell asleep on the coach, as she'd had some samples of the new IPA at the brewery. She woke at 6:00 a.m. No Larry. She called all their friends, the hospitals—no Larry. She called the police. Larry had not been missing for the requisite hours. She drove to his office. He wasn't there.

She came back and sent the kids to school, although Zach and Kirsten both volunteered to stay with her. JJ tearfully told them that it was all right, he'd be home soon. They both went to school in a daze.

They got home that afternoon. Steve Fortunato was there, talking quietly to JJ with his two assistants waiting in the car. JJ was making a list of Larry's family members: cousins in Opelousas, an aunt in Slidell, college friends in Baton Rouge, Beaumont, and Houston.

Kirsten felt a cold terror when she saw Fortunato. He had commented on her nervousness last night and now maybe he'd look at her twitchiness in a new light with Larry missing. She steadied herself.

"Your foster father is missing," JJ said tearfully.

Kirsten and Zach both hugged JJ and Kirsten worried her hug felt insincere. "What can we do?" she asked.

"We're going to call all the people on this list. His friends, his family, in case anyone has heard from him."

"Okay," Kirsten said.

"You were the last person to see him, sweetheart," Fortunato said to Kirsten. "Can you tell us anything, anything at all he said? Any place other than the office he mentioned where he might go?" There was no accusatory tone in his voice and it made it easier for her to stick to the story.

"No…he seemed in a hurry. He put down the food and his phone and told me to go ahead and eat if I was hungry. Then…" She paused. "He went into y'all's bedroom. I went and got my plate and sat in the dining room and ate and read a history chapter for school. I was hungry and I didn't want to wait for Zach, plus I had homework." She stopped again, thinking, taking it step-by-step. "Uncle Larry went upstairs and then went out to the garage; I heard the door open and shut. And then he came back in and told me bye, and he'd be back in a bit. And then he went out again."

"So he went to the garage twice?" Fortunato asked.

Kirsten nodded, as if she hadn't thought of it that way. "Yeah, I guess he did."

Kirsten saw Fortunato and JJ exchange a look. They were trying to figure out how he'd loaded his missing suitcase without Kirsten noticing.

"Did you see him carry out a suitcase?" JJ asked.

"No," Kirsten said. "I would have mentioned that. And I would have asked him where he was going. But I was in the dining room and I didn't see him going out to the garage."

JJ and Fortunato looked at each other again. He cleared his throat. "I don't think we need to have the kids help with the phone lists," Fortunato said. "My staff and the other football parents are happy to make the calls."

"So he took a suitcase? Where do you think Uncle Larry has gone?" Kirsten said, her voice rising slightly. "Has he left us? Am I going to another family?" Now her voice trembled in fear.

"No, honey, I'm sure he hasn't," JJ said, trying to sound optimistic. She embraced Kirsten and Kirsten forced herself not to tremble. She hugged JJ back, closed her eyes. "No one is going to move you again, I promise you that," JJ said.

"Maybe he's hurt," Zach said. He looked at Steve Fortunato, not at Kirsten.

"I called the hospitals," JJ said. "Kids, please, think. Has he said anything unusual, anything that might help us make sense of this?"

"Shouldn't we call the police?" Kirsten said, feeling that someone had to say it, hoping they wouldn't.

"They won't do anything for forty-eight hours," Fortunato said. "And, well, we'd like to find him on our own."

Of course he didn't want the police involved. Find Larry, maybe find the money. Was the money even still in the attic? She had thought last night, as she lay burrowed under her blanket, that they should have dumped the money with Larry—it would appear he'd taken off with it—but if the Fortunatos got their cash back, maybe they'd leave her little foster family alone.

JJ patted her shoulder reassuringly.

And Kirsten realized that she and Zach weren't suspects. At all. At least not so far and not to JJ or Fortunato. The possibility that Kirsten had accidentally killed Larry and Zach had disposed of the body did not occur *at all* to the grown-ups. They were kids; they wouldn't have been capable of such a thing. Kirsten thought a large neon sign might as well be on her forehead flashing "Killer," but she just looked like the boring, studious girl she had always seen herself as. She tried to be normal. Or to act as the innocent Kirsten would act.

People brought food. Football parents and Fortunato people started to call the friends and relatives on the long list. JJ wrote an impassioned Faceplace plea. Finally the police got involved, when Larry's aunt in Slidell started demanding to know why they hadn't been called yet.

Larry's car was found near the airport. The missing suitcase wasn't in the trunk (it was with him in Bayou Sauvage, Kirsten suspected, but she did not ask). Kirsten and Zach stood behind JJ in the front yard with the news stations filming as JJ tearfully pleaded for Larry to come home, or if someone had taken him, to please let him go. Zach had his arm around Kirsten and she wondered what would happen if she shoved JJ aside and confessed on camera. But then Zach and Henry would go to jail. They were both eighteen. She would go to juvie and there would be a bad TV movie made about her life.

Or the Fortunatos would arrange to kill them all. If she confessed, she would have to talk about the money. The reason why Uncle Larry had tried to kill Zach.

The Fortunato people, when they were over at the house, never searched anywhere or went into the attic. Maybe JJ didn't know about the money. Kirsten herself did not dare go up into the attic to see if it was still there, and there wasn't a time in the weeks that followed when she could have because other people were constantly around. JJ was on leave from her job, and there were always other parents there, lending support.

Did you tell them about the others? Did you tell them about her?

She wanted to ask Zach what Larry's last words meant, but she didn't dare whisper any strand of the truth, not with JJ in the house, or Fortunato, or anyone else. They talked, but not about this. Never about this.

The crank calls and tips poured into the police: Larry had been spotted in Houston, boarding a flight for Brazil; Larry had run to Mexico; Larry had been kidnapped; Larry had turned on the Fortunatos and gone into witness protection, leaving JJ and the kids to fend for themselves.

For ten days the vanished accountant was the lead story, until three men were shot near the French Quarter, and then the story lost momentum. Kirsten and Zach didn't go to school for a week, and then they went back and everyone was so nice to them. Especially Paul, who seemed to think they might know where their foster father was and asked gentle questions about it until Kirsten finally snapped at him, "Of course we don't know. Why would he tell us? We're moving out of his house in a few months. We're not his actual kids, you know."

And that shut Paul up.

"He suspects," Henry said to them both as they stood alone after school in the St. Gentian courtyard. It was the one place they could talk and not be noticed or heard. "Paul mentions what he overhears to Zach and then that night Larry vanishes."

"Larry could have already known he was in trouble." The thought of the Fortunatos believing that she and Zach knew where Larry was scared her. But they'd never cornered her or Zach to question them.

A local reporter wrote a story mentioning that Larry Melancon was, after all, a missing accountant with ties to the Fortunato family, but Steve had his lawyers respond that the Fortunato businesses were entirely legitimate and he deeply resented any suggestion they were not. The police and the FBI dug into Larry's files, but his computers had been wiped clean. The Fortunatos had erased any possible trails that law enforcement might have followed.

JJ sank into a depression. The disappearance undid her and Kirsten's heart ached for her. JJ was waiting for the impossible—for Larry to come home.

The school year inched along. Zach and Paul both played varsity basketball, and JJ and Fortunato would not sit near each other; JJ, Kirsten decided, had started to figure out that Fortunato's interest in her missing husband was not just the concern of one football father for another. She wondered how much JJ knew about Larry's activities. Kirsten and Henry would sit together on the top row of the bleachers, watching St. Gentian play St. Martin or Newman, away from everyone. They could whisper and not be overheard.

"How is she?" Henry asked during the last home game.

"She still has that list of relatives and friends. I think she believes one of them is hiding him. There's a name circled on there. Linda Davidson. I think she was Larry's college girlfriend at LSU. JJ calls her and keeps asking if she's sure she doesn't know where Larry is. If she's hiding him, JJ just wants to know if he's all right."

Henry closed his eyes. "I feel for her. When you and Zach leave she'll be alone in that house."

"I think she'll just keep fostering kids. Like, forever, so she won't be lonely. I don't know. She and Larry were a good team." Until he tried to kill Zach.

"A good team," Henry murmured. And for the first time, he took her hand.

She could tell he was waiting to see if she pulled her hand away. She didn't.

They were bound together like he'd given her an engagement ring. He had done the unimaginable for her, with a steady resolve and cool that belied his years. She used to wonder about Henry, but then she read accounts of extraordinary bravery and resourcefulness shown by soldiers his age, and she realized: *This was Henry's battlefield, and he fought for me.*

"I did it because I wanted to protect you and give you the life you deserve," he said very quietly, but she could hear his words under the cheers as Paul sank a basket and St. Gentian regained the lead. "You don't owe me. You will never owe me. I don't want it to be that way between us." He was looking straight ahead. Not at her.

She looked at him. A boy in glasses. But he was a warrior underneath that calm facade, a coolheaded knight with fire in his eyes who had saved her and Zach.

She squeezed his hand. She had grown to love his plain, unremarkable face. She wanted to kiss him. So she turned his chin toward her and she did just that. A sweet, short kiss, since they were out in public. He smiled and he lowered his eyes and then she saw JJ watching them, ten rows down, and then she turned her attention back to the court because Zach had the ball, driving down toward the basket.

-

The school year ended, then a long awkward summer, mostly spent out of the house. Zach hung around with Paul a lot. Kirsten wondered how he managed, his guard always up so he wouldn't betray any knowledge of Larry's fate. Kirsten tried to make amends by helping JJ around the house. But JJ sank into a blue funk. She went to work at the microbrewery, came home, sat on the couch, then stared into space or mindlessly watched TV for hours. Kirsten did the cleaning and the cooking (sometimes making Zach help), worked a part-time job at a mall candy store, went to movies with Henry, and thought, *I just have to make it until the day we leave for college.*

That day finally came. They were up in their rooms, and JJ was downstairs on the couch, sinking into it, staring off into nothing.

"You can't let Steve Fortunato pay for college," Kirsten said. "You'll be bound to them forever."

"I don't have a choice. I don't have scholarships like you." Zach was packing. She was already packed. Henry was going to drive Zach to Baton Rouge to attend LSU, then take himself and Kirsten farther west to Lafayette and ULL. Henry's parents were following in an SUV full of Henry's stuff. Zach and Kirsten barely had anything to take.

"Don't go to work for them after college then," she said.

"I have to, for a while," Zach said. "It will be fine. I promise you, it's okay." His voice was steady and she didn't know how to say: *I'm scared for you. I'm scared for what your life will be.*

Then they heard the noise.

The creak of the attic ladder being lowered outside their bedrooms. They looked at each other. Zach went and opened the door in time to see JJ climbing up the steps.

They stared at each other. Kirsten had a sudden vision of having missed a bloodstain. The bat was gone, in the bayou with Larry.

They could hear JJ rummaging around up there. Pacing. Walking. Kirsten looked at Zach in wordless terror. Zach opened his door.

"That's odd," they heard her say.

Kirsten slowly climbed up the ladder. She saw JJ looking around the attic. "What is it?" she said.

"I had a rug up here I was going to give you for your dorm room. Blue and gray."

The rug Larry's body was wrapped in. "Oh. I really don't need a rug," Kirsten said. "My roommate said she'd bring one in school colors."

"Well, but where is it?" JJ put her hands on her hips. "I'm sure I didn't throw it out."

Kirsten glanced in the other direction, through the path of the old boxes.

The stack of coolers was gone. She stared at the emptiness.

She looked back at JJ, and JJ was watching her stare at the space where the money had been.

"I don't know," Kirsten said.

"I guess you'll have to do without a rug," JJ said, but something had shifted in her voice. Something that made Kirsten want to run.

"Thanks for thinking of it for me," Kirsten said. She went down the stairs.

JJ lingered in the attic another five minutes before she came down.

The coolers were gone. Had JJ found them and taken the money? Or had the Fortunatos? It didn't matter; the coolers were gone. Thousands upon thousands of dollars.

She wondered: *Zach, you knew the money was there. Did you take it?*

She didn't dare ask. She didn't want to know. She was glad the money was gone; it wasn't something she could have looked at again.

When they were all gathered outside, the good-byes were awkward. JJ told them they could always come back for Thanksgiving and to call her if they needed anything. She didn't have more foster children coming right now—she needed a break from it, she said, and it was hard without Larry—but she wanted to hear from them. Kirsten tried to hug her and JJ allowed it, but she felt stiff and awkward. Kirsten stepped back quickly.

"The house is gonna feel so empty now," JJ said.

I'm sorry, Kirsten wanted to say. *I'm so sorry.* But she said nothing.

"We'll call you," Zach said. The hug JJ gave him was awkward too. Her gaze kept flickering between the two of them.

"I'll be fine," JJ answered. But this was in front of Henry's parents, and Kirsten thought it had the air of a performance, that same bright-toned reminder her first day with JJ that studies came first.

She suspects, Kirsten thought. *The missing rug. Me looking at the spot where the coolers were. She suspects.*

But she can't prove anything.

-

Finally in the car and headed down the interstate, Henry's parents not far behind, it was the first time the three of them had been alone in a long while. Truly alone.

"What did Larry mean," Kirsten began, "when he said did you tell them about the others? Or her? Do you think he meant JJ? Maybe she knew all about that money."

"Why are you asking me that now?"

"Because I think about it every day."

Zach didn't answer for a long minute. "I can wait you out," Kirsten said.

"When we would go fishing, sometimes he'd get a blue cooler from the attic and a green cooler from the garage. We'd go to a park and fish and I wasn't allowed to open the blue cooler. One time I did when he went to go piss. The blue cooler was full of cash. I closed it and acted like I didn't know. He'd leave behind the blue cooler. Just on the shore, or by the picnic table. Once I watched in the rearview and a woman and a girl came out of the woods and grabbed it. Like they were waiting for us to leave."

"Where did you fish?" Kirsten asked.

"Sometimes we'd go all the way to Baton Rouge. Sometimes much closer. Never the same place."

"Why didn't you tell me this?" Kirsten asked.

"Because why would I? Knowing about cash he was spreading around Louisiana would only make trouble for you," Zach said.

So he had been leaving money for these two—at least, and maybe other people; maybe those were *the others*—to pick up? Accomplices in his plot to stash and squirrel away stolen money. Was he doing this for himself? For a rival mob?

"If you knew about the money, you could have taken it."

"Do I look crazy?" Zach said. "Hell no."

"Did you tell the Fortunatos it was there?" she asked. Maybe they came and took it away.

"No. We all agreed."

"So either JJ found the coolers and realized it was theirs and gave it back to them, or she took it and they don't have it back," Henry said.

"That's not the point," Kirsten said. "She saw me looking right where it was."

"You were just looking around the attic. You're being paranoid," Henry said.

"Paul hasn't said a word to me about the money," Zach said. "They don't ask and I don't tell."

"But they're paying for your college," Kirsten said.

"I'm not putting that in jeopardy by bringing up Larry."

"So maybe if it's not JJ, then that's who he meant by 'her.' This lady picking up the cash."

"I guess so. He told me nothing. I think he didn't give a crap about fishing and I was cover for him so JJ wouldn't suspect. I don't know who the *her* is."

"What did they look like?"

"Didn't really see them. Baseball caps and sunglasses. We were speeding away." Zach glanced at her. "Kirsten?"

"What?"

"This is the very last time we discuss this. Never again. Okay?"

"All right."

"We got to stick together." Zach glanced at Henry, who was driving. "You're my sister."

"Not really," she said, her standard answer.

"Always really," he said.

She believed him.

-

So Kirsten started college with anxiety about her scholarships and if she'd be able to ace her courses, and wondering if she'd get along with her roommate, and being nervous about being smart enough and good enough and wondering if JJ or the Fortunatos would appear at her dorm room asking, *Where is he? We know you know.*

JJ called her once a week for the first few weeks. The conversations tried to be pleasant but always ended up strained.

"Odd thing," JJ said at the end of her first month at college. "I found something of Larry's."

"What?"

"It doesn't matter. But it's just something he wouldn't have left behind if he had a choice. If he just left us all. He would have taken it with him."

"What was it?"

JJ didn't answer.

In the spring semester of their freshman year, Henry's great-uncle died in New Orleans and he went home for the funeral. He called her when he got back and asked her to meet him downstairs. Something in the tone of his voice sounded off.

It was raining lightly, and people weren't out. No one was near them.

He didn't waste time.

"I saw JJ. She's moving out of the house. It's for sale."

"Oh. Why?"

"She said she can't afford to keep it, not without Larry's income." He stuck his hands in his pockets.

"Where is she going?"

"I think into an apartment. There was a girl there, helping her. Her new foster."

"Oh." Kirsten felt a sick mix of relief and worry. She had spent Thanksgiving at school, studying, and then Christmas break with her roommate's family in Natchitoches, who were wonderful and very parental and had taken Kirsten into their hearts. Zach had spent it with Paul and his family. JJ had presumably been alone, but Kirsten, once freed of the house, could not face going back to it. It would be like reentering a prison. "Did she ask about me?"

"Yes. I told her we were dating and she said to tell you hi."

"That moment when she saw me looking at the spot where the coolers were. And she couldn't find her rug. I still think she suspects we know something."

"She doesn't. She hasn't gone to the police."

"But..."

"If she suspected, she would go to the cops. She hasn't. We're fine."

"Is she okay?"

Henry took her hand. "I don't know. It's probably a good sign she's fostering another kid. Keeping herself busy."

"A little kid?"

"No, a year or two younger than us, I'd guess. She was helping JJ load the U-Haul. We didn't talk."

"She must miss Larry terribly," Kirsten said suddenly. "I think if someone took you from me…"

"Hey. Hey." Henry ran a thumb along her jaw. "She'll be okay. In a way maybe she's better off without Larry."

"She just lost her house, Henry. Don't pretty up what we did."

"Have you talked to her?"

"Not since I didn't come back for Thanksgiving. Maybe that was a mistake. Maybe it made her more suspicious."

"Or maybe you're just another foster kid moving on with her life. They had a total of six of them over the years. The others didn't come back, did they?"

She shook her head. "The others weren't there when she lost her husband."

He took her in his arms and kissed her. She rested her head on his shoulder. "I want her to be okay," she said. "I can't make it okay, but…"

"I know. I know." He held her. "I stopped at LSU before I got here. To see Zach."

"Is he all right?" They talked once a week at least, and Zach had come twice during the first semester to visit her and Henry. It was only an hour-long drive along I-10.

"Yeah. He's living with Paul."

"Oh, no," she said. "He was staying in the dorm…."

"Apparently Paul likes having a roommate in the condo that his dad bought for him. So Zach's moved in." He shrugged. "They seem fine."

"Zach can't be on his guard all the time."

"Kirsten, let's say the Fortunatos found out about Larry." He lowered his voice, even though no one was around. "So what?"

"So what?" Her knees felt weak. "I don't think they'll shrug it off."

"The money is gone. Either they have it, or JJ has it, because we don't."

"Or whoever he was giving it to..."

"What, broke into the house and took it? No." He put his hands on her shoulders. "My point is he was stealing from them, and I don't think they care if he's dead or who killed him. His death stopped the stealing. You did them a favor."

"I did...them a favor."

"Let's say JJ goes to them. Says she's suspicious of you. What are they going to do about it—not that you know where he's hiding, but that you killed him? Nothing. He was a problem. He's not a problem anymore."

"Isn't the Mafia about honor and blood vengeance and stuff?"

"They're not the Mafia and I don't think that applies to their accountants."

"You think Zach has said something to them?"

"You saved Zach's life. He's your brother. Zach would never betray you." He slid an arm around her shoulders. "I'm just saying, let JJ go on with her life, and we'll go on with ours." He paused. She thought he was going to say something else. But he didn't, not in that moment, talking of dark things, but two days later, at dinner, he told her that he loved her.

39

The past

They graduated college. Henry popped the question. She said yes.

Henry's mother did a post on her Faceplace page, like an old-fashioned engagement announcement you'd have seen in a newspaper, and described Kirsten as the "daughter of Dr. Erik Plumm of Copenhagen, Denmark, and the late Jacquia Deslatte of New Orleans." Henry had asked if she wanted to try to contact her father before the wedding, and the very thought made her ill. That Henry's mother even listed her cowardly father had infuriated her, and despite Brenda North's apology Kirsten had been at a low simmer of anger for two days.

But it was on Faceplace, and then the phone rang at Henry's parents' house and Kirsten answered it as the Norths were outside and she'd just come back in to grab a beer. Booze calmed her, if she didn't overindulge. Even being next door to the house where *it* happened made her nervous. The new people living there seemed nice—young family with two kids who would attend St. Gentian. She wondered if it was now haunted as she cracked open the beer. If Larry's ghost rambled in the attic…looking for the teenagers who ended him when he tried to end them…it made her not want to look out the windows at night.

The phone rang. She answered it. "North residence."

Silence for four beats, then: "Kirsten?"

"Yes?" She knew who it was.

"It's JJ."

"Hi. How are you?"

"I'm all right. Congrats on your engagement." She paused. "I hope you're very happy."

"Thanks, JJ." She felt she should apologize for not being in touch. But the words wouldn't come. JJ might be calling in hopes of an invitation. "Are you still in New Orleans?"

"Oh, yes. How is Zach?"

"He's fine."

"I wonder…if you and Zach would meet me for a coffee."

Kirsten said, "Okay," although she wanted to scream *No!* "Are you all right?"

"Yes. I just want to talk…about something maybe we should have talked about before."

I put this behind me. I'm happy. I'm finally happy and I have a good life ahead of me and now you call me.

"Um, okay, when?" *She suspects. She knows something.* But there was no evidence to be found. So it was just a coffee, and maybe she just needs to talk about Larry. To someone who knew him. Kirsten told herself she could do this.

"Tomorrow. Café Duris?" It was a cool little coffee place not far from the microbrewery.

"Sure," she said.

"Say around eleven, before lunch? Would that work?"

"Sure, JJ. I'll see you then."

-

"Do you want me to go with you?" Henry asked.

"No. She said me and Zach."

"I could come and sit nearby…."

"Quit trying to fix it, Henry." She put her hand on his cheek. She didn't know she could love another person this much.

"Okay," Henry said. "I just…"

"I can handle seeing her. Maybe she just wants to wish me well to my face."

"Then she would have asked for me and you, not you and Zach."

The thought was unsettling. "I'll be fine."

"What does Zach say?"

"He told me he'll be there." She hadn't seen Zach in a month. She talked to him on the phone, but the Fortunatos kept him busy on the weekends. She was afraid to ask what they had him doing.

"All right. But if she accuses you, admit nothing. Nothing. We stick with the story."

"I don't need you to tell me that."

"I'm sorry." He hugged her. She hugged him back.

You can do this, Kirsten thought. *It's just coffee. She has no proof.*

-

Café Duris had outdoor seating, and it was a fine spring day in New Orleans. She parked in a lot two blocks away and walked to the café. JJ was already there, sitting, a cappuccino in front of her. Zach wasn't there yet. She had told him to get there early so she wouldn't have to be alone with JJ, and of course he wasn't here.

Put on your smile; make this work, Kirsten thought. She waved at JJ, went inside to the counter, got a coffee, and then went out onto the patio.

"Hi," JJ said.

"Hi," Kirsten said. She set down her coffee and wondered if she should hug JJ, but JJ made no move to stand so Kirsten sat down.

"Where's Zach?" JJ asked.

"We didn't come together.... He'll be here in a minute. You look good." Which JJ didn't; she looked like she hadn't slept much, frazzled. But JJ nodded and gave an awkward smile and said, "Thanks."

"How have things been going?" Kirsten said. "Henry said you were still fostering."

"Oh. Sort of. Just once more. Not again." She cleared her throat. "I'm happy for you and Henry."

Maybe this was nothing more than wrangling a wedding invitation, Kirsten thought, and just saying hello. She didn't want to invite JJ, but she also didn't want to raise questions among Henry's parents' friends by not inviting her. "Thank you. I need your new address to send you an invitation." There, done; she couldn't fight with herself anymore about it.

"Oh. That's kind of you." She bit at her lip. "Is Zach still friends with the Fortunatos?" Something in her voice. Worry. Concern.

"Yes. He's been working for one of their real estate companies during the summers."

"I guess he'll go to work for them now?"

"Yes. I think so."

"Be nice if you talked him out of that."

"You know what he's like. I can't."

"And you and Henry? You're staying here?"

"Henry and I both got jobs here, so we're lucky."

"Good. Congrats."

"Are you still at the microbrewery?"

"Oh, yes. They can't run the place without me." She sipped at her coffee. "The police don't have any new information in Larry's disappearance. I thought you should know that." Then her gaze met Kirsten's.

"I'm sorry." She didn't know what else to say.

"It's strange how he could just vanish so thoroughly. I don't know how he's managed to stay under the radar for four years."

What was she to say to this? Did she honestly believe he was still alive? Or was this just a test to see Kirsten's reaction? Kirsten took refuge in her coffee.

"I mean, he loved me, I thought he loved me…."

Kirsten wanted to say the comforting words. She needed to say them for the story. "He did."

"He didn't love me as much as I thought…he…Oh, there's Zach!" She waved and Kirsten turned and saw Zach about two blocks away, walking fast because he was late and JJ said, "He's gotten even bigger."

And he had, and instead of his typical baseball cap and shorts and T-shirt he was wearing all black, the black dress shirt and the blazer tight across his frame, and his thick hair grown long and slicked back, dark glasses on.

They had...changed him. Deeper than the clothes. She could see it in the arrogant way he walked, the way his gaze shot around, surveying his surroundings, and then his stare found her and he gave this little half smile that seemed like a distant echo of the boy who saved her a place at lunch, who told her she was, in every way that mattered, his sister.

The boy she'd killed a man to save.

That boy was gone.

"Oh, Zach," she whispered to herself.

And then there were two loud pops, and she saw Zach doubling over and running and it was only when the car coming up the street accelerated like crazy and roared past them and JJ screamed that Kirsten realized it was gunfire.

And that someone was shooting at Zach.

And he was *shooting back*, crouched behind a parked car, aiming at the car as it sped away from them.

The car was gone and Zach looked at her. Making sure she was all right. Kirsten bolted from the patio to him. "Are you okay? Are you hit?" She felt along his chest, his shoulders.

"No. I'm fine." He stilled her hands, put the gun in the holster under his jacket. His gaze shifting past her to see if the danger was returning for a second try.

"Why is someone shooting at you?" she screamed. She couldn't even begin to talk about him returning fire.

"I don't know. I don't know." He was shaken and Kirsten hugged him. He didn't hug her back.

"What do they have you doing? What?" And she didn't even have to say their names: the Fortunatos.

"I need to get out of here," he said. "I can't be talking to cops right now." And he hurried away, not the way he'd come, but walking onto a side street, vanishing from sight.

Kirsten watched him go. She turned back and walked to where JJ stood by their table, her face pale with shock.

"Is he all right?" JJ asked. A crowd was gathered in front of Café Duris now that the shooting had ceased. Talking and pointing at where windshields in parked cars had been starred, someone calling the police and trying to describe the shooter's vehicle. Kirsten couldn't have told anyone what car it was or what the driver looked like—she'd seen a flash of dark glasses and a baseball cap, the window lowered, but nothing helpful that registered.

"He doesn't know why anyone would do that," Kirsten said to JJ. Her voice was hoarse.

JJ grabbed her arm and hustled her away from the crowd. All the way to the street corner where Zach had turned and gone from sight. JJ was shaking. "You tell him…not to work for the Fortunatos. They're…Tell him, don't do it." Her voice was jagged. "He should leave New Orleans. Maybe you both should."

"Why?" she asked JJ. "Why should I leave?"

"Nothing good will come of this. Just go. Put distance between yourself and them."

"I'm not leaving. No one is chasing me out." She couldn't leave Zach…not because of this. And her life with Henry was here.

JJ blinked for a moment. "Okay, then. Good-bye, Kirsten." She turned and hurried away, just as the NOPD cars were pulling up.

Kirsten watched her leave. She walked away too; she didn't want to be pointed out as a witness who had spoken to the target, the police figuring out the man she rushed to comfort was her foster brother, and that they were the former foster children of a missing CPA who worked for a criminal syndicate.

She had her wedding to plan.

Kirsten kept her word and invited JJ to the wedding, but she didn't respond or come. Kirsten suspected it was because Steve Fortunato and his wife and Paul were going to be there (Zach begged and insisted and she gave in); and someone told her at the wedding that JJ had left town. She had taken the advice she'd tried to give Kirsten.

Kirsten hoped she found peace.

Zach was her choice to walk her down the aisle. They stood in the church foyer, alone for a moment, about to head down, her a sudden bundle of nerves, Zach calm.

"Are you going to tell me what happened at the café?" She thought asking him right now, in this moment, might throw him off guard.

His gaze held hers. "I honestly don't know what happened," he said, and for a moment she believed him.

He hugged her and said, "Be happy. I want that for you."

"Be safe," she said. "I want that for you."

"You're my sister," he whispered.

"Not really."

"Always really." He kissed her cheek.

She wondered if he had a gun on underneath his tuxedo jacket. She hugged him back; he didn't.

"Don't cry," he said. "It's a happy day."

"One tear is not crying." She wiped at her cheek quickly, and it was gone.

He gave her his arm and they started walking forward, surrounded by the music and the beaming smiles of the guests. And Henry, the handsomest man in the world to her, waited for her at the altar.

During the large number of toasts at the reception, Steve Fortunato wished her and Henry every happiness. She smiled and sipped the champagne. She looked for Zach. When she spotted him, she saw Paul Fortunato whispering in his ear, Zach nodding and smiling.

They went on a cheap honeymoon cruise out of New Orleans, and that night lying next to her husband, Kirsten thought, *God shuts a window and opens a door.* Her old life was finished; her new life could start now.

40

Morgan fell asleep on the couch.

"So," Kirsten said. "Let's figure this out."

Flora had wiped away her tears and Kirsten could see a new resolve on her face. *But how far would she go?* If Kirsten killed the person who was framing Flora, it wouldn't help Flora unless there was evidence of the frame as well. Kirsten pushed the thought away. First things first. Step one: find the killer.

Flora followed Kirsten to the penthouse office. Kirsten had used the inside of the closet door, which could be closed and therefore hidden, to reassemble her printouts and notes so she could look for connections. Articles and photos of Adam, of Flora. She put the news accounts of her husband's murder in the middle.

Flora silently studied the printouts. "This is what you think is interesting about me?"

"It's what the world says about you. Why did you give up journalism?"

"It made Adam uncomfortable."

"So?" *You have no idea how uncomfortable Henry could make me*, she thought. Try falling totally in love with a guy who can hide a body at age eighteen with the cool of a serial killer. "He could have adjusted."

"I know," Flora said. "I think I liked the theory of journalism more than the practice. That you could coolly gather the facts and tell the story. I was good at it, but there's so much...bull you run up against, especially as a woman. I never thought I'd let a husband—oh, 'dictate' isn't the right word—let's say influence my decision so much. I had been doing business reporting and after I met Adam everything seemed like a possible conflict of interest. He might invest in a competitor of someone I wrote about, or hire away a CEO I'd profiled...and it just seemed easier in that moment to make a change. I got the job running PR for the foundation. And then when the founder retired, I got the top job." She sighed. "I always wondered if it was because I was really good at my PR job or that I had money—Adam's money—and therefore more connections."

"I'm sure you were good at your job," Kirsten said. It seemed the right thing to say.

"I'm not sure I was. Writing for online, the level of burnout is extreme. I felt like the quality was dropping. I was a hard worker, but I was supposed to be doing in-depth stories and fast web stories. My new editor had TV anchor experience and no print. I had specific experience writing about medicine and business and I got taken off those beats. He wanted me to write about the social stuff, local Austin tech millionaires doing good, profiles of how they were changing the city. It got tiresome. I lost my energy, my appetite for it. And Adam talked me into leaving it at the right time." She swallowed. "I used to think when Morgan got older I'd go back to it. Maybe start a magazine or a news website, something niche but that I could grow. Something of my own."

"Look," Kirsten said, pointing at one of the pictures she'd found. A photo of Flora when she was writing for the Austin paper, following the governor of Texas as he stormed away from a podium, asking a question, caught by a photographer in a moment of intensity. She was going to get her answer, Kirsten could tell. Flora's face was softer, less severe than now, less of a mask.

"I've not looked at that picture in years. I look different."

"Forceful."

"Could you stop elevating the old me and dismissing the now me?"

"Am I doing that?" Kirsten raised an eyebrow.

"Just a bit."

"Why isn't Flora Zhang asking questions of her little circle of suspects like she was still a journalist?" Kirsten said. "You know how to do it. You're calling your political buddies and the response is to arrest a homeless guy. Norman is in jail and the real killer thinks he's the smartest guy in the room. On the planet."

Flora didn't answer. She looked at the limited printouts tied to the "Greenkey" search. "Nothing substantive on Greenkey still."

"Nothing." There was a Green Key Antiques on Burnet Road—but what could an antiques store have to do with anything? There was a Green-Key Recycling Center located in far north Austin. It didn't look like an Adam Zhang–style investment on its website, more of a mom-and-pop operation. And there were meanings for "green key" in the urban dictionary—a synonym for marijuana, or a fake item used as a conversation starter when you wanted to flirt with someone. Flora read those definitions aloud and shook her head.

"Was Greenkey an idea? A project name? A product? It almost sounds like a code name."

"I asked Melinda. She said she hadn't heard of it, but I think she was going to see if she could find anything on the name."

"Has she gotten back to you yet?"

"No."

"Adam told Marco about Greenkey just days before Henry got here. So it has to tie to them."

"'Key' suggests security. 'Green' suggests money," Flora said. "Let me call Marco."

She tapped her phone, put it on speaker. *Be how you used to be. Remember that girl who yelled at the governor until she got her answer.*

"Marco. Hey. It's Flora Zhang."

"Flora. Hi."

"You told Kirsten North about a project of Adam's called Greenkey and I need to know more."

"It was just something Adam mentioned to me; he said I would want to write about it, but he couldn't share details yet; the deal wasn't through."

"The deal. So he was negotiating with someone."

"I guess."

"Look, I get why you didn't want to say more to Kirsten. You wanted her to just tell you what it was and not ask too many questions if she didn't know anything. But I need to know everything you know about it. One journalist to another."

"Oh, are you a journalist again?"

"Not on this story. But Marco, if you help me, I'm going to help you. I can get you interviews with Kirsten. With Shawn. I'll even ask Melinda Alari to talk to you."

"I'm talking to her right now," Marco said. "I mean, this very minute. I'll put you on speaker."

Melinda's voice came on the line: "Hello, Flora."

Kirsten and Flora stared at each other. Kirsten pointed at herself and shook her head, mouthing, *Don't tell her I'm here.*

Flora kept her voice steady and crisp. "I don't know what I ever did to you, other than exist, but you seem very sure I killed my husband."

"I simply suggest it as a possibility."

"Melinda, I did not kill him."

"You had the most reason to want him gone."

"And yet...he hadn't divorced me. Or left me. And he'd bought me a penthouse. Maybe you realized he was never leaving me. Because he loved me and you were only a distraction. And that fragile little ego of yours couldn't take it and you killed him."

Kirsten gave Flora a small twisted smile.

"Tell yourself what you need to," Melinda said. "He'd outgrown you."

"No, he was just testing the new model. Kicking the tires. But he wasn't going to leave his child." Flora had no idea if this was true. But it sounded good, and she hoped her words were like a needle under Melinda's skin. "I know someone's trying to frame me. I'm going to find out who, and then I am going to bring the full force of all the money Adam left me—left me, not you—into bringing them to justice. So, this is fair warning. If I find out you had anything to do with this, I'll bury your company. I'll fund every competitor. I'll call every CEO prospect you're selling to and let them know what bad publicity they're getting just by purchasing your product."

For the first time Melinda sounded uncertain. "You're just mad because he preferred me."

"No, sugar, I'm not. I don't care. You could have had your affair and left me out of it and been done, but no, you had to come after me and mine. So you get what you get."

Silence then.

Flora continued as if at a business meeting and moving on to the next agenda item: "Marco, if you still want to talk to me, you can. I hope you have a productive interview with Ms. Alari. I'll see you tomorrow night at the fund-raiser. And I'll be quotable."

"You just were," Marco said.

Flora hung up.

And then she caught her breath and sank into the desk chair.

"If she's the killer, she's on notice," Kirsten said.

"Then maybe she'll make a mistake and we'll all see it," Flora said.

"Fund-raiser?"

"Oh. For the foundation. Hosted by the Townsends at their place on Lake Austin. My first public appearance since Adam…and Henry died."

Kirsten nearly told Flora that Henry had been to the Townsend house. But she decided not to. She didn't have to tell Flora everything. "Big event?"

"Several hundred of Austin's wealthiest."

"I hope you raise a lot of money then." Kirsten cleared her throat. "Tell me about the others in Adam's life. Teddy, the Townsends. Like a journalist, not a friend."

"Shawn is very by-the-book. He wants things done a certain way and there were times he and Adam had knock-down, drag-out fights because Adam did something innovative or not what Shawn expected. He's from New York, not Texas. He came here to work as chief marketing officer for a software company that wouldn't make him CEO and it pissed him off; and so after it had gone public and he'd done very well he founded another company as CEO, proved he could do it, sold it, and became Adam's partner."

"What's his dark side?"

"What?"

"Everyone's got one. What would spur him to commit murder?"

Flora considered. "He always acted like he was in Adam's shadow. I think he resented that. Like he was mad for a bit that the firm was Zhang Townsend and not Townsend Zhang. He'd said it would be better to be further along in alphabetical order, which was petty and silly. A little thing. But sometimes people show you who they are with the little things."

"They do," Kirsten said. "And Taylor?"

"I actually introduced her to Shawn—at a party at our house. She came along one evening because she knew our neighbor Milo; she worked for another charity here in town and Milo and his wife, Jeanne, were sponsors. She and Shawn hit it off easily. Then I ended up offering her a job at my foundation, which she kept until she wanted to do to the full-time mom thing. Their daughter is six; Taylor's a terrific mom. I've tried to get her to come and work PR at the foundation, but she's happy doing volunteer work for us."

"And her dark side?"

Flora hesitated. "You can tell sometimes she grew up without much. She can be a little money-obsessed. I love her, but I think sometimes she urged Shawn to be more like Adam. If they weren't getting along…I think she might have been throwing fuel on the fire."

"How did she get along with Adam?"

"They got along fine. They were only around each other when the four of us socialized. She was my friend, not his."

"Do they have alibis?"

"For each other. Home watching TV."

"And Teddy?"

Flora folded her arms. "Adam insisted he live with us."

"Melinda says you insisted."

"Melinda's just blowing smoke. Adam wanted to show Teddy the stability of a family. Teddy hadn't really had that. His mother had a history of mental instability from a young age. She had him young, she couldn't care for him, the father wasn't in the picture. She died of an overdose—Adam never wanted to say it was suicide, but I've always wondered. Some other cousins in San Francisco took him in for a long while, but he got passed around and he hadn't had a normal life."

"I get that," Kirsten said.

"And the house is so big…it was just the two of us then. I said okay. Teddy's sweet. He's like a little brother to me. Maybe like you and Zach are."

Zach was pure big brother, not little, but Kirsten said nothing.

"Adam heard about his situation when Teddy was in high school and took charge of him.…He paid for Teddy's college and brought him out here."

How sweet, Kirsten thought. She wondered what she would have done if her father had swept in like Adam, the rescuing hero. She thought she would have had the courage to tell him to go back to Denmark, she'd never needed him. "His burst of generosity didn't strike you as odd?"

Flora started to object and then didn't. "Adam could help a poor relation and he did. He did a lot of regrettable things, obviously, but people are complicated, aren't they?"

"Sometimes," Kirsten said. "Sometimes not."

"Teddy was Adam's good deed."

"And what was that like for Teddy? Coming from a difficult, insecure situation to all this comfort and security?" *Because I know what that's like*, Kirsten thought.

"He's always been grateful."

"Did Adam expect him to be grateful all the time? Bend the knee, kiss the ring?"

"No. Teddy never resented him."

"Did he try to control Teddy, keep him under his thumb? They lived together; they worked together."

"Once…once I came in on them talking and they both fell silent in the way that tells you they have a secret. That they don't want you to know something. He hasn't told me."

"And he was at home that night?"

"No. At the office. And then he went to dinner by himself." She cleared her throat. "My neighbors—Jeanne and Milo—told me they witnessed a document Adam brought them that might have been assigning shares to Teddy in Zhang Townsend. Adam started the company before we married. He can treat it as separate property."

"Why would he give Teddy some of his shares? Why now?"

"I don't know."

"Maybe Teddy knew about the situation with Melinda and this was a way to buy his silence."

"Oh, no. No," Flora said. "Surely not. Adam's done everything for him…."

"Adam has. Not you. Teddy might be happy to keep Adam's secrets. Has Teddy produced this document? Waved it around and claimed his shares, which must be worth a considerable amount?"

"No."

"Maybe it wasn't Melinda or Shawn that Adam wanted hacked by Henry. It might have been Teddy. He put a camera in his room, after all. He was watching him like he was suspicious. And then he rewarded him. But maybe it wasn't enough. Maybe Teddy wanted more and…"

Flora put her face in her hands. "So now Morgan and I are supposed to go back there? Teddy's at the house and you're saying he could have killed our husbands." She gave a jagged laugh. "I know Teddy. I know him. I know all these people. Except Melinda. It's her."

"We know no one! You don't know what people are capable of when they're cornered, when they have to survive, when they're scared of losing what they've got. Adam cheated on you. Henry lied to me. Didn't we know them best? Wrong. None of us truly know each other."

The silence grew long. Then Flora said, "I have to be able to return to my house with my child and not freak out, so please, unless you have hard evidence, quit trying to theorize me into blind panic."

"Adam and Henry have to have spoken or talked. If there's not a trace on Adam's side, then there has to be one on Henry's." Kirsten opened her laptop and started typing.

"What's that?" Flora asked.

"We assumed they talked through text or email or phone. But there's no sign of that. So maybe it was through social media. Or a shared document where they both had access."

"Do the police know you could check that?"

"They've not asked yet," she said, not looking up.

Henry didn't much use social media—he thought it a terrible security risk—but they had an old Faceplace page. She remembered the log-in and password. He hadn't posted anything in months. But in his account's message center he'd gotten several notifications from an account called A2Z, with requests that Henry create an online shared document and send the link to A2Z, that this was a serious and lucrative offer for an assignment of the utmost secrecy. The message had been sent three times before Henry responded with a "Fine, we'll talk," and a link to an online document from a private service.

A2Z.

"Adam Zhang," she said aloud.

"What?" Flora said, staring.

Kirsten clicked on the link to the document. "I think this is it," she said.

It asked for a password.

She teased Henry sometimes: the security expert who relied on a pattern for passwords. But he said it couldn't be easily guessed, and he changed the pattern often enough that it wasn't a risk. Lately the pattern had been the number 54 (part of their street address with her foster parents the Melancons); the letters BEU (the initials of his favorite science-fiction author); the alphanumeric # symbol; and then the letter tied to the software or website he was accessing—such as A for Amazon or e for eBay. This was a shared doc, so she entered S at the very end.

It didn't work.

She tried again, with *s* now lowercase.

The file opened.

It was the kind of document where anyone with the password or a link granting permission could view, comment, or edit, depending on the settings. Kirsten knew that these online documents could serve as a work-around for sending potentially compromising emails or texts that could be traced. Someone could access the doc, leave a note, and others with access could respond there. Then the document, once its purpose was served, could be deleted, no one the wiser for the communication that had taken place.

> —Hey thanks for agreeing to talk this way, Henry. I have to be careful. You understand, I hope. I need absolute discretion.
>
> —Who is this?
>
> —My name is Zhang. I really need to stay under the radar. I want to hire you for a security analysis.
>
> —OK, so why not just make an appointment? This isn't how I do my work.
>
> —This situation is extremely delicate. I know you must respect a need for privacy and security. I need your utmost discretion and I can pay you well for it. It involves my wife. I believe she's planning a move against me—divorce or worse. I need her computer systems hacked.

—This isn't what I normally do. You want a private investigator. Or the police, if you feel you're in danger.

—You mistake me. I need a digital security audit and confirmation of my fears. It will enable me to keep her from making a terrible mistake and also to protect my son. I'll make it worth your while.

—Seriously I don't do the cheating/crazy spouse bit.

—I'll pay you a hundred thousand for this work, and it will be simple. I can't have my wife knowing about this. She's made threats to me and to our son. If so the answers would be on her computer or phone. I can't access them. I need your help.

—How do I know you're serious? Maybe you're the bad guy and she's the one in trouble.

—Come to Austin, tell no one. I'm in a position to help you grow your business, find investors to build your practice into a large and sophisticated consultancy, take care of your wife.

—How do you know I'm married?

—I checked you out. Please come to Austin. Meet me tomorrow night at a property that I own. 1413 Junipero. It's a warehouse. We can talk there, candidly, and if you decide you don't want the job then I'll still pay you $10K for your trouble and your travel.

—I'll think about it.

And then:

—Fine. I'm coming. I'll stay at Hotel Byte so I can hack without worry. I'll need the following information from you: your home's IP address, any passwords you know your wife uses, her system specs, her OS. Also the password for your home internet.

And then those last details, entered with a sign-off:

—Thank you, Henry.

41

The surveillance report. The computer analysis from Henry. Now this, showing that Adam had secretly, stealthily reached out to Henry and hired him.

Flora read it over her shoulder. "I never ever gave him reason to doubt me. I don't know what he was thinking."

Kirsten thought: *A hundred thousand dollars? For one job. For one consultant who sometimes struggled to pay off the monthly mortgage. Henry could not have said no to this. Not with his business flailing.*

"None of this is true!" Flora said, her voice rising. "But the police will see this; they're going to think I killed them...."

"We don't know that this is Adam. We can't be sure."

"Isn't there a way to trace who accessed it?"

She went to the account that had sent Henry the message on Faceplace. It was in the name of Adam Zhang, but it looked like a burner account. No friends, no postings, no groups.

There was a picture of Adam, though, smiling in sunlight.

"We could show this to the police," Flora said.

"Not yet."

"The killer could delete it."

Kirsten took a screen capture of the page. She glanced at Flora. "We could say hi."

"If the killer thinks anyone's found this, they'll delete the page."

"Maybe. But this is part of the false trail that frames you, Flora. That's why they've left it up. This incriminates you."

Flora got up and paced the room.

"Could this document be traced back to someone?"

"I don't know. We can see. But I think we leave it in place right now."

Flora stopped at the assortment of printouts. As if there was an answer there, in the tangle of lives Adam had gathered around him: Shawn, Melinda, Teddy, Flora.

Kirsten watched her stare at their faces.

"I agree. Leave it in place," Flora said.

"Okay."

Flora saw the edge of a sticky note under the printouts. She pulled it free. Read it.

"Did you write this?" Something sounded off in Flora's voice.

Kirsten took the sticky note from her.

Your brother is lying to you.

Block letters. Someone had to have been in her hotel room to leave this...or here. Flora and Taylor had been here. That was more likely. But why accuse Zach? Just to make her suspect her one true ally here? A note couldn't do that. This group had no idea what she and Zach had survived together.

What was Zach lying about? He had nothing to lie about. He had come here when she needed him, he had found Henry's car, found the GPS data that told her where her husband had gone...

But had he told her everything?

And who would know if he was withholding information? Who would tell her this?

"Kirsten?"

"Someone posted this in my room," she said. "All this was up on the wall in my hotel room. I thought...I thought someone had been in there." The jacket knocked off the chair.

"Oh, no," Flora said.

"Why accuse Zach? There's no point to it," Kirsten said.

Morgan woke up then, crying, and Flora hurried to him. Kirsten followed her into the living room.

"I need to take him home. I need to figure out what to do," Flora said. "My mind's a mess."

"You mean about Teddy?"

"Yes. And everything else. I can't put my child in danger."

"Just pretend you know nothing for now. You're the grieving widow."

"All right," Flora said. "I'll talk to you in the morning." She scooped up Morgan and headed out to the elevator. She turned back to Kirsten when the door opened. "You believe me. That means everything. Thank you."

Kirsten said nothing because she believed Flora right *now*, because of small reasons about Henry and his habits. But a terrible gnawing had started in her stomach. What if she was wrong about Flora? What if she'd just let Henry's killer worm her way into her confidence?

"Bye," Kirsten said. The doors shut, Morgan asleep on Flora's shoulder.

Kirsten ignored the wine in the fridge and drank a glass of water. She tried to text Zach. No answer.

Someone other than Zach had been in the room. She paced. She thought. She studied the downtown lights.

The intercom from the garage buzzed.

She answered it. "Zhang residence."

It was the downstairs guard. "Ms. North?" He remembered her name. "This is Carl, at the security desk. There's a Mr. Couvillon at the parking gate asking to be given access to the garage; that okay?"

"Yes, please. Thank you."

"Yes, ma'am."

She waited for Zach to buzz the express elevator intercom. "Are you alone?" he asked.

"Yes."

"Can you let me up? And hurry?"

"I'll come get you." She took the elevator down to the garage. The doors slid open.

Her eyes went wide.

"I brought you a present," Zach said. "His ID says his name is Mender."

42

Flora entered the house, Morgan asleep on her shoulder; he'd fallen back into slumber on the drive home.

She walked through the den to take him upstairs and there was Teddy, on his laptop. He raised a hand to her in a gentle wave. She took Morgan upstairs. As soon as she laid him down she thought, *I should have put him in the bed with me. So I can lock the bedroom door. In case Teddy is…not the Teddy I know.*

She moved as if in a dream, taking Morgan from the crib and to the master bedroom, settling him on the side of the bed where Adam had slept, feeling slightly better and worse all at the same time.

She couldn't suspect Teddy. But.

She went back to the den.

"Hey," Teddy said. "You all right?"

"Yes, fine." Check: her voice sounded normal. "How are you?"

"Fine. Where did you and Morgan go?"

"I went to check on Kirsten at the penthouse. And then we just drove around a bit. Morgan slept and I thought about things."

"I wish you'd let me know where you are. I got worried."

"I'm fine," she said.

"Okay. Let's talk about Kirsten North." He gestured at the couch. She sat, keeping a space between them.

"First," Flora said, "let's talk about you."

"What about me?" He grew very still.

Five beats of them staring at each other. "Why did Adam help you so much?" she said.

"Because he's Adam."

"Being Adam has taken on all sorts of dark tones."

Teddy said nothing for several seconds. "People are complicated. I don't know why. I'm just grateful." He took a deep breath. "He flew out to San Francisco. He had just finished his MBA and was coming out there for a job interview he ended up not taking. I was maybe ten. A cousin I was staying with took me to his hotel lobby. We talked. He asked me to do math for him. He..."

"Wait, what?" She had never heard this before. She thought Adam had entered Teddy's life when he was older.

"To do math. He wanted to see my homework. My school papers—my essays, everything. He read through it all."

"He evaluated your academic work? You were ten?"

"Yes. Later I would realize it resembled showing a client a portfolio." His voice quavered. "He told me he saw a lot of potential in me."

Potential. "That's what he'd say about a company to invest in," Flora said slowly.

"Yes. I never thought of it that way, though." Teddy glanced away. "And he would be sure I wouldn't be passed around the family more or end up in foster care. He got me settled with some other cousins who were willing to keep me long term. Got me in a good school. Got my life in order for me. And then after I graduated college, he brought me out here and you know the rest."

"Your mother was his second cousin, right?"

"They weren't particularly close. Why?"

Oh, now he was suspicious. She'd pushed too hard. "I'm trying to understand Adam. I feel...in some ways he was a stranger to me. I'm trying to reconcile the man I knew with the man who could have gotten involved with Melinda and...I just don't understand."

"He did good and bad things. That's it. Okay. Can we go back to Kirsten?"

She nodded.

"I know you mean well in trying to help her."

"Yes."

"But you should know her foster father vanished her senior year in high school. He was never found."

Teddy had a collection of news stories up in browser tabs. He turned the laptop so she could see. They were news articles from an archived site. "His name was Larry Melancon. He was a CPA. He and his wife took in Zach Couvillon and then Kirsten Plumm when they were freshmen in high school. About a week after Zach turned eighteen, Larry Melancon vanished. He brought home dinner to Kirsten, no one else was there, and then he said he was going to his office, but he was never seen again."

"Was she a suspect?" *You never know; Kirsten had said that herself.*

"She was the last person to admit to seeing him. Melancon had been a CPA for some people called the Fortunatos, who are a crime family in New Orleans. The theory became that Melancon either stole from or crossed the Fortunatos and they did away with him."

A murder in her past. "Okay, but that's not Kirsten's fault."

"No. But guess who funded Zach Couvillon's college? And who now employs him at one of their real estate companies, of which they have several?"

"This crime family."

"Exactly." He pointed to one of the articles on his screen. "This was written a few years after the unsolved disappearance. The reporter talked to the next-door neighbor as well—Jim North. He provided these details."

"North."

"Yes. Jim North was Henry North's father."

Flora sat down. "Zach Couvillon is basically a mobster?"

Teddy shrugged. "They're more into financial crimes. And he's...something. And so I'm wondering if Henry and Kirsten are connected with them too. Jim North basically argued that Melancon didn't vanish because of the Fortunatos but because his marriage was unhappy and he disliked being a foster dad. Being one was his wife's idea. And that Zach wouldn't take help from the people who killed his foster dad; therefore, there's no crime, just a man walking away from his life. Mrs. Melancon did not comment for the article."

"I don't see how this connects to Adam."

"We keep thinking Adam hired Henry."

"Yes," she said. Then she shut her mouth.

"What if that wasn't the relationship? These mob guys, they're always looking for ways to clean money, right? According to the TV shows."

The thought was jolting. "You think they approached Adam to clean money for them."

"These guys set up front companies. The front companies invest with Zhang Townsend. The money's in a high-growth but high-risk investment; could be lost, but it could multiply several times over. At least it's not sitting under a tarp in a furniture storage rental. But then they have ownership in a legit company and when it goes public they sell their shares and reinvest them in legit stocks. Cleaned."

"Henry was a hacker, not some financial programmer."

"I'm just saying his brother-in-law is tangled up with these bad people. Maybe this wasn't Adam hiring Henry. Maybe this was these mobsters pressuring Adam and he said no and something went wrong and he and Henry North ended up dead."

This theory didn't mesh with the shared document, but she said nothing. Instead, she said: "Adam was shot neatly and Henry wasn't. Like he was made to suffer."

"Maybe Zach hated his brother-in-law."

"No. Zach Couvillon didn't come to Austin until the morning after Kirsten did. She told me. She called him on the way here and talked to him and then he arrived the next day."

"I have a friend who works in airline reservations," Teddy said. "Zach Couvillon flew here the night of the murders."

Your brother is lying to you.

43

Saturday

It had been a long night.

Zach had given Mender too much of the sedative and he'd been out for hours. Zach carried Mender inside the penthouse and put him in the office's bathroom, in the tub, wrists and ankles securely bound with Mender's own zip-ties he'd intended to use on Kirsten. He left Mender in his clothes—he'd found the gun, the syringe, and the wallet full of fake Frederick Mender ID. Zach had made a few phone calls and procured more of the sedative—some local friend of the Fortunatos delivering a bland package politely to Carl downstairs and a shaken Kirsten going to retrieve it from him. Mender had a black eye and a split lip that Zach had given him but didn't otherwise seem too badly hurt.

"He thought I was you. He came to the hotel to kill you." They stood over the unconscious Mender in the tub.

"I've seen him before," she said. "I don't know where, but I've seen him."

Zach looked at her. "This guy has all the markings of a hired killer. Did you see him following you before?"

"Maybe...I just can't remember."

"Whoever hired him is clearly threatened by you being here. What you're doing. You're going back to New Orleans in the morning. This is too dangerous."

"I am not," she said.

"I'll guard him," Zach said. "I'll wake you if he stirs and we can talk to him. He might sleep all night."

"He might be the one who killed them."

"Yes, or he might not be. We'll talk to him."

"And then what? We really can't take him to the police. You drugged and kidnapped him."

Zach shrugged. "Self-defense."

It wasn't, but she said nothing.

"Go get some sleep, Kirsten," he said. "You need it."

"You realize this clears Flora, right?" she said. "I was right about her. If she sent a killer to get rid of me, she wouldn't have invited me to the penthouse and sent the killer to my old hotel room."

"The rope, zip-ties, and sedative mean he was going to kidnap you. Maybe kill you, maybe not. Maybe just make you disappear. There could have been a miscommunication about where you were. Let's not clear Flora just yet. We'll see what Sleeping Beauty says about his employer."

"You said before you wouldn't help me kill the killer," she said.

"He came after you," Zach said. "That changes the math."

And if you kill him and we have to get rid of another body, Henry's not here to tell us what to do, she thought. Of course the Fortunatos could make Mender disappear forever. It was not a reassuring thought.

She nodded and went to the futon in the office and tried to relax. She didn't think she could, but exhaustion crushed her and she fell into a deep sleep.

Saturday midmorning, Zach shook her awake. She followed him back to the bathroom. The man was awake, if not alert, watching them through lidded eyes.

Zach sat on the toilet, lid down, and Kirsten pulled a chair into the bathroom.

She thought of the French widows. She could do this. This could be the guy who killed her husband. Someone's hired gun. Who did he work for?

He was a Nazi; she was a French widow.

"Who are you?" she asked as her first question. "I know your face. Where do I know it from?"

The hit man didn't answer.

"Is Frederick Mender your real name?"

"It's what you can call me," he said. His voice was raspy, thin.

Zach took a photo of Mender on his phone. "I work for some very influential people in New Orleans. You may or may not have known that. I think you're hired, and they're going to be able to circulate your photo to ID you. This will end your employability, of course, and your client is going to be identified, eventually. Henry didn't work for my employers, but he was my brother-in-law and they take family matters seriously."

"You're going to kill me anyway," Mender said. "My employability is not really a factor at the moment."

"I don't want to kill you. I want information from you," Kirsten said.

"You being the good cop is kind of sexist and transparent," Mender said.

Zach handed her three phones. "He must have a sky-high cellular bill."

All were encoded. She grabbed his finger and put it on the reader on the first phone. It opened. No apps. Just a phone. Call history deleted.

She did the same on the second one. No apps. Just a phone. Cleaned call history.

Third phone. The finger scan didn't work. The screen's keypad appeared, asking for a code.

"Tell me the code."

"No."

Zach punched him, hard. Mender's head bounced off the tiles.

"No, don't do that, please," Kirsten said. She kept her voice steady. Zach was so comfortable with this. She felt chilled. "We're up thirty stories. It's a very long drop down. But if I tell this man to drop you off a balcony after you tried to kill him, he's likely to do it."

"He could have killed me at the hotel."

"He didn't because he made a promise to me." *Your brother is lying to you.* "I know you think you're going to get to make a deal. I'm your only option."

They stared at each other.

"Did you kill Henry?"

Mender said nothing.

She got up and went to the office. She came back.

"My husband was a hacker. Four-digit phone passwords are fairly easy. You can hook up a phone and put a password cracker against it and you'll get the data. It'll ding when it's done, like popcorn in the microwave."

Mender closed his eyes.

This phone mattered to him, Kirsten saw. Someone on the other end mattered to him. She wondered why a hit man would carry a phone that could lead back to his loved ones. It was a terrible risk, but he had taken it so there had to be a good reason.

"Did you kill my husband?" she asked him.

Mender opened his eyes, staring straight ahead. "No, I did not."

"Did you kill Adam Zhang?"

Now his gaze met Kirsten's. "I don't know what you're talking about."

"Then who hired you to come after me?"

He looked at Zach and then her. "I don't have a client name. I have an intermediary, a handler who...handles that."

"Is that your encoded phone, your handler?" Zach asked.

"No," Kirsten said. "He's not scared for his handler. He's scared for whoever is on the other phone."

Mender looked at her. Then looked away. "I would like to make a deal."

"Listening," Zach said.

"I tell you what I know and you don't crack that third phone. Just leave it alone."

"Wife and kids?" Kirsten asked. "Or a girlfriend? Or boyfriend? That would be such a liability in your line of work."

"Do we have a deal?" he asked.

"Yes," she said. "Who is your client?"

"I absolutely don't know. That's what my handler is for. And you can threaten to kill me; it won't make a difference to him. He won't talk to you over the phone. He'll vanish."

"Did he tell you to come after me?"

"Yes."

"So I'm somehow a threat to his client."

"Presumably."

"Were you to kidnap her or kill her or both?" Zach asked.

"Make her vanish. If that failed, make her look like a suicide."

"Are you saying you didn't kill them but were sent to kill Kirsten?" Zach asked. "You got a partner?"

The thought chilled Kirsten. Someone else out there. Mender's gaze slid back and forth between them.

"Maybe the encoded phone is his partner," Zach said.

But she thought not. He hadn't asked to be spared or turned over to the police. Just that the person on the other end of the phone be left alone.

The stare Mender gave her was flat, but she could feel a hatred in it. He would have put a bullet in her and thought it wasn't personal, but now that they had fought back…now that he was vulnerable, it was personal.

"The night they died. Tell me," Zach said.

His gaze settled on a spot above Kirsten's head. "I was told to go to the warehouse. By my handler, with orders to kill the two men there. But I got there and one had already shot the other."

"Who?"

"The Asian man had shot the guy in glasses."

"Did you even know their names?" Kirsten heard herself say, and Zach put a hand on her arm.

"I shot the Asian guy. Twice, neat and clean. I checked the pulse on the other guy. He was gone."

"Adam Zhang was shot in the head, two precise shots," Kirsten said. "Henry was shot four times, in the chest. One precise, one not. It wasn't a fight. It was two different shooters." And the shock of it washed over her as another thought nagged at the back of her brain. Shouldn't there be different bullets from different guns? Wouldn't the police know that by now?

"How did you know Adam shot him?" Zach said. "Did you see him?"

Kirsten thought: *Why would Adam Zhang kill my husband?*

Mender considered. "No, but he was there with a gun and a dead body. I didn't ask a lot of questions of him. I did what I was told."

Kirsten said, "Did you see anyone around? Like someone maybe smoking a cigarette near the warehouse?"

She could feel the burn of Zach's stare.

"I would not have entered the warehouse if I saw someone," Mender said.

"They might have been there when you left," Kirsten pressed.

"I didn't see anyone. I moved his car, per orders. I took a taxi back to where I was staying and reported in. I thought I was done. I was told instead to sit tight and wait for further orders."

"That's not usual." Like Zach knew the protocols.

"No, it's not. There was an offer of additional compensation."

Compensation. Kirsten punched Mender. She did it before she could think. Blood gushed from his already battered nose. "Who is your client?"

"I don't know."

"Who do you think it is?"

"I don't…I don't understand."

"You must know the players here. The candidates. Is it Shawn Townsend? Teddy Chao? Melinda Alari?" She paused. "Flora Zhang?"

"I don't know."

"But you were told to wait."

"Yes." A pause, though, before he answered. Then she realized it. He had sat next to her, on the flight from New Orleans to Houston. In a cap and sunglasses, but it was him.

She stared at him. "Told to wait in Austin."

"Yes."

"Assuming I would arrive soon once Henry was identified."

He gave no answer.

"But then the client changed their mind and sent you to New Orleans. To kill me."

"Yes. Then I was told to go to New Orleans."

"And kill me."

"Yes. Make you look like a suicide." Mender closed his eyes. "Grieving widow."

"That was the point of the phone call. It wasn't to get me to Austin. It was to explain how I knew my husband was dead. Someone told me and I killed myself out of grief?"

"That would only work if you told other people first about the call, and you didn't," Zach said. "You just headed immediately to Austin."

"Maybe your client didn't account for my weirdness," Kirsten said.

Mender shrugged.

"Why would someone want me and Henry and Adam Zhang dead?"

"I was to kill you and to take all your husband's hard drives," Mender said calmly. "I surmise that maybe they were worried about you being a witness or finding evidence on Henry's drives."

"Surmise," Zach said. "Big-word man."

"Are you framing Flora too? Did you plant the report in Henry's hotel room?"

"No. She's of no interest to me."

"Did you put a cell phone in Norman's cart?"

"Norman?"

"He's the guy in jail for your crimes." She felt sick. She had to get Norman out of jail. But she also had to find the client before the police did. *Norman would understand. Wouldn't he?* Her choices were changing the lives of other people.

Mender shook his head. "No, I didn't plant a phone. I do my work; I get out. I'm not a ramifications guy." He smiled at her. “He the one smoking outside the warehouse you’re worried about? We can get him handled.”

“Don’t you even think about it,” she said.

“So if you call your handler, and you ask him to tell you the client’s name or we’ll kill you, he’ll talk, right?” Zach said.

“I’m not really his favorite, so no.”

“If you’ll leave him with me,” Zach said, “I will get the handler’s name. That’s our leverage. We can put this guy’s picture out there. If we have the handler’s name as well, they’re both done. Former clients might even put a contract out on the handler so he can’t negotiate with the feds.”

“Taylor might be sending over more furniture. I’ll tell Flora to ask her not to. They have a big shindig tonight, so they’ll be busy getting ready for that.”

“Who are these people, throwing a party after her husband dies?” Zach asked.

“Fund-raiser. Honoring him.”

Zach made a noise. “You’re not going?”

“I wasn’t invited, which is fine.” She glanced at Mender. “Were you invited?” She raised an eyebrow.

“I don’t like parties,” Mender said. “Don’t leave me with him. I didn’t kill your guy. I failed to kill you. Honestly not much of a threat, and I’ve seen the error of my ways.”

She had been ready to put a bullet in Henry’s killer. Now she was flinching at Zach threatening to beat Mender to a pulp. It wasn’t the same as Larry. With Larry she hadn’t had time to think.

She looked at Zach. “Is there a way to confirm a name or phone number or anything he gives with the handler?”

“Yes. I can make some calls when he tells me.”

Kirsten went to the office. She texted Flora: R U OK? All OK with Teddy?

Flora answered: Yes, fine.

A little abrupt. Kirsten texted: Pls tell Taylor no furniture or other stuff sent over today, just can’t handle. It’s like the reality hit me. I know you’re busy with your event tonight and I hope it goes well. I'm sleeping a lot today. The grief caught up with me and I need some alone time. I need to think. Can we talk tomorrow? Please? Thank you again.

And the answer from Flora: sure. R U OK? Did u learn something else?

Flora was already getting to know her. She wrote back: I will be.

She picked up Mender's phone. She took it with her. Zach left the man in the bathroom and closed the door and followed her to the elevator.

"If I leave him with you, will you not kill him?" she said.

"Do you think I normally murder people?"

"I don't know what you do."

"Where are you going?"

"I don't entirely believe his story."

"You going to tell Flora the hit man said her husband killed your husband?"

"No. Because that's hard to piece together. He might be lying. He doesn't want me to think he killed Henry. But I took his photo on my phone while he was unconscious last night." She showed him the picture on her phone.

"Kirsten..."

"What would his client do if they thought he was telling us everything he knew? Panic, maybe, enough to show themselves. He hasn't reported in to his handler. He must be overdue. If the handler's told the client, then maybe there's a really nervous person in that circle of people around Adam Zhang and I can make them nervous enough to stumble and show themselves."

"You really are my sister," he said. He blinked. "Be careful. This guy is someone's attack dog, and we've leashed him. The homeless guy getting arrested isn't enough for whoever hired him. They could get real desperate real fast."

"I know the feeling. Don't kill him."

"I'll try reasoning with him. But nothing works like pain."

She cleared her throat. "He normally wears a wedding ring. I can see the mark on his finger. My guess is it's a wife. So make him scared we'll find out about her."

"Just between us, I'm not going to hurt his wife. I want you to know there are boundaries."

"You really are my brother. I'll be back."

44

Kirsten drove her rental car.

Your brother is lying to you.

She'd wanted to ask the hit man that question—*Did you leave a note in my room?* It must have been him; he'd had access, clearly.

She didn't want to ask Mender in front of Zach. She didn't want him to know that she could believe such a threat, and…she didn't want him to know she wasn't sure what to think. His going to work for the Fortunatos and staying there had never sat well with Henry.

Someone else—maybe Adam Zhang—had killed Henry and then Mender had killed Adam Zhang. That was the story he was peddling. Was it a lie?

She stopped at a light. Glanced at herself in the rearview.

She had as much as told Flora she was going to kill the killer. The hit man was one killer, but the client, the architect of the ruining of her life, that was the one she wanted.

Oh, Flora, she could have said. *The entirely trustworthy hit man said he killed your husband, but yours killed mine first.* Sorry we can't be friends. She took a deep, gulping breath and steadied herself.

Would she have to buy a gun to do what she planned? She should have taken the gun from Mender. It was one thing to say you would kill someone and then another thing to actually do it. What if Mender never told them who hired him? What if she didn't have time to plan or carry out her revenge? She kept telling herself she could do this, but now she wasn't sure.

It wasn't the same as Larry. Talk, especially to one's self, was cheap.

She had put the Townsends' address into her phone and the calm, reassuring voice directed her west from downtown and onto a road called Old Travis that wound through the wealthy suburb of Lakehaven. It looked like a nice place to live, the kind of place she might have wished for as a child, but she knew there was an ugliness underneath it. Someone here had hired the killer, wanted Adam and Henry dead, been willing to end lives to help themselves. *For what? Position, wealth, security?*

Past the main part of Lakehaven the map app told her to turn and she went on a winding road through impressive hills that led to huge houses on the banks of Lake Austin. She reached the Townsends' address.

She boldly drove down the huge circular driveway.

People were already at work preparing for tonight's event.

Four vans for a catering service. Workers putting up fancy decorations in the stretch of land between the massive house and the boathouse that sat slightly to the left and behind the house.

No sign of Taylor or Shawn—she had seen his picture on social media—among the people there.

A woman with a clipboard glanced at her and gestured for her to roll down her window. Kirsten, after a moment, did.

"Can I help you?"

"Yeah, sorry, I think I have the wrong address. Is this 452?"

"No, it's 462."

"Oh, sorry," Kirsten said. "Wow, a big party happening?"

"Yes." Her glance was stony.

"Well, I certainly hope it won't be loud enough to disturb our family reunion at 452."

"*This* is a fund-raiser for rare-disease research," the woman said, as though offended. Kirsten thought it was funny how people would tell you things out of a need to defend themselves. *I'll have you know...*one of her foster mothers, Momsy, had raged at her, and told Kirsten her salary and her bank account balance, because she wasn't taking Kirsten in for *charity*, because she didn't need it. And once Kirsten figured out her PIN number, well, it wasn't hard to take an extra twenty now and then when she needed it. In the name of charity.

"Oh, that's a worthy cause. Well, good luck and sorry to have bothered you." Kirsten drove the rental car back onto the main road and turned right to head down to the address she'd given the woman.

So. There was not going to be an easy way to get into the house during the setup, and even with all the workers around, Lady Clipboard was a sentinel.

The best camouflage was going to be the party itself. Hundreds of people, Flora had said, and she would have to find a way in. Without Taylor or Flora seeing her. Taylor would be busy hosting. Flora would likely be surrounded by a constant stream of people wishing her well and expressing sympathies and donating in Adam's name to her foundation's cause.

At 452 she turned into the driveway and stopped long enough to check her phone for the nearest clothing resale store.

-

Kirsten went to Goodwill and bought shoes and that rarest of resale shop finds, a serviceable little black dress, one that looked nicer than the price tag indicated. Her lucky day. She couldn't do much about her hair, but at a drugstore she bought a curling iron and a nicer brand of lipstick than she usually bothered with.

Henry had driven to that grand, beautiful house. To learn more about Adam? Or for another reason? Why not go to Adam's house?

She tried on the dress and the shoes. They would have to do. She looked fine but not glamorous and maybe that was for the best; she just needed camouflage. She also picked out a black clutch for her phone, which rang just as she approached the cash register.

Henry's number. Just like when she'd been called and told Henry was dead.

But the phone was in police custody. So there was a cloned phone out there.

She stared at the screen while five feet to her right a child loudly pleaded with his mother to go home, he was *bored*. She stepped away from the noise and answered the phone. "Hello?"

The same voice that had called her before. Raspy, disguised, electronically altered. "Hello, Kirsten."

She took a deep breath. "Did you kill my husband?"

A woman in the aisle glanced at her in surprise, moved away.

A deep breath from the caller. "Where are you?"

Kirsten dropped the dress and shoes, along with the clutch, and bolted outside to the parking lot where no one would hear her words. "We have your pet on a leash. He'll talk."

Silence for five seconds. "He can't say what he doesn't know. Well, he killed them, so do what you want. It's done."

"Yet he tells a different story."

"Of course he would." And then the electronic voice gave…a yawn.

Rage filled her. Kirsten made her voice a knife. "You think you can't be found? I will find you. I am coming for you." The last five words she carefully enunciated, made each one a punch. "You wanted me here? You got me here. Although I don't know what you thought you would gain from it."

She realized she was shaking, not in fear but anger.

The caller said, "Adam Zhang was a bad guy. So was your husband. They got what they deserved. So will you."

"You're only calling me to scare me. Because you're worried your pet or his handler will talk. And they will. To save themselves, they'll turn on you. You're scared. You should be."

The call ended.

She stared at the phone.

Kirsten went back into the Goodwill store. The shoes, dress, and purse, thankfully, were still where she'd dropped them. She bought them and left, ignoring the few stares from the other shoppers.

She drove to Flora's address. Seeing the Townsends' grand home made her want to see how the Zhangs lived. Plus, she wasn't eager, after this morning and the phone call, to deal with Zach.

She found the cul-de-sac and turned in. The houses were…huge. There were two news vans there, not broadcasting at the moment. She didn't want to be seen. She paused just to look at the house, like a curious person drawn by the news. It was gigantic, and comfortable, and surrounded by an iron fence. All the houses were. She saw an older man coming out of the house next door, walking a thick-bodied dog. He raised a middle finger to the press and kept walking. She turned her car around and parked down by where the circle met the cross street, also full of grand houses built by software and tech and the other businesses that had forever transformed Austin. She lowered her window and as the older man went by she said, "Sir? Is that Flora Zhang's house?"

"Yes, and can't you please leave her alone in her grief?"

"My husband, Henry, died with Adam. He was the other shooting victim."

This stopped him and the scowl vanished, replaced by an immediate sympathy. He seemed to study her as if to make sure this wasn't some other journalism trick and decided that it wasn't. "Oh. Oh, really? I'm very sorry."

"I just wanted to see where she and Adam lived. She's letting me stay at their place downtown."

"Oh, goodness. Hi. I'm Milo Hobson." He offered his hand and she shook it.

"Kirsten North."

He leaned down a bit closer to the car. "My wife, Jeanne, helps Flora with her little boy, and she's over there right now. So Flora is home. If you want to see her?"

"I talked to her this morning. I don't want to deal with getting past the press."

"I'll go chase them off." Milo seemed to relish the idea.

"No, don't, please," she said. "Can I ask you a question? What was Adam like? I mean, as a neighbor. Were you friends?"

"Oh, yes, a good man, and I don't believe that woman who said they were shacking up for a minute. I mean, Adam was a family man. He worked very long hours, but he did it all for his family."

Kirsten wondered. Men made this excuse a lot—all the work done for their family. She was sure it was true sometimes, but she wondered if the work, to more than a few, was more interesting than the family.

"That homeless man killed them," Milo said.

"Yes. I understand that. It's just not clear how Adam and my Henry knew each other."

"I'm sorry, but I don't think I can help you with that."

"Y'all sound so close to Flora." She pulled out her phone, found a photo of Henry and her together. Leaning together, smiling. It still did not seem possible that he was dead. "You must be around them a lot. Did you ever see Henry at their house?" She showed him the picture.

"I don't think I'm the one to answer your questions. Maybe Jeanne, she spends more time over there." But politeness won out, and he looked at the photo. "No. I don't recognize him. I'm sorry. I did see a picture of him on the news." Her possession of this photo seemed to reassure him that she was telling the truth about who she was.

"What about this guy?" She pulled up a picture of Zach. Alone, smiling as much as he ever smiled. It had been taken at his last birthday party and Kirsten had made him wear a little pointy hat, which looked ridiculous on him.

"No. Don't know him either. And I keep my eyes open around here; we've all got those doorbells with cameras, I like to see what's happening."

"Thank you, Milo." This was pointless.

"You know Milo's Gin?"

She remembered seeing large billboards for it on the way from the airport into downtown. "Yes. It's you on the billboards with those movie stars."

"That's me. Milo. My wife and I built it up from nothing to being a celebrity brand."

"Congratulations," she said, unsure where his ill-timed bragging was going.

"Well, we've done well, but we want to go global, you know, and Adam was going to help me with that. Find investment partners that wouldn't boss me and Jeanne around, people that would finance us in different markets, distributors...We got offers from the big beverage companies, but I like being my own boss. Big project."

A question she'd asked Flora earlier fell into place. "Did Adam buy that warehouse for your company's expansion?"

Milo blinked, then shook his head sadly. "He didn't tell me that he had, but it would make sense. We need warehouses. Oh, gosh, how awful. He said he thought our brand had so much potential. Adam...losing him this way, it's a huge loss for us personally but also professionally. No one else I'd trust. I mean, if Flora still wants to invest. I haven't brought it up. Not the time. It can wait. But if your husband was going to launch a company with Adam, then...well. He picked a good man. I'm so sorry."

"What about Teddy?" she asked. "I guess he'll take over."

Milo's mouth twitched. "I suppose. Or be involved."

"You don't approve? Flora told me she relies on him so much."

"He...I shouldn't say."

"He's kind of a leech," Kirsten ventured. Guessing this was the gripe.

"I mean, ambition I admire. But to want to live with your boss. He's a grown man; he should get his own place. I've seen how he looks at Flora. Like he wants to tell her something but can't." He shut his mouth then, as though he'd said too much.

She thought Milo might dislike the press because he worried he'd say too much around them. "Flora said he's like a little brother to her."

Milo rolled his eyes. His dog barked. "Flora's an only child and sometimes it shows."

"Why did Adam keep him around; I mean, with that living arrangement?" Maybe Adam was right to be suspicious.

"I think he felt that he owed Teddy. You can tell when a man feels an obligation. And Teddy took advantage. Free place to live, room and board, and he had the ear of his boss all the time. I don't think Shawn Townsend much liked it."

She hadn't thought about Shawn having a reaction to Adam's generosity to Teddy, or even their relationship. Could it have been a threat to the partnership? There were already so many secrets at Zhang Townsend. Maybe there was an even bigger one. "Thank you for talking to me, Milo. I'll be sure and try some of your gin."

"Are you…not to be awkward…there's this big fund-raiser tonight that's been planned forever. Milo's Gin is one of the sponsors. It was Adam's idea and so I guess Flora is going ahead with it. To honor him."

"Oh, yes, I've heard. But I don't think I'm up for a party." She said this in case he reported back to his wife or Flora. "I told Flora I was going to sleep most of today."

"I sure understand. I'm sorry for your loss."

"I am glad Flora has y'all to support her. Thank you again for talking to me."

"It will get better," he said unexpectedly. "I know right now it feels like the end of the world. It is, but it's not. You're young and pretty and you seem real smart. You're strong. I can tell that. He'll live in your heart always, but you'll go on." Milo Hobson seemed to realize he'd said too much, too quickly, and he blinked and stepped back.

She knew he meant well. And maybe he was right. Maybe she would go on. People did. But she couldn't, she wouldn't, until she had justice.

Milo headed off with his dog, who seemed more than happy to finally get their walk underway. And her phone chimed with a text from Melinda Alari: Can we talk?

Kirsten texted: Yes. She's talking to me. I think you might want to know what she says. She's not happy about you talking to Marco.

Meet me for coffee. And she gave Kirsten an address.

45

Jeanne had texted Flora to see if she needed help, and Flora said yes. She found it hard to say no to Jeanne when she offered. She was so competent with Morgan. Even when she thought to herself, *I need to get better at this; I need time with him*…Jeanne was there. If they'd moved to the penthouse, she would have lost that support.

Jeanne was in the kitchen, having fed Morgan while Flora showered and got recharged with some coffee.

"There are press downstairs," Jeanne said with a frown.

"Of course there are."

"There were three vans, but one left," Jeanne said. "That's a hopeful sign. They might just do a news update from here and then leave."

"I need to get over to Taylor's to help with the fund-raiser." She nearly said the word "party," but that felt wrong in her mouth right now.

"I feel certain Taylor can handle all that, and your staff at the foundation can help her. You don't need to do a thing. How did you sleep?"

"Not well." She glanced up at Jeanne. "I've let this Kirsten North into my life and…well, into my other home and I don't know much about her." Into her other home. Who could have come into *this* home and planted the computer files about murderous wives?

Someone who didn't have to sneak in at all. Teddy.

"Mrs. North is a widow like you; what's to know?" Jeanne asked.

"I think her brother might be involved with some bad people in New Orleans. Teddy's checked into them."

Jeanne patted Morgan's back. Morgan giggled and played with Jeanne's necklace. "You think somehow Adam got involved with these bad people?"

"I don't know. I just don't know if I can trust this Kirsten."

"Then don't let her stay at your penthouse. Send her on her way back to New Orleans. You got a babysitter for tonight? If not I'll stay here with the little punkin." Jeanne softly rubbed her nose against Morgan's and he giggled with delight.

"I've got a babysitter. I want you and Milo at the event. I need your support. Put on your best dress."

"Are that woman and her brother coming?"

"Oh, no. No. I didn't invite her and I'm sure she wouldn't have come anyway. It would be cruel to her, not knowing anyone, and all the people staring. I don't feel at all like going, but it's a memorial and at least it's for a cause I support and I'll know the people staring at me. Wondering if my husband cheated on me."

"I'll get between you and the stares," Jeanne said.

Teddy came downstairs then, dressed in khakis and a dress shirt.

"Well, don't you look handsome," Jeanne said.

"Thanks, Jeanne. Good morning." A coolness in his tone.

"Coffee's made," Flora said.

"Thanks. We need to talk," Teddy said.

"That's our exit cue, sugar pop," Jeanne said. "I'm going to go read this fellow a story in the nursery, if that suits."

"Thanks, Jeanne, seriously."

"Of course."

Teddy watched Jeanne go up the stairs, talking to Morgan about which story he might pick. He waited for the door to shut.

"What?" Flora asked.

"We know Zach was in Austin before he told his sister he was here. Do the police know this? Either I'm telling them or you are."

"That doesn't mean anything," Flora said.

"It means he lied to his own foster sister."

"I know. I know. I'm thinking."

"What is there to think about?"

"Because…I made a promise to her. Widow to widow."

"That's…not a thing, widow to widow."

"It is to me and her."

"We need to tell the police."

"Like you needed to tell me about Melinda and Adam?" The anger she felt—the rage—broke free.

He took a step back as she took a step toward him. "It wasn't my place."

"You keep saying that; so what the hell is your place? I welcomed you under this roof."

"That was Adam, not you."

"You don't know how marriage works, do you? If the wife doesn't want you here, you're not here."

"So you want me here?" He was looking at her as though he were giving a business presentation and she'd lobbed him an unexpected answer.

"I was willing to do it to make Adam happy."

Emotion tore at his face. "I'm staying here for you. And Morgan. So you're not alone. But if you want me gone, I'm gone."

"Teddy. Why are you here? Why?"

"What?"

"I want to know what was going on between you and Adam, because I was shut out. Why he took such an interest in you."

"I don't want anything. I just want to help you. Please believe that."

She stared at him. "Edward. Just tell me."

His breathing grew ragged. He moved past her, poured himself a mug of coffee, sipped it as though steeling himself. "I don't want you to judge him harshly."

"We're already there." First the Melinda secret, and now what was coming? She felt dizzy.

"Adam is my father."

She stared at him. And then she laughed. "No, he was too young. Just...fourteen years older than you."

Teddy said nothing. Then he lowered his stare to the floor.

"Wait, your mother was his cousin. She..." Flora stopped. "How old was she?"

"Fifteen. He has the DNA tests proving paternity. He's kept them in a safe. They're probably in the safe at the penthouse. He knew from the beginning, or suspected. But his parents kept him away from me; he was too young, it might have upset his future. He only reached out to me when he finished business school. He was twenty-four, I was ten. I'd always been told by my mother and her cousins that my father was someone she barely knew. She was never stable...mentally. I thought...whoever my father was just didn't want to deal with her. It wasn't like that. For the longest time I thought Adam was only my cousin who wanted a better life for me."

"How long have you known?"

"He told me a few months after Morgan was born. The DNA test confirmed it. He asked me not to say anything and of course I said I wouldn't. I was so happy, but I couldn't tell anyone."

"No." Flora shook her head. "He would have told me."

"Not when you'd just had Morgan. And you'd accepted me as his cousin....There was no point in telling the truth until there was a better time."

"He's given you shares in the company."

"I didn't ask for that. I don't want anything. He's given me an education and a job and...being part of this family."

All this time. All this time his own son had been living here, under her roof.

"If you want me to stay, I'll stay. I'll be a good brother for Morgan. A good influence. I can do that. For Adam. I can't take his place, but..."

Her mind swam. What had Adam done, bringing his first son here and not telling her? It was staggering. This whole "There was never a good time" excuse was garbage.

"Could you give me some space, please?" she said tonelessly. "I need to think. Alone."

"All right. But Flora, I haven't done anything wrong."

"You participated in an unforgivable lie," she said.

"I had to do what Adam wanted." He started up the stairs. He didn't seem like a grown man right now; she could see the confused, hurt boy he must have once been. Or was being again. Imagine being asked to be someone's greatest secret.

"Teddy," she said and he stopped.

"Have you told me the truth about that night?"

"What do you mean?"

"I mean exactly what I've asked."

"Are you asking me if I killed Adam?"

"I think I am," she said.

"Why would I? He's given me everything."

"Except telling the world who you are. Forcing you to keep the secret. Letting you live here but not be his son. Seeing him with his other son, acknowledged, loved. That might have eaten you alive. Him acting ashamed of you." The last part was cruel, but the words came out.

"I think he was embarrassed. Not by me, personally. By being a fourteen-year-old who got an unstable, impressionable cousin pregnant." He grimaced. "You don't put *that* on a résumé. You don't introduce your oldest son and heir that way."

Heir. Morgan is his heir too. But you used the singular, Flora thought.

Teddy continued: "You don't introduce your junior associate that way during a pitch to investors. It's not a story the world needs to hear. I was happy to be his cousin. It could only matter to him and me." A tear rolled down Teddy's cheek and he swiped at it with the back of his hand, like it was offensive.

"And to me. And to Morgan."

"You don't seem happy about it. This is why he didn't want to tell you."

Flora pounded her fist into her own chest. "I just lost my husband and I thought I knew who he was and I don't. He's a stranger to me and now so are you. I mean, if someone wanted to frame me for killing him, you'd have every reason. I couldn't profit from my crime if I was believed to have killed him, so you and Morgan would be his heirs. Half of this is still a lot."

Cui bono?

Teddy stared at her and shook his head. "You've made a couple of criminals from New Orleans feel more at home than me." Bitterness finally twisted his voice. "My father's dead. I couldn't let what I really felt show this past week. At all. I couldn't breathe. I've needed you; I've needed Morgan; you've acted like I'm your errand boy." He took a deep breath. "He said he was making provisions for me. In life and at Zhang Townsend. I think he bought the penthouse for me and was working up to telling you. So don't fight it in court. I'm his as much as Morgan is."

He went upstairs and slammed his bedroom door and Flora thought: *He's Morgan's brother. He'll always be connected to us. But can I trust him ever? No more secrets, no more, no more. What do I do now?*

Jeanne—who had to have heard some of that screaming match—came down with Morgan clutching a book, her face pale, and said, "Morgan's been such a good boy; let's get him a little snack. Some of Jeanne's lemon cake."

And Flora grabbed Morgan out of Jeanne's arms and held him tight.

46

The coffee shop was in the corner of a Lakehaven shopping center, and Kirsten wondered how much damn money was in this town. The parking lot held a higher percentage than normal of BMWs and Mercedes and high-end pickup trucks that Lakehaven teens apparently favored (several had shoe polish writing on the back windows, team numbers or names or hearts). She remembered when Henry talked about moving to Austin because there were so many tech jobs there and she hadn't wanted to leave New Orleans. It was all she knew, except for during Katrina when she'd gone to Shreveport. New Orleans was its own world and it was the world for her. What if they had come here? They had every reason to leave New Orleans. Put distance between themselves and the bad memories, and the Fortunatos. But she couldn't leave Zach.

She went inside the coffee shop. She saw Melinda's large friend David, sitting alone near the door, like a sentinel. He nodded at her, jerked his head toward the back of the café. Where she saw Melinda…and a man she recognized as Shawn Townsend.

That was unexpected. And not good.

"How is she?" Kirsten asked David.

"Lively," David said. He had a low voice.

"She's using you."

"Maybe I don't mind being used." He sipped his latte.

Kirsten walked toward the back.

"You said I'd thank you for the slap," Melinda said as she approached the booth. "I haven't felt like thanking you yet."

"I'm staying at the penthouse. She's talking to me."

"Is she saying anything interesting?"

Let Melinda stew. Kirsten looked at Shawn. "I'm Kirsten North. You're Shawn Townsend." She sat down.

"Yes, I am," he said. "I'm sorry for your loss."

"I'm sure losing your business partner is a blow."

Shawn raised an eyebrow. "Well, Taylor likes you, but you've walked in here like you're ready to fight."

"She hits," Melinda said. "I can vouch for that."

"It helped Flora and I make a separate peace."

"Clearly." Melinda frowned.

"This," Kirsten said, waving a finger at the two of them, "also looks like a separate peace."

"Melinda has the single most promising company in our portfolio. I don't want to see the initial public offering derailed by other factors," Shawn said.

Kirsten said, "You mean your partner's murder."

"Which has nothing to do with our company," Shawn said.

"That would be nice for you, wouldn't it? He's dead and if Flora is guilty, once the legal wrangling is over, the company will be yours."

Shawn had the air of a slightly bored professor talking down to his students. "Adam was a huge loss for us. I'm assuming your grief is why you are making unfounded accusations."

Kirsten gave him a slightly withering look and turned to Melinda. "What does your software do?"

Melinda glanced at Shawn. "It pulls together data from multiple sources—banking, online shopping, social media—to give our clients a much more detailed and predictive picture of someone's financial health."

"You mean, like, if their accounts were low on money," she said very softly.

Melinda nodded.

"Like if a guy was in desperate need." *I'll offer you a hundred thousand for this work.*

Melinda and Shawn glanced at each other.

Either Adam had used this software to find a financially desperate security expert who would respond to his unusual plea, or someone close to Zhang Townsend had used it. And faked the communication from Adam to frame Flora.

"Who has access to this software so far?"

"Our customers, obviously; we have a dozen already."

"And you all do, right? You're in the office, correct?"

Shawn said: "What does this have to do with anything?"

"Why did you want to talk to me?" Kirsten countered. She should throw in his face that Henry came by his house, but if she did, he'd want to know how she knew and she wasn't ready to play every card yet. She decided to wait and see what he said.

Shawn cleared his throat. "In view of your tragic loss, although it had nothing to do with Melinda's company or Zhang Townsend, we're prepared to grant you shares in her company. Not as compensation. We carry no liability. Just as…a gift."

"Wow," she said after a moment. Her phone buzzed and she went and retrieved her coffee from the ready counter. It was hot, and as she sat down, Kirsten wondered how much damage she could do to Shawn's face if she threw it at him.

"And I presume this buys my silence. So I'm not out making accusations against y'all when you're prettying up your company to sell public shares. This generous gift would lose some of its value." Kirsten could see it—the attention of the business press would be on this company more so because of Adam's murder. No such thing as bad publicity. Maybe the institutional investors would shy away if the new company's CEO was tied in any way to her lover's death.

Shawn and Melinda were guarding their own.

"What's Greenkey?" she asked Shawn.

"I already told you, we don't know," Melinda said.

Shawn shook his head. "She's right. I don't know either."

Play the biggest card. Shake the cage. She tapped on her phone, brought the picture of the sleeping Mender up on her phone. "Know this guy?"

She held up the phone.

They both leaned forward to look. She watched their faces. For a hint of recognition, a surge of panic.

"Is he asleep in a bathtub?" Melinda asked.

"He's had a hard day."

"I don't know him," Melinda said. "Who is he?"

"No idea," Shawn said. He leaned back.

Kirsten had seen nothing in their faces, but they were both businesspeople, negotiators, deal makers, and they weren't folding.

"I hope you'll consider our generous offer."

Generous offer. *Every life is worth something*, she thought. What we were willing to spend on medical care to save someone, or willing to take out in insurance, or willing to spend to educate or incarcerate. But she looked at the two of them and decided: *Henry was worth more*.

"Basically it's a bribe."

"It's not that. It's a recognition that Adam and Henry died together and us wanting to help you," Melinda said.

"You could talk your new best friend Flora into selling her shares to me and consider it a consulting fee," Shawn said blandly.

Selling her shares. Did he not know about the supposed grant to Teddy? Oh, she almost wanted to drop that bomb on him. But that was Flora's news to share.

"I don't want your money. I want my husband back. Is everything a business transaction with y'all?"

"I pushed for this for you," Melinda said. "I got Shawn to agree."

"If Mardis, Melinda's company, does well," Shawn said, "it would be worth a great deal to you. You don't have much; I'm sorry to be blunt, but we've assessed your financial holdings."

She nearly laughed. "My holdings. Of course you used your little software on me."

"A nicer house. Maybe a master's degree in your field. Security."

"And I'm sure the last thing your initial public offering needs is an extended murder investigation."

"Extended? An arrest has been made; the case is solved. Soon as there's a trial, justice will be served," Shawn said.

"Shawn, I do like your wife. But I don't like you. This is gross and offensive. I don't even have my husband's body back. And you're hosting a party tonight to celebrate Adam's life and…" She stood up. "Melinda, thanks but no thanks."

"Then I don't want to hear from any lawyers representing you," Shawn said.

She nearly said *I'll see you tonight*. Her anger had made her blind to the fact that Shawn would now know her face. This was going to make it that much harder to get into the party.

She'd have to figure it out.

47

Mender knew he was likely to die. The woman was indecisive about it, full of bluster, but she didn't have the nerve to kill him. The brother, though, was the one who would end him. Turning him over to the police would implicate his sister in multiple crimes and Couvillon wasn't going to do that. They would do what he had planned to do to Kirsten: make him disappear. It was what he would have done in their position.

He told himself to make peace with it. It was always a possibility in this line of work. But if he thought too much about it, he thought of Annie growing old without him, of her raising their child alone, of him missing the baby's smiles, the first steps, the first day of school. It made his heart feel like a fist was squeezing it.

Haven't you taken that away from people? he asked himself.

Yes, but it was different, he told himself next. *Those were people who made bad choices. Very bad choices. My job was to rectify bad choices.*

He had one job now: protect Annie. He never should have dated her. Ever. But he'd gone into the bar that night to have a drink with an old buddy, and the buddy canceled via text and he decided to still have a drink, alone, because he was so used to being alone, and there was a trio of girls laughing at the table behind him and then the night's band started up and he decided to ask the pretty brunette to dance, certain she'd say no, but she said yes and that was it.

He shouldn't have gone to the bar; as a hit man, he shouldn't even have had a friend.

Now he was tied up in a bathtub, hoping he could save his wife and their soon-to-arrive baby.

Zach Couvillon kept injecting him with stuff that made him dopey, but Mender hadn't given him the name of his handler. Zach hadn't started in with fists or pliers or some other crude method of persuasion. He wondered if Zach knew about the note Mender had left for Kirsten. He thought not. Or they knew about it and saw it as a transparent attempt to divide them. It hadn't worked.

Zach reentered the bathroom. "I admire how you've kept your mouth shut and tried to deal with your failure professionally."

"Thank you," Mender said. He tensed.

"So my boss has sent your photo to a number of handlers who work with guys like you, and not a single one of them is owning up to you. No one wants to claim you as their employee. Which means no one is willing to negotiate on your behalf."

"If I tell you his name, will you please just go after him? And not anyone else? Please. Please."

"Because of your professional and pleasant demeanor, I will not go after anyone connected to you. There's nothing in it for me."

"Or your bosses. No one goes after her."

"I know you're not in a position to trust me, but this is business—even though you came after my sister. I'm not that guy who goes after innocent people."

Mender took a deep breath. "My handler's working name is Pierson. I don't know his real name. But if he's on your list..."

"There is a Pierson here." Zach's gaze met his.

Oh, good. He knew there was a guy named Pierson in the business. He didn't much like Pierson. His handler's name was Garrison; he was a short African American guy, and he was charged with taking care and relocating Annie if something went terribly wrong. If he betrayed Garrison or the client, that deal would be off.

So Garrison had to be protected—at least long enough to get Annie to safety.

But Mender said: "Pierson might be able to identify the client."

"I get why you are telling Kirsten you didn't kill Henry, but part of the deal is honesty."

"Okay. Honesty. That seals the deal."

"Yes."

For Annie, then. Tell the next lie. "I killed them both."

Zach activated the video camera on his phone. "Say it. For her."

Mender looked into the camera's lens. "I killed them both. Henry North and Adam Zhang. I did it. And I'm sorry."

Zach turned off the camera.

"Professional courtesy." Zach sat back down. "Okay, Pierson. Where's he located?"

"His phone's area code is Atlanta, but of course he could have just bought it there." Pierson, last he heard, was in Atlanta. Garrison was in Chicago.

"You must have met him before. What's he look like?"

"Fifties, tall, ex–football player type. White guy. Bald the last time I saw him. Around six four, three hundred pounds." Nearly the opposite of what Garrison looked like. Let them chase shadows. Save Annie.

"Thank you for your cooperation."

"You promised me," Mender said.

"I did," Zach said quietly. "And if you've lied about any details of Mr. Pierson to me, our deal is off."

Then they heard it both: a woman's voice, raised in bright query: "Hello, Kirsten? Are you here?"

Mender opened his mouth to scream and Zach grabbed for the syringe.

48

Flora had come to the penthouse because the safe was there, and she needed to know for sure if Teddy was telling the truth. Kirsten would just have to understand and forgive the interruption.

She had parked in the garage when she saw Detective Bard getting out of another car.

"Ms. Zhang. I was coming to see you and thought you might be here."

"Oh. Yes. I'm letting Kirsten North stay here."

"Can we talk upstairs?"

"Sure." Flora felt uneasy. She thought the police detective would have called or texted first and then it occurred to her: *Maybe she didn't want you to be ready for her. But she's made an arrest.*

They took the elevator up to the penthouse. Flora stepped out, calling for Kirsten.

When she didn't get an answer right away, she glanced at Bard, who was looking around. "It's not fully furnished yet," Flora said.

"What a view." Bard drifted toward the window.

"She said she might sleep most of the day," Flora said.

"Mrs. Zhang," a low voice boomed. Flora turned to see Zach Couvillon hurrying from the bedroom area in a gray T-shirt and jeans. She'd offered the place to Kirsten, not him, and Flora knew she shouldn't be irritated but she was, knowing what Teddy had found out about them. About this man and their past.

"Hello, Mrs. Zhang." He offered Flora his hand and she shook it because she had to. He shook hands with Bard. "Detective. If you're looking for Kirsten, I expect her back at any moment. She texted me that she was on her way."

"I thought she was feeling overwhelmed today. She came by my house, according to my neighbor Milo." Flora folded her arms.

"She needed some fresh air and time alone, so she went for a drive. I think the reality of Henry's death is sinking in."

"It can take some time," Bard said.

"Detective Bard and I didn't come here together. I need to pick up something. Excuse me," Flora said. She turned to the hallway and made her way to the room Adam had set up as an office. Hardwood floors. She checked under the rugs; no safe.

She noticed the bathroom door was closed but didn't think anything of it.

Then she heard Kirsten arriving and saying hello and Flora went out to see her.

-

"With the arrest of Norman Murphy," Bard said, "the case will proceed. We've completed the autopsies and the bodies will be released to you both. I thought you would like to hear that from me. You can take your husband's body back to New Orleans, Kirsten, and we will help you arrange that if you'd like."

"Thank you," Kirsten said. "Do you really think Norman did it?"

"We did find your husband's phone on him. That's the most conclusive evidence."

"But you didn't find a gun."

"No, we did not."

"Has he said why?" Flora asked.

"He has not. He hasn't cooperated. We think he camped near there and saw two men go into the warehouse, one driving a rather nice car. A moment of weakness, he must have thought it would be easy money. He may not have intended to kill them, but we believe Henry must have fought with him for the gun, hence the greater number of shots, and then he killed Mr. Zhang. I'm sorry."

"Are you the type," Kirsten asked, "to admit if you've made a mistake?"

Bard frowned. "Yes. But I cannot ignore evidence."

"It doesn't seem likely that a homeless guy would just chuck a valuable item like a gun," Kirsten said.

"If he used it in a murder, it does seem likely."

"So the case is closed."

"Of course we're open to new evidence, but we believe it was a crime of opportunity and we have our man."

Flora cleared her throat. "I know you and your brother must be ready to get home. I'll be putting the penthouse on the market soon and I need to get it ready."

"Sure," Kirsten said. "Thanks for the hospitality." She could sense the hostility under the words. Flora was upset. She glanced at Zach. Was Mender still in the tub?...Zach was out here, being calm, with a police officer.

It was like being in Larry's den with Steve Fortunato, except Bard could arrest them.

"We appreciate it, Mrs. Zhang," Zach said. "Thanks for your kindness."

"You're welcome," she said in a flat tone.

"Mrs. North," Bard said. "Since you seem concerned about Norman Murphy, if you have further information that would clear him or implicate someone else, I want to know that."

"Of course. No, I don't. Is Norman all right?"

"Yes. I'm surprised at your concern for him," Bard said.

"He's an old man. And I'm not convinced he's guilty."

Flora glanced at Kirsten.

"Like I said, he's not talking," Bard said. "I just wanted to give you the information about the bodies' being released in person. I know this has been a horrible time for you all. You have my number if you need to reach me." Bard turned to leave, then stopped and turned back. "Not to bring up past tragedies in light of the current one, but did the police in New Orleans ever solve the disappearance of your foster father?"

Flora glanced at the other two. Zach's face was impassive. Kirsten's started to go crimson.

"No, they did not," she said.

Bard said, "He was a mob accountant, right?"

"He was an accountant," Kirsten said. "I don't believe he was ever accused or convicted of a crime."

"And one of his…clients, really, his main client, put you through college, right, Mr. Couvillon?"

"Yes, ma'am."

"And you work for them now?" Bard continued.

"I work for Magali Investments, which is a real estate firm."

"Owned by the Fortunato family."

"They own many businesses."

"They must need many accountants then." Bard gave a smile with no warmth. "It's tough, Kirsten. Losing both your foster father and your husband to violence this way."

"My foster dad left us. That he met a violent end was never proven."

Bard gave a little nod. "Be in touch with the morgue about getting Henry home. Good night."

They watched her go to the elevator and leave.

The silence was awkward. "I don't know why she brought that up. I was a child," Kirsten said.

"Zach," Flora said. "When did you get to Austin?" Kirsten's head jerked up.

The look he gave Flora was searing. But he said: "The night of the murders."

Silence among the three of them; Kirsten stared at Zach.

"I knew that," Kirsten lied. Zach glanced at her.

"You didn't know. You told me that first day we met he'd just arrived. Why did you lie, Zach?" Flora said.

"Well, you've lost your timidity," Kirsten said.

"I've lost a lot more than that," Flora said.

Zach kept his voice steady. "Kirsten, I didn't want you to know I'd failed to protect him. Henry asked me to come that night," he said. "He was afraid."

"Of whom?" Flora asked.

"He didn't say. Late Monday afternoon, he asked me to fly to Austin, right then. He said it was extremely important and so I did. And he said not to tell you, Kirsten. But there were storms between Houston and New Orleans and my plane was delayed. By the time I got here...he wasn't answering his phone. Or texts."

"You knew he was dead and you didn't tell me. I cannot even," Kirsten said.

"I didn't know where he was; he said for me to call him when I got to Austin and he'd tell me where to meet him. I started calling hotels and hospitals. Then the next day I saw the news about a shooting at the warehouse. It wasn't until they released Adam's name...that I knew for sure."

"The caller..."

"Would be able to see I'd texted him. Unless he deleted all the texts. Which Henry might have done to protect me before he went into a dangerous situation. It would be like him to be careful."

"I still can't believe you," Kirsten said. "How could you not tell me this?"

Flora said, "This is between you two; I have something I need to do." And she marched down the hallway and they watched her, keeping her in sight, as she made the turn toward the master bedroom and away from the office—and its bathroom.

-

The safe was in the floor of the main bedroom closet. She tried the current combination for the safe at the Lakehaven house. It didn't work. Then she tried the combination they'd used previously—and it worked.

The safe didn't have much in it. A file folder with the label CHAO, EDWARD on it. She paged through the contents. There were legal documents in there as well, including the death certificate for his mother and older papers from the authorities in California about Teddy's guardianship status.

But there was the DNA test. She read it. He *was* Adam's son.

And at the back of the file, a document. Granting shares in his company to Teddy, witnessed by Jeanne and Milo, just as they said. Signed by Adam. But he hadn't given this to Teddy or his lawyer; this was the original.

Had he changed his mind? Told Teddy he wasn't giving him the shares?

She felt shell-shocked.

For a moment she nearly tore it up. Destroyed it. Grief and anger, a fury that she didn't understand, welled up in her.

How could Adam have not told her about Teddy? How could he have his own son, a young man she liked and had welcomed, living under their roof and never share that with her? And how could he have cheated on her with Melinda?

He had wanted a wife. He hadn't wanted to share his life.

And at the bottom, more file folders, each tabbed with a company name. One was a surprise, labeled Milo's Gin—printouts of financial reports, with Adam's handwritten notes. It looked like from the notes he had been advising Milo on expansion plans, a new round of investors. Other companies with odd names: Canary Tech, Grinke, Acceleran, Meeble—the list was long. Mostly handwritten notes on financial statements, which she shuffled through quickly.

Wait. Grinke—could that be Greenkey? Marco hadn't seen it written down, just heard Adam say the word, and maybe he interpreted it as the words "green key."

She opened the file. It was empty. No papers.

Adam must have taken them somewhere, or hidden them in another place, or destroyed them.

If Zhang Townsend was fracturing, then maybe these were the companies he was helping.

Her gaze went from the file labels to what was beneath the folders: a gun.

Adam had a gun. She didn't know about it. She stuck the folders of notes back in the safe. She checked it. It was loaded. She made sure the safety was on. She didn't want a gun in the house with Morgan. So she stuck the gun back in the safe, relocked it, and took Teddy's papers with her.

It didn't look like the argument between Kirsten and Zach had been resolved. She didn't care. She never had to see these people again, except maybe at Norman's trial.

"It's not Greenkey, it's Grinke." Flora spelled out the name.

"How do you know that?"

"I saw it in Adam's notes. It's just another company he might have been considering for investment, something he hyped up to Marco. Probably because he was going to end his partnership with Shawn and he needed to sound like he was working on the next big thing. It can't matter at this point. And my husband's business really isn't your concern anymore."

"I'd still like to know more about that company," Kirsten said.

"I don't know if I'll see you again," Flora said. "Leave the key with the guard when you go."

"Flora. I'm sorry," Kirsten said. "Why are you mad at me?"

"I just am. I feel like you weren't honest with me."

"Last night I was more honest with you than I've been with anyone in a long time," Kirsten said. "I told you what I was going to do."

"Well, it didn't matter. They arrested Norman."

"The killer called me again. This morning, when I was out. Warning me off."

Flora shook her head. She didn't know whether or not to believe her. "Can't you tell who it is?"

"The voice is disguised. But I was telling them off and they...they yawned. *Yawned* at me like I was boring them by threatening them." Her voice shook. "Whoever is behind this...whoever arranged this...thinks they've beaten us."

"Then tell Bard. Tell the police. Or maybe it's just someone cruelly messing with you." Flora took a deep, calming breath. "I hope you get your life sorted out, Kirsten."

The words were like a slap. "Well, I hope you do, too, considering yours is a bigger wreck than mine. We'll clean up before we leave. Give Morgan a hug for me. Thank you again."

Flora started to say something but didn't. She went to the penthouse elevator and left without looking back.

-

"I'm going to her fund-raiser," Kirsten said.

"You can't," Zach said.

"I can't stay around you and look at you right now," she said. "And what are we going to do with that guy in there? How did he not make a noise with Bard here?" Suddenly she caught her breath. "Did you..."

"He's sedated. I had to give him a solid shot. He'll be out for hours. His handler is a guy named Pierson. Some friends of mine in Atlanta are looking for him. They'll make him talk. They'll make him say who the client is. I made a deal. No retribution against his family."

She did a slow clap.

"I mean, the Fortunatos wouldn't. And I wouldn't do anything like that."

"Wouldn't you? You're a paragon of brotherly virtue."

"I failed Henry. How could I tell you that? I screwed up. I messed up. If I had been there...maybe it would have gone down different or maybe I'd be dead too. But I got this guy; I'm going to find out who ordered this, and I will make them pay. I will make it right for you." Zach looked like he might cry.

"Zach. Stop," she said. "I can't do this right now. He was at the Townsend house. I need to know why. That's the hole in this, the why. What did Henry find once he got here and started digging into Flora? The only answer is in what he did...before either of us got here."

"All right."

"But I'll ask again: What are you...going to do with Mender?"

Zach said nothing.

"Just in cold blood. I can't..."

"You can't what? Henry and I covered for you."

"Not the same. It was an accident."

"You did what had to be done. This is the same. You think we can let him go? He'll come after us."

"We need him to clear Norman," Kirsten said.

"I have a recorded confession. We'll find a way to get Bard to believe it."

"I don't want you..."

"We argued when you said you were going to kill whoever killed Henry. Now you're too delicate." He held up his phone, played the recording. She heard Mender admit to the deaths. She closed her eyes.

"Send that to my phone," she said.

"Why?"

"Because I'm going to find a way to anonymously send it to Bard. Maybe it will help. Maybe the police or the feds will recognize him. His face. Maybe he's wanted."

"I'm pretty sure this is the first time he's been caught."

"I have to think," she said.

She went into the office and opened her laptop. Copied the video from her phone to the computer. Chatted online with her online researcher group, learned a way to send a digital file through a cloaked server. She took Mender's confession and set it up. Watched the video. He was lying in the tub. You could see the decorative gray tiles.

Would Bard know this was in Flora's penthouse? It wouldn't be hard for her to check.

And if the killer was at the gathering at the Townsends, then maybe having the confession on her phone would be useful. A card to play.

If she got no answers tonight, then she'd send it to Bard. She couldn't let Norman stay in jail.

She couldn't help herself. She searched online for Grinke. There wasn't much—a famous author from years ago, a town in Mississippi, a pastor in Minnesota. No indication of a new company with that name. She went back to her online research group and put in a request for information from anyone who had an idea what it might be, because it appeared to be a company that wasn't a company.

Maybe it folded, a participant in Iowa answered.

Or it's a front company, someone in California said. A throwaway.

It felt like a dead end to Kirsten. She was absolutely drained. She had used the excuse of the reality of Henry being gone sinking into her for staying here, but now her excuse had become the truth. She lay down. She could hear Zach moving in the other room. She closed her eyes. Exhaustion swept over her.

-

She awoke hours later. The sun was setting. She got up. Zach was on his laptop and his phone. Trying to find the handler. No luck yet. She peered into the bathroom. The hit man still looked asleep.

She showered in the master bathroom.

Put on the little black dress. Realized she didn't have jewelry that really went with it. She hadn't packed any in her haste to get here. But she didn't need to look nice to attend a party where she wouldn't be welcomed.

She came out.

Zach was sitting on the couch. He looked haggard. "You look nice."

"I just have to fit in long enough to get in."

"I wish you would not do this."

"Maybe if you had called me as soon as you knew, all this would have unfolded differently."

"I'm sorry. I did what I thought was best. Because you're my sister."

"Not really," she said, and this time she meant it.

His "always really" was a faint whisper on the air as the elevator doors closed.

49

Kirsten had turned her rental car over to the valet, and then pretended to check her phone while she waited for a group of four women, glamorously dressed, to walk just a few feet ahead of her toward the Townsend house. She trailed slightly behind them like she was part of that squad. It would be easier if any security or screeners thought she was with a group. She was ready to plead she'd forgotten her invitation if asked but no one asked, and near the front of the house—which, wow, looked really beautiful and grand, the event decorations done with tasteful restraint given the situation—she saw the attractive redhead who was at the head of her useful group dash toward a tall, gorgeous woman and exclaim, "Meredith! You look stunning!" and they did the embrace and air kiss that wouldn't muss their makeup and the other women, like birds, flocked around their friend. *Okay, improvise then.* Kirsten put her phone up to her ear, waved generally at them all, and wasn't noticed as she entered the house.

The crowd was large, but muted.

She thought Taylor or Flora might be at the check-in, but of course they weren't; there were foundation staffers to handle that chore. And no sign of her morning nemesis, Clipboard Lady.

Name tags were laid out on a tabletop. When the older gentleman running the table was distracted, she swiped one that read "Elizabeth Martin," pushing the tag next to it into the empty space. She stepped away for a few moments, again pretending to be on the phone, then returned to the table with a bright smile.

"Hi, I'm Lizzie Martin."

"Ah..." The man checked his list. "Ah, here you are." And he checked her name off.

"I don't seem to see a name tag." She aimed her finger at the rows, pointing toward the M names.

"Oh, we can fix that," the gentleman said. "I'll make you a new one."

"Can you make it Lizzie? That's how everyone knows me. I thought I had registered that way." Just in case the real Elizabeth Martin was five minutes later. Two women named Martin with a similar first name was entirely possible.

"Ah, of course," he said again, and a printer spit out a name tag as he consulted his tablet. He slid it into a plastic cover with a lanyard and presented it to her with a flourish.

The fake Lizzie Martin thanked him. When his back was turned a moment later, she replaced the stolen name tag on the table. She then sailed off into the celebration of life for Adam Zhang, benefiting the Zhang Global Rare Diseases Foundation.

-

Kirsten snagged a glass of champagne off a passing tray; a drink was just more camouflage. She might not have much time if the real Elizabeth Martin showed up and the check-in guy got suspicious. She'd prefer not to answer questions.

She did a quick scan. No sign of Taylor or Flora or Shawn. She knew what Teddy looked like from his social media picture; she didn't see him either. Or her new friend Milo, but she had seen the sponsorship signs for Milo's Gin. She doubted Melinda would be in attendance, with Flora here.

The house was large and furnished with care. Elegant, understated, but cold. One back wall of a massive den was glass, and it fronted out onto a huge yard that sloped down the shore of Lake Austin. The lake looked more like a river to her, with towering limestone cliffs on the other side. A boat crept past leaving a small wake. Dozens of people were already outside, where there was a bandstand and many tables set out. No doubt Adam Zhang's death had raised attendance. She could see items on some of the tables; it looked like a silent auction.

Shawn must have a home office in this huge, gorgeous home. She needed to find it.

Her glance ran across the room. There was a well-built young man in the corner, wearing a dark suit and not holding a drink, with a visible earpiece. Security. He was near the stairway, presumably to keep partygoers from heading upstairs. Kirsten walked away from him. She wandered, pretending to sip at the champagne, glancing into rooms. There were bathrooms. And a media room, and guest bedrooms, but she hadn't seen an office.

It must be upstairs.

She went into a kitchen so large she could hardly believe it was in a residence. Workers bustled in from the catering trucks outside. She glanced around.

"I'm sorry, this is a work area, miss," a woman in a gray polo shirt with a catering company logo on it said very politely.

"I apologize." Kirsten lowered her voice. "I'm trying to get upstairs. My sister had…an issue…and needed something from me…she texted me that she'd hidden in an upstairs bathroom."

"Of course," the woman said, understanding. "There's a stairwell just past the kitchen."

"You're a darling, thank you!"

50

Mender woke up in the tub. He felt weirdly alert, not drowsy. He didn't know how long he'd been unconscious, but his muscles ached.

He listened.

He heard someone, presumably Zach Couvillon, puttering around in the kitchen. Maybe making a snack. Or boiling up some water to throw in Mender's face. He'd heard Flora Zhang's voice and nearly yelled out to get her attention, but Zach had been too fast, the hand clamped over his mouth, the needle in his neck.

He still had on his shirt and pants. And in the cuff of the pants, where the big New Orleans jerk hadn't searched, was the little Japanese blade. He had not been conscious or alone long enough to attempt to use it. He was able to pull his legs up slightly, even with the zip-ties, and he felt the hidden blade in the cuff.

He pulled it free.

Carefully, carefully, he turned it so the edge faced away from his fingers.

Slowly...slowly...he cut through the zip-ties around his ankles. It took fifteen minutes, but Zach Couvillon didn't check on him during that time. He must have thought Mender was still out from the sedatives.

The zip-ties around his ankles parted and he had to keep himself from crying out with relief. His legs felt cramped; he slowly stretched them out to get the blood circulating.

He heard a humming noise approaching the bathroom.

He had just folded his legs back into position when Zach returned. Zach looked at Mender, not closely, just a bundle of arms and legs inside the tub, his hands out of view. His gaze was cold.

"What?" Mender said.

Zach leaned down and punched him. Not too hard but enough to make his ears ring. Mender had the blade behind his back and stayed still.

"You've cost me the only family I've ever had," Zach said.

"I'm sorry," Mender said. Defiance was not an option right now. He cleared his throat. "I admire your devotion to your sister. My sister died of cancer when she was thirteen." This wasn't true, but it never hurt to paint oneself in a sympathetic light.

"It's too bad she's not here to save you then," Zach said.

"There's no point in being mean about it," Mender said.

"You're right. Let's keep it professional," Zach said and went back out as the oven timer pinged.

He didn't shut the door all the way, but the kitchen was down the hall. He'd still have to be quiet.

Another agonizingly slow fifteen minutes and Mender was through the ties on his wrists, although he had a nasty, careless cut on one finger to show for it. He stood, so careful, so careful not to make the tub creak and signal to Zach that all was not well.

He could hear a television playing in one of the rooms. A basketball game.

He removed, carefully and so quietly, the towel bar on the back of the door.

It felt good in his hand. It felt so good.

He had a plan.

He stepped from the bathroom toward the sound of the basketball game, down the hall.

51

Kirsten smiled and nodded and hurried up the stairs; the security team must have decided that no intruder would brave the crowd in the kitchen. She crept down a hall, suddenly remembering that the Townsends had a young daughter and wondering if the kid was up here with a sitter.

What would it be like to grow up in a house like this? A kind of paradise, she thought. She checked two doors: one a small study, clearly Taylor's from the decor. It was spotless and looked like a magazine's idea of a small, quaint office. Next to it, another guest bedroom.

She heard a toilet flush.

Someone else was up here. She ducked into another room, left the door cracked, and saw one of the security guys exit a bathroom and shut the door behind him. He moved down the hall and took up a position near the stairs.

She was trapped.

Okay. She looked at the room she was in. It was full of…action figures.

Shelves covered the walls. On one side were action figures from a huge variety of film and TV franchises, still in their packaging, carefully arranged. On the other side were action figures freed from their plastic and cardboard coffins, posed in moments she recognized from the films. In the middle of the room there was a desk with printouts. She scanned them in the dim light of a lamp that had been left on—valuations of rare figures from forty years ago, from TV shows she hadn't heard of, some highlighted with a yellow marker. The prices on some were in the thousands.

Great, trapped in a room with a rich man's toys, she thought. There was a door on each side of the room. She tried one and found a small bathroom; she tried the other and found…an office. Desk, laptop, two large computer screens, a flat-screen mounted on the wall.

Jackpot. Shawn's home office.

She closed the door to the action figure room. The lights were off in here, so she risked turning on a small desk lamp that gave off a modest glow. The office's windows offered a view of the lakeshore and the crowd of people; she quickly lowered the shades.

Kirsten took a deep breath. If someone had seen her in the lighted window where she shouldn't be…but it was a party, no one should have noticed.

She wouldn't have much time. She had to think, be orderly about this. She sat down at the computer keyboard, which snaked to the laptop, which was closed, moored in a bay with a multitude of computer ports.

The screen awoke at her touch and asked for a password. She started opening the desk drawers and after finding a small black notebook, she raced through the pages. It listed internet passwords for stores and sites, with the password for each. Henry had told her this bad security practice was far more common than people thought. She found the system password and logged in—it was a variation of the name of one of the action figures. *Boys and their toys*, she thought.

She saw an icon on his screen for SecurityVideo. Of course a house like this had better-than-average security. She clicked through and the browser kindly filled in the password automatically.

A list of digital videos by date. She went to the date for when Henry drove here.

There were red flags on the feed; she guessed that was when significant motion or activity picked up. First flag was Shawn, leaving for the day. Second flag, a cleaning person arriving for work—the relevant video feed jumping to the right camera. Third, Taylor heading out in exercise togs. Normal things. Taylor returning. Cleaning person leaving.

Fifth flag, Henry approaching the door. Looking confused.

He was here.

He rang the doorbell and stepped back politely.

She couldn't hear, but she could see him speaking. The sound might not have been working or was turned down.

Then there was a figure stepping into the frame, apparently closing the door behind her. It was Taylor.

Talking to Henry.

Henry was holding his laptop, which Kirsten thought was odd. They spoke briefly, then Henry turned and left.

Taylor stood in the doorway and watched him leave. Then she shut the door.

He must have come here to see Shawn. But…why not go to Shawn's office downtown? It appeared, from the shadows, to be late afternoon.

She jumped to the other flags—approaching the fateful hour. She found cameras aimed at the driveway, the garage. Shawn came home; he drove off again. Taylor walked out the front door, earbuds in, like she was going for a jog.

They had been each other's alibis, though. That they were both home.

She went straight to Shawn's email and searched for Henry's name. No match. She searched Henry's various email address.

The account name accessing the shared doc had been "A2Z." She searched for that name. And saw an email notification about an edit to a shared doc.

She clicked on it: I've established that you're the one who sent me the shared document from this IP address and offered me money. I think we should talk face to face. I should know as much about you as you know about me.

Adam hadn't hired him. It was Shawn. And Henry had somehow managed to track the source of the shared document, perhaps through a vulnerability in the private service's access logs, and come here to the Townsend house. But Shawn hadn't been here.

She took a picture of the email, with the address of the sender, a glob of numbers and random letters.

She searched the emails but didn't find anything else. She looked through the documents file. So much stuff, all tied to his business. She searched for "Grinke" and "Greenkey."

Nothing.

Then she went to the Downloads folder. Maybe she'd find something there that had been downloaded from a now-deleted and erased email. Proposals from work, PowerPoint presentations, documents for review. Nothing that indicated it might be Adam's or Flora Zhang's secrets or reports.

Where was it?

Voices, female. In the hallway. She put the computer to sleep. Nowhere to go. She went under the deep desk, tried to scoot out of sight.

–

The door opened and then closed.

"I can't be gone long." Taylor's voice.

"I don't want to wait longer." A woman's voice. Not Flora's. Not Melinda's. But a voice she had heard before.

"I don't know where he is," Taylor said. "I can't just keep...doing this. You wanting one result, me wanting another."

"We're nearly there. If he got rid of Teddy, it would crucify Flora. She'd be done."

"Her I don't care about. I can get Shawn to bury your problem. It's the other two."

"Let time pass. You've waited this long."

She knew that voice. Kirsten stopped breathing.

Taylor said, "Flora says they're leaving. Fine. I don't have to see it happen to them. Let them leave. Let them get away from us, back to New Orleans, and then wait a bit and then be done with them. It won't be a question; look at the scum he works for. A hit on him that also catches his innocent bystander sister…it won't even be a story for a week. Then we dance on the graves."

"You have to do as I say. You wouldn't even know about them if it weren't for me. You tried before and you failed. You screwed this up by calling her because you wanted to hear her pain. But we'll get back on track. Stay strong."

"I need a drink."

"I know you do." A soft laugh. "And I know someone who can get you one. So, let this party happen. Tomorrow is a new day, and we'll be one step closer."

"That my contacts are not answering me at all is a problem. What if they really found them? The shooter could talk."

"He doesn't know our names."

"He could describe us."

"She's bluffing. Get ahold of yourself. Put on that pretty smile and be sympathetic and charming and go help that idiot Flora get some donations. She'll thank you and never see the knife coming. And we don't talk again. Not for a week, at least, and then maybe we can run into each other casually at Flora's. You just make sure there's no more questions."

"All right. All right."

"You've been so brave. He'd be proud of you."

The sounds of an embrace. A heavy sigh. Then the door opening, fake laughter from Taylor and the words: "Oh, I'm glad you think he's gone overboard with the action figures too!" Maybe for the benefit of the guard.

And then the door shut.

Kirsten remained under the desk for a moment, her hand closing into a fist. A rage that defied anything she'd ever felt filled her and she pushed it back down to a level that would allow her to function.

She thought: *Will Flora believe me? She thinks Zach and I are practically criminals. This is her best friend.*

She considered her options.

Finally she unfolded herself, pushed the chair out from the desk, and stood on her wobbly legs.

Get out. Now.

She went to the door of the action figure room. Barely cracked it. She could see the security guard standing there. He was looking at his phone screen.

She eased the door shut. She went back into the office's door that faced out on the hallway. Opened it. She couldn't see the guard from there; the angle was just barely farther along the hallway. But he might sense her movement. She went slowly, not worrying about shutting the office door behind her. She moved down the hall.

And into Taylor's office. She eased the door shut. Waited for a knock from the guard. None came.

She could hear Flora on a microphone outside, thanking everyone for their kindness, their support, their generosity, their remembrances of her husband.

Kirsten started on the perfectly arranged little desk, going through the drawers. Pens, pencils, stationery, thank-you notes with TT as the monogram.

In the third drawer, a silver package with a blue fleur-de-lis on it.

Gaudet cigarettes. Like the one Norman had found near the warehouse.

Underneath it, a gadget that looked like a toy: a red plastic miniature megaphone.

Something shifted in her chest. She took the cigarettes out and put them in her little clutch. She set the megaphone down on the desk. This little laptop unfortunately didn't have a book of passwords next to it or in the desk. She straightened up. The cigarettes weren't enough. She stepped to the bookshelf. Framed photos atop it.

Taylor and Shawn. Taylor and Flora, laughing at a party. An older picture of a teenage Taylor and...Uncle Larry.

She stared at it and then the door opened and a little girl came in.

"Why are you in Mommy's room?"

"Hi, sweetie, are you Amelia?" She thought that was the kid's name.

"Yeah. I have to stay up here and watch movies. Why are you in Mom's office?"

"She asked me to bring her something."

"That's my toy," Amelia said. "Mommy keeps borrowing it." She picked up the megaphone and spoke into one side of it. "Hey there, let's go to the party." The girl's voice now sounded like a low rumbling electronic scramble.

Just like the caller.

"How fun," Kirsten managed to say. "Mommy asked me to bring her this." She held up the picture. "Is this Mommy and a special friend?"

"My granddad. He died before I was born." She said it into the voice modulator toy. Now her voice sounded high, like a cartoon mouse.

"What was your granddad's name?"

Amelia lowered the toy and used her normal voice. "Larry. I like your dress."

Kirsten could see the girl had eyes like Larry's. Hand shaking, she stuck the picture in her purse. "Well, Mommy wanted to show Granddad's picture to an old friend, so I came up to get it and now I have. Let's get you back to your bedroom."

She took Amelia's hand and led her to another bedroom, got her settled in with a cartoon, and told her it was nice to meet her.

At the far end of the hall was the grand staircase that fed down to the foyer, where another guard waited farther down the stairs, one who would remember that he hadn't let her up and would likely contact the other guard to ask about her.

The guy closer to the kitchen was probably more junior. That didn't mean he was more gullible.

She turned back toward the grand stairway. She ran a hand across her lipstick, smearing it just enough. She made sure to stagger slightly as she came down the stairs.

The guard glanced at her. "Miss? The upstairs is not accessible at the moment."

"It's totally okay, he took me up there, I'm just coming back down five minutes later like he said," and she made an exaggerated shush motion with her finger. His eyes went to her finger and the smeared lipstick and his mouth tightened. She kept moving, hopeful he wouldn't reach out and stop her and that she was convincing as a party girl who'd already had a bit too much to drink and might talk if she was stopped. She moved past him downstairs, quickly, and out of his sight. She found a bathroom near the entrance foyer and repaired her makeup.

Okay. That worked. What do you do now?

The framed photo didn't fit well into her purse, so she dumped the frame into a trash can, secreting the photo back in the clutch.

She had to find Flora. Talk to her alone, which would be nearly impossible here. She was the center of attention. The crowds milled as she hurried out of the house.

Then she saw her. Flora, facing toward Kirsten, chatting with an older woman in a lovely blue dress, and next to her stood Milo, the neighbor who'd been so nice to her earlier.

Part of her thought of running up to them, slamming her fist into the woman's face, screaming at her. But it was a lovely, crowded party and there was security and this called for a knife, not a hammer.

She hid behind a corner of a hospitality tent, watching. Waiting.

Flora moved away from Milo and the woman—hugging each of them—and another person began talking to her. There was no way to get her alone, not easily.

But Kirsten had to, and now.

She hurried over to Flora, said "Excuse us" to the woman who was in the middle of saying how sorry she was for Flora's loss, and started to steer Flora through the crowd toward the front, where the cars were.

"What the hell are you doing?" Flora demanded. "Kirsten, let go."

"Please just listen to me. Please, we have to talk, away from here."

People kept trying to stop them, to offer Flora condolences. Kirsten kept moving her along, trying not to look like they would break any second into a frantic run.

"Get your hands off me, right now," Flora hissed. "Don't touch me."

"I know who hired the hit man. Henry came here. The day he and Adam died. I know why."

"I can't just leave here; people are staring."

"Let them stare. They're talking about killing Teddy and framing you for that as well."

"They. Wait, here? You mean Shawn?"

"No. I mean Taylor. We have to call Bard, now."

"You have completely lost your mind. Get away from me."

A hand closed on her arm as she tried to pull Flora along. She turned. Milo, wearing a slight but kind smile, said, "Oh, that's nice! You decided to come."

Flora pulled free of her, but Kirsten reached out and snatched her hand.

Kirsten slipped her arm through Flora's. "Milo. You made me realize that now that Flora and I are friends—bonded through tragedy—I should be here to support her and to honor Adam." She looked several feet past Milo, where another woman stood, unmoving. "Oh. Hi, you! I'm just thrilled to see you after all this time. How are you?"

The woman behind Milo first turned away as though about to run.

"Honey," Milo said. "Come say hi."

The woman turned back and moved forward like she was walking a plank. She made herself smile, but it took effort. "Hello, dear," Jeanne said.

"Hi, JJ," Kirsten said.

52

"JJ?" Flora said. "This is my neighbor Jeanne." Milo looked confused.

"JJ is my foster mother. Or was; we haven't seen each other in many years. I nearly didn't recognize you with your elegant haircut and beautiful dress." Kirsten patted Flora's arm, but Flora wasn't trying to pull away now. "Henry's mother made us invite JJ to our wedding, but she didn't come, and I can't blame her."

Flora said, "You knew Henry? You never told me. You…" Now she was staring at Jeanne.

Milo said, "What is this?" He looked completely confused.

"You see, JJ and Larry Melancon fostered me and Zach. All through high school. They were really good to us. Then Larry took off and was never seen again and JJ didn't really want to be our foster mom anymore."

"Because you all killed him." Jeanne Hobson's voice was low, barely audible.

"We were kids, and Larry was a money launderer," Kirsten said. "He was funneling money and dropping it off at various locations when he took Zach fishing." She turned to Flora. "At least once there was a woman and a girl who picked up the cash." She held up the photo of Larry and Taylor. "That's Larry. With Taylor."

"Is this true?" Flora asked Jeanne.

"Milo, I'd like to go home now. This has upset me," Jeanne said.

Milo frowned. "Sweetie, answer Flora's question."

Suddenly two of the security guards were on either side of Kirsten, pulling her off Flora, manhandling her.

"Her," Taylor said to them. "She's trespassing."

"Hey, hey!" Milo yelled, but Jeanne pulled him away, crying now, asking him to protect her from Kirsten.

Flora said, "Stop, stop!" but the guards ignored her and kept Kirsten moving along toward the house. Flora scanned the crowd. Saw him. "Teddy! Teddy, please! Help her!" Pointing at Kirsten.

Teddy looked confused, but he didn't hesitate; he ran toward them, but a third guard intercepted him and held him at bay.

Taylor rushed up to the guards, whispered something. Kirsten was screaming, "Flora! Flora! It's the truth!"

Taylor snatched the photo from her, yelled, "You cheap little thief!" and slapped Kirsten.

The crowd near them went silent as Taylor retreated.

Kirsten screamed again, "Help me! Please!" as the guards dragged her off, a woman with a clipboard following them.

The people in their finery kept their places, certain that the hostess and her security team had the unfortunate disturbance under control.

Flora tried to followed the guards. "Let her go! Now!"

"Flora, don't." Taylor was next to her, blocking her. "She's crazy."

"I saw the picture. That's the man in the article Teddy found."

"I can explain all that."

Flora could see the guards. She thought they would be escorting Kirsten off the property, but now, clear of most of the crowd, they were taking her to a side entrance of the house.

"Where are they taking her?"

"Obviously I'm pressing charges. She stole something from my house. My child is up on that floor. She's dangerous. You know she is." Taylor seized Flora's arm.

Flora looked at her. "Let go of my arm."

Taylor steadied her voice. "Flora. I will remind you that you are my best friend. I've tried to protect you from all this…"

"Take your hand off my arm, or I will snatch the hair from your head," Flora said in a low voice. "Now."

"I love you like a sister," Taylor said. "Jeanne and I tried to protect you. These people are mobsters. They have wanted to shake down me and Jeanne. . . ."

"And you've told all this to the police?"

"Please. Please. Not here. Think of Adam. Think of the money we can raise tonight if there's not more of a scene."

"Where are they taking Kirsten?"

"They're detaining her."

"I'll take her home. Less of a scene that way."

"We're calling the police."

"That will make more of a scene. Let me remove her and we'll talk later."

"Flora . . ."

"Or I will go to that microphone and give another speech. This one about you and Jeanne and everything you didn't tell me."

Taylor let go.

Kirsten was still struggling when Flora spoke to the guards. They looked toward Taylor, who nodded, wilting under the gaze of the watching guests. The guards released their grip on Kirsten's arms. She stumbled toward Flora.

Kirsten said, "We have to get out of here." They walked to the driveway, cognizant of the stares and the whispers in the thinning crowd.

"It's crazy to think Taylor is involved in this. And Jeanne takes care of my child."

"They're not who you think they are."

"Like how you and Zach aren't who I thought you were." They stopped at the parking stand and Flora gave the valet her ticket.

"Does Taylor smoke these?" Kirsten said as she pulled the Gaudet cigarette pack out of the clutch.

"It's a joke; she says she smokes only when she's super stressed."

"Norman found a Gaudet cigarette outside the warehouse. He kept it to smoke, then he thought maybe it had belonged to someone watching the warehouse that night. I think Taylor and Jeanne were there. Waiting for our husbands. Maybe they wanted to hear Henry die."

"Why would they want that? And they didn't have any reason to hurt Adam."

"They think…I hurt Larry. Taylor's real dad, apparently. And JJ's husband. They killed Henry to hurt me."

The valet pulled up and they both got into Flora's car. Kirsten saw Jeanne and Taylor hurrying toward the valet. No Milo, no Shawn. Teddy following them.

"Go, go," Kirsten yelled and Flora took off. She roared down the residential street. Kirsten looked back to see if a car was following yet. "Call your sitter. Tell her to take Morgan and go to her own home or somewhere where there are people."

"Jeanne wouldn't hurt Morgan."

"I know they hate me, but they hate you, too, for some reason."

Flora told her phone to call the sitter. They spoke quickly, the girl agreeing to leave right away with Morgan. When they hung up, Flora said, "She's going to her parents' house with Morgan. Jeanne doesn't know them."

"But she knew Henry and never told you." Kirsten tried to piece it together. Two women who loved Larry. The money gone from the attic. JJ married to a successful entrepreneur who was relying on Adam to grow his business.

She thought she saw it and she gasped. "Milo told me he wanted to expand his business. That Adam was helping him. He bought the warehouse for Milo, so he must have been serious. He said in one of those articles Marco wrote that he always looked deep at their initial funding." She remembered the words in the interview she'd read that first, sleepless night in Austin: *I look at the history: How did the company start, how did they first make their money…* "And I think maybe Jeanne—JJ—took mob cash Larry had siphoned away to help fund Milo's gin operation. And Adam discovered this."

"Would that come up in an audit?"

"I don't know. It might. Maybe Adam found money fed into Milo's companies that couldn't be accounted for by loans or proper investors. Maybe it was just a front company."

"Why wouldn't Adam go to the police?"

"Marco said Adam always had to have the upper hand. He proved that to be true, in the way he treated you and Teddy, the way he acted with Melinda, the way he reacted to his firm falling apart. He could have threatened Jeanne with exposure if she didn't play along. Maybe he thought he could get a valuable company very cheaply."

"But Milo's our friend."

"That didn't matter, Flora. That is who your husband was."

"Where should we go now?" Flora asked. She wiped her mouth with the back of her hand.

"The penthouse. We have the hit man they hired tied up there."

"What?" Flora screamed.

"He's a contract killer named Mender. His client is Jeanne or Taylor or both of them. I think they were there when our husbands were shot. To see it done, especially to Henry. And then…I think Jeanne hired Mender to get rid of me in New Orleans. But Taylor was the one who called me. She knew if I knew Henry was killed here, I'd come and I'd bring Zach and then maybe she could see us both die." She took a deep breath. "Henry traced the anonymous document that Adam supposedly sent him. He traced it to the IP address at Taylor's house. That was why he called Zach. He must have recognized Taylor…." The realization hit her then.

"There was a young woman who moved in with JJ after we left for college. We assumed JJ was fostering her. And we know there was a young woman who picked up at least one of Larry's money drops. One and the same. It must have been Taylor. Henry saw her just the one time when he went back to New Orleans for a funeral, but he recognized her when he went to her and Shawn's house. She and JJ must have found each other after Larry died. Adam didn't hire Henry. Adam never met Henry, until the warehouse. That was Taylor offering him the job. They each lured our husbands there for different reasons and then had them killed."

"I don't know your whole history, but...why have they waited until now?"

It felt like the past had made a fist and punched her in the head. "Oh. They tried once before. Someone fired shots at Zach when he was on his way to join me and JJ at a coffee shop the last time I saw JJ in New Orleans. Now I think it was Taylor." She thought. "And then JJ told me we should leave New Orleans. She made it sound like she was scared of Zach being involved with bad people. But JJ was just trying to throw us off from the fact that Taylor tried to kill Zach that day. Not long after, they moved. And they ended up in Austin."

"I met Taylor through Jeanne. They said they met through a charity."

Kirsten tried to fit it together. "Why now? Because Adam was a threat to JJ *right now* if he exposed that she'd funded Milo's Gin with mob money. If they killed off Adam and Henry, the whole point of the investigation would be uncovering their connection—which didn't exist, unless they made it look like Adam needed to have your own computers hacked for some reason. And you would be framed. Two birds; one stone. JJ saving herself; Taylor getting revenge."

"But why hurt me?" Flora whispered. "They loved me."

Kirsten glanced at her. "Flora, you're nothing to them. Maybe you were once. But not when they needed a fall guy."

Flora made a noise in her throat. She told her car phone to call Teddy. A young man's voice answered. "Flora? Where are you?"

"Teddy, listen to me. What's happening there?"

"People are leaving. The party has definitely broken up."

"There is a laptop in Shawn's office. Get it. Steal it if you have to. It has evidence. About what happened to your dad."

"There's security dudes all around; I can't...All right. I'll figure it out."

"And then call Detective Bard. Tell her we have evidence against the real killers."

"Uh, okay. I guess you're not mad at me anymore."

"No, Teddy, I'm not mad at you anymore. Please don't go home. Don't be alone around Jeanne or Taylor."

"Teddy. This is Kirsten North. I heard them talking in Shawn's office. They said if you turned up dead, it would be a nail in Flora's coffin."

"Oh, did they?" Now he sounded mad. "I'm getting that laptop."

"Okay, but then go someplace safe."

"Morgan...," he began.

"...is safe," Flora finished for him.

"I'll come help you."

"You'll end up an accessory," Kirsten said. "Stay clear of the penthouse; go to a friend's house."

"I'll get that laptop," Teddy said again. He hung up.

"So, Taylor is...what? This man Larry's daughter?"

"Zach knew Larry was leaving coolers of cash near Baton Rouge. He thought it was for another accomplice. But once he saw the pickup, and it was made by a teenage girl and a woman. Too distant for him to see them well. I think Larry had another family in Baton Rouge. He had a college girlfriend that JJ called a lot after he went missing—she must be Taylor's mom. And somehow, that way, after Larry vanished and stopped bringing them money, JJ and Taylor must have connected." And they fed off each other's hate. JJ's suspicions shared with a girl who blamed Kirsten and Zach for killing her father. How Taylor must have hated her and Zach; they'd had a life with her father when she had so much less.

Flora felt sick. "What do we do now?"

"I bite the bullet. We take the contract killer to Bard and turn him over. I'll probably go to jail. Or we'll cut a deal with the prosecutors."

"Will Zach go along with that?" Flora sounded scared.

"I don't know."

53

They drove into the building's garage and parked.

"Let me go in first and talk to Zach," Kirsten said.

"He was going to get rid of this guy, wasn't he? I mean, that's what mobsters do."

"'Mobster' is just not a term I use with him. And I don't know that," Kirsten said.

"He'll want to get rid of me too."

"Flora, I promise you, my brother won't hurt you. He's not like that."

"Oh, he only hurts the 'bad people,' right?"

"He won't hurt either of us," Kirsten said. "I'll text you when it's okay to come up."

"Did he kill your foster dad?" Flora asked.

"No, he didn't." Kirsten got out of the car then and left Flora there.

-

The elevator door opened.

The penthouse was dark—one light on in the kitchen. Kirsten hurried forward, down the entry hall, into the kitchen. She couldn't remember where the main light switches were; there was only the feeble backlight glow along the kitchen countertops.

"Zach?" Maybe he was gone on his…unpleasant errand. How would she explain this to him? Could Flora stay quiet? And without a witness how could she get Norman cleared?

"Kirsten." The voice came sliding out of the dark and then he stepped forward from the back hallway. Mender. Holding a gun. Aimed right at her.

"Zach!" she screamed.

Mender shook his head slowly. "You look lovely. How was your party?"

"Where is he?"

Mender stepped toward her, the gun unwavering in his hand.

"Are you going to kill me?" She said it and then realized it was a stupid question.

"I'm supposed to, but who I'm really annoyed with is my client for putting me in such a chaotic situation. I don't feel I was set up for success. I have an idea of who it is, but I want you to tell me her name. I know the faces."

"Your client is in a great deal of trouble and I don't think she's going to be able to pay you."

"You would say that."

"Check social media in Austin. There was a huge blowup at this fund-raiser. Accusations flew."

"The name."

"Taylor Townsend."

He took a deep breath. "That's what I needed to know."

"I have my laptop set up to email your confession," she said. "It had to be scheduled because it's going through a server to hide where it came from. If I don't turn it off, it goes."

"That's unfortunate," he said. Her announcement didn't panic him. He didn't lower the gun.

"I want to see that Zach is all right before I cancel that for you and you leave," she said carefully. Like they were actually negotiating.

Mender shook his head. "I'm not ever going to get to see my kid because of you."

"That's not my fault. I didn't bring you here."

"I just get the sense," Mender said, "you were the cause of it all."

He raised the gun.

-

Flora saw the car pull into the parking garage. Jeanne's Porsche Cayenne. Milo's birthday gift to her last year. She and Taylor got out. Flora dove down to hide. She could hear them arguing, blaming each other, with Taylor saying they had to stick together because then they could afford the best lawyers and nothing could be proven, and Jeanne complaining that she never should have let Taylor talk her into doing it this way.

Two murders was "doing it this way." *Just keep going*, Flora thought. *Please don't notice this car.*

Then silence, then rapping on the glass. She looked up. Jeanne, with a gun. An actual gun, aimed at her. "Get out, Flora."

Flora obeyed.

Jeanne kept the gun pointed at her. With the hands that had cared for her child.

"When did you ever get a gun?" Flora asked. Trying to delay, wondering if Jeanne would just shoot her dead right here.

"Larry," she said. "To protect myself if things went bad."

"You," Taylor said, "are such a disappointment."

"I cared about you. Both of you." Flora glanced at Jeanne. "And I trusted you with my child."

"And you still could have done those things, but you chose that bitch," Jeanne said. "She and that brother of hers killed my Larry."

"And you killed my husband," Flora said.

They got into the elevator. Taylor had a key.

"Where did you get that?"

"From Adam."

Flora thought: *She took it off his body. He had it and she took it off his body.*

"You were the one up here that night I came up alone."

"I was looking for something."

"I have what you were looking for. More evidence on Jeanne's financing Milo's Gin with mob money?" It was a careful lie, bolstered by Kirsten's theorizing on the way. And the Grinke file in the safe was empty—but Jeanne didn't know that. Flora steadied her voice to tell the lie. "It's in his safe."

And so was that loaded gun.

She had to get to it. Had she left it on top of the file folders? Or under them? Jeanne would force her to open it. If Jeanne let her reach in…could she grab it before Jeanne shot her?

Could she actually shoot Jeanne?

They want to take you away from Morgan. She felt her heart harden.

"I'll need that evidence," Jeanne said.

The elevator doors opened. Jeanne gestured with the gun for Flora to step out.

A dim glow came from the counter lights in the kitchen. No sign of Kirsten. Flora felt a breeze and realized that the sliding door to the balcony on the other side of the room was open to the beautiful night.

Jeanne prodded her forward with the gun.

-

"Don't you want me to disable that email?" Kirsten said, her voice rising.

Mender paused. "I'm weighing the relief that would give me versus the relief of killing you. I'm not sure I trust you near a laptop. But thanks for telling me; I'll put a bullet through your system before I leave."

The gun centered back on her.

Henry, she thought. *Zach. Mom.* The three people she'd let herself love in her life. And now they were all gone; everything was about to be gone.

She heard the elevator door open.

Mender froze. He shifted the gun away from her and toward the corner of the kitchen where the arrivals from the entryway would first show themselves.

Flora appeared. With Jeanne right behind her.

And they both saw Mender with the gun and Flora gasped and Jeanne aimed at him and screamed, "Drop it, drop it! Right now! I mean it!" Her voice was full of hysterical bravado.

Mender didn't. His bullet slammed dead center into her forehead and she dropped.

The sound was deafening in the penthouse. Kirsten saw Flora turn and run. But she was not fleeing; in the hallway back to the elevator, Flora tackled Taylor, who was running and screaming.

"Stop, stop!" Mender yelled. He ran past Kirsten—and she ran toward the kitchen. Knives. There were knives in the drawer. Taylor's house stylist had sent over all that fancy stuff. She grabbed the biggest one.

Mender had his back to her, aiming at the two fighting women. He seized Flora hard by the hair, flung her aside.

So he could see Taylor. *I know the faces.*

And Kirsten sank the knife into his back.

He howled. He pulled away from her so she couldn't pull it out and stab him again.

Flora ran in the other direction, sprinting back toward the master bedroom.

Mender screamed in agony. He leveled the gun at Kirsten, but then he saw Taylor, the key card in her hand, the elevator doors opening, escape just inches away. He grabbed her foot; she turned and then he saw Jeanne's gun in her hand and she fired but missed. A huge window at the end of the hallway behind him starred with the impact but didn't give way.

He fired and hit Taylor in the chest. She writhed and gurgled and clawed at the floor, but she was down. He started to turn toward Kirsten.

But before he could face her, she jumped onto his back and twisted the knife. She pulled it free and he slammed her backward into the wall.

"Flora!" she screamed. But Flora was nowhere to be seen.

Mender threw Kirsten over his shoulder. She still had the knife in her hand, though, and she slashed with all her strength into his leg. He growled in pain and released her but then grabbed her by the throat.

And started dragging her toward the balcony.

"That blonde shot your husband. She and the old woman argued about it. Messy job. She begged to do it, even though I was being paid. He begged for his life. Begged. They laughed at him and they told him I would kill you. Then she shot him and she made sure it hurt. I want that to be your last thought," he taunted as Kirsten felt the night air on her face.

He's going to throw me off, she thought in blinding panic.

"Here you go," he said through gritted teeth as he lifted her toward the railing.

She heard the shot.

He staggered and she fell to the balcony floor. She saw Flora, ten feet away, a gun in her hand. Flora, timid, don't-rock-the-boat Flora, eyes of new steel, was aiming again, swallowing and then firing and Mender staggered once more. He raised his gun toward Flora and fired as Kirsten shoved him, pushing and lifting his legs, up and over the edge. All thirty stories down, he screamed something that sounded like *Annie*.

The sidewalk was empty where he hit.

I want that to be your last thought, he had said.

She ran to Flora. Mender's final shot had missed.

"Flora..."

"I shot him," Flora announced. "I shot him. I shot him and you shoved him. I felt the bullet go past me. Right past me." She sounded dazed. "I shot him."

"Zach..." Maybe he lied. Maybe he'd killed Zach. *Oh, please...*

Kirsten ran to the bathroom. Zach had been badly beaten and was tied up inside the tub, just as Mender had been. But he was breathing. Alive. She screamed, "Flora, we need an ambulance!"

Flora called the downstairs security, the police, and Detective Bard. Then she looked at Taylor, still breathing, and waited for the ambulance.

Taylor's eyes opened. "Flora, please...please...I didn't do anything she said. She's lying. Lying...She's a murderer. Please."

54

Morgan Zhang toddled across the floor. He had decided again that Kirsten's lap was his favorite spot, and so he crawled back into her arms.

Weird little kid, she thought.

Teddy Chao sat across from her. He'd grabbed the Townsend laptop, as promised, and immediately called Detective Bard. The police had examined the video footage of Henry with Taylor. Taylor was not cooperating from her hospital bed, but Shawn was, and he had also gotten her the best defense lawyers in Texas. It would be a hard-fought battle to convict her, but that was tomorrow's problem. The police and the feds were searching for Mender's handler, as he could testify against Taylor and Jeanne for having hired a hit man. So far they hadn't found him.

On the TV in the den, the local news was airing a report on the case: a concierge at a lodging called Hotel Byte was cooperating with police, saying that a woman who fit Taylor's description had come to the hotel and, using his passkey, accessed Henry North's room on the night of the murders. Apparently to plant a faked report by Henry North that would implicate Flora Zhang. Mrs. Zhang's neighbor, Jeanne Hobson, had allegedly earlier used her easy access to the Zhang house to plant incriminating data on Flora's laptop to seal the frame. Melinda Alari was interviewed next, apologizing for her announcement that Flora was guilty—but she had been told by Taylor that if she didn't help them drive Flora from the business, her funding would be withdrawn in the next round. Part of that help involved giving Taylor access to Melinda's software—she had used it to identify that Henry

North was in financial trouble and to lure him to Austin with an offer he couldn't refuse. Records of phone calls from Taylor's home to some of Henry's clients confirmed she had been behind the scheme to discredit his business. Shawn found himself facing tough questions on how much he knew about his wife's alleged crimes. He claimed to know nothing.

"They would have destroyed Flora just because she was the easiest scapegoat for Adam's death," Teddy said. "It's disgusting."

"If you don't want shares in that company now," Kirsten said, "no one would blame you."

"Oh, I'm going to have my shares and then I'm going to run Shawn out of my dad's company," Teddy said. He smiled and she believed him.

Kirsten thanked Flora as she set down a serving tray with coffee for them all. She had been Flora's guest the past several days since the penthouse was officially a crime scene.

"Are you sure about going back to New Orleans? You could stay," Teddy said.

"I'll be back. I don't know if I'll be able to stay in our old place. It holds too many memories of Henry." She didn't want to say she couldn't afford it.

"Are, um, Zach's employers feeling the heat of the Larry Melancon case?" Teddy asked.

"It's back in the news, but no new evidence. Except that Jeanne thought we had gotten rid of Larry, which was crazy." Kirsten cleared her throat and sipped her coffee. "It seems she found letters Taylor had written to Larry. That explained something she said to me earlier—that she found something Larry would have never left behind if he'd gone of his own free will." She cleared her throat again. "JJ had an affair with Steve Fortunato after Larry vanished, which shows you how crazy she was. He swore to her that he hadn't taken out Larry. So she convinced herself Zach and I had." Because of that awkward moment in the attic that raised JJ's suspicions, but she didn't say so. "She told Taylor she suspected us, and Taylor tried to shoot Zach.

She failed, and JJ got her out of town before she could try again and bring down the wrath of the Fortunatos. They settled here, they met their husbands, and then Adam threatened JJ and they decided they could be rid of him and settle their score with us, all at once."

Teddy said, "And both she and Taylor's mom had cash from the money laundering Larry did."

"Well, not exactly. Adam had found the trail. The first investor in Milo's Gin was a front company Jeanne set up called Grinke, with an *ee* sound at the end. Named for the little town in Mississippi where Jeanne was from. But Marco heard Adam pronounce the name and thought he said 'green key.' Grinke was a front for Fortunato money, but Jeanne told Milo it was old friends of hers who put up the funds. From the start Milo was funded by the mob and he didn't know it because Jeanne ran the finances. And they've had a share of Milo's profits ever since. When Adam started digging into the finances, he found that Grinke was a front and he threatened Jeanne with exposure. He wanted to buy that company at a huge discount and he made the wrong enemy in her."

"Poor Milo. Jeanne worked for a brewery, so working for his distillery wasn't much different."

"I dug into that to help Marco with his research yesterday," Teddy said. "To re-create Adam's notes that were missing from the Grinke file in the safe. If you took a casual look, you'd see Milo's Gin was Grinke's only investment. It could have been a red flag."

"So where were the notes Adam made?" Kirsten asked.

"Adam took them to what he thought was a meeting with Jeanne at the warehouse to negotiate. Jeanne took them off his body. But Taylor came to the penthouse the night I spotted the lights on to be sure he had no other evidence. They got anxious and risked using his passkey."

"She never thought Milo's Gin would get so big," Kirsten said. "The blessing became a curse."

"Morgan misses her. But the thought of her with my son..." Flora shivered.

Morgan laughed and grabbed at Kirsten's necklace and Kirsten fended off the attack with a smile.

"Naptime, mister. Say bye-bye to Kirsten," Flora said.

Morgan did, and Flora took him to his room. When she came back down Kirsten and Teddy were sitting silently.

"Are you and Zach going to be okay?" Flora asked.

Kirsten sipped at her coffee. "We've been through more together than a lot of real brothers and sisters have. He meant well in trying to make it right. We'll be fine." Although she knew they might never be exactly the same. They'd have to work through it.

"You and I both have to figure out what to do with our lives," Flora said. "And I have an idea."

Kirsten looked up at her.

"I used to be a journalist. I was a good one. I stopped. You're a good researcher. I think we would make a good team. You could come to Austin, make a new start."

"Work for you?"

"Yes. Remember what Bard told us; we're an ambush of widows. I told you I'd thought of starting some kind of digital media company or a magazine...maybe called *Ambush*. I can fund it for quite a long time. Maybe help people who need a little extra help. Do something with all this publicity."

And there had been a lot. Two widows who solved the murders of their husbands and escaped a hit man—the very idea of it was made for modern media. In the past several days, there had been national news articles about them, and requests from cable network shows for interviews, four film producers trying to option their story, calls from a book publisher, and agents asking if they needed representation.

"I don't think I like that much attention," Kirsten said.

"This is our moment, so let's take it. Let's own it."

Kirsten considered. What was left for her in New Orleans, other than inertia? Zach was there. Zach wouldn't, or couldn't, leave. But it was a short flight away. Maybe the distance would help heal the hurt.

Austin could be a new start.

The doorbell rang. Flora answered it. Zach Couvillon. And to her surprise, he held a beautiful bouquet of flowers.

"Thank you for taking care of my sister," he said, handing her the flowers. "I know we didn't get off to a good start, but you saved her life."

"Oh, Zach. Well. Thank you." Flora had invited him to stay at her house as well, but Zach, hurt and beaten, seemed to prefer his privacy when released from the hospital. He still had two black eyes from Mender's fists and a bad bruise on his jaw. He looked awful.

"Hey, Kirsten. You ready?"

"Yes." It was an eight-hour drive from Austin to New Orleans and Kirsten thought it would give them time to talk. About the future, about the past. But she wanted this said, in front of Adam's family.

"Zach," Kirsten said quietly.

"What?" He glanced at her. His poor face.

"You're my brother."

"Not really," he said faintly.

"Always really," she said.

He took two huge deep breaths and amended his relief into an embarrassed sigh. "I love you."

"I love you too. And what happened was not your fault."

He stared at her.

"That you weren't at the warehouse with them. At the meeting as you'd planned."

"Um." He didn't know what to say. He glanced at Flora and Teddy as if mortally embarrassed.

"It's not your fault. It's not. It's not," Kirsten said as she stepped toward him and put her hand on his broad shoulder.

"Okay," he said hoarsely. "Uh..."

"It's not, Zach," Flora said. And Teddy rose to shake his hand.

Zach gathered himself and managed to nod. "Okay, well, are you ready to go?" he said, looking at the floor.

"Let me say good-bye to Norman." Kirsten went upstairs to a guest bedroom where he was lying on the bed, clean-shaven, bathed, and well fed for the past days. Right now he was watching *The X-Files* on a streaming service. He had identified Jeanne as a woman who had stopped to give him money—and slipped the cell phone into his cart. The police had found a duplicate phone, cloned with Henry's number, hidden in Taylor's desk.

"We're leaving," she said and Norman paused the screen. He had told her earlier he'd not watched TV in years and she hated to take him away from his joy. "I'll call you, though. You going to be okay?"

He nodded. "I don't feel the itch to wander right now. I forgot how good a bed feels."

"I might come back and work for Flora," Kirsten said. It didn't sound completely crazy.

"Me too. Office manager. Or office intern. Office something."

"Could you do that?"

"Yes." Norman cleared his throat. "Teddy found where my daughter's living. In Houston. I called her. She said she'd talk to me if I could stay off the streets for six months. So. I could do that, I think."

"I think you could too."

"Teddy's going to take me to every place on my old beat where they wouldn't let me in and we're gonna eat lunch and then I'm gonna see if they recognize me in my new clothes." He said this with a bit of glee.

"You're too handsome now," she said.

"You got me out of jail."

"I took a day longer than I should have." The shame welled up in her.

"I'm not mad. We're okay."

"Well, the truth is out there; get back to your show."

-

In the driveway Kirsten gave Teddy an awkward hug—she really didn't know him, but after the whole insane experience a handshake didn't seem to be enough—and then Flora. But Flora hugged her hard. It was strange. Tragedy had brought them together, but it didn't have to define them.

"Think about what I said," Flora said.

"An ambush of widows. You just know that's a term a man invented."

"We can make it work."

"I wouldn't remind you of all that you've lost?"

"I think we'll rise above that. New memories. New experiences."

"I'll think on it." Kirsten hugged Flora again and whispered, "You deserved better than what you got from him. But you have Morgan. That's the best part."

Flora whispered back, "I don't believe what Taylor keeps saying. That you murdered Larry in cold blood. I know it's not so."

Kirsten just gave a wordless nod and stepped away.

Flora blinked back tears. "Remember, think on what I said. The job is here if you want it." And she pressed some papers into Kirsten's hands and turned to go back into the house.

Kirsten glanced through the papers. "Hey, Zach, I'll drive so you can rest." Zach, who had been putting their luggage into the trunk, nodded and got in the car as she laid the papers, with her purse, in the backseat.

The day was sunny. Kirsten lowered the window so the cool air could play across her face. She drove through the hills, heading east.

"Zach?"

"Yeah."

"I'm going to move here."

"Fast decision."

"You could move here too."

"And do what?"

"Well, Flora appears to be handing out jobs."

"Can't take it." He sounded beaten. The old confident Zach needed to be rebuilt. "It's not easy to quit the Fortunatos. You don't just resign."

"Flora gave me all the notes on the Fortunatos funding Milo's Gin."

"What?"

"JJ found the cash and gave it back to the Fortunatos. They made their peace. She knew Milo needed an investor and they needed a way to clean funds. I'm sure they'd prefer this not be exposed. I think Flora just gave us your ticket out."

Zach blinked at her. She tried on a smile. First one in many days.

"You," Kirsten said, "are my and Flora's first project."

55

Annie let the baby nurse. She closed the laptop and didn't let the rage build inside her until the baby was done. She didn't want the baby feeding on her dark mood. But then she'd think, *My little avenging angel; maybe I should fill you with anger.*

Garrison had gotten her and her mother new names and relocated them to a new city. Mama wasn't happy, but it was necessary, at least for a while. No one knew she was connected to the hit man in the big news story.

Her husband had been identified after his plunge from the balcony. His real name was Scott and that was her baby's middle name, even though it was traditionally a boy's name. She had watched the news from Austin, the story of these two widows who had solved the murders of their husbands and brought both the contract killer and his clients down.

She watched the media firestorm after she gave birth and she watched it when the baby was down for her brief naps until her mother made her turn it off. Annie would turn it back on. She recorded the coverage and watched it again. And again.

Not now, Annie thought. *Not yet. Not while my baby is this young. I'll let you get comfortable. I'll let you get lazy. And then I'll come for both of you.*